REVIEW ACCLAIM FOR JAMES NOLAN'S SHORT STORIES

"A fine debut collection . . . Nolan's prose is both languid and biting. He has a tender-tough sympathy for even his most wayward and marginalized characters. And he's wildly inventive in how he launches a tale."

-Michael Upchurch, *Seattle Times*

"The real deal . . . The city's long conversation with itself has never been louder or more insistent than in these stories, with all their exuberance, despair and wit."

-Susan Larson, *Times-Picayune*

"Call me a gusher, but this is a standout collection, one of the best I've read in years, and it deserves a place in the most august company."

-Garry Craig Powell, *Arkansas Review*

"Most of these stories are darkly comic, some of them deadly serious, all of them poignantly delivered. Do yourself a favor: read this book."

-Terry Dalrymple, *American Book Review*

" . . . stories that feel vital and necessary. Nolan's sentences are impeccable. Each contains a small surprise, or killer image, or turn of phrase that both moves the story forward and thrills the reader with a poet's economy and precision of language."

-Sean Ennis, *Southern Literary Review*

"A peculiar, dream-like quality suffuses each of Nolan's stories, punctuated by intervals of disbelief, disgust, profound sadness, and laugh-out-loud humor."

-Nathan Tipton, *Lambda Book Report*

"There is something universal in the stories. Something that I, a software engineer from India who shares hardly anything with the characters, can relate to . . . a human smell of sweat and follies."

-Parth Vasa, *Gently Read Literature*

Also by James Nolan

FICTION

Higher Ground (University of Louisiana at Lafayette Press)
Perpetual Care: Stories (Jefferson Press)

POETRY

Drunk on Salt (Willow Springs Editions)
Why I Live in the Forest (Wesleyan University Press)
What Moves Is Not the Wind (Wesleyan University Press)

POETRY IN TRANSLATION

Pablo Neruda, *Stones of the Sky* (Copper Canyon Press)
Jaime Gil de Biedma, *Longing: Selected Poems* (City Lights Books)

CRITICISM

Poet-Chief: The Native American Poetics of Walt Whitman and Pablo Neruda (University of New Mexico Press)

ESSAYS

Fumadores en manos de un dios enfurecido: Ensayos al caballo entre varios mundos (Madrid: Editores Enigma)

You Don't Know Me

New and Selected Stories

For Karl,
Now you know me,
Best wishes,
James Nolan

YOU DON'T KNOW ME

NEW AND SELECTED STORIES

New Orleans
Nov. 20, 2014

BY

JAMES NOLAN

University of Louisiana at Lafayette Press
2014

Front Cover Art: Adrian Deckbar

University of Louisiana at Lafayette Press
P.O. Box 40831
Lafayette, LA 70504-0831
http://ulpress.org

Library of Congress Cataloging-in-Publication Data

Nolan, James, 1947-
[Short stories. Selections]
You don't know me : new & selected stories / by James Nolan.
pages ; cm. -- (Louisiana writers series)
ISBN 978-1-935754-34-3
I. Nolan, James, 1947- Reconcile. II. Title.
PS3564.O36A6 2014
813'.54--dc23
2014024293

Printed in Canada.

in memory of
Olga Glaudot Partee, Lenow Partee,
and Marguerite Glaudot:
Mémère, PawPaw, and Reete,
who raised me right

CONTENTS

I. INSIDE THE COURTYARD GATES

II. FROM *PERPETUAL CARE*

I.

Inside the Courtyard Gates

Like many of the Creole houses, the façade presented a commonplace and unattractive aspect. The great green doors of the arched entrance were closed, and the green shutters of the balconied windows half shut. . . . But beyond the gates lay a little Paradise.

-Lafcadio Hearn,
"A Creole Courtyard" (1879)

Reconcile

ZOLA LEANS OVER the wrought-iron balcony railing, growling in that husky voice of hers, "Sherene, hon, look across the street."

Three pink kibble feeders are set out on the sidewalk below, and these enormous rats have lined up as if they were at a food court. And they're fanged wharf rats, nothing like the itty-bitty mice that scurried around inside my greasy stove before Zola's cat moved into the building and scared them away.

"Just yesterday," I tell her, "I cornered one of those animal rescuers and said, 'Sugar, please don't feed the rats in the Vieux Carré.'"

We're on my balcony, where Zola has been busy brushing out the matted fur of Boom Boom, her Angora with the wedge-shaped noggin and bushy tail. Whenever my neighbor rings the bell to my apartment, which is practically every evening at cocktail hour, she'll be standing there on the landing, a vodka tonic in one hand and Boom Boom clutched like a rag doll in the other.

"When I got back from evacuating to Waco," Zola says, "the out-of-town animal people were already setting up feeders for pets stuck here after the storm. Guess there are no hungry river rats where those folks come from."

"Been more hurricane aid pouring in for pets than for people,"

I say. "You lost your home, they direct you to the FEMA website. You lost your Chihuahua, they put you on prime-time TV."

Although there's no denying pets did suffer. The night before the storm, we assumed we'd be back to New Orleans in three days. As it turned out, Boom Boom was locked inside Zola's apartment for three solid weeks before her insurance adjuster brother-in-law from Houston was able to come get him. Boom Boom had clawed open a bag of cat food and was drinking from the aquarium. So now the cat suffers from "acute separation anxiety," according to his pet psychiatrist. At first, whenever Zola left the apartment, Boom Boom would scratch open sofa cushions and leave claw marks on the new paint job. Got to the point where she had to incarcerate him inside a cat carrier while she was at work. So the doctor put Boom Boom on Reconcile, a cat tranquilizer. Now when Boom Boom starts to climb the walls, Zola will slip him a Reconcile mashed up in tuna fish.

Sounds like what this whole town needs: Reconcile.

Ours is the only streetlight working in this block of Ursulines, and with the 6 p.m. curfew, the street is dead quiet. Since the bars are closed, I wonder where Julius is. We're three single souls living in this Creole town house, all getting on in age, and we take care of each other. Julius and his spotted pooch Weasel have the courtyard slave quarter, Zola is upstairs in the attic apartment with Boom Boom, and I'm in the second-floor balcony unit, happy as a clam finally to be by myself. Julius has been here since the Civil War, although it's Zola who has drawn us together. She seems so lonely, always with a drink in hand.

"She's not even a real woman," Julius said after she first moved in.

"What *ever* do you mean by that unusual remark?" I replied. Of all people, how would he know what a real woman was?

"Look at that five-o'clock shadow and those big clodhoppers. Girlfriend almost passes, but not quite. And that wig!"

"But two years ago she had a lumpectomy and started wearing the wig during chemo. Now she just hates to fuss with her hair."

"Bet I know what lump they cut off."

True, Zola is mannish, but in a hyper-feminine way. She's built like a linebacker and has one of those smoke-and-whiskey cured baritones. But she always dresses real cute, usually in color-coordinated red and white outfits, with round red sunglasses that take up half of her pie-shaped face. She favors big plastic earrings that match her bangles, which coordinate with her belt and shoes. Look, I'm from Mississippi and can recognize a small-town Texas gal in search of big-city sophistication. Besides, I saw her once in bra and panties. Even they matched, but she was all woman.

We've both grabbed a handful of last year's plastic Carnival beads dangling from the railing and are slinging them at the rats when Julius comes staggering down the street.

"You're out after curfew," I shout from the balcony.

"Johnny White's Bar is still open," he says, breathless, "but a National Guard just stopped me at a roadblock. Stuck his huge gun thing in my face and said I couldn't go home. Told me this area is cordoned off for security."

"So how did you get past the roadblock?" Zola asks.

"I made a date with him."

I roll my eyes. "Thought the bars had to shut down at six now."

"The owner said he hadn't closed Johnny White's in thirty years, and so he couldn't find the key. Hey, what are you ladies doing? Practicing your throwing arms for Mardi Gras parades?"

"We're getting rid of the rats having a picnic down there," Zola says.

Julius studies the red and fuchsia beads scattered next to the kibble feeders under the lone street light across the street. "What rats?"

BOOM BOOM IS missing.

"I turned my back one second," Zola says, eyes red and swollen, "and *zoom*, he scooted down the staircase lickety-split and out onto the street."

"He'll be back," I tell her. "But in the meantime, he'll have to fight the river rats for the animal-rescue kibble."

"That, doll baby, is not a comforting thought."

Zola flies into a panic, Scotch-taping photocopied flyers on every lamp post in the neighborhood. "Pet Alert," they read, followed by a color snapshot of Boom Boom. "Adorable gray Angora missing from 700 block of Ursulines. Call (504) 538-7026. Reward! Boom Boom come home and take your meds! Mommy misses you."

What Zola doesn't know—but will find out during the coming week—is that CNN is in the Quarter shooting a special on the plight of pets after the storm. One night I'm tucked in front of the TV with my knitting, next to the big stack of books I keep meaning to read, when I catch a pan shot of those kibble feeders, followed by a close up of Zola's poster. And there's Boom Boom's pointy puss on the poster, followed by Zola's phone number, clear as it can be.

"'Mommy misses you,'" the reporter reads. "And that's the tragic fate of many pet owners in this devastated city struggling for survival. This is Anderson Cooper for CNN in New Orleans."

It's only ten o'clock, so I ring Zola. She's a night owl who detests mornings—claims she doesn't *exist* before she draws on her eyebrows at noon—and has forbidden her friends to call her until sundown, when she straggles in from her part-time bookkeeping job at the Postal Emporium.

"You're famous," I say. "Just saw Anderson Cooper on TV with Boom Boom."

"A reporter found Boom Boom?" Ice cubes rattle in her glass.

"No, but he showed your pet-alert poster on TV and said 'Mommy misses you.' Aren't you absolutely thrilled?"

The next morning I can't figure out what Zola is doing up so early. My ceiling rumbles all morning while she stomps around upstairs, screaming her head off. As she lets me in her door, the phone is cradled to her ear. Looks like she's barely had time to slip on a quilted robe, and dark bags sag under her eyes. I've never seen her without makeup before, and her face is as stark as a Kabuki mask. The shaved eyebrows are extraterrestrial.

"No, Boom Boom has *not* come home," she spits into the receiver, "and thanks ever so much for your goddamned concern. Give me your number, and I'll call you at three in the morning tomorrow in Rhode Island to see how you're doing." Then she slams the wireless down onto the flowered arm chair.

"It hasn't let up for one minute since dawn." Zola sweeps into the Pullman kitchen to splash more vodka into her tomato juice. "They're calling from Montana and Nebraska and California and frigging Birmingham, England. Want to talk to Boom Boom's mommy. Wait till I get my hands on that Anderson Cooper. You can't put somebody's private phone number on international TV."

"CNN is no place to hide," I say. "Just turn off the ringer, sugar."

"There's no ringer button on this stupid phone. Besides, what if somebody in town really has found Boom Boom? What I really can't stand is when people call to tell me how much they hate the President for what he let happen to New Orleans after the flooding. Pinko fools want to *sympathize* with me. 'Look,' I tell them, 'I'm from Texas and I adore that man. His daddy and my daddy once had breakfast together.'"

Zola Coates is on the ball about most things, but not about politics. Her daddy was a bankrupt cattle rancher who wound up working for a petroleum company, where he did so well that he was able to send his kids to fancy colleges. When Zola's mama was still lucid, she swore up and down that studying medieval art history at Tulane University was where her daughter picked up "those funny notions" and wound up as a spinster in the trampy French Quarter working at no-account jobs. But Zola still swears by Texas and the President. Claims she has crude pulsing through her veins. Now that I've seen her without makeup, I believe it.

The phone bleats.

She drags herself to the arm chair. "No, Boom Boom is *not*

back. Don't you nitwits in Schenectady have anything better to do?"

EVERY TIME JULIUS plunks himself down on his white leatherette couch under the squiggly op art paintings that make me dizzy to look at, he bolts up again to let Weasel scamper in or out of the French doors. He fusses with that feisty dog as if she were a disabled child, swatting at her when she gnaws on the rug or that metronome tail knocks a gewgaw off the glass coffee table.

"I'm really concerned about Zola," I say. Having neighbors is so much like being part of a family. What binds us together is complaining about each other.

"Saw her on the corner today, calling 'Boom Boom come home.'" He adjusts the straining waist of his faded jeans, and combs the dyed black mustache with his fingernails. "The girl doesn't look well."

"Of course not. She's worried sick, and can't sleep because everyone in the United States of America keeps calling day and night about that cat."

As I almost told Zola—but of course I'd never dare—*just get another damn cat.* Boom Boom probably has found himself a foxy lady cat and is busy screwing under a house. He's not pining away for Zola Coates. But you can't tell that to an old maid about her house cat. I've been married three times, and I suspect that's where my exes are right this minute, screwing under a house. After the husbands took off reeking of somebody else's hair spray, and then the two boys finally grew up and went away to college, I just closed the door, locked it, folded my arms, and said, "At last."

And then I broke a blackboard pointer over my knee in front of the seventh-graders, crammed as much of my stuff as I could into the back of a Chevy station wagon, and hightailed it from Natchez to the French Quarter. Do I miss my boys? Of course. Do I want them to come live with me? Not on your life. I'm all mothered out. I have three dieffenbachia growing on the balcony, but they're not doing so well.

"It's time for Weasel's nap," Julius tells me. I know what that means. The bars have reopened, and he's going for happy hour to the Mary-Go-Round. He used to invite me along to shoot pool, but I couldn't help but point out that the scuzz muffins he hit on weren't worthy of him. So now when he goes trash picking, he goes alone. Any evening I expect to hear a shrill scream for help from the slave quarter, then tear down the stairs in my lace nightie waving a fire poker to rescue Julius from some homicidal maniac running around in his drawers.

"And I have some urgent knitting to attend to." I hoist myself to my feet from the Barcelona chair, woozy from facing the op art paintings that cover the brick walls. The gallery Julius once had on Royal Street was the rage during the seventies, so he decided to stick with what he knows. Don't we all feel that way about when we were young? As long as his butt is tightly blue-jeaned and his art is bold metallic stripes, he hasn't grown old. Although he couldn't sell any of that today, and I don't just mean the paintings.

Weasel burrows into the dhurrie carpet with his claws, digging a hole in the meticulous decor to uncover some phantom bone buried decades ago by Iggy Stardust.

Julius claps his hands in reprimand, just like I used to do teaching English. "She's a rat terrier and loves to dig."

"Of course. She's part of the natural world. You know, 'bloody tooth and claw,'" I say, hanging quotation marks in the air. "So send her across the street to scare those rats scarfing kibble from the animal-rescue people. She'd have a ball."

"Rats?" Julius gasps, scooping up the muscular dog into his arms. "Not my little Weasel."

JUST BEFORE THE Carnival parades start to roll in February, Boom Boom comes home. He must have climbed over the ivy-covered brick wall into the courtyard, because there he is, prancing in a circle mewing when I take out the garbage late one afternoon.

"Zola," I scream up to the top floor, "get down here, girl. Boom Boom is back."

The way she staggers down the sinuous curves of the staircase hanging onto the railing, I suspect she's the one who has been popping the Reconcile for acute separation anxiety. During the past three months she's become a washed-out ghost of her insouciant self. Her outfits don't even match. She didn't take her own daddy's death this hard. All she does is mutter into her cocktails about Boom Boom. So it's my distinct pleasure to hand her the gamey ball of tattered fur, which smells exactly like sex under the house.

Zola is weeping, cradling the cat like a Flemish Madonna with child. As the sun sets through the branches of the sweet olive tree, bathing the courtyard in a golden filigree of winter light, I want to hum "Ave Maria."

Julius and Weasel scurry out, and our silent triptych poses in the ethereal gloaming as if after a visitation by the Holy Ghost. Even the rambunctious Weasel sits still with an ear cocked, no doubt mesmerized by angelic choirs. Then we pop the cork on a bottle of bubbly, crank up Julius' stereo with a cassette of the Village People, and have a "Boom Boom is back" party in the courtyard. We jig in hilarity to "YMCA," passing Boom Boom from arm to arm. My daddy was the president of the YMCA in Natchez, Mississippi, and I've never fathomed what those lyrics are supposed to be about.

Champagne glass poised in midair, Zola slips on the flagstones and takes a tumble, sending Boom Boom swooping with rampant claws onto the top of Weasel's head. The hissing is punctuated by fierce barks until Julius separates the two. I grab the wobbly Zola from behind and steady her to her feet, holding the silky auburn wig that has slipped off her head.

"This is what cancer looks like," she says. The downy gray stubble on her scalp is like something you'd see in a concentration camp. "My hair never grew back."

"But you're a survivor," I say, almost bawling.

"I thought Boom Boom was never coming home," she sniffles,

"so I booked a flight to Waco for Mardi Gras. I'm going to spend some quality time visiting Momma in the memory unit, if she still recognizes me. I didn't feel like celebrating without him."

"So stay," Julius says. "The mayor tried to cancel Mardi Gras, but we wouldn't let him. This is going to be the best Carnival ever."

"I can't." Eyes watering, Zola nuzzles the cat's head. "I got the ticket by auction online, and I'd lose the whole fare. Can y'all look after Boom Boom for four days? I'll be back on Mardi Gras evening."

"Of course," Julius and I murmur in unison, cutting each other concerned looks.

"You know, y'all and Boom Boom are the only family I have left. I never expected to find myself so alone at this stage of my life." The wig tucked under one arm, Zola mounts the twisting staircase, Boom Boom's furry tail swishing back and forth behind her turnip-shaped backside. "You're all I have to live for."

Julius circles a finger around his ear.

"Don't listen to her," I whisper. "It's the Reconcile talking."

THIS MARDI GRAS I've decided to go as Marie Laveau, so I'm trying on a checkered turban and gold hooped earrings. Later I'll string these chicken bones that Boom Boom has been licking clean into a voodoo necklace, weaving in some Spanish moss and those darling dried baby alligator heads that Zola gave me for Christmas. That should spook people out. I'll take Boom Boom along on a leash as my spirit familiar, although I hope it won't be too nippy out. A cold front is moving in, the TV warns, and we should have a hard freeze by tomorrow night.

Paws splayed, Boom Boom is sprawled in a patch of sunlight on the couch. The cat usually watches TV with me, snuggling against my leg when I go to sleep. After so long, it's comforting to share the apartment with another breathing creature. Last night while I ate dinner, Boom Boom perched on the window sill in the kitchen over his bowl of Reconcile à la King, so sweet that I gave him a second helping, meds and all.

"How are you, my little bugaboo?" I slide onto the couch next to my house-guest, my voodoo familiar, my dining partner, my fuzzy wuzzy. His paws are unusually stiff, so I turn over the sleeping cat.

Blood is oozing from his mouth. Next to his whiskers is a pile of throw up that smells like tuna fish, chockablock with jagged pieces of chicken bone.

I shake the rigid cat, pump on his stomach, blow air into his mouth and ears. Wind pipe, I think, wind pipe. I ease my index finger down his throat, trying to clean it out. There's no protest.

That's because he's not breathing.

Nothing I can do—water, massage, prayers, screams—will make him come back. Just a while ago he was breathing on the couch, luxuriating in an afternoon cat nap, probably dreaming about sex under the house. And now he's not.

I dial the vet's number that Zola left, along with the cat food, treats, kitty litter, rubber mice, and big bottle of Reconcile. The recording gives me an emergency number that then rings and rings and rings. After all, it's Carnival weekend, and nothing normal will happen here until Ash Wednesday morning. I pick up the phone to dial Zola in Waco, then put it down. I lift it again.

Then I throw down the phone. She'll go to pieces.

"Boom Boom," I implore, shaking the dead cat, "come back. Mommy misses you."

This can't be happening.

I pour a couple of fingers of bourbon into a glass and slug it back.

"Julius," I shout down to the courtyard from the kitchen window, "get your butt up here on the double. And bring some garbage bags."

After he arrives, it's soon decided that we can't allow Zola to waltz in here on Mardi Gras evening only to discover Boom Boom stashed next to the ice cream in her refrigerator. I can hear the screams already.

"So your freezer or mine?" Julius asks.

Turns out that neither of us wants a dead cat next to the frozen shrimp and sausages for our Mardi Gras spread. Just like before the storm, we're hosting an open house in the courtyard and both of us will be cooking. Julius's specialty is gumbo, and I'll be doing a pan of jambalaya. What if Boom Boom has some feline fever like those birds you hear about over in China?

"It'll freeze this weekend," Julius says, "so we can double-bag Boom Boom inside these plastic sacks and leave him in the courtyard until Zola figures out what to do."

"What are we going to tell her?" I plead. "You can't imagine how hard she's going to take this."

MARDI GRAS DAWNS bright and sunny, so unseasonably warm that I strip off the woolen shawl I've draped over the shoulders of the white linen voodoo-queen dress. The copper-colored makeup smears immediately—I haven't worn makeup since my last ex ran off to a motel with his alcohol-abuse counselor—and winds up looking like a fright mask.

"Who are you supposed to be," Julius asks, fingering the chicken-bone necklace, "Etta James cleaning out the garbage disposal?" He's bare-chested and leering, with a hard hat that reads FEMA. "I'm a plumbing inspector," he says, waving a suggestively shaped rubber wrench. "Want your plumbing inspected?"

We agree that the frozen cat needs to be buried before it thaws. A rotting cat in the corner just wouldn't be festive. We dig a trench next to the blooming camellia bushes, unwrap the cat, and shovel dirt over it. We bow our heads and mutter a prayer.

"Here's the story." I feel a lot better now that Boom Boom is buried. "We'll tell Zola that Boom Boom ran away again. And how we looked and looked, but couldn't find him anywhere. Then after a few weeks, I'll give her an Angora kitten called Boomlette. She'll be ecstatic, just wait and see."

We clink glasses just as the first guests arrive, a group costumed as moldy refrigerators. Never before have I seen anyone drink a piña colada and eat a bowl of gumbo while dressed as a moldy refrigerator. So then everyone starts to rehash the encounters with their fetid refrigerators the day they came back after the hurricane. By now the whole Quarter is home from wherever people were exiled to, and we're laughing and crying all at once, retelling for the hundredth time our evacuation sagas as we lick jambalaya off our fingers and pour another drink. Since the storm, we've seen the thin skin between civilization and savagery ripped asunder in this town, with cadavers rotting in flooded houses and people shooting each other in the head over copper pipes, and now all we want is to return to a normal life that, as my mama would say, is *reeeal niiice.*

Gangs of friends come and go, their necks layered like surgical braces with bulbous Carnival beads, throwing their arms around each other and toasting our return. At one point the entire Mary-Go-Round is here, bald and bare-chested, pumping meaty paws in the air as we dance to "I Will Survive." At the beginning of the party, nobody can decide whether to stay in New Orleans or leave. By the end, everyone takes me aside to swear they're staying. Maybe it's the Reconcile talking. The truth is we've loved and lost and will never be the same.

The whole time I'm beating on a tom-tom and shaking my feathered voodoo staff in everyone's faces, prophesying who would make the perfect couple with whom. It does my heart good to be home, not in the place fate tossed me but in the place I chose. As the sun sets and the last wave of people ebbs away, we lock the carriageway gate. Only a few of us are left under the sweet olive tree, seated in a circle of candlelight on cast-iron chairs next to trays of congealed food. I've just frightened myself to death by glancing in the bathroom mirror. The turban is askew, my face flecked with feathers and bits of chicken bone, and the copper makeup is smeared down the front of the white linen dress like dried blood.

On the way back from Julius's bathroom, I notice a frantic shadow darting from one end of the courtyard to the other. I blink, sure that I'm seeing things.

"Julius," I ask, dragging my chair closer toward the candle, "what's that shape-shifting mythical beast in the corner? Looks like two creatures in one."

"Weasel!" He rises, claps his hands, and the dog edges closer toward the circle of candlelight. "Come here, you bad girl. What have you got in your mouth?"

The dog emerges from the shadow, dragging the muddied carcass of some animal.

A furry gray one whose tail is sweeping the patio.

"Has she got a rat?" I curl into a ball in the chair, gathering the dress around my ankles. "Damn those animal-rescue people."

"Look, Sherene," Julius shrieks, "Boom Boom is back."

We both leap up at once.

Pointy ears erect, the rat terrier is galloping around the courtyard, dragging Zola's just-exhumed cat. We race after the snarling dog, lunging to grab the mucky corpse out of her mouth. Weasel is spinning in a frenzied circle, flailing the animal by its neck to the right and left, as if trying to knock her stiff prey even more unconscious.

At that moment, a key clicks in the carriageway lock.

Then the gate slams.

"Civilization at last!" Zola's baritone echoes along the brick corridor. "Boy, am I glad to be home."

I straighten my turban, smooth the voodoo dress, then turn to face the high heels clacking along the flagstones toward us.

Hard Freeze

BY THE TIME the famous pianist arrived in New Orleans, everything was already dead.

Walking through the courtyard, Émile Jackson turned up the collar of his wool overcoat as he followed behind the ebullient Mrs. McNamara from the Save Our Symphony Committee. She never stopped talking, even as they sidestepped the gummy leaves of tropical plants collapsed onto the flagstones in ochre piles. Overhead, an icy wind whipped through the frayed fronds of banana trees, the trunks gone soft and purple with the piercing cold. Jangling a ring of keys, the white lady with the dyed red hair was babbling about her "vacation slave quarter," a phrase she used with no trace of irony, considering to whom it was addressed. Émile doubted she even saw who he was.

"This courtyard was such a jungle," Mrs. McNamara said, fumbling with the keys at the French doors, "but after the past four nights of 23 degrees, just look."

As at a grave, Émile stood with bowed head over the fish pond coated with a slick of ice. Refracted through the surface, a golden fishtail flashed, and he wondered what life might linger below, frozen in slow motion. A beard of icicles sprouted from the fountain spout, each crystal reflecting the grey light. This wasn't how he remembered the city. He had been here once before at his mother's request, in June five years earlier, but only for the few hours it took to slip in and out of his father's funeral. The humid heat had wilted his starched white shirt in a matter of minutes, and nobody in Papa's dark-hued family seemed to recognize the light-complexioned stranger perched alone in the last pew of the clapboard Baptist church. Yet shortly after his heart attack in November, when Émile had received Mrs. McNamara's invitation to headline a benefit concert in New Orleans, something stirred inside, as if he'd been given one more chance. Now, as he searched for his father's face along the courtyard wall stubbled with brown ferns, he wondered why he had come.

"Sad for you to see it this way," Mrs. McNamara said. "*Quel dommage.* It was so lush."

"I'm sure the lushes will return this spring," he said, green eyes twinkling, "like the swallows to Capistrano." Mrs. McNamara's breath was probably flammable, and after one whiff at the baggage carousel, he'd felt relieved that she wouldn't be driving them to the French Quarter herself.

"You're so. . . ."

"French?" Three times in the limo between here and the airport she'd told Émile that he seemed "so French."

"Now we know your mother was French, and you were raised over there," she said, throwing open the apartment doors, "but didn't I read somewhere on the Internet that your father was from here?"

"The Seventh Ward, as he called it. But he was a military man and lived everywhere, long before my mother and me, and long after us."

"So you must have family—"

"We were never encouraged to stay in touch."

ONCE INSIDE, ÉMILE ducked under a grandiose chandelier and plopped into an overstuffed armchair while Mrs. McNamara scurried about, flinging open doors, flicking on lamps, and fiddling with the thermostat. Spot lit in one corner was a Steinway baby grand, as he had requested. A wall of French doors opened onto the courtyard, and Émile closed his eyes at the desolate vision of drooping foliage.

The stem of a flute glass was pressed into his hand. He opened his eyes, blinking.

"Champagne?" Mrs. McNamara said, holding an unopened bottle of Veuve Cliquot.

He massaged the bridge of his nose. "Since the coronary three months ago, I don't drink."

"I lost my husband to that," she said, pointing to her heart. "Here, let me rest this pillow behind your neck."

As he stood, the pillow slid to the floor. "This is my first journey in a while, and I'm tired."

Everywhere he had ever been in the world—his mother's house in Nevers, the forlorn Army bases where his father brought him during several interminable summers, his ex-wife's flat in the Marais, his apartment on the Upper East Side, a piano stood in front of a window. While swallows swooped by in spring, summer drizzle fell, falling leaves drifted past, and snow flurried, he lost himself in the chords of Liszt and Chopin as his temples greyed and muscles sagged. And even here in New Orleans—the only place ever called home by that gruff man with a green duffel bag in one hand and a pint of gin in the other— was another piano.

Years ago, after his divorce, Émile realized that he had little talent for whatever part of living came in between the various rooms, each with its own piano. Herself a pianist, Mamam always told him, quoting her favorite poet, Verlaine: "*De la musique avant toutes les choses.*" Music before everything. He had kept his eye on the prize, and for years it was all he could see. Except that now, after collapsing on stage during the Cincinnati concert in November, that vision was beginning to blur. The rest of the autumn tour had been cancelled, and the spring bookings the agent made were tentative, contingent upon further test results. Until a few weeks ago, it seemed that his concert career might be over. But then, out of the blue, he'd received Mrs. McNamara's call. Maman would have indulged his illness, hired a nurse and sent him to her family's farm house in Dordogne to recuperate.

But even from the grave, Papa wouldn't let him quit.

New Orleans, of all places in the world.

"I'll leave the champagne here," Mrs. McNamara said, "in case you feel naughty later, and will be by tomorrow at six to bring you to the patron party before the concert. The tux is hanging in the closet, the thermostat set to Miami Beach, and the fridge chock full of goodies from Whole Foods. Monsieur Jackson, we are so honored to have you here, and so touched you've agreed to do our benefit. I know you're booked three years in advance to play before the crowned heads of Europe, so this. . . ."

She stood a foot taller than Émile, and while he looked up like an obedient child at the lipsticked mouth working the pasty face, his chiseled features remained impassive, wide nostrils flaring like a thoroughbred's. His square head, topped with a nimbus of tight curls dusted with grey, was set like a marble bust on the delicate frame of a compact body. As the last rays of daylight filtered through the marquisette curtains, his latté complexion turned ashen. No matter how he felt, he had to go through with this—how did Papa put it?—"come rain or come shine."

"Au revoir," Mrs. McNamara chirped, stumbling backward out of the door. *"Bienvenue à la Nouvelle Orléans."*

It never failed, Émile thought, sliding the dead bolt behind her. Like the double-faced Roman god Janus, he was always on the wrong side of every door. To the Europeans, he was *un noir américain,* and even though his mother raised him to be one-hundred-percent French, he didn't look the part. One glance at him, and the French expected someone rollicking or angry, Louis Armstrong or James Baldwin, somebody who would thump the piano and set the house to rocking. But it wasn't him. And here, even among Americans of his father's race, as open a tribe as you could find anywhere, there was still an invisible wall. They saw him as the hothouse product of some unidentifiably foreign clime, and shouted at him as if across a wide canyon so he could understand their language, one he spoke perfectly. Or, feeling threatened, they saw him as an uppity so-and-so who needed to be taught a lesson, as if he were a Pullman porter lording it over the ordinary folk. Here in New Orleans, with its French history and African blood lines, where he had long dreamed he would melt in like chocolate, he felt particularly foreign.

He sat at the piano bench and stretched his tapered fingers into the rolling first chords of Beethoven's "Moonlight Sonata," trying to perfect the tricky half-pedaling technique that the piece called for. Outside, a full January moon rose over the ghostly garden in the courtyard, casting shadows as long and dark as memory. Not that they had ever talked much, but he wished that he could tell his father about this "vacation slave quarter" in New Orleans. That would have made the old man cackle. But the last time Émile had spoken with him, a mere three weeks before the heart attack that sent him in a flag-draped coffin to the family tomb in St. Louis Cemetery, he wasn't laughing. His papa had only whispered "we so proud of you" and then hung up. And Émile had returned to practicing—on yet another piano facing another window—the echo of a dial tone pulsing in his ear.

STILL GROGGY WITH sleep, Émile stood in Mrs. McNamara's kitchen, baffled by an American device called a Mr. Coffee, wondering what the blinking red light meant. Outside a roar was building, as if a motorcycle were revving up in the courtyard, the same infernal noise that had woken him earlier. Émile gathered the terrycloth robe around his neck, grabbed a mug of the coffee that had mysteriously filled the pot after the red light stopped blinking, and opened the door, bracing for an arctic blast.

Although the light was still dishwater grey, the air was warmer. The garden had been scalped. A desiccated prune of a man, wrinkled and molasses-colored, was chasing leaves into a heap with a leaf blower. He glanced up at Émile with rheumy eyes, and as if he didn't like what he saw, examined the shriveled elephant-ear stalks at his feet.

"Good morning," Emile shouted over the noise.

"How do." The man clicked off the machine. "They didn't tell me nobody was back here. That white lady never come except at Carnival time. Usually this whole place empty," he said, gesturing toward the locked doors and windows at the back of the Creole town house, now a warren of expensive condos.

Émile stepped across the worn flagstones in his slippers, observing the stubs of beheaded plants sticking up everywhere like broken teeth. "It's too bad the frost killed these plants."

"They not dead. This spring they all be sprouting and blooming, wait and see. Anything what got a root come back." "Root" came out like *rut*, and the old man looked at the ground as he spoke. "You from away?" he asked, brow furrowed.

Émile squinted, trying to understand the man's English. "I live in New York City."

"Thought you talked funny. My cousin Tyrone went up there once and say he near about froze to death." With creaky movements, the gardener bent to scoop a handful of debris into a trash bag. "Y'all used to that weather. Got to come down here just to warm up," he said with a grunt.

"How long will you be working?" Émile glanced at his Rolex. "I have to rehearse for my concert."

"What you play?"

"The piano." Émile pointed at the elephantine shape in the window

"Me, I play the trumpet. Nothing fancy, just second lines and barbeques. Most everyone down here play something or other."

"That's what my father played, the trumpet." Before Papa enlisted, he'd recorded an LP, one with a frayed blue cover that said "Basin Street Stompers." As a boy, Émile had worn the record grooves smooth on his mother's phonograph, although she slammed the living room door shut whenever he played it.

"What club you gigging at?" the gardener asked.

"I'll be soloing with the New Orleans Philharmonic."

"Don't know nothing about that. Must be Uptown. I'm from the Seventh Ward."

"So was my father," Émile said, moving closer. "He spent most of his life traveling with the military. But he did come home to die, as he always said he would."

"So y'all from here." A smile widened the old man's face as he reached over to pump Émile's hand. "My name is Ducote, Cyril Ducote. Who your people?"

"I'm Émile. My father was Linton Jackson."

"I known some Jacksons live over by the Picou Bakery on Bayou Road way back when. Had a big old gal taught school, and a horn-playing son my age shipped out. Smart move, if you ask me. Or the brother'd still be here," he said, kicking the leaves at his feet, "mopping up like me. That's what I tell my knucklehead grandson, out dealing drugs and shooting people every night of the week. I say, 'You wanna kill people? Well, the gov'ment got a job for you. Make you more money than on that street corner.' Where you say you come up?"

"I was born in Nevers, France, where my mother raised me."

"Whoo whee," Cyril Ducot said, slapping his thigh. "France! 'Didn't he ramble, didn't he roam?' like the song say. Come to visit your daddy's folks?"

"Not exactly. Are you still in touch with that Jackson family?" Émile asked, excited. The Picou Bakery rang a bell. "Papa always talked about the jelly donuts at that bakery."

"Place be long gone. But a few Jacksons still stop by the old barber shop."

"I looked in the phone book, and there were four pages of Jacksons. If you see any of that family you know, please tell them I'm Linton's son and to come hear my concert tonight at the Orpheum Theater. After they can call for me backstage."

"I'll run it by Loretha," the old man said with a wink. "You know, wanna get the word out, only three ways: telephone, telegraph, or tell a woman."

A chill wind picked up, and Émile's coffee turned cold. "I have to rehearse now."

"Mind if I listen while I finish up out here?"

"It would be a great honor, sir."

When Émile slipped inside, he left the door cracked open despite the cold, not wanting to break his connection with the gardener. This was as close as he had gotten to his American family since his father's funeral, when he left without speaking a word. Papa had always fumed about "those people down there," saying they were narrow-minded and willfully ignorant. As a captain in the United States Army, Linton Jackson had considered himself a man of the world—"good as any white man, better." He treated his son like a recruit, demanding order, discipline, and respect, and during the boy's infrequent summer visits to his father in officers' housing, those few hours that Émile wasn't practicing the piano were spent shining his father's boots to a high gloss. A chart hung on the kitchen door, listing his chores and practice sessions by the hour and day, and he had to check them off as they were completed. When, with great relief, Émile flew back to France, his father shook his hand at the airport, as if he had completed an assignment. Émile half expected a grade, and was never quite sure if he had passed, either as a son or a pianist.

As a boy, practicing on the rented upright in his father's living room, Émile could always hear his father listening, even if the old man's face was hidden behind a newspaper, slurping a gin and tonic. And if the truth be known, every time he played a concert anywhere in the world, he could still feel his father listening. But as he stood to acknowledge with a bow the standing ovations he had come to expect, he didn't hear the applause, no matter how thunderous.

Because it was never Papa's.

His father's face remained behind the newspaper, critical, disapproving, and Émile's playing was dismissed with an irritated wave of the hand, as if to say *enough of that noise. Time to hit the sack.*

Now as the pianist's fingers relaxed into the first chords of Beethoven, he could hear the gardener listening. When Émile lifted his eyes from the sheet music and out onto the patio, he spotted Cyril Ducote. Elbows propped on his knees, the old man was seated hunched over on a white cast-iron bench, head bowed and eyes closed, as if lost in prayer.

AT THE PATRON PARTY in a drafty ballroom of the Roosevelt Hotel, across the street from the Orpheum Theater, Émile ate three Godiva chocolates, washed down by a glass of Perrier. He could never eat before a concert, although he would be ravenous after, and had requested that his sponsors leave him the usual ham sandwich in the dressing room. As Mrs. McNamara led him by the elbow from group to group of symphony supporters, the mind-numbing chatter calmed his nerves. So this was Papa's mythic New Orleans, another accident of history like Émile himself, not really America yet not quite Europe, a self-contained island that reminded him more of Martinique than of either Dallas or Paris. The only uncomfortable moments came when tipsy people tried out their Louisiana French on him and he couldn't understand the pronunciation, instances that proved even more taxing than when he'd tried to make sense of the gardener's English this morning. These had been perfect occasions to stop a circulating waiter and reach for a chocolate. Leaving, he pocketed a fourth chocolate to eat just before the performance.

He was now in the backstage dressing room, listening on a staticky speaker to the local orchestra saw through an uninspired performance of the "Eroica" symphony, savoring the fourth chocolate. Maman kept an empty chocolate box tucked behind the hat boxes in her musty bedroom armoire, and every once in a while the young Émile would take it down to run his fingers over the quilted rose cover and to smell the story inside. As she told it, this was the box of Belgian chocolates that a dark, handsome American soldier had given her as she scavenged for food in the ruins of a public market the day after the war ended. "It was the first time I'd eaten in days," she said, "and you can imagine, chocolates!"

Whatever happened later between Émile's moody father and austere mother, she claimed it was the best present she'd ever received. She never spoke ill of her ex-husband, not even of the disastrous months she spent on the segregated army base in Oklahoma the year before Émile was born. For a long time in Nevers, before his father began to sporadically send for him in the summers, the ratty copy of the "Basin Street Stompers" and that empty chocolate box were all he knew of the Negro American in the black-and-white photograph framed on the sideboard in the dining room. He was wearing a wide tie and striped, double-breasted suit, resting a trumpet on his shoulder, and looked like just about the happiest guy in the world. He paid for everything, of course, but never visited. Émile always assumed that was because life was so wonderful for him everywhere other than in boring old France. Or at least he thought so until he got to know his father's temper tantrums and inability to get along with anybody.

Émile could play anything by Chopin or Liszt blindfolded. Mamam had seen to that. But he always considered Beethoven devilishly tricky, almost as much as he found his father to be, which was perhaps why he chose for this concert the Sonata in C-Sharp Minor, Opus 27, Number 2, the one written during the year the composer was diagnosed as deaf. He'd worked all morning on the triplet figuration of the right hand and the half-pedaling required by the Adagio, a haunting pianissimo that took absolute mastery to sound both soft and strong at the same time. He was also anxious about the tempo of the rapid arpeggios in the third movement, which could have used one more run through. But now it was too late. As tepid applause crackled through the speaker, he stood and brushed the chocolate crumbs from his fingers.

Knuckles rapped on the door. "Monsieur Jackson?" The door cracked open, and the stiff red peaks of Mrs. McNamara's coiffure appeared. *"Nous allons?"*

"Yes, of course." Émile took a deep breath. "Lead the way."

"Your adoring audience awaits you."

Émile smiled stiffly. Although Mrs. McNamara didn't know it, tonight he had a special audience. The St. Louis Cemetery where his father was buried was only a few blocks away.

As soon as he was seated at the piano bench under the arc light, he spotted them, the only dark faces visible within the first three rows. The two old ladies were staring straight at him, smiles of recognition lining their faces. Among the highlighted blond hairdos, waxed eyebrows, and porcelain skin sparkling with jewelry, they stood out. The older one, a ragdoll of a woman with all of the sawdust shaken out, wore Coke-bottle glasses and a shabby blue coat, frost-white hair pulled tightly back into a bun. The younger one had a rouged, corpulent face, elaborate lacquered curls, and a corsage of artificial violets pinned to her ample bosom. Émile cocked an eyebrow at them before he nodded at the page turner. He raised his fingers above the piano, hushing the tittering auditorium as the first notes slid from the keyboard like a spool of plaintive moonlight spilling across stilled midnight water.

Although he never glanced up again at the two old ladies during the performance, he could hear his father listening, especially when he blew the pacing on the final arpeggio. Émile winced, detecting an impatient rattle from the newspaper masking Papa's face. Yet later, when he stood with head bowed to the standing ovation, he could hear a sound coming clearly from the direction of the old ladies, one he hadn't heard in a long time.

It was applause. Not quite his father's, but almost.

EVEN BEFORE THE TWO old women entered the dressing room, Émile could smell the mothballs. The odor became even more pungent as they stood in the doorway, waving at him over the beefy shoulder of a security guard with an apologetic air.

"Mr. Jackson, these two ladies says they knows you," he said, barring the doorway with a licorice-colored hand resting on the door knob.

"I told you," protested the hefty one in a rich contralto. The corsage of artificial violets jiggled as she tugged at the lapels of a black silk jacket, trying to close it over her mountainous breasts. "This is my brother Linton's boy, Émile."

"Are you Papa's family?" Émile gulped, put down the ham sandwich, and leapt to his feet. The floorboards of the old theater creaked under the acrylic carpeting.

"I been telling everybody at church my grandson coming to town," the older woman said, "and when Loretha Ducote ring me this afternoon to say you looking for us, I knew we had to come. Of course, had to hock the house to get tickets, but I been hearing about this young man for the past fifty years. Everybody this side of Canal Street know I'm Émile Jackson's grandma. And if they don't know who he is, I sure enough tell 'em."

"Should be proud of that." With a bashful smile, the security guard ushered the ladies in and shut the door.

Hands clasped together, the two women stood there, visibly percolating with joy.

"Please sit down," Émile said, drawing up two chairs.

The large lady, who made Émile think of the daintily toe-dancing hippos in *Fantasia*, was shifting from one foot to the other. She sank onto a chair with apparent relief, loosening the strap of a stiletto heel. "That sonata you played—"

"Oh hush up, you." Émile's grandmother hobbled over in orthopedic oxfords and threw her bony arms around him, smothering him with the scent of Vicks Vap-o-Rub and mothballs. "You look just like Linnie," she said, staring into his face with a wide display of dentures. "Don't know why he never brought you round before. That son of mine sure could be peculiar."

"If I'd have known how to contact you," Emile stuttered. "Papa never—"

"Linton didn't talk about anything else except how proud he was of you. Isn't that right, Mama?" The younger woman reached her stubby hand over to shake Émile's. "I'm his youngest sister, your Aunt Didi, a retired school teacher. Beethoven is my favorite composer, and I've never heard the "Moonlight Sonata" done with such exquisite—"

"Okay, Didi, we know you smart," the grandmother said, wagging her finger. "Just like Émile here know he a good piano player. Look, he eating a ham po'boy, just like Linnie used to do after he play his horn at the clubs. Let the man tell us how he is." She looked up at her grandson, as if expecting a full report.

"Well. . . ." Émile started to say they'd just put a stent in his heart and that he felt afraid and alone, but he didn't. He glanced at the half loaf of French bread stuffed with ham, lettuce, tomato, and pickles. "This sandwich doesn't look so poor to me." Speechless, he wiped his watering eyes. "I've been dreaming of this day for so long."

"How your mama over in France?" the grandmother asked. "What her name, Giselle?"

"She died last year."

"And your wife? I read somewhere you were married, more than I can say about this unclaimed jewel." Didi fluttered her fingers in mock melodrama. "How many kids?"

"Françoise and I divorced a while back." Émile looked down at his empty hands. "No children. After my own, I never wanted to preside over somebody else's unhappy childhood. I wouldn't have been a much better father than Papa was."

In the ensuing silence, each member of the Jackson family studied a different corner of the dressing room.

"That man sure had his ways," the grandmother finally said, shaking her head. "After he come home, we had a time with him. All that gin drinking and hollering didn't help none. Nothing ever be good enough for Linnie Jackson. He was too proud. But always was a lot down here to hurt his pride."

"He was a good man who felt bad about himself." Didi caught Émile's eye, then turned her face. "Like he didn't measure up to some inner standard. Before he passed, he told me that his only success in life was you. Late at night, he'd sit alone in the dark listening to your records and get all choked up, the only time I ever saw my brother cry."

"I remember during the few summer months I spent with him," Émile said, studying Papa's high cheek bones in his grandmother's face and blinking at the recognition, "he'd put me on the phone to somebody called Big Momma in New Orleans when he phoned on Sunday afternoons. That was *you*." At the funeral, he'd caught a glimpse of a weeping old lady he was sure was her. He had agonized over what to say, but his feet wouldn't carry him toward her. If his father hadn't wanted him to meet his family, he figured there were reasons, although the old man had been wrong about almost everything else.

"You had the cutest accent," the grandmother said. "*Oui, Mémère. Non, Mémère.* Sound like those French people out in the country. When you coming over to dinner, my little French boy? Forget about that old ham po'boy." She dismissed the sandwich with a wave. "You ain't never tasted my chicken."

"I'm flying to New York tomorrow morning."

"You'll have to come back real soon," Didi said. "You're related to half this city. You belong to us."

"Nobody has ever told me that before." In France he'd never really believed it, and now it would take some getting used to.

"What time is it, Didi? We don't want to miss that ten o'clock Esplanade bus. After that they come so irregular. TV say it gonna rain, and it so cold outside, I had to dig my good wool coat out the cedar chest."

As they stood to leave, Émile fished in his wallet for a business card, which he handed to his aunt, wrapped in two bills. "Here's where you can reach me. And please, on a night like this, take a taxi."

"This should be enough." Pursing her lips, Didi handed him back one of the two twenties. "I see somebody raised you right, although I doubt it was my brother."

"Didi, the present," the grandmother hissed, fumbling with the buttons on her blue wool coat.

"We have something for you," Didi said. "We weren't sure they would let us back here to see you, so we wrote our address and phone number inside this." She took a small box wrapped in Christmas paper from her enormous shoulder bag and handed it to him.

After Émile escorted the ladies along the corridor to the stage door, hugging several times along the way, he returned to his dressing room, flushed and exhausted, his heart racing. He carefully unwrapped the Scotch-taped package, peeling back the wrinkled Santa Clauses.

It was a box of chocolates.

Inside was a note scrawled on lined tablet paper, signed "Gloria & Didi Jackson," followed by an address and phone number. The mismatched top layer of chocolates looked as if they had been put together from other boxes of candies, and several had crusted white with age.

He threw back his head and beamed. It was the best present he'd ever received.

WHEN ÉMILE EMERGED, Mrs. McNamara was standing at the stage door under a sturdy black umbrella.

"I apologize for the weather," she said, extending the umbrella over his head. "But a limo is waiting. As I mentioned, we have dinner reservations at Antoine's for ten o'clock. My husband and I used to go there after every concert. Tonight it'll be you and I and a few members of the symphony board."

"That ham sandwich was quite filling." Émile tucked the box of chocolates into his overcoat pocket. "How do you call it, a 'poor boy'?"

"Hardly fare for someone of your stature. Wait until you taste Antoine's pompano *en papillote. C'est marveilleux.*"

"Mrs. McNamara, if you don't mind, I'll just walk back to the apartment. As you know, I'm still recuperating, and there are medications I need to take now." Emile touched his chest. He doubted that he could get through a whole besotted evening of being French with Mrs. McNamara. He longed for the musty smell of his war-bride mother's armoire, the mothball scent of his grandmother's coat. What had his father been so ashamed of all along? Those smells were where the music came from.

"But in this downpour?" Mrs. McNamara looked stricken. "We'll give you a ride."

"I never feel as if I've been somewhere until I've walked the streets myself. Madame, *s'il vous plait,* may I borrow your *parapluie*?"

She handed him the umbrella, turning up the collar of his coat. "It's just that. . . ."

Above their heads rain drops drummed on the umbrella.

"I'd so hoped. . . ." She seemed on the verge of tears, then her face crinkled with a flirtatious smile. "I heard you had a visitor backstage. You must have a lady in every port."

"It was my grandmother."

"Your grandmother!" She looked flustered. "Why in the world didn't you tell us? We could have arranged for a limo, a box seat, another reservation at Antoine's."

"She's very old." Émile smiled at the thought of his grandmother and Aunt Didi riding in the limo with Mrs. McNamara to Antoine's. Papa would have liked that. "Besides, we just met."

"Just met?" Mrs. McNamara folded her arms. "Your own grandmother?"

Émile felt old himself as his shoes squeaked across the slick cement of a deserted Canal Street. Entering the dimly-lit French Quarter, all he could make out under the rim of the umbrella were puddles lining the slippery bricks on Dauphine Street as rain lashed down around him. He felt a slight tightness in his chest, although nothing like the two-ton elephant that had been sitting there before the heart attack. When the orderlies wheeled him in for the angioplasty, he was petrified by the possibility that he would never give another concert. The cardiologist warned that he might require bypass surgery. His agent was alarmed by the news that he might retire from the stage, in which case Émile knew that he wouldn't live much longer. He had even drawn up a will. So tonight's concert was a triumph of sorts. Tomorrow, as soon as he got back to New York, he would ask the agent to confirm his spring bookings. In spite of the rough ending to the sonata this evening, he would tackle more of a Beethoven repertoire. He had already started to practice "La Pathétique," which together with tonight's piece might work well for the Denver date in April.

And he would get to know his father's family, perhaps during another concert stop in New Orleans this fall. Under the rim of the soggy umbrella, he took in the worn wooden stoops of the Creole cottages along Dauphine Street. Maybe his grandmother and Aunt Didi lived in just such a house. He imagined Papa sitting on steps like these to practice the trumpet, driven outside by the bustling ladies of the house into the warm, thick folds of a summer evening. Émile longed to sit on these steps to take in the dank, loamy smell of the city, but his shoes were already soaked and an icy wind whipped the overcoat around his knees.

When he reached St. Louis Street, he knew from the map he'd studied that St. Louis Cemetery Number Two was a few blocks to the left, and Mrs. McNamara's "vacation slave quarter" was two blocks to the right. He veered to the left. *Don't be a damn fool,* his father's voice commanded, *go home and take off those sopping wet socks.*

Once inside Mrs. McNamara's gate, he sloshed through the shadows of the dormant garden, past the thawing fish pond, and made it inside just as another downpour burst across the French doors. With a smile, he took the box of chocolates out of his pocket and studied the note. His first impulse was to call his grandmother, to ask her and Aunt Didi if they had made it home safe and dry. And he wanted to hear them ask if he were all right. But he glanced at the kitchen clock, kicked off his shoes, and changed his socks. Once dry and comfortable, he popped open Mrs. McNamara's bottle of champagne and set a bubbling flute on top of the baby grand, a tear of foam spilling over the lip.

His problem, Émile knew, was the build up of arpeggios in the third movement of Beethoven's sonata. While a torrent of rain lashed against the windowpanes next to him, he flipped through the sheet music until he found the right page. Then he touched his fingers to the keyboard, and as the gusty chords matched the force of the thunderstorm over the city, he could feel Papa's presence outside, nodding in approval.

UNDER THE HOUSE

ROBERTA THOUGHT IT ridiculous that a father couldn't babysit for his own four-year-old daughter, even if he was an ex-crack addict. At least she hoped the "ex" part about Trevor was still true, but maybe that was why she'd been asked to come keep an eye on things this weekend.

Trevor's parents, her sister and brother-in-law, were at a wedding in the Florida Keys, and Roberta was on her way to their organic vegetable farm in Folsom, across Lake Pontchartrain from her home in New Orleans. Although the farm was hidden away in a backwoods of scrub pines, this once rural area had become a booming exurb of cloverleaves and strip malls. Roberta was used to walking three blocks to the grocery trailing a granny cart, chatting along the way with porch-sitting neighbors, and wasn't sure which of the extremes over here made her more nervous, the bumper-to-bumper traffic she was just stuck in or the utter isolation awaiting her once she reached the farm. As she passed the familiar Waffle House on the right, she strained to spot the red mailbox to the left that signaled the long, winding road to the house. On the seat next to her she had an emergency supply of Xanax in an overnight case, and under the mohair shawl piled on top—these country nights could be chilly—her pistol.

The exuberant blackberry vines clawing their way through

the azalea bushes on the drive to the house were ripening, and Roberta decided that would be the perfect outing for her great niece, to take Carolyn berry picking. Wasn't that what kids did in the country, dressed in denim overalls and carrying wicker baskets? For thirty years she had administered the pathology lab at Touro Infirmary, and didn't have a rural bone in her body. At home she had a molting parakeet and a bed of sun-scorched petunias, and except for fighting the spiders that infested her house every summer, that was about it as far as she and nature were concerned. Nothing was going to get her, not if she could help it, and her interest in protecting small, vulnerable beings ended with herself. She'd endured the shooting lessons required to properly license her pistol, and in her laundry room had a whole shelf devoted to cans of bug spray that promised to "kill on contact."

Her woodsy-fernsy sister was the polar opposite. Over twenty years ago the younger sister and her psychologist husband, who had met at college in Santa Cruz, California, moved across the lake scouting out, as they put it, "enhanced wholistic options" for bringing up their only child, Trevor. They insisted on "going back to the earth," were dedicated to organic gardening, and raised their kid like a hot-house seedling. At an expensive private school, the antsy boy was prescribed Ritalin by age seven, and as a teenager finally landed in a drug rehab program set in a pine forest. Then, instead of college, came two years in jail over some crack transaction gone bad. The mother of his little girl was still locked up on distribution charges, and Carolyn would have wound up in foster care if her grandparents hadn't agreed to take her in.

As Roberta pulled her Nissan next to Trevor's pickup under the moss-draped oaks in front of the two-story house, she wondered whether she also might start smoking crack if she lived out here. What in the world was there to do except watch zucchini grow?

"Hey, Aunt Berta." Heavy-set Trevor came pounding down the wooden front steps, longneck beer in hand. Even with the scraggly new beard, he was still a handsome young man, except for the squiggly tattoos up and down his arms and those round Ubangi-looking thingamajigs weighing down his earlobes.

Roberta stuck her avian beak out of the car window, the meticulously made-up face topped by a curly bob dyed a shade too blond. She took a deep breath, clearing the freeway from her lungs and sucking in the piney, cut-grass smell. Here goes, she thought, popping open the car door and planting her sturdy oxfords in a thick matting of leaf mould.

"Let me help you with your luggage."

"That's okay." She reached over to embrace her nephew, almost bowled over by his beery breath. "It's just an overnight case." She walked around to the passenger side of the car, slipped her pistol into the valise, and draped the shawl over one shoulder. "Sorry I'm late. Traffic was terrible."

"I heard. Mom and Dad just called to say they made it to the airport in time."

"Where's Carolyn?"

"Playing with her dolls under the house."

Roberta turned to take in the filmy expanse of tree tops along the distant property line, and the neat rows of cucumbers, poled beans, and trellised squash plants soaking up the last rays of the setting sun. It was like Farmer McGregor's garden.

Under the house?

Wasn't that where kids went to hide when their parents abandoned or abused them? Three years after she'd moved into her own house, a news story gripped the Uptown neighborhood where she lived: drug thugs had kidnapped a young wife, fed her LSD, and for two weeks kept her chained naked and hallucinating under their house. Just thinking about it made Roberta shudder, wiping imaginary spider webs off her arms.

Trevor got down on his hands and knees next to one of the three-foot-high brick pillars that raised the clapboard house above the flood line and shouted, "Look who's here. Aunt Berta! She came all the way from New Orleans to see you."

A blond child with grubby knees and a necklace of filthy sweat crawled out, dragging two naked dolls by their matted nylon hair.

"That's no place for a young lady to play." Roberta shot her nephew a stern look. "Under there must be crawling with pathogens. Carolyn, come upstairs with me, I'll put you in the tub, and then we'll see about dinner."

"She says under there is her make-believe world," Trevor explained.

"I see," said Roberta, studying up close the Ubangi thingamajigs in her nephew's ears. "And what's so wrong with the real one?" Then stooping to kiss her niece, she gestured toward Farmer McGregor's garden. "Look at all the cute bunny rabbits hopping around out there."

The first thing Trevor did when they entered the house was to warn his aunt, "If the landline rings, don't answer it."

Roberta was standing under the cathedral ceiling in the renovated living room lit by a massive bronze chandelier, its eight spidery arms holding out twinkling bulbs. With one hand she lugged her overnight case and with the other gripped Carolyn's grimy fingers.

"Your parents always call me on my cell, but may I ask why I shouldn't answer the house phone?"

"It might be some bad people calling."

"Bad people?"

"Some dudes that have been harassing me about stuff."

"From the 7-Eleven?" Roberta knew that he had a job at a convenience store, part-time work mandated by his probation officer.

"Yeah," he said, looking down. "You know how some people are. Out to get you."

Roberta shook her head, tugging Carolyn toward the stair case. "No, I don't know how some of the people you know are. Come on," she said to the child, mounting the staircase. "Let's go see about that bath."

"Just don't answer the landline, okay?"

Under the House

SMELLING OF TALCUM and baby shampoo, the freshly scrubbed girl perched in flannel bunny pajamas on a kitchen chair, watching her aunt steam broccoli fresh from the garden, slice Creole tomatoes, and broil trout that her grandfather had caught earlier that week. Night had fallen around the farmhouse, now aglow with amber light and filled with nutritious smells. As if to impress his agnostic aunt, Trevor said grace over the carefully set table, and then toyed with the food he'd just thanked the good Lord for, sticking toothpicks into broccoli spears to fashion little boats that he sailed across the tablecloth onto his beaming daughter's plate. Over the years, Roberta had never seen him eat a single bite of vegetables.

In the middle of dinner the house phone rang. Roberta was halfway out of her chair when Trevor eyed his aunt, as if to remind her not to answer it. Later, washing up, Roberta noticed him standing in front of the freezer, eating from a half-gallon of ice cream with a serving spoon. So much for dessert. Her sister had specified that Carolyn wasn't to be fed sugar in any form.

While tucking Carolyn into bed upstairs, Roberta hoped that her sister wasn't making the same mistakes in raising her grandchild that she made with that wayward son of hers. Roberta was childless and had never married, a career woman, as she called herself, and had few regrets. She'd had to study long and work hard for what she put together in life—her own home, a professional pension, and personal independence—which made her less than indulgent of other people's bad choices. Her only sister had given up a post-grad biology fellowship to marry and have a child, one whom she'd raised by the book as if he were a Pavlovian science project, like the hamster in grammar school they'd taught to spin faster and faster on his wheel by withholding food until he'd made a calculated number of rotations. Roberta had stood by helplessly as Trevor was brought up in the same way, spinning through an endless round of archery lessons and psych-evaluation appointments and math tutors, with no sugar or television or toy weapons or violent video games allowed in the house. Was it any wonder that he sought illicit rushes elsewhere? Or that he'd fallen open-armed into the embrace of the first person to ever really accept him, warts and all, even if Carolyn's mother was a drug-crazed hotel maid from a trailer park whose only discernible interest in life seemed to be collecting toothbrushes?

Carolyn was sound asleep by the time her aunt finished reading aloud the bedtime book she begged for, *Where the Wild Things Are.* When Roberta tiptoed down the stairs, she recognized the sweet musky odor even before she spotted Trevor's back through the arms of the chandelier, smoke rising from the kitchen doorway that opened onto the screened back porch.

As she approached him, he swiveled around to ask her if she wanted a hit.

"What did you say?" Roberta skittered away.

"A toke of this blunt," he said, exhaling. "It's twenty-four/seven, you know, that medical-grade shit from California."

"I don't care if it's seven/eleven from Tangipahao. How dare you," she sputtered, face reddening, "smoke that thing in the same house with a child?"

"I'm her father."

"Well, that's a fine how-do-you-do." Sometimes it shocked her how much she'd come to sound like her mother, not only in the expressions that popped out but in the quivering timbre of her voice.

"Come on, Aunt Berta," Trevor said, waving the fragrant joint in her face. "Mom told me you used to be a real stoner. And pretty foxy, too."

Roberta turned around to face the sink, grabbing a dirty glass to wash, so that Trevor wouldn't see the trace of a smile playing around the corners of her mouth. She hadn't smoked marijuana in what—thirty-five years?—and couldn't even remember why she'd once been so fond of it. What did they call it then? A doobie? A number? It occurred to her that she still had a vintage doobie tucked inside a college textbook, the *Norton Anthology of British Literature,* Volume Two, in case she ever again felt the craving, but she hadn't thought of it in years. Of course, it wasn't that she was against pot. It had nothing to do with addictive trash drugs like meth and crack that ruined people's lives these days, but the thought of it simply bored her. Like the LPs she used to listen to, grass seemed to belong to another time and place, and now to another century, her century, the one that had passed her by.

"Finish that outside on the porch, if you don't mind," Roberta said, holding the washed glass up to the light.

"Sure thing," he said with a knowing grin, shooting a stream of smoke in her direction. "After that, I need to go out for a while. Just to the 7-Eleven, to relieve a guy who got sick until the store closes."

Ten minutes later his truck peeled out, headlights flashing through the kitchen window. Roberta felt relieved to be alone in the house for a couple of hours. Maybe she'd make potato salad for tomorrow's lunch while listening to the NPR weekly opera broadcast.

First she wandered out to the back porch to collect her thoughts. Frogs were chorusing their steady *knee-deep knee-deep*, and moonlight pooled among the poled and trellised vegetables. It was peaceful on the farm, she had to admit, and staring through the screen, hoped to catch sight of a deer. No police sirens, wailing car alarms, or neighbors' TVs intruded, and certainly no firecracker pops of distant gang gunfire. It amused her that she'd thought to bring the pistol, without which she didn't feel safe living alone in the city. Yes, indeed, she'd have no trouble getting used to the plush green quiet out here.

Trevor had left his half-smoked joint in the ashtray on the white wicker coffee table, and Roberta picked it up to sniff. The pungent smell brought her back. In college one of her long-haired boyfriends, who dealt a little weed on the side, had taken to calling her Birdie instead of Berta because he claimed she was always either pecking at him or chirping. He hadn't lasted long. None of them had, disappearing in clouds of pot smoke.

She put the joint back in the ashtray and reminded herself to bring it inside later. You couldn't leave something like that lying around with a child in the house.

Then she picked it up again. What could one or two tokes

hurt?

She fired it up with the Bic lighter next to the ashtray and held the first puff in her lungs. Goodness, that felt better. The godawful traffic, the rushing around the house trying to appear motherly and in charge, and the concern about being stuck out here in the middle of nowhere melted away. Another puff should do it. Then she'd deposit it in a Ziploc bag to return to her nephew with the proper reproach. By the third toke she was floating along with the frog choruses, feeling her heart beat to their soothing rhythms. What a lovely night it would be to bathe in moonlight, to stroll among the rows of ripening tomatoes and leafy kale, paying respectful tribute to the elements of nature missing in her life.

The house phone was ringing off the hook. Roberta ignored it.

She had no sooner creaked open the screened door and descended the steps when she spotted it, the long sinister shadow creeping along under the oak trees. Whatever it was, it was moving, and she could swear it was topped by a pair of beady amber eyes. The way that it swayed sent shivers down her spine, and her jaw tightened. It must be an alligator from the drainage ditch behind the tree line. Hadn't her sister told her something about alligators, either here or on a neighbor's property? Could the toothy reptile climb the steps, chew through the screen door, and get into the house?

Scurrying back onto the porch, she latched the screened door and dragged the white wicker settee over to brace it closed. Then she switched off the porch light, sweating and gasping. She stood paralyzed on the darkened porch a long time—it felt like forever—staring at the creeping shadow through the screen.

Only now it wasn't creeping. And there were no amber eyes, only a sporadic flitting of fireflies. In the darkness, the long shape resolved itself into a tree limb that must have fallen from the oak above and lay rotting in a pile of leaves. The moonlit clouds that seemed to animate the shadow had stopped racing through the sky.

She was safe: there was nothing out there.

She dragged the settee away from the door, flicked on the porch light, and walked down the steps. Now she remembered, giggling with relief. Grass. Paranoia.

What had they called it in college?

Panic grass.

At that moment, two bright headlights were moving toward the house. Trevor, she thought, at last. Was it eleven already? But the beams weren't from her nephew's beat-up old pickup but from a monster black truck raised high off the ground by eighteen-wheeler tires, roaring like something in a Nascar race as its icy blue lights flooded the front of the house. Head-splitting hip hop blared through the tinted windows, a thumping woofer rattling the glass panes in the kitchen door.

Two figures, one tall, wiry, and quick-limbed, the other slower and squat, jumped down from the truck. Roberta scampered up the steps, latched the screened door, and stood hands on hips, glaring at the truck's elaborate grille as it it were Darth Vader's helmet.

"Turn down that racket before you wake the baby," she shouted, the words catching in her throat.

"Trevor here?" asked the tall one, his ferret-like face pointing toward the porch.

"He's out."

"You his mom?"

"What?" Roberta screamed, hands over her ears.

The squat one reached up inside the truck to kill the music and headlights.

The frogs resumed their chorus, the moonlight its shimmer.

"You the mother?"

"None of your business," Roberta said, unwilling to give out any information to such people. "Are you his friends from the 7-Eleven?"

"Yeah, in a way," said the squat one, spitting on the ground. "From the 7-Eleven parking lot, that is. And he's got something of ours."

"That's where he is right now, at work." Roberta still felt exceedingly odd from the joint. Could this possibly be happening, or was it another illusory alligator emerging from her pot-addled brain? Did they call that weed twenty-four/seven because its effect never wore off? "You can probably catch—"

"No, he ain't. We checked. And we been calling the number he give us all night."

"Come back another time."

"You here alone?" The tall one smirked.

"Certainly not. We have a houseful of company."

"Mind if we come in to wait with y'all's company?"

This was getting out of hand. "I told you—"

"And I done told Trevor we not putting up with his shit no more," bellowed the tall one. And with one swift thrust of his steel-toed boot, he kicked at the wooden base of the screened door. The latch popped off, clattering to the floor at Roberta's feet, and the door swung open.

BEFORE SHE KNEW IT, Roberta was standing with the two young men next to the granite kitchen island, where she got a better look at them. Like Trevor, they both had spider webs tattooed on their elbows, although unlike her nephew, they displayed no pretense at good manners. The tall, ferret-like one ransacked the place with his jumpy eyes while the bald, squat one with the low forehead and pug nose stared Roberta down, as if daring her to return his gaze.

While the tall one sauntered into the living room, subjecting every corner to his scrutiny, the squat one tried to strike up conversation with the old lady frozen in front of him.

"Where's your company?"

"My son, who just got back from deployment in Afghanistan, is upstairs watching TV, and his father—"

"Can the company bullshit, lady. I know Trevor ain't got no brother."

"I'm not his mother, but his aunt."

"Where his parents at?"

Roberta folded her arms across her chest and lashed out. "If you two hoodlums aren't out of here in ten seconds, I'm calling the cops." She could hear drawers being opened in the living room, chairs scraped across the floor, and cushions thrown around. "I don't need to put up with this."

The man just smiled and shook his head, as if he appreciated her stab at humor.

The tall one strode back into the kitchen, where he threw open cupboard doors.

"What in the world are you looking for?" Roberta asked him. "The cookie jar?"

"We'll be out of here right away if you show us where the dude keeps his stash."

"Of marijuana?"

They both cracked up.

"The rocks, lady," explained the squat one. "The coke we fronted him to sell that he never paid us for or returned. Trevor's a bad businessman, hear what I'm saying?"

"Oh that." Roberta's mind raced. "I know just where he keeps them. The rocks. Upstairs."

"You lead, and we'll follow."

"I am not, under any circumstances, going to take you into a room where a baby is sleeping. You'll have to wait here while I go get them."

"Jeez, keeps crack in his kid's room?" The two exchanged baffled glances, and the tall one nodded. "You not back here in five minutes, we're coming up after you."

Roberta sprinted through the living room and up the stairs, heart racing. On the second floor, she eased open the door to the child's room, where Carolyn lay curled in slumber, holding a felt bunny rabbit with long, dirty ears. Roberta blew her a kiss, and then slid the door shut. Her next stop was the guest room, where muttering to herself she rooted around inside her overnight case until she found it. She clicked off the safety, threw a plaid robe over her lacy blouse and navy skirt, and then tucked the pistol into the robe's sagging pocket.

Minutes later, she stood midway on the staircase, staring down onto the heads of the two home invaders.

Then she pulled out the pistol and aimed it at them.

They glanced up.

"I want you to turn around, walk out this house, get back in your truck, drive off this property, and never come back. Whatever then happens between you and my nephew is none of my business."

"Come on, lady," said the squat one. "This ain't cops and robbers, but business. We not gonna hurt you or take nothing but our merchandise."

They both lunged toward the staircase.

Just as she'd been taught at the firing range, Roberta stiffened her arm, took aim at the bronze chain holding up the chandelier, squinted, and fired. The massive light fixture came crashing to the floor, missing both men by inches.

"Holy shit," the tall one said.

"The next shot's aimed at you," she announced.

Among the shadows in the dimmed room, now lit by a single table lamp, their silhouettes backed toward the kitchen door. Roberta stood planted on the staircase, arm steadied, muzzle aimed at the kitchen, until the screened door banged, a flash of headlights flooded the window, and a motor revved up. Tires squealed, the lights disappeared, and the engine roar faded into the distance.

Roberta collapsed onto the step where she'd been standing and burst into tears. Then she blew her nose on the robe's sleeve. Nothing like this had ever happened to her before, but now she knew exactly what she needed to do. And she didn't have a moment to lose.

Those drug thugs could be back any minute with their arsenal.

"COME ON, HONEY, we're going for a drive." Roberta slid the sleeping child into her arms, brushing the hair out of her eyes.

Carolyn woke, staring wide-eyed at her aunt.

"Where we going?"

"To my house in New Orleans. To make fudge!" That was what Roberta needed at the moment, a Xanax and a chunk of pecan fudge.

"Why?"

"Because I have a present for you there that I forgot to bring. And your MawMaw and PawPaw will be there tomorrow to help us eat the fudge."

"Is Daddy coming?"

"He's not here."

"Where is he?"

"Playing under the house."

"At nighttime?"

"In his enchanted garden, where it's always a terrible day in the neighborhood."

Roberta scooped up the girl's sundress from a chair, grabbed her hair brush, and then propped her up on the guestroom bed while she threw her own things into the valise. Then still in her plaid robe with the bulging pocket, she crept down the stairs, overnight case in hand, the child thrown over her shoulder. She stepped around the splintered bulbs and splayed wiring of the smashed chandelier, and nudged open the screened door.

Carolyn was fast asleep by the time she laid her on the front seat of the car and covered her with the mohair shawl. Spinning around, Roberta was startled by the headlights zeroing in on the house, and yanked the pistol out of her robe pocket. But they weren't the glary headlights of the monster black truck but the blurry ones of a rattling old pickup.

Trevor's.

She slipped the pistol back in her pocket and leaned inside to start the car engine. Then she turned to her nephew, who was sliding out of the front seat of his truck, a six-pack dangling from his finger by the plastic holder.

"Whassup?"

"I'll tell you what's up," Roberta hissed, trying not to wake the child, "and I'll tell you what's going down." She jabbed her index finger into his chest, steering him toward the house so fast that the Ubangi thingamajigs in his earlobes swayed. "The 'bad people' who have been calling you paid us a little visit tonight looking for your supply of goddamn crack cocaine, and they scared the bejesus out of me. So I shot down the chandelier in the living room and drove them off."

"They came *here*?" Obviously dazed, Trevor just stood there, fingering the six-pack.

"I don't know or care what you're smoking or peddling, but what you're going to do right now is get inside, pack your things, and by dawn be gone. If you ever poke your nose in this house again, I'm going to call your probation officer about the crack dealing, speak with Child Protective Services, and then ring the St. Tammany sheriff's office to report the home invasion tonight. When they pick up your two business associates, they'll rat you out faster than you can roll a joint, and all three of you will be slammed for a good long time. Have I made myself clear? Want me to clarify any doubts in that foggy mind of yours?"

"What about Carolyn?"

"Your mom and dad will pick her up tomorrow at my house. I'll call them on my way home with a full report, don't you worry."

"And my parental rights?"

"You forfeited your parental rights the minute you started dealing drugs. You and that mother of hers."

"Can I tell her goodbye?"

Roberta reached into her robe pocket. "If you wake up that baby, I'll shoot you, swear to God. Now get in the house and start packing."

"Aunt Berta," he said, face caving in, "aren't you being, like, a little harsh. I love you."

"Go study that mess on the living room floor if you want to see what love is made of. A bunch of hot wires jumbled together with shards of light and hard, hard choices. And there's no use in you hanging around here waiting for any more of it. You're never going to get what you want from your family until you go somewhere else to finish growing up on your own. The longer you stay here, the littler you'll get, until soon your daughter will be more grown up than you are."

Roberta left her nephew standing in front of the screened door swinging the six-pack with a shell-shocked look on his face. Then she gunned the Nissan, whirled it around, and shot back down the winding, blackberry-laden road to the two-lane highway. She put off calling the child's grandparents in Florida, afraid to wake her, still clutching the bunny. Besides, how could she explain to her sister what had happened? That Roberta—the spinster, the sensible sibling—got stoned on her nephew's weed, had another one of her panic attacks, shot up the whole damn place, and kidnapped her niece? Or that crack dealers invaded the house looking for Trevor's drugs, threatening her safety and Carolyn's, and would probably come back, armed to the teeth? As Roberta squinted through her night vision at the road ahead, the fuzzy line between these two versions blurred like the yellow stripe dividing the lanes in front of the car.

Somewhere past the Waffle House, the little girl woke up, rubbing her eyes. "Why we have to go to New Orleans to make fudge?"

"Because your grandmother wouldn't allow it." Roberta shot her a sly smile. "But I have a stash of chocolate at home."

The child frowned. "Is Daddy still under the house?"

"Looks like it."

"What's he doing there?"

"Playing make believe."

"With my dolls?"

"No, with his own scary dolls."

Theirs was the only car on the road, and the headlights illuminated the menacing tangle of vine-covered underbrush on either side of the tarmac. In the hazy distance, sparsely spaced arc lights led the way back to the blazing snarl of cloverleaves and strip malls ahead. No wonder her nephew grew up the way he did, Roberta thought, if that was the only thing people around here knew as civilization.

"Will Daddy come see us in New Orleans?"

"He'd better not." Roberta reached over to tuck the shawl around her niece. "Now hush and let Aunt Berta drive. You go back to sleep, hear?"

Mary Sorrows

THIS WAS SUPPOSED to have been the big day, but my boyfriend Joe stood me up, the little *hijo de puta*. Again. This time at the clinic. The son of a bitch was supposed to pay for it, since I'm waiting to start classes at Holy Cross College and don't have a job yet. So here I am outside the clinic in the teeming rain, texting him like crazy, while these red-faced loons are prancing up and down on the sidewalk out front waving signs that say "Baby Killer" and "Abortion Is Murder." This wrinkled old witch straight out of a fairy tale comes up to me and points her knobby finger at the gold cross around my neck that I got for my First Holy Communion.

"Are you a Christian, honey?" she asks.

I blow a stream of smoke in her face. "That's so none of your beeswax."

"If Mary had an abortion," she goes, "we wouldn't be celebrating Christmas this year in America. What country are you from?"

I turn my back.

Look, I want to tell her, my name is Delores and I'm, like, an American, born in bread. Which is more than I can say about some of the people hanging around our house who don't speak English so good. I was raised here in New Orleans, and just graduated from Mother Cabrini High School. So, lady, don't be going, "You Spanish or something?" I've never even been to Spain or any of those other countries down there where my family came from hundreds of years ago when my mom was a little girl.

You'll notice that my name is spelled like the black girls do—Delores—not like "María Dolores," which it says on my birth certificate. What retard would name someone Mary Sorrows? I mean *heeello?* Let's try to be more modern, okay? My mom's name is Marisol, which I always thought sounded so bright and outdoorsy because *sol* means "sun." But then she tells me her official name is María Soledad, which is like Mary Loneliness or something. And my grandmother's name Angus—it fits her to a T because she's as big as a cow—is really María Angustia, or Mary Anguish. So there you have it, three generations of anguish and loneliness and sorrow, only you can count me out.

I'm Delores, with an *e*. An American.

Bet I know why Joe isn't texting me back. He probably spent the abortion money on a lid last night or did some lines with his homeys. Tears are streaming down my cheeks and my mascara is running as I plop down on the curb under an umbrella, slowly figuring out that Joe isn't going to show. We've been together forever—six whole months—and I can't understand how he could do this to me, leave me pregnant and parked in the gutter. If I'd told my mom, she would have put on her high-heeled tap shoes and clacked over to his house waving a shotgun. Right now we'd be hitched and I'd be living with him in that scuzzy room in the back of his folks' carport in Marrero, watching him take apart one of his greasy lawnmowers while I smoke and polish my nails. That's not going to happen, so I explained to him over and over that this was the only way out. He said that I was trying to trap him by forgetting to take my pill, which is no way true.

I forgot because I forgot.

Period.

Then I go to the Winn Dixie for a six-pack of water, and the check-out lady in my line has this religious conniption fit, with angels probably floating over her scanner. She's the color of a

Tootsie Roll, with a mole in the middle of her forehead and oily hair wrapped up tight in a hair net and I don't even want to look at her she's so scaly, but she starts shaking, eyes popping up at the fluorescent lights.

"Girl, Jesus just spoke to me," she goes, staring straight at me, "and said *don't do it*."

"Do what?" I ask, like this Tootsie Roll knows what's going on inside my head.

"What you about to do. I can feel it right here," she says, grabbing her fat stomach. "The Lord loves you and that child."

Oh my God, I totally freak, and take my water to another line, where the only thing the check-out lady says is "paper or plastic?"

"Plastic," I go, trying to act like a normal person. Meanwhile this Tootsie-Roll prophet is eye-balling me from the next cash register, mouthing *don't do it, don't do it.*

As usual, my mom is at rehearsal, so when I get home, I just scram into my room and slam the door. I really need to talk to her bad, but my mother isn't like other moms. She loves me and makes me clean my room and has an ordinary job as a secretary at a hospital, where she has to wear a regular skirt and speak English all day long. I've hardly told anyone, not even Joe, but my mom is—I don't believe this—a flamenco dancer. With those clicky-clacky things on her fingers and the long ruffled skirts that go on for a mile and the screaming and stomping around, like she just drank ten cups of coffee and is trying to stamp on a million cockroaches at once.

She says it's her "tradition" and "expresses her soul," but really she just likes to put on those gold hoop earrings and tons of makeup and go running the streets, speaking Spanish. My dad was a famous flamenco guy over in Spain—bet you haven't heard of him—but I never met him and now he's dead. Whatever. These days Mom dates flamenco guitar players and singers who moan like they've got the flu and even this one dork who plays the *cajón*, although I don't know how you can call anyone a musician who sits on a wooden box, banging it with his fingers. That's so lame, like something we used to do for extra credit in Music Appreciation. This year I finally told my best friend Dana. She's a cheerleader and spread around school that my mom was a flamingo dancer. For months everyone was after me to "do the flamingo," which is this humongous pink bird in Miami that stands around on one leg all day and doesn't even move, much less dance. And so one day I went to my desk and somebody had left a plastic flamingo on it to make fun of me and I just about died. If you want to know the truth, kids can be so cruel, even the smart ones. So don't tell anyone my mom is a flamenco dancer, hear? I've got enough problems already.

"*NO ME DIGAS. ¿Un aborto*?" my grandmother says, stirring the eternal pot of vegetable soup on the back burner in the kitchen of her shotgun house in Mid City. Abuelita's face is scrunched up into a scowl, and she crosses herself, lowering her big booty into one of the vinyl dinette chairs as if her glass bones were about to snap.

"Joe has a good job cutting lawns, and just hired someone to help him." I can't believe I'm telling her about my boyfriend and the abortion, but she knows how to listen, even if she can't speak English too good. "But we're not ready to do the marriage thing." I can't imagine where I'd hang all of my clothes in that bedroom of his. He doesn't even have a closet, and his clothes are piled on the floor. I'd rather raise my baby in a manger like the Holy Mother because even barnyard straw is cleaner than Joe's skanky socks and boxers.

"*Casarse o no casarse*," Abuelita says, shaking her head, "what you do is *pecado*, a sin." She reaches over and grabs my hand. "Marisol wanted to do the same thing. With you. I put my big foots down." She stomps like a flamenco dancer. "And *otra vez* for you." She stomps again, rattling the light dangling over the dinette table. All we need is a *cajón* and we could charge admission.

"Mom wanted to abort me?" What do you expect from three

generations of anguish and loneliness and sorrow?

She revolves her hands in a circle like a tumbler dryer. "*Lo mismo.*" She explains in Spanish that right here, nineteen years ago, her daughter sat in the same chair crying after she came home from tramping around Spain, telling her the identical story. Says America is good for certain things—freedom and Walmart and Pop-Tarts—but women suffer more here because they make bad choices they wouldn't be free to make in Honduras, where girls are kept behind the barred windows of their papas' houses until delivered as virgins into the hands of their husbands. But Mom grew up wild in America because her own papa was killed by the government in Honduras when they stole his farm, and then look at me, she says, with no papa around to say "no." "Look," she says, pointing at me. "*Mira qué desgracia.*"

Okay, maybe I am a disgrace, I realize, sinking into the dinette chair as I think of what my abuelita and mom have gone through. "*¿Entonces qué voy a hacer?*" I ask, wondering what the hell to do now.

"*Sea fuerte,*" she says, clenching her fist.

"How?" I don't know how to be strong. All I know how to do is shop, shave my legs, tint my hair, and look pretty. Although I'm a whiz at algebra and can dissect a frog in ten seconds flat.

Abuelita gets up and moves around the kitchen, washing plates and wiping counters. She's singing a song about a girl who nobody wants, a girl who decides to love herself so she can love her own baby. "*Ay niña linda, linda, la niña a que nadie quiere.*" Spanish really is a more beautiful language to sing in. It does something to my heart, like a firecracker exploding inside. Abuelita puts a bowl of soup in front of me, a spoon, and a hunk of her crusty homemade bread. She wants me to be hungry, but my stomach is tied up in knots.

"How to be strong like you and Mom?" I ask again. I'm starving for something else.

"Eat," she says, pouring me a glass of Pepsi. "And sing." Her fingers are bunched together, gesturing toward her mouth.

I DRIVE AROUND AND around the city, waiting for my mom's rehearsal to be over, but when I get to the garage Uptown where she's been practicing, they tell me she's already at the *tablao,* which is like the name for their cockroach-killing concerts. The show is at some joint on Canal Street called Chickie Wah Wah, and while I'm heading back downtown I finally get a text from Joe: *sorry luv u.* All I can think to text back is *LOL @ yr luv bye,* and then hit the accelerator. I have to talk with Mom about what I'm going to do, and at this point Joe is so out of the picture. As if he loved me, snorting the abortion money up his big fat nose. I'll never be with anyone again.

Ever.

The so-called nightclub is a long dark cave with a bar on one side and a spot lit wooden stage at the back. Walking in, I already hear canned music of some old guy groaning in Spanish like they just sawed off both his legs. A woman stationed with a basket near the door wants me to pay fifteen dollars, but when I tell her that I'm looking for my mom, Marisol, she jumps up to go find her. I try to melt into a dark corner near the video poker machines, wondering if now really is the best moment to bring this up. But after the show Mom will be out until all hours, tooling around in those gold hoop earrings and clapping and singing dumb Spanish songs, and then in the morning before she goes to the hospital, she'll be hung over and hunched over a cup of coffee, staring at the newspaper cross-eyed. I know her.

She finally comes sweeping out in a red polka-dot dress, heels clacking along the cement floor. She's short, with wide hips and legs like overpass posts, and walks like she owns the earth. Coal-black hair is piled on top of her head, her shoulders draped with a silky shawl fringed like a tablecloth. *"Mi hija!"* she shouts in a hoarse voice, and everyone turns around to gape at her daughter. I can tell from the stagey voice that she's already on, doing that stormy diva thing of hers, talking a mile a minute with arched eyebrows painted up to her hair line and scarlet lips flashing like a stop light. I feel so pale and little, like some sick kitten on a cold night that the nuns would take pity on.

"Hey, Mom," I mew, shivering with the enormity of what I have to say.

"*Mi amor*!" Like some crazed parrot, she swoops down on me with smooches as if I've just come back from a year in, like, Borneo. "*¿Pero qué haces aquí?* Have you come to see the show? Paco," she screams to a bony guy with stringy gray hair, "Dolores is here to watch me dance. At last!" She strikes a haughty pose and snaps her fingers above her head.

"We need to talk," I say.

"Back at the house." She cuts me a look that could slice chorizo.

"I'm in trouble." My eyes are leaking, and then my shoulders shudder.

Her face falls shut, and the clown mask slides off. She grabs me by the elbow and marches me outside, where couples are lounging around tables smoking. They applaud when she walks past, calling out flamenco stuff like *olé* and *elé*, only now her face is as stern as a cast-iron skillet. She kicks out the chair at an empty table and shoves me into it. When she leans into me from across the table, the beauty mark penciled like a mole on her cheek is twitching.

"Thought I smelled something funny in your room." She lowers her voice to a raspy whisper. "So much like your father. You on drugs?"

"Mom?" I whine. "As if."

"Then what?"

"I missed my appointment today at the clinic."

"What clinic?" Her brow furrows.

I stare down at the cigarette butts on the sidewalk. "The abortion clinic."

She doesn't miss a beat. "Joe?"

I nod.

"No good *hijo de puta*," she curses, sucking in her cheeks and staring into the distance. "I warned you about that son of a bitch." She splays out her polka-dotted skirt and crosses her legs. "Okay, I knew something like this was going to happen. It's our fate."

"I talked to Abuelita," I say, trying to get back at her. "She said you tried to do the same thing with me."

"They didn't have pills back then in Spain. Or foam or IUDs or nothing. By the time I got home from Sevilla, it was a done deal."

"I forgot to take—"

"You didn't forget. You're just out of high school and don't have a job and are trying to come up with the next step in the dance. Only nowadays women can do other things beside pop out babies. I hope you realize this ruins your chance for starting college. Who'll take care of the baby while I'm at work and you're in class?"

I shrink back into the chair, shaking my head. "I'm not having—"

She leans over, grabs my wrists, and shakes me. "God be my witness, you are."

"Mom? I'm not strong like you and Abuelita."

"And what do you think makes us strong?" She jumps up and slaps her stomach. "It comes from here. I was just a scatterbrained nitwit with ratted hair chasing guitar players all over the earth until you came along. You don't remember those first years when we lived with Mama and I worked two jobs while I took night classes at the community college. You didn't know I cried myself to sleep every night because my girlfriends were out whooping it up at rock concerts while I was home learning computer programs and nursing you. I became somebody," she says, "*because* of you. And you will, too."

"I don't know how to be somebody."

"See these shoes." She raises her foot and practically lays it on the table, like I'm dying to take a look at her clunky black dance shoes with those spastic straps. "These aren't metal taps that you pick up in some dime store. Oh no, young lady, you don't just waltz into Dillard's one day and buy yourself a life with a credit card. There are one hundred nails in each heel, pounded in by hand, one by one. That's how you become somebody. One nail at a time, until you can do this." She starts vibrating her feet in a staccato rhythm like horses galloping. Heads turn, and somebody shouts, *"Baila, guapa."*

"Now I've got a show to do. After your news, I don't much feel like it, but I keep my word, no matter what. And you're going to watch." She takes my hand and squeezes it, pulling me back into Chickie Wha Wha.

It's all I can do to to keep from running back to the car screaming. First Joe treats me like trash, then I'm supposed to have a baby I don't want, and now I have to watch my mother do the flamingo in public. Why can't we just bond at the bowling alley like everyone else?

WHEN WE WALK in, a long-haired guitar player is already strumming, the *cajón* player is drumming his box, and the chunky singer with a red carnation stuck in her hair is screeching about the moon and a gypsy lover. I so can't wait for this to be over. Mom plunks me down at a table on the first row, next to the bony guy with the stringy gray hair, and pecks me on the cheek.

"Hola." He turns to me, smooth as the gypsy lover in the song. *"Soy Paco."*

"Hey," I say with a tight smile. "Delores."

"Pretty name."

"Not if you know what it means."

"María Dolores," he practically sings, "I knew you before you were born."

He smells like rum and cigars, and his eyes are boring a hole in me. His craggy face looks like it has traveled over some pretty bumpy roads. This afternoon I sat abandoned in the gutter of one of them, and don't want to walk down any more. I know where they lead, to the cobwebby ghost town in some antique land where my father plays guitar while my mother hammers nails into her heels and Abuelita sings songs that break your heart. I'd rather go with Dana the cheerleader to hook up with Joe at the Mrs. Fields in the West Esplanade Mall, only now you can leave out the Joe part. And come to think of it, scratch back-biting Dana. So what would Mary Sorrows do there, eat a chocolate-chip cookie in the food court alone?

"Knew your old man in Sevilla. Great artist." Paco smiles, flashing a scary gap where a front tooth should be. "They did an homage concert to his music in Madrid five years ago."

"My dad is dead." I swivel around to look for a vacant chair at another table.

"I know," Paco says. "He ODed at my house. You have his hungry eyes." Then he points his chin at the stage.

My mom is pacing across it with measured steps, head down, face half in shadow. One arm is held straight over her head, fingers grasping at the air as if she's trying to claw her way up to heaven. The arm falls, slaps her thigh, and then she pivots around on one heel, head raised high in profile, staring straight at me. It's Mom all right, but at the same time it's not her, like some snaky spirit has descended into her body, twisting it into fierce angles. Arms arched and wrists cocked, she's oozing through the air, swimming on land.

"*Ay qué dolor*," screams the singer in a voice made of mud and gravel.

I can't take my eyes off the stage. Every movement is sharp, glinting like a knife blade. I see muscles I didn't know Mom had. Her body curls into a crescent moon, then whips around and stomps, not like she's killing a cockroach but as if she's daring to place her foot down on the earth for the first time. Then another determined foot. She lands, then marches forward, yanking bloody daggers out of her heart and hurling them at the audience.

Directly at me. I cringe.

"*Quita una pena otra pena*," the singer wails, "*y un dolor otro dolor*." Just like the singer says, Mom's body is getting rid of one pain with another, one sorrow with the next. The heel with a hundred nails taps, then repeats the rhythm, then taps again. The singer is really going at it, as if blood were pouring out of her mouth. "*Ná, ná, ná . . . es eterno.*"

And now I can see that it does go on like this. Forever. Anguish and loneliness and sorrow, each love replacing a lost one like the generations. I wrap my arms tight around my stomach to feel the new life moving inside me. Honey, I don't know if you'll even be born, much less what your name will be, but this hug is all I have to give you at the moment. This, and what is happening on stage, where Mom's and Abuelita's faces blend into my own.

Whistling and thunderous applause break my trance. I turn to the bony guy next to me to ask him about my dad, hoping to reclaim some part of my real name—María Dolores—the one that just landed like a hatchet in my heart. But already Mom has jumped down off the stage and is hovering over me, wrapping me in that fringed shawl. And all I can do, like some blubbering baby, is to blink back the tears and mumble "awesome."

The Whole Shebang

FINALLY, AT SUNSET, the dreaded knock came. The rapping on the battered green shutter sounded tentative, unlike the call of fate it would turn out to be. As usual, Justin was stuck on the first paragraph of the book he was writing about Friedrich Nietzsche, and almost didn't answer.

He knew who it was.

All afternoon he'd heard Janine dragging heavy pieces of furniture across the herringbone pattern of old bricks that paved their courtyard. The new neighbor in the slave-quarter apartment next door had a screw loose, no doubt about it. Earlier today, coming home from his summer class, he'd run into her at the gate, so now he couldn't pretend to be out. Besides, much as he sometimes hated it, he was a gentleman. His grandparents had raised him that way. Maybe that was why he was still stuck as an instructor teaching intro philosophy courses. Of course, he could offer a million excuses for not answering the door: he was napping or in the shower or on the phone to Europe or had food poisoning. But much as he admired subterfuge in others, he couldn't pull it off himself. He was at the mercy of what his grandfather had called "your word—the only thing a man has." Nietzsche would have approved of PawPaw.

What he really wanted to do was hang out the sign his girlfriend Rosalie had snatched from a biker bar: "I'm Busy. You're Ugly. Have a Nice Day." Instead, he slouched downstairs to the living room and cracked opened the shutter.

The neighbor bunched up her face into a forced smile. "Oh Professor Stark—"

"Please call me Justin." He looked down at his flip flops.

"Hope I haven't disturbed you." Janine's face once might have been pretty, but now was puffy and misshapen, as spongy as if fashioned from Play-Doh. Behind her cats-eye glasses, a disturbing indistinctness danced around the eyes, blinking erratically as if they didn't quite believe what they were seeing. The corners of her thin lips twitched between a smile and frown, and her bright red drunkard's nose looked as if any minute it might fall off.

"I wanted to invite you over to my house for cocktails and hors d'oeuvres." She pronounced "house" like *hoose.* "Another couple from my former life in Old Metairie is coming over, and it's a good chance for us to become better acquainted."

"I'm going out with my girlfriend at seven." This lunatic must have been at least fifty, more than twenty years older than Justin, and he had no idea what she meant by "another couple." He intended to deep-six any such notions right away.

"Then come cut up with us for an hour before," she said, doing a wiggly dance step. "Get a buzz on."

Last week their landlady, Mrs. Amadee Comeaux, had brought over the new tenant to meet Justin. Janine Biggens at first reminded him of someone you might see at a Bloomington shopping center loading groceries into the beige family van covered with politically-concerned bumper stickers. Short, pudgy, in a sleeveless pink-flowered top and baggy gray shorts, her glasses kept sliding down the bridge of her nose on perspiration. The landlady proudly explained that Justin worked at Tulane University, where the new neighbor mentioned that her husband taught.

"We'll be all Tulane back here," Janine had said, shaking his hand as if at a library sherry after a lecture. She looked like what she claimed to be: a faculty wife. And that certainly would stick out in the French Quarter.

"I know your husband." Justin recognized the name: Dr. Geoffrey Biggens was the chair of the History Department. Justin often heard the man's arrogant bray coming from his corner office, and noticed Professor Biggens's brusque manner when they passed each other in the corridor. He was said to run the department like Pol Pot.

"Make that ex-husband," Janine explained with an untimely belly laugh, pushing the heavy black-frame glasses back up her nose. Something about her quite ordinary face made Justin think of a cubist portrait, the way in which the planes and angles didn't quite connect.

Now Justin glanced at his watch, wondering how he could worm out of cocktails with Biggens's former wife. "Guess I do have a few minutes," he mumbled.

"Hey, is that ever nice. I've got it set up out here." There it was again—*oot here*—the odd accent. She clapped her hands together, then pointed.

In a corner of the dank courtyard she had arranged the facsimile of a suburban living room, right under the exuberant fig tree. A moldy sectional sofa and two sun-bleached wingback chairs were gathered around a warped coffee table. In the shadows was a vinyl recliner with the stuffing leaking out. A rusty pole lamp was plugged into an extension cord that ran from the laundry room, and potted dieffenbachia had been stuck into two cone-shaped plastic planters resting on corroded chrome tripods. A half-empty bottle of cheap vodka sat on the kidney-shaped table, next to a plate of what looked like Triscuits smeared with Cheez-Whiz and a triangular ceramic ashtray heaped with peanuts.

"This is what's left of Old Metairie," she said.

"It reminds me of my childhood." Justin's parents' living room in Nashville had been set up like this before his mother got sick. Most of his early memories were a blank until that decisive moment when he ran out in the middle of her funeral. Later came the string of schoolyard fights he provoked that almost landed him in juvenile detention. Eventually his father gave up trying to raise the considerably pissed-off little boy by himself and dumped him with his grandparents. PawPaw, a retired Episcopal minister, enrolled the kid in a Catholic prep school, where he insisted that Justin join the Latin Club. "You'll never amount to anything if you don't know Latin," PawPaw said. Soon Justin was so busy working with his grandfather on a translation of *Caesar's Gallic Wars* that he never gave anyone a black eye again.

Now he winced at Janine's ghostly diorama, longing for his parents' suburban living room even as the very thought of it made his skin crawl. He figured that the new tenant must have moved directly from her sprawling ranch house in Old Metairie into this tiny efficiency, with everything she owned in tow. The morning Janine had arrived, the landlady stood with arms crossed and ruby lips pursed as a huge moving van in the driveway disgorged room after roomful of furniture into the courtyard of her Creole cottage. Justin's eyes bugged out, wondering how his new neighbor was going to squeeze all of that furniture into the upstairs bedsitter next door, a fourth the size of his own two-story apartment. Although the movers tried, little fit inside. Later that afternoon a goateed young man with a shaved head, whom Justin recognized as a bouncer at the Dungeon, stacked the mattresses, bed frames, and night tables inside a narrow alley that led to the laundry room. The bouncer turned out to be Janine's son, Spike, who lived up the block and went out with an unsavory woman from a tattoo parlor. That was the last Justin saw of him. The rest of the furniture remained strewn about the courtyard, exposed to the caprices of a hot, humid summer.

That night it rained. And didn't stop for a week.

When the furniture began to swell, molder, and stink, the immortal Mrs. Amadee Comeaux, dressed in her peasant blouse, gypsy skirt, and sandals over bobby socks—exactly what she had worn when she was a painter on Jackson Square during the sixties—threw a fit.

"Get that crap out of my courtyard," she screamed at Janine.

"Trina, I don't think it's appropriate for you to yell at me," the new neighbor said, sniffling.

"*Appropriate?* What do you mean by that crack?" The landlady surveyed the courtyard filled with sodden furniture steaming in the sun. "And don't you forget, my name is Mrs. Amadee Comeaux."

Now Justin took a deep breath as he approached the spectral rumpus room set up in the courtyard.

"How about a vodka tonic?" Janine asked, escorting him into her impromptu den. Bees buzzed around the fig tree laden with clusters of ripe purple fruit.

"A small one." When he sat on the sofa, the cushions squished beneath him. He leapt to his feet, brushing off his damp backside. "I'd rather stand. Been sitting all day."

"Here's a serviette," she said, handing him a paper napkin along with an iced tea glass of vodka and flat soda. "What's your field?"

"I teach logic," he said, dabbing the napkin on the back of his pants. "Actually, my doctoral thesis was on Nietzsche's transcendence of good and evil."

"Geoffrey's specialization is the Inquisition. Do you think that's why he's fucking that bimbo from Barcelona?"

"Beg your pardon?"

"Did you say logic?"

"Yes. That's what I teach, but—"

"Well, I've never been very logical, according to Geoffrey." Weeping, Janine drained her tumbler and poured herself another. "'Hormonal' is what he calls me. Says all I do is cry and bitch."

This wasn't going well. Justin had lost his mother to cancer when he was ten and wanted to be sympathetic about other people's families. "So sorry to hear about your troubles. . . ."

"Oh don't worry your handsome young head about it," she said, blowing her nose. "I'm sure Nietzsche is much more interesting than I am. I'd be fine if they hadn't foreclosed on the hoose. You see, I lost my health insurance with the divorce, and after they found the lump in my breast I took out a second mortgage to pay the medical bills, and just couldn't keep up. Meanwhile, all Geoffrey could talk about was Carmen, Carmen, Carmen, who he met at a conference in Barcelona. Carmen! Sounds like an opera." She swiveled her gaze toward the gate. "Where the hell are they?"

"Who?" A cockroach scampered under the coffee table, making a beeline for a squashed fig. Justin took aim at the bug with his flip flop but missed.

"The other couple. I should have known the bastards wouldn't show. They're probably at Commander's Palace right now with Geoffrey and Carmen, stuffing their faces with enchiladas." She burst out laughing. "Olé! And here I am, a farm gal from Calgary with one tit to the wind, sitting on this sofa that Geoffrey and I picked out at Hurwitz Mintz the month we got married. Oh no, he didn't want to spend the money, but I insisted. After all, it was what I'd earned as a secretary while putting him through grad school in Illinois, and finally he had a position and we could have our own hoose and start a family. Dr. Geoffrey had to have the right sofa to entertain the right people so he could tippy-toe his way up the ladder of success." She caressed the mildewed fabric. "You're logical, Justin Stark, Professor Just-in-Time. What do you think it means?"

Justin glanced at his watch. So this was what happened to people who tippy-toed up the ladder of success. He edged over to the tree and popped a ripe fig into his mouth. Never had he tasted anything so satisfyingly sweet. With his back turned, he splashed the vile vodka onto the ground.

The wooden gate rattled with a loud bang. Then another.

"That must be them." Janine staggered across the courtyard, drink in hand. "My dear old friends from dear Old Metairie. Okay, I'm coming," she screamed. "You don't have to tear down Mrs. Amadee Comeaux's hoose."

As the gate swung open, a goateed face loomed in the doorway.

"I'm on break," Spike said, glaring down at his mother, whose head reached his shoulders. "You said you'd stop." He grabbed the glass from her hand and smashed it on the courtyard bricks. "You promised if you moved around me, you'd stop."

"I'll stop tomorrow," she said. "Come on in. I'm entertaining

Professor Stark from Tulane. Look how I've set up the furniture, just like on Beaumont Drive."

Wild-eyed, her son took in the courtyard living room.

Janine handed him the plate. "Care for a Triscuit?"

IT WAS A SURPRISINGLY balmy July night, cool enough for Justin to kill the rattling air conditioner and sleep with the French doors thrown open to a breeze from the river. The screened doors, a rare anachronism in the renovated French Quarter, kept the blood-thirsty mosquitoes out, and the ceiling fan hypnotized him as it whirred over the thin futon where he tossed and turned, agonizing over Nietzsche and Rosalie Russo.

Justin was trying to picture himself in ten years. Wasn't that the question job interviewers asked, where do you see yourself in ten years? He was settled down in an Arts-and-Crafts cottage Uptown with Rosalie and two brilliant children who attended the arts magnet school. The way he imagined it, already tenured at Tulane, he could afford to be remote and eccentric, a free spirit sweeping late into his classes in a belted trench coat to lecture on German Romantic philosophers and the existentialists. Maybe he'd even grow a fierce hedgehog mustache like Nietzsche's. His students, of course, wouldn't care about their grades but would be enraptured by this fierce *überman* who, temple pulsing with cerebral intensity, would draw back the curtain to flood them with the blinding sunlight of reason and truth. He would wake them from their religious superstitions and instill in them a passion for the life of the mind, for which they'd be grateful their entire lives.

But he'd never get tenured until he published his book, and the only way he could ever start writing the damn thing would be if he scaled back his full load of intro courses and stopped teaching these summer-session classes. Of course, then he'd have to ask Rosalie to cover his hefty student-loan payments with her paychecks from Pan American Life Insurance Company, where her old man was a senior agent.

The book.

He was tired of her nagging him about it as a prelude to any discussion of their marriage plans. The book was to be a revision of the thesis he submitted at the University of Indiana, where he'd slaved over it at his monk's carrel in the library stacks for three years, long before meeting Rosalie the month after he started the entry-level job at Tulane. It was titled *Beyond Good and Evil: Nietzsche as a Precursor to the Existentialist Dilemma,* was four hundred pages long, had 643 footnotes, and all of three people in the world had read it.

Those three scholars on his committee said it was pretty good, but as a mere thesis not good enough to land him a tenured position. To get that, the dog-eared thesis manuscript hanging like a cinder block around his neck would have to be published by a university press. Justin doubted that the world needed yet another Nietzsche book, but Rosalie's old-fashioned father wouldn't give his blessing to the marriage without a secure job under his future son-in-law's belt. Mr. Russo, shrewd as he was gregarious, wasn't about to throw a big Italian wedding for someone with only a year-to-year contract, and Rosalie insisted on a wedding even bigger than her kid sister's: St. Louis Cathedral, a second-line parade through the Quarter, a reception in the Blue Room, little meatballs on toothpicks, the works. So to sail past the little meatballs, get laid regularly, and have kids, Justin first had to solve the existentialist dilemma. Jean-Paul Sartre had taken a crack at it in nine hundred pages, and what did *Being and Nothingness* get him?

Nothing.

Justin yanked up the plaid boxer shorts that kept creeping down his skinny hips. He wondered what the final payoff for all this was—the student loans, the thesis, the book, tenure, the little meatballs on toothpicks? He knew most of Nietzsche by heart: "You are young and ask for a child and marriage. But I ask you: Are you the victorious one, the self-conqueror, the commander of your senses, the master of your virtues?"

No, he had to admit that he wasn't the victorious one but the passive one, an innocent bystander to the crime of his whole life, beginning with his mother's illness. It was as if he were scuttling along the narrow ledge of a cliff and couldn't afford to cast a questioning glance either to the right or left, terrified that at any minute a single misstep could plunge him into the emptiness yawning below. Perhaps he should have entered divinity school like PawPaw wanted him to do. But in some seminar or other he'd subscribed to the notion that Nietzsche was right and God was dead, along with the bourgeois family and its stale Christian values. Yet even if the whole shebang were over, he still craved tradition and stability, everything his interrupted childhood had denied him.

And what, he wanted to know, would take the place of the whole shebang?

Justin froze.

A floorboard creaked on the balcony outside.

Then, out of the corner of his eye, he spotted her on the other side of the screen door, staring in. Through the rusted screen, her face looked like smudged newsprint, and her white nightgown glimmered in the moonlight. Justin remembered that he'd latched the screen doors. What was it, one o'clock in the goddamn morning? And there was Janine, creeping around outside his bedroom door. He lay flat on his back, feigning sleep. This was the limit. He would speak with their landlady in the morning.

Her eyes burned into him like shards of dry ice. He coughed, struggling to lie still. She would have to go away eventually, wouldn't she? She didn't move, barely breathed, and he could feel her glare taking in the tuffs of curly hair on his chest, his pale torso, and the long white scar along his ribcage from the motorcycle accident.

Justin's eyes popped open at the sound of a slap, as if somebody had smashed a mosquito against an arm. Wrapping a sheet around himself, he bolted out of bed and stomped to the door. "Just stay the hell away from me, okay?" he shouted.

Janine jumped. Her arms shot up to cover her breasts, as if she were the one being spied upon. "I'm not trying to steal your thoughts, you know," she stammered.

"Keep the fuck away." Justin was shaking with rage. If she were a cockroach, he would have stepped on her.

Glasses perched at the end of her nose, she stumbled along the balcony in the moonlight, and then her door clicked shut.

ON THE AFTERNOON the email arrived, Justin trudged along the fluorescent-lit corridors of Fowler Hall, past History and toward Philosophy. He took this path every Monday, Wednesday, and Friday, but today it felt as if he were shuffling shackled through a prison yard. The summer session was almost over, and except for a few bleary-eyed students slipping late papers under faculty doors, the building was abandoned. Most of the tenured professors were off on summer research grants or tooling around Europe. A travel poster for Barcelona marked Professor Biggens's door, along with a *separata* of his latest scholarly publication on Tomás de Torquemada, as if anyone would linger in such a dismal hallway to study his bibliography. This morning Justin had planned to stop by the department to drop off the corrected exams, but now felt as if he were dumping what was left of his life into a plastic garbage bag.

He was being fired, or rather, not rehired for the fall. Toepfer's email was curt, and the reason left vague. Stunned, he'd called the department to make an appointment with the chair.

He had to find out.

Bernie Toepfer, chair of Philosophy and the department's Hegel guy, was in his office, packing books and papers into a worn leather briefcase. When Justin rapped on the opened door, Professor Toepfer shuffled sideways like a hermit crab to usher him into the cramped office, baggy brown eyes lowered. Then he did something that unnerved Justin: he closed the door. In conferences with students, Justin always insisted that his office door remain open, to dispel even the slightest suspicion that any untoward intimacy might be taking place. And he never saw his students after class, not even for a cup of coffee. One misinterpreted gesture, he knew, and his career would be kaput.

"Bernie," Justin blurted out, "I'm flabbergasted by your email. I understood that my contract would be renewed annually for five years, pending favorable evaluations. I've been here for two years, and my evaluations—"

"Have been outstanding," the chair said, never taking his eye off the worn heel of his oxford. "We had great hopes for you here. My old pal Arnold at Bloomington told me you were the most promising grad student he'd ever worked with. How's that Nietzsche book coming?"

"It's coming," Justin lied, staring at the Venetian blinds askew behind the desk. Rain drops were pelting the dusty window pane. As the sky darkened, the office lamp brightened into an inquisitorial glare.

"A woman called me last week," Toepfer said, turning his face to flick off the computer that dominated his desk. "She was crying and sounded, well, hysterical. She claimed you had sexually harassed her daughter, who is in your summer logic section, and then after sleeping with you, the girl tried to commit suicide. Now I know how these things start. A young woman develops a crush on an instructor, and perhaps he says or does something that makes her believe—"

"Preposterous!" Justin brought a hand down on the arm of his chair, and the sudden smack obviously alarmed Professor Teopfer, who brushed back his comb-over. "I can barely recall what those women looked like or any of their names. I have a fiancée, Rosalie—you've met her—and nobody else turns my head. Does this mother have a name?"

"She didn't leave one." Toepher fiddled with a stack of papers.

"So you're letting me go on the basis of an anonymous phone call?" Seven years of preparing for a career had come to this?

"She also called the dean."

"I see."

"And he claims the details she gave him were convincing. The girl described to her mother certain of your physical attributes that one might only observe, shall we say, in an undressed state.

She swore you have a long white scar on your chest, along the right ribcage." Teopfer cocked an eyebrow. "Do you?"

Justin squirmed. "Well, yes, but—"

"But what?" Toepher's face shut down.

"Say, what did this lady's voice sound like?"

"She was distraught, of course, but I could detect an accent, perhaps Commonwealth, the way she elongated certain vowels, that would make one believe she—"

"Might be Canadian?"

"You could say that."

"It was Janine Biggens." Justin dropped his head into his hands, conjuring up the distorted features of her face like some fanged Asian serpent mask. A thunderstorm exploded outside, lashing the window with sheets of rain.

"Did you say Biggens?" Toepfer straightened up in his swivel chair.

"Professor Biggens's ex-wife, my new neighbor in the Quarter." The story poured out in a rush: the phantasmal cocktail party in the courtyard, the moonlit voyeurism outside of Justin's bedroom, her drinking problem and illness, her husband's affair. "She saw me naked—almost."

Toepfer looked Justin in the eye, as if finally interested. "I've heard Biggens went through a messy divorce, but he's away for the summer—back in Spain, I presume—and I wouldn't want to be the one to confront him with these personal issues. You know, he chairs the Humanities Budget Council. Look, if you were tenured, this could be arbitrated by a committee and perhaps cleared up, but fact is, as of the last day of this week, you're no longer employed here. The college can't afford any lawsuits, and the dean won't rehire someone with a standing complaint of this nature. Personally, I hate to lose you, and was hoping to give you the existentialism course somewhere down the line."

Toepfer stood and offered his hand. Justin, lost in a vision of his neighbor's splotchy face, didn't take it.

"What if," Justin said, rising from his chair, "Janine calls the dean and recants her absurd story?"

"He just left for a conference in Berlin."

"Faxes him a notarized affidavit?"

"That's between you and Mrs. Biggens." Swinging open the door, Toepfer flashed a wide smile revealing teeth white as bathroom tile. "And how has your summer vacation been?"

THE FIREBALL MOVING CO. van was parked inside the courtyard driveway when Justin swerved his battered Volvo into a rare space in front of the Creole cottage. Mrs. Amadee Comeaux stood at her back door chewing on an ice cube, and shot him a complicit smile as his gaunt profile raced past, mouth twisted into a determined grimace. Now was the hour to strike, and what luck to find Janine there just before she moved away to God-knows-where.

"We finally got her out." The landlady lifted her plastic go-cup in a toast, face flushed with victory and a piña colada. "Bitch's new landlady called me yesterday for a reference, and I said, 'Honey, she's the best damn tenant I ever had.' Told her not to miss out on this jewel." She threw back her head and cackled.

Right after Justin had reported to his landlady the moonlit encounter on the balcony, Mrs. Amadee Comeaux returned Janine's uncashed rent check, explaining how sorry she was that things weren't working out. The new tenant refused to move, and the landlady asked Justin to pull the fuses from the locked box that contained the circuit breaker to her apartment. When Janine still stayed put, the landlady said she worried about a drunk stumbling around with lit candles inside her two-hundred year-old investment. These days the former artist was a woman of property who lived off rentals, not paintings, and couldn't afford a vacancy. Justin heard that she'd done well for herself when she had her looks, shacking up with a string of ailing arts patrons just before they kicked the bucket, and then inheriting their houses. So the landlady, already scouting for a new tenant, changed the lock on the gate and shut off Janine's water.

"Know what that evil witch did?" Justin sputtered. "Got me

fired."

"No." The landlady's splayed fingers landed over her heart.

"Said I sexually harassed her daughter in my summer-school class."

"She even have a daughter?"

"I don't know, but I checked and no Biggens was registered. You know I didn't touch any of those snotty brats."

"Rosalie would kill you if you did." Mrs. Amadee Comeaux looked horrified. "When you two tying the knot, babe?"

"Her old man will never let her marry a loser with no job. And now with this on my record?"

After the thunderstorm, a scorching sun was setting behind the peaked roof of the Creole cottage. There under the fig tree stood Janine, nudging the coffee table with a knee toward a mound of drenched furniture, which two burly men were hauling, piece by moldy piece, into the van. Wisps of thinning hair were plastered with sweat to her scalp, above a florid face whose features looked more disconnected than ever. Trying to catch her breath, she glanced over at Justin and the landlady standing in the shade of the cottage awning.

Although the merciless afternoon glare was exploding inside his skull, Justin knew what he had to do.

As he approached, Janine pushed the cats-eye glasses back up the bridge of her nose.

"Need any help?" After all, he was a gentleman.

"These two plants have to go into the truck," she said, wheezing. "The movers will probably break the leaves. But they're heavy."

"Here, grab one edge and I'll take the other." They hoisted one of the cone-shaped planters a few inches off the ground and, doubled over with the weight, scurried across the bricks.

Justin fixed her eye in a barbed stare. "Why did you call Bernie Toepfer and the dean with that ridiculous story about sexual harassment?" He could smell her stale, boozy breath as he spit out the words two inches from her face.

"How is everything at Tulane?" she said, blinking. "I'm so out of the loop."

"You heard me," Justin shouted. "You got me fired."

"I don't know what . . . ." The planter slipped from her fingers and crashed onto the bricks, splitting in two.

"Now look what you've done," she screamed.

"What I've done!" Beside himself, Justin kicked at the cracked flower pot as it rolled out. "You've flushed my career and marriage plans down the toilet."

"*My career.* You people are all the same. I was trying to help you."

"Help me?"

"Avoid all this," she said, gesturing at the mound of mildewed furniture. "So your girlfriend would never have to stand in my shoes. So you and that bimbo from Barcelona—"

He grabbed her wrist. "Look, nut job, you will write and sign a confession to the dean before you set one foot out of this gate today." Justin motioned to one of the movers. "Stop loading this stuff."

"This lady's paying me, bud, not you," the mover answered, throwing the pole lamp over his shoulder.

Justin tightened his grip on her wrist. "You'll confess, or I swear—"

"Help!" Janine's panicked face sought out the landlady and the movers, who stood watching. "This man is harassing me."

"I'll harass you all right," he said, taking aim. "You and your make-believe daughter." As when a small fire races up the wall and suddenly engulfs a room, exploding through the windows, Justin reached his flashover point in a moment of startling clarity. He didn't have to remain forever on the narrow ledge where he was trapped, could do anything he wanted, really, as long as he accepted the consequences.

And raising his fist, he accepted them.

The blow to Janine's face knocked the glasses off her sweaty nose as she crumpled to the ground. Justin squinted as the setting sun blazed in his eyes, blinded by a brilliant ray that seemed to be focused directly on him. Heat rose to the crown of his head and his mouth tasted like ashes. He knew they were his mother's, the cold metal urn a numb little boy had refused to touch before he ran from his grandfather's church.

How dare she leave him when he needed her the most?

He felt a soft touch on his arm and lowered his clenched hand.

"Stop, you've hurt her." Mrs. Amadee Comeaux bent over the body stretched out on the bricks, running an ice cube from her cocktail over the woman's forehead and clucking as she wiped blood from her mouth with a handkerchief. The landlady reached into a pocket of her voluminous gypsy skirt and pulled out a cell phone. "I'm calling 911."

"Where's Geoffrey?" Janine slurred through the pink froth on her lips. "Supposed to take me home to Beaumont Drive today."

The landlady shook her head. "People don't know how to act any more." She cut a cold eye at Justin. "With those big ideas, I thought you educated types would be civilized. You got three days to get your butt out my building."

JUSTIN WAS ALREADY in his second-floor study when the wailing sirens approached the house. He parted the marquisette curtains to glance out of a smudged pane of the French door. Backfiring, the Fireball Moving Co. van was backing out of the courtyard as the still shrieking ambulance was angling into the driveway. Then there was silence. Below, the refrigerator motor revved up in the kitchen and his grandfather's mantle clock chimed the hour.

It's time, kid, PawPaw said, *to stand before God as a man.*

Two paramedics were strapping Janine's body onto the gurney when Justin appeared on the balcony with a granite expression on his face, the thick thesis manuscript tucked under one arm. Janine's goateed son Spike, the movers, and the landlady were gathered in a huddle around the ambulance driver. Mrs. Amadee Comeaux turned to point an arthritic finger at the thin figure perched like an idol on the balcony.

The two movers conferred and nodded. Spike glowered.

The driver looked up at the balcony then spit into his cell phone, "Send a squad car. Code 34, assault and battery, perp still on the premises."

Justin tossed the manuscript high into the air, the pages fluttering down one by one into the courtyard like a flurry of white doves. Unemployed, evicted, and soon to be unengaged, he felt naked standing there, exposed to the early evening's mosquitoes swarming around him. He studied the decaying suburban furniture piled below while a snowfall of footnotes blanketed the herringbone pattern of worn bricks. As though waking from an opalescent dream, he rubbed his temples, aware for the first time of exactly what he was capable of.

And if only for a moment, felt free.

Then he marched down the stairs and stepped into the courtyard, next to the gnarled fig branches heavy with fermenting fruit. The sky over the stifling port city turned pink, a few clouds drifting overhead as a tropical sunset was refracted off the crumbling garden walls. When Justin appeared, the people watching him lowered their eyes from the intense stare of the young man striding like a Roman soldier toward them.

The List

ON THE NIGHT of my fortieth high-school reunion, a drunk tourist accused me of stealing her purse.

It was early September, and the sticky blanket of murderous heat made me feel like hauling off and punching somebody. Until I reached the arctic chill of the Marriott's ballroom on Canal Street, the plaid shirt I was wearing was soaked with sweat and strands of wet gray hair were glued to my forehead. I raced inside, gulped a glass of ice water, and glanced around at the reunion shindig, shocked that I was even there. That was when I spotted Amos Roemer, of all people. I hadn't seen him since the F.B.I. ran him out of town during the sixties.

Some bald geezer with a clipboard asked who I was, then handed me a nametag with my mug shot from the senior-class yearbook. As a group, we really needed those pictures to identify each other. Everyone there looked like jack-o'-lanterns left out in the sun for three days after Halloween. Some of the jack-o'-lantern faces were still glowing inside, but you could tell that most hadn't had anything burning inside for some time now.

Forty years can do that to you.

Amos didn't recognize me right away, but was the only person there I had anything to say to. He was a tall, lanky egret of a man, and seemed all Adam's apple as I stared up at him from my squat Sicilian perch on earth. He'd played basketball until he grew his hair long, and then the coach kicked him off the school team when he refused to cut it. Now, like the controversy once surrounding men's long hair, there wasn't much left of his, only a monk's tonsure of gray wisps.

"Nick Fazio," he said, "you're the last person I expected to find at one of these square clam bakes." Then he bent down to wrap me in a full body hug.

We'd been the class misfits, ersatz beatniks with guitars slung over our shoulders, dressed in black turtlenecks and sandals in a sea of madras shirts and Bass Weejuns. Now, just as we once had in the school cafeteria, we found ourselves hiding in a corner of the cavernous ballroom, whispering in conspiratorial tones. And again, we were glad to have found each other. Amos said that he needed to go outside, and even though I wasn't crazy about heading back into the steam bath, he led me onto a terrace next to the ballroom where the tattooed caterers were smoking. He lit up, then slipped on a pair of glasses hanging on a lanyard around his neck and fished a list out the back pocket of his slacks.

"The list," as he called it, was a six-page, single-spaced print out, with columns of names and places that he remembered from New Orleans. He showed me my name on page three, in between "Johnny the Greek" and "Phil Manslow (narc?)." He told me that nobody else from high school was on the list, and that he hadn't been back since he'd tossed that bucket of pig blood on the files at the draft board office. An oil-industry brat, he grew up all over, and the few remaining members of his family were in California, where he was living now. He was dying to go down to the French Quarter, he said, shoving the list in my face. It was as if New Orleans had left an indelible watermark on his soul, and Amos needed the list to remind himself of who he once was here. He was back to excavate his youth.

I scanned the column of long-defunct places: the Seven Seas, La Casa, the Acropolis, and the Quorum Club. "Man, these places haven't been in the Quarter for thirty years or more."

Squinting, he tilted his head to one side, just as he did in high school. "What's there now?"

"It's all inside out. Used to be a place where ritzy visitors came to slum with poor dagos, sailors, and artists," I said. "Now it's hordes of blue-collar stiffs staggering around with two-buck beers looking for the movie stars and millionaires who live there, hiding behind high courtyard walls."

"Must be something left," he said, shaking his head.

"Remember the Dream Castle on Frenchmen Street, the blues bar we'd go to on Saturday nights to hear old Babe Stovall play his steel guitar?"

Jake put on his glasses and dug in his back pocket for the list, scanning the pages until he found the Dream Castle. "Sure do," he said, pointing at the name. "Used to do my chemistry homework in the men's room whenever the cops raided for underage drinkers."

"That's because it was integrated, and they were trying to find a reason to bust it. Long ago the Dream Castle became the Dream Palace, the hippest music joint in town. But the whole street now is lined with clubs. After I talk to a few people inside, I'll take you down there."

"Kind of a rough neighborhood, isn't it?"

"Wait till you see it now," I said with a slow whistle.

Truth was, I was dying to get back into the air conditioning. But I didn't last long, even in the crisp cool of the ballroom. The tedious conversations were about children, careers, divorces, cross-country moves, how much people missed New Orleans. Hardly anyone lived here anymore. Everyone seemed to be practicing proctology in the Sunbelt like Hortley Craig, or was married to somebody who did, like Monica Peal, the former cheerleader now hanging on his arm. I stared down at their pristine jogging shoes and didn't say much.

"So you've been in town this whole time?" Hortley drained his drink, the same frat-boy smirk plastered across a wrinkled face. "We kept waiting for you to make an album or start some famous band. What the hell do you do here?"

"Library technology stole my heart," I told him. How much

was there to say about living with your eighty-year-old mother, sleeping in the same room you had in high school, and cataloging books at the public library?

"The rest of us had to leave to find good jobs," Craig said, grabbing another Sazerac off a passing tray. "It's tough in New Orleans, even for someone with family connections like mine."

"Oh, there are opportunities galore here, if you know where to look." Such as the "Hourly Help Wanted" section of the *Times-Picayune*. "Especially in entertainment solutions." Like bar tending and pole dancing, I wanted to say.

"Not in my field."

"Nope, we don't have a lot of proctologists, but we sure have a lot of . . . ."

We cracked up.

"You'll never change, Nick," Hortley said, patting my head. "And congratulations to the only guy here who still has all his hair. We knew you'd make good in the hair department, if nowhere else."

AMOS TOLD ME his life's story as we trudged down Decatur Street, mopping our brows. His face lit up as we stopped in front of what used to be Sidney's Newsstand, now a wine shop still called Sidney's. It was as dilapidated as ever, with the same rusted wire grating covering the smudged window and door panes. Out came the list from Amos's back pocket as he slid on his specs.

"Wait," he said, "this is the place where I used to buy the *Village Voice* and pick up *The Courier*, that underground rag from the Quarter. But Sidney's isn't on the list."

"Try 'Dirty Book Store.' That's what we called it then. First place I ever saw a pussy up close, although I didn't have the bread to buy it. The magazine, I mean."

Amos beamed. "Hot diggity, here it is. The Dirty Book Store." Seemingly satisfied, he made a small check mark on the list, an archeologist taking inventory. "Didn't they also sell cheap jugs of wine?"

"That we used to pass around in Jackson Square while Babe Stovall played. Unruly long-haired white kids mixing it up with black street musicians and civil-rights workers. No wonder the cops were always after us."

Amos caressed the padlocked door like an old friend. Three gutter punks with green hair and pierced eyebrows were slumped in a nearby doorway, studying us two old guys loitering in front of Sidney's. Nested in a pile of filthy rags, they were swallowed by shadows, except for the apple-red cheeks that beamed at us. One of them let loose with a dissonant riff on his battered guitar, then a grubby hand appeared. "Spare change?"

Amos put a dollar in their tip box. "Peace," he told them. Turning to me, he asked, "Was that what we used to look like?"

"I like to think," I said, huffing up, "that we had a political purpose and could actually play the guitar, unlike those members of the Whatever Generation."

"But that's what the cops saw," Amos said, pointing at the punks. "And the kids still say 'spare change,' just like we did. Think they'd mind if we sat with them for awhile?"

I rolled my eyes and yanked at the sleeve of his sports coat. "So what do you do," I asked as we continued walking, "in your uncle's bomb shelter in Sacramento?"

"Well, I feed my five cats. I've been on disability for the past ten years, ever since I left the merchant marines. All my life people called me crazy," he said, "so I figured I might as well cash in on it. Truth is, I never wanted to grow up in their world."

"Ditto," I said. I certainly understood what he meant by *their*. Hard to forgive the people who planned to send us off to die in a rice paddy before we drank our first legal beers. When I was starting to shave, black folks who wanted to sit at lunch counters were being attacked by snarling police dogs, and guys a couple of years older than me were being shipped to Southeast Asia to napalm kids and burn down villages. It was a domino game with the Communists, the old men told us. We bought it as much as those gutter punks now believed in the war in Afghanistan. Even back then, we knew it wasn't about democracy but oil.

"So you actually live in a bomb shelter?" I asked.

"My uncle built it in the fifties, and for years it was his wine cellar. Now he likes having me around, so I have my own free place. I feel like Dostoyevsky's underground man. I could have been somebody else, maybe the poly-sci professor I always wanted to be. But the F.B.I. got me kicked out of Cal State after a takeover of the president's office in '71, when we were trying to ban R.O.T.C. from campus. Fat chance, with all those Defense Department contracts rolling in."

"No wife or kids?"

"Never got hitched, but about ten years ago this nurse pops up who says I'm her daddy. She was raised in a foster home after her mother—a crazy chick I'd rather forget—ODed on drugs. So my daughter got me on S.S.I., and now fusses at me about high blood pressure and stuff. I'm a granddaddy, too. Two boys, already in college. Business and tech majors. They can't wait to join the rat race, same one I spent my life running from. Except now the rats are broke. Those two don't believe in anything but the almighty buck, just like my dad. You? Kids, I mean."

"Look," I said, wiping sweat out of my eyes with a handkerchief, "it's simple. If you grew up in a happy family, you want to repeat the experience on your own. If not, you don't. So no kids. That's my one contribution to humanity. Remember what my old man did when I was in high school?"

THE DREAM PALACE on Frenchmen Street was packed. Inside was as sweltering as outside, only smoky and loud. On the stage, a busty brunette in a green velvet dress was crooning "Why Do You Do Me Like You Do?" I'd been coming here off and on for years, if only to get out of the house when Mama had one of her bad spells and got up at midnight to scrub the kitchen floor. During my senior year, Daddy put a gun in his mouth and blew his brains out while he was sitting at the table with her. Mama was still trying to clean up the mess.

"Yeah," Amos said, taking out his list. "I remember these

dirty tile floors and that long oak bar. But it seems so much bigger now."

"They knocked out that side wall into what used to be a storage space," I said, pointing. "Put in a stage and book local bands."

We shouldered through a crush of tattooed girls with dyed black hair and goateed guys in fedoras.

"Whoa, white and black people together," Amos observed. "Never thought I'd live to see this day in New Orleans, Louisiana."

"Yeah, baby, remember integration and the Soviet Union, end of the fucking world," I said, scratching my head as if waking from a long sleep. "What the hell was that all about?"

"Fear."

"Want a beer?"

He shot me a thumbs up. "First let me go see if that bathroom's the same."

"Don't worry. Hasn't been cleaned since 1967."

I pulled up a stool and sat at the bar. The Gypsy Vipers were playing World War II swing music with a funky Dixieland sound. I could dig it. Always dreamed that I'd be up on that stage one day, but now who wants to hear acoustic folk music? For years I kidded myself that I would "get back into my music" once I retired from the library, but now, even working part time, I saw that was never going to happen. Years ago I'd done some studio work in L.A.—even played back-up guitar for Carly Simon on "You're So Vain"—but then Mama had to be hospitalized. The selfish bastard blew away more than his brains when he stuck that gun in his mouth, like Mama's mind and my own dreams. Around then I dropped out of "Armageddon Sect," this band I was touring with, and started to care for her full time. I played the occasional gig at coffee houses and even went to the trouble of putting out a solo CD, but that jerk Hortley Craig was right.

Only part left of who I used to be was my hair. *Let the sunshine in . . . .*

Right next to me, a drunk in a pink feather boa started whining in a New York accent that she'd lost her purse. "Had it just a second ago."

Everyone glanced to the right and left, as if they could care, then looked back up at the stage. The pink boa lady borrowed a flashlight from the bartender and searched under the stools around us, making everyone move. One eyebrow cocked, she kept coming back to me.

"I was standing right here. Sure you haven't seen my purse?"

"What's it look like?"

"Fake black alligator with a gold clasp. About this big."

"No fake black alligators in sight," I screamed over the sax solo on stage.

"Get up," she ordered. "It must be under your feet."

"Look, lady, I told you I haven't seen it." I wasn't about to let this drunk push me around.

"You have it. I'm sure you do. Bartender," she screeched, "this guy stole my purse." The bartender shifted his eyes and moved to the other end of the bar. Then she whipped out a cell and punched in a few numbers. "Help, police! I want to report a robbery."

"What's going on here?" Amos turned up at my side.

"Bitch thinks I stole her purse," I said, handing him an Abita Amber.

She swiveled around. "Look, buster," she said, spittle flying from the peach lipstick smear of her mouth, "I'm on to you. Everyone back at the hotel warned me to be careful in this joint." She turned to Amos. "You see this creep grab my bag?"

Amos burst out laughing. "Just got back from the bathroom. Anyway, this creep is my pal from high school."

"Oh, I see." A slow smile cracked the foundation on her plump face. "So your accomplice here passed you the purse, and you emptied the wallet and then stashed the bag in the men's john. I know how you guys work. Who you bums supposed to be, Mutt and Jeff? You look like pickpockets straight out of the Port Authority bus station." The palm of her hand shot out. "Give me back my cash and credit cards before the cops get here, and I won't press charges. You can keep the knock-off bag."

"Get lost," I said, batting her away with my hand.

"I said hand it over."

As the band finished its set, everyone around us broke into applause and whistles. Soon the singer in the green velvet dress was edging her way through the crowd with a basket. I tossed in a dollar, and then another one. "This buck is for me. And the second for this crazy lady who lost her purse and won't let me listen to you sing."

"Okay, scumbags," spit the lady in the pink boa, "you'll be sorry." Then she marched toward the front door as if on a mission.

Amos and I looked at each other bug-eyed, as we used to do in algebra class. He hummed the theme from *The Twilight Zone*, our favorite TV show in high school, and I circled a finger around my ear. After the earth had orbited the sun forty times, here we were again, beers in hand, standing on the tiled floor of what used to be the Dream Castle, snickering like teenagers at the absurdity of it all.

What more did we need to complete this picture?

RIGHT IN THE MIDDLE of the second set, the caps of two policemen sailed over the top of the crowd toward us, the fleshy shoulder of the lady in the pink boa clearing a path. Much to their credit, the Gypsy Vipers continued their version of "On the Sunny Side of the Street," as everyone's gaze shifted toward the cops. The dancing stopped, and several out-of-towners put out their cigarettes.

"These two slime buckets stole my purse," the lady said, pointing at us.

People around us cocked their ears to eavesdrop on the drama.

I burst out laughing. "This tourist has had one too many. We don't know anything about her purse. Think we'd still be here if we swiped it?"

The lady shook her fist in my face. "This guy handed it to his friend, who stashed it in the men's room." I could picture her jumping up and down, arguing over a parking spot in Brooklyn.

"Wanna take a look in the men's room?" said the graying officer with sagging jowls to the younger cop with a buzz cut. The older one crossed his arms, studying me and Amos with a wary eye.

"I know you," Amos told the cop.

"Yeah?"

"You ran me in at that anti-war demonstration in front of the Federal Building. June of 1968. Officer Marvin Blanks, right?"

His eyes widened. "You got a good memory. I was just a rookie then."

"Look," Amos said, digging into his back pocket. "You're on my list." He flipped through the pages. "Here you are."

"Your list?" The cop's brow furrowed. "Lemme see that."

"He's been away for forty years," I offered, "and these are the people and places he remembers."

"Hey," said Officer Blanks, flipping through the pages. "Here's my brother-in-law, Johnny the Greek. You knew that character? He was a pool shark on the back patio of the Seven Seas."

"Showed me everything I know about the game," Amos said. "He still around?"

"Died ten years ago. My wife's only brother."

Buzz Cut appeared, holding out empty hands. "There's no purse in that john, although some queen lingering in a stall looks as if he might like to carry one."

Officer Blanks shot a look at the lady in the pink boa. "Satisfied?"

"I'm telling you these guys stole my purse. Like I should know where they hid it?"

The crowd erupted in raucous applause, and Officer Blanks clapped both hands over his ears. "Okay, let's take this outside. Can't hear a damn thing in here."

Once again the lady in the pink boa led the way, elbowing through the crowd.

"Now that you mention it, I remember that demonstration you was in," Officer Blanks said to Amos as they walked toward the

door. "My first month on the force, same week my older brother got drafted. Never made it back from Nam. Haven't voted for any of them bozos since." He shook his head. "Now my son is in Afghanistan. Tell you the truth, I wish he was out demonstrating against the government instead."

Under the balcony outside, club-goers streamed down Frenchmen Street. Clumps of skinny young women in little black dresses wobbled along on stiletto heels, staring down at glowing iPhones in their palms. Their pudgy dates were in baseball caps and baggy shorts, clutching green plastic cylinders of some boozy concoction. I could see that the street was becoming the hipster tourist's answer to Bourbon Street, a galaxy away from the clandestinely integrated blues bars that first drew Amos and me down here.

"Afraid I'm going to have to ask you for some ID so I can write up a report," Officer Blanks told us. Then he turned with an annoyed look to the lady in the pink boa. "Listen, lady, sorry you lost your purse, but these gentlemen don't have it."

"But I saw him—"

"Okay," I blurted out, sick to death of the whole thing, "we'll empty our pockets and you can pat us down, if it'll make her happy. Come on, Amos, let's make like we're at the airport."

Amos and I spread the stuff from our pockets across the hood of the squad car. We had no sooner raised our arms over our heads to be searched when Hortley Craig and Monica Peal turned the corner, still wearing their reunion nametags.

"Nick!" Hortley said. "And Amos Roemer. What's going on here? You bad-asses still in trouble with the law?" He wobbled from side to side, slurring his words.

"You know these bums?" the lady in the pink boa asked. She was probably staying at the Marriott, too.

"Know them? They've been my buddies since high school. Look officer whatever-your-goddamn-name-is," Hortley said, getting right up in the cop's face, "my old man is a retired Criminal Court judge, and one phone call from me could get your ass fired." He waved a cell phone above his head as if it were a club.

"Sir, I'm asking you to step back." Officer Blanks held up his palm.

"Did you hear me?" Hortley grabbed him by the collar. "My dad is Judge Hortley Craig, Senior. So leave my friends alone."

"Honey?" Monica Peal said.

"Look, asshole, I said step back or—"

"Who you calling an asshole?" Red-faced, Hortley did step back, then swung forward to slug the cop.

Before Monica Peal had finished shrieking, the buzz-cut young cop had Hortley in a choke-hold. Blanks rubbed his jaw, then spun Hortley around, twisted the arms around his back, and cuffed him. "Okay," he said, lifting a wallet out of his back pocket, "let's see some ID. You coming with us."

"Monica," Hortley blubbered, "call Daddy."

"And give him another coronary, like after your last bar fight?" his wife whimpered. "Officer, as usual my husband has had a few too many but he—"

"Public intoxication and assaulting an officer," Blanks said, pushing him toward the back door of the squad car. "Get in. Guess your daddy will know where to find you."

Then Officer Blanks turned toward us. "You two can go." He nodded toward me, then reached out and shook Amos's hand. "Sorry," he said. "I mean it. And thank you."

"Hope your son makes it home in one piece," Amos said.

Officer Blanks slammed the squad-car door shut on a bilious-looking Hortley Craig.

The crowd of gawkers parted at the door to let the bartender through, a black purse held high above his head. "Somebody found this in the women's room," the bartender shouted, showing it to the pink boa lady. "Yours?"

"YOU'LL HAVE TO PUT hothead Hortley on your list," I said. "He sure distinguished himself in action tonight." We were walking down Chartres Street, back toward Amos's hotel on Canal. The heat had finally lifted, and a breeze was blowing in from the

Mississippi, where an approaching freight train moaned along the wharves.

"Did you hear what Officer Blanks told me?" Amos asked, eyes gleaming.

"About his brother in Viet Nam?"

"No, man. When he said *thank you.* Nobody has ever told me that before, much less somebody in a uniform."

"Must have meant for putting up with that woman's bullshit."

"Don't you see? It was for what I did all those years. The demonstrations." He spun around, shaking. "That war pretty much blew my life to hell, as much as it did to the guys who went over there."

"Come on. Think a cop congratulated you for wrecking the downtown draft office?" Amos evidently had forgotten what the New Orleans police were like.

"During the same stupid war his brother was killed in? The one everybody regrets so much today? And now the sequel, the one his son is in? Fucking-A that's what he meant, bro."

"Afraid the times haven't changed in our direction. 'For the loser now will be later to win,'" I sang with a nasal twang, "'For the times they are a-changin. . . .'"

Amos didn't sing along. "Look, I'm not asking to be buried in Arlington goddamn Cemetery. I'm no hero. But I'm not a coward either. When you see something wrong, it takes guts to say *no* to everything you were brought up to believe in. That *no* took everything out of me, man." Amos's voice was breaking, Adam's apple bobbing as if he were choking. "It blew my fuses. I'm lucky to have a bomb shelter to hide in."

He was becoming agitated, talking a mile a minute, his voice booming down the length of empty Chartres Street.

"Yeah, you right," I said, patting his back.

"And nobody ever told me thank you. Nobody *ever.* . . ." He was sobbing now, his chest heaving. "Nobody."

Was this how my high-school reunion had turned out, stuck with this Ichabod Crane of a sad-sack war resister freaking out because he never got a commendation from the President? I really didn't know this man anymore, and his tears really got my goat.

"Listen, buddy," I said, "while you were out in California balling nurses' mothers, I was here at home . . . mopping up."

Amos pulled himself together. "I remember what you said about your mom."

"And nobody ever thanked *me*—much less a word from my mother—for giving up my music to take care of her after what my old man did."

Amos turned to face me. "So we're both losers."

"Not losers or heroes. We just did what was right. Nobody asked us to, we just did it. War, suicide . . . the ripples go on and on. Somebody's got to be a grunt and carry the ball forward. Someone's got to suck it up and do the decent thing."

"Decent," he said, nodding. "We did the *decent* thing." He seemed to like that word. "But we'll never get our pictures in the paper for that."

"At least I made it onto your list."

The freight train finally passed along the riverfront, its whistle slicing through the night with such a solitary wail of pure blues that I thought I'd die then and there. It was Babe Stovall back at the Dream Castle, eyes squinted in his old lined face, stretching a mournful note on a single guitar string for forty years into the future, toward the far horizon where we were now standing. Then the train was gone, leaving Chartres Street at midnight so quiet that, except for our echoing footsteps, you could hear the fountains gurgling inside the brick courtyards of the rich and famous.

Latins on the Loose

MY EX-FLAME Tremaine has been calling all afternoon, probably to ask if I want to meet him at one of the bars in the Quarter. I know it's him because he lets the phone ring three times and then hangs up, thinking, as he always does, that if I don't pounce on the receiver after the first ring, I don't want to speak to him. Tremaine is what we used to call "simple" when I was a boy. Only now they've come up with more complicated words for being simple.

"Hey," I say, finally managing to grab the phone after the first ring. "Is that you?"

"You know it be me, Kirby," Tremaine growls. "Just don't want to talk to me."

"That's not true," I lie. I picture the nut-brown brow furrowed with suspicion, the crossed eyes, and the fleshy lips set in a peevish pout. His personality has only two speeds: darkest paranoia and childish sunshine.

It seems that I specialize in crackpots, easy enough to do here in the French Quarter. What I actually do is to glue back together broken pieces of antique porcelain, a tedious task that calms my frayed nerves. It began with my great-grandmother's turkey platter, shattered during a move, and now as a hobby I do porcelain repair jobs for several Royal Street antique stores. It doesn't bring in much money, but gives me something else to do in my free time besides haunt the bars looking for love.

This is the third Saturday in a row I've spent moping around the apartment alone, pruning azaleas and mending porcelain. My fingers are caked with epoxy and my lower back aches. No, I inform Tremaine, I don't want to meet him at a bar. Last year I spent two months dating him, and now every time we run into each other he asks me for a buck. "I'm hongry," he whines. The next moment he's feeding the dollar into a video poker machine.

But later I get to thinking. If I went out dancing, maybe Donna Summer could help me to unkink this stiff back. Although I'm tired of hanging out in raunchy gay bars, stumbling home full of well drinks, saturated with stale cigarette smoke, and if I get lucky, hauling home somebody whose name I can never remember. Rather than admit I've forgotten a trick's name, I call them all Doug.

"Touch me there, Doug," I say. "Take it off, Doug."

When he finally corrects me, I go, "Sorry, but you remind me so much of my best friend, Doug." Then he snuggles up to me until, sooner or later, one of us passes out.

What taxi drivers call the "fruit-loop" in the Quarter never closes, and the bars are just hosed out at dawn before the after-hours crowd shows up. They're filled with nothing but tourists and conventioneers and party-circuit revelers, you know, here today, Palm Springs tomorrow. The guys may be rich and beautiful, but where is the follow up?

When a stranger approaches me in one of these joints, his opening comment is the inevitable, "Where are you from?" As if we were at some airport departure gate rather than the quirky city of my birth.

"Around the corner." I always deliver my response dead pan. "Just out to get a quart of milk. You?"

That always flusters the guy: the very nerve that someone else hasn't spent millions of dollars to fly thousands of miles to waste endless hours choosing exactly the right outfit just to meet him, spot lit at the epicenter of his own fabulousness. *Who does this local yokel think he is?* I can hear him wonder. *Why, he might not even be gay. And look at those shoes.*

I've finally had an earth-shattering revelation: that sleeping with tourists is not the path to true love, and that the only people you meet in bars—*hellooo?*—are people who go to bars. So I'm no longer looking for Mr. Doug, that conveyor-belt party animal from New York or California. Until the Tourist Commission puts me on payroll, I resign from being the anonymous boy who pops out of the cake during everybody's wild weekend getaway in New Orleans. I imagine the trick the next morning, staring out of the airplane porthole and slapping a palm to his throbbing forehead, thinking *oh my god, and then there was Kirby, that skinny redheaded guy with the freckles in the decrepit slave quarter. What was I thinking? Nobody's going to believe this one back in the support group.*

So here I am, lolling around the house on a Saturday night listening to Billie Holliday and catching up on my email before I have to drag myself back to the AT&T personnel office on Monday morning. I just read a letter in "Dear Abby" that urges you to make a list of the qualities you're searching for in a mate, promising that once you have a clear image of this person in mind, presto, you'll meet him. It's too easy, the letter claims, to be distracted by attractive riffraff, and that you need to conjure up your dream Romeo beforehand. So if this technique works for Eunice, age 29, from Greenville, South Carolina, why won't it work for Kirby, age 32, from New Orleans, Louisiana?

Who I'm looking for, I decide after much deliberation, is somebody tender and easy-going, somebody also interested in porcelain and gardening, somebody with a depth of feeling, the courage to be himself, and in touch with the magic of the cosmos. You know, someone hung like a horse. Someone totally adorable who will never forget that I'm the cute one. Someone who knows how to roll over and play dead the minute I'm sick of the sight of him. Not someone else I'll have to throw out on the street at three in the morning along with his stack of boring action flicks, his mother's cheesy pole lamp, and his ex-boyfriend's collection of Madonna re-releases.

I hear Eunice chortling all the way from Greenville. Who am I trying to kid?

Okay, let's simplify, I tell myself. Age or race or weight or physical disability no barrier, I'm seeking another breathing male in the city of New Orleans with a job.

I sling on my shorts and turn off the air conditioning.

I'll be out looking for a while.

THE FIRST PERSON I run into at the Mary-Go-Round is the last person I want to see. Tremaine is wearing one of those enormous velvet Mexican sombreros and towering head and shoulders over everyone else like some Watusi mariachi.

I brace myself for his greeting. No, I don't have a dollar.

"Hey, Boogers," I call out. "What's with the sombrero?" His family calls him Boogers, he once told me, after his niece seared his ear with a hot curling iron. They said the scar tissue looked like boogers.

"You like it?" Tremaine twirls around like a runway model, face crinkling into a toothy smile. I can usually lighten up those features so often shadowed by a distrustful misapprehension of the world.

"Where you staying by?" I ask.

"By my auntie's house in Westwego." He puffs out his chest. "I took the bus here all by myself."

"You took the bus from across the river in that big Mexican hat?"

He giggles like a ten-year-old, even though he's as tall, dark, and handsome as a *GQ* model. "You got a dollar?"

"When are you going to get a job?"

"I had me a job," he stammers with impatience, "but now I got my disability paper. Say I'm schizophrenic. You understand what this mean?" He pulls an enormous wad of papers from his back pocket and hands it to me.

"You took a bus from Westwego in a big Mexican sombrero with your schizophrenia papers?" Tremaine never ceases to surprise me. The second time we slept together, he dropped by shaved bald, dressed to the nines and reeking of cologne, and told me he'd just starred in a Hollywood movie. Then he asked me for a dollar.

"What them papers say?" he asks. "I going to get my government money?"

The electronic music is thumping like a car factory, and some bare-chested queen with his tank top stuffed into a back pocket bumps into me, spilling his drink on my sandaled foot.

"Hey, buddy, watch out," I tell him.

"Where are you from?" he asks, sidling up to me. It's the only line these boys know.

"Look," I tell Tremaine, ignoring the tourist, "I can't read these papers in here. It's too dark and noisy. Let's take them back to my house."

"But then I miss my way back cross the river. Met this nice man say he ride me to auntie's."

"Go tell him you'll be back in an hour."

How do I keep getting myself into these situations? I wonder if the epoxy on the cup from the Occupied Japan demitasse set has dried by now, and if the handle will hold.

A moment later Tremaine's sombrero is looming over me. I'm being introduced to a balding creep in a checkered button-down shirt and wrinkled beige Dockers. He looks like a Home Depot clerk, and I bet he really does live in Westwego. Man's name is Stan.

"Stan ax can he come by your house," Tremaine says. "On his way home now."

"Have anything to drink at your house?" Stan asks, as if he's already been invited.

"I can offer you a beer." I'm from a good Southern family and not known to be inhospitable to anyone forced into my presence, even under the most trying social circumstances.

"Got any porn at home?"

"Beg your pardon?" Did this Home Depot clerk just ask me if I had any porn?

"You know, movies of homo sex acts. I'm not gay myself," Stan tells me, "but I'd like to watch some porn. I live with my momma."

Tremaine giggles.

It's already two in the morning. I glance around the Mary-Go-Round, where Donna Summer is cranking up one of her retro torch songs. Reflected infinitely in the mirrored corners of the dance floor, hunky Dougs in tank tops are embracing other hunky Dougs in tank tops, faces aglow with lust, no doubt swapping hotel room numbers.

And here I am, shopping local, stuck with Tremaine in his sombrero and momma's boy on a porn safari.

"My DVD is broken," I say. It really is. "But I suppose I have a VCR and some old tapes you can watch."

"I ain't picky," Stan says with a wicked gleam in his eye.

I INSTALL STAN upstairs in the bedroom with my VCR and a video cassette beaded with dust balls that I find under the bed.

"Know how to work this thing?" I ask.

"Sure." His gray skin is glazed with a sheen of sweat.

"Okay, Boogers," I say, seated again at the kitchen table downstairs. I put on my glasses and squint at the stack of papers from the Social Security Administration. Here's the diagnosis: paranoid schizophrenia. And a notification of S.S.I. benefits is pending. Attached are forms that need to be notarized and returned within ten (10) business days, papers that require the signature of both the recipient and the legal guardian or caretaker.

"Tell your auntie to notarize these," I explain. "Look up 'Notary of Public' in the yellow pages, and then you both have to go—"

"She in a wheel chair." Tremaine's face clouds. "We don't have no money to take a cab to some big office."

How do they expect poor, crazy people—and you don't qualify for this unless you're poor and crazy—to face these complex legal maneuvers. Is it a test? If you can understand what you need to do to get the money, then you don't qualify for it. And if you can't figure it out, then you deserve the checks but will never receive them. What a brilliant ploy to save taxpayers millions.

"Hey Kirby, I think it's broken," Stan hollers from upstairs. "Got a screwdriver?"

"What for?"

"To get the damn tape out."

As I bound up the stairs with a screwdriver, Tremaine cracks open the refrigerator door.

"I tried hitting eject." Holding the remote, Stan crouches befuddled in front of the VCR, where the cassette is jammed in backwards. The room smells of singed hair, and an aluminum-foil pipe smolders on top of the TV.

"You've broken my machine," I shout, beyond exasperation. "What the hell are you on?" I'm not sure what he's smoking, but I've heard that people on crack flip out into twisted sexual trips like cross-dressing, public masturbation, and porn obsession.

"Wait," he says, grabbing the screwdriver with a manic gleam in his eye, "I know how to get it out. This happened to my momma's once." His sweat smells like burger grease and his breath, stale beer.

Somehow he manages to pry out the cassette, the tape unspooling from inside in loopy spirals. The label reads *Latins on the Loose.*

"I know how to fix it," he says. "Just have to rewind it by hand."

"The tape is broken," I insist. "Besides, I don't want you doing drugs up here."

"Got another one?"

"No," I lie. "That's all I'm into, day and night. *Latins on the Loose.*"

"Don't worry." He grabs the tape. "I can fix it."

"Got any luncheon meat?" Tremaine yells from below.

I stomp down the stairs, back to Tremaine in his sombrero and the schizophrenia papers. Tears are dribbling down his cheeks, and from under the elaborately braided brim of the hat he observes me slit-eyed, as if I'm Lucifer himself. I've seen this murderous look before.

He then accuses me of not having any luncheon meat. "Ate it all up cause I was coming over. I know you."

"How about some nice cheese?" I ask, leaping toward the refrigerator.

"You trying to stop me up?" He pouts, pointing at the papers. "And cheat me, too?"

"Look, I'm explaining what you need to do—"

Stan bolts down the stairs, the unspooling cassette of *Latins on the Loose* in hand, shouting that he just needs to get something from his car.

"Be back in a sec," he says, racing out the door.

The courtyard gate slams shut, and then a car engine revs up. I arrive panting at the gate just in time to see taillights streaking down the street into the night.

Then I run back into the kitchen. "Your friend on crack swiped my videotape. He just took off."

"Mean I lost my ride to Westwego?"

"What am I running here, a crack house? Why would that idiot hightail it back to his momma's with a broken porn tape? This is your brain on drugs."

"Can I spend the night?"

"Absolutely not." I'm over any more psychodrama with Tremaine. I pick up the cracked demitasse by the handle and smile. It holds.

"Can I leave my sombrero here?" he asks, taking off the hat and laying it on a chair.

"No." I don't want any reason for him to come back. "Take your schizophrenia papers and your sombrero, and I'll walk you back to the bar. God knows what Stan would have done with you in Westwego. Tied you up and made you smoke crack."

"I only smoke menthol."

I decide to give Tremaine, cracked-out Stan, *Latins on the Loose*, and the evening's mariachi theme a military escort out of my life. We trudge down Bourbon Street in silence, Tremaine weeping under his ridiculous hat as he clutches the wad of schizophrenia papers. A lone squad car passes, and the cop shoots the sombrero-wearing black man a dirty look.

"I'm leaving you here, Boogers," I say, as we step through the door of the almost deserted Mary-Go-Round. A refrigerated wave of booze, sweat, and smoke almost shoves me back outside. "I'm sure you'll find a ride."

"You got a dollar? I'm hongry."

"Why not?" I take out my wallet and peel one off. Then I peck him on the lips.

Tremaine giggles, his scowl softening back into sunshine. Why does the world expect so much of him? What makes him happy is luncheon meat and dollar bills. He struts over to the video poker machines, king of the universe.

On my hasty retreat from the bar, I collide with a shirtless blond with sculpted pecs and a sun-bed tan. His buzz cut is bleached the color of an American Express Gold Card.

"Hey, cutie," he slurs, eying me up and down, "where are you from?"

The rest of the broken demitasse set is back at the apartment waiting for me, along with a trash bag filled with azalea clippings I need to haul to the curb. On Monday morning, at eight sharp, I'll be back behind my desk in personnel. As I study the guy, I hear the click of a key card unlocking a hotel room and smell the chlorine from the patio pool.

"Pasadena," I lie. "I'm Kirby. What's your name?"

"Doug."

I smile. "That's easy to remember."

"How long have you been in town?" he asks. The pale light of dawn is seeping over the sagging balconies of Bourbon Street as Doug quickens his pace to walk alongside me.

"Only three hours." I spread my arms to take in the trash-strewn street. "And isn't this the most fabulous place in the world?"

The Empty Throne

THE MESSAGE WAS waiting for Wally Wiggins on his answering machine when he came home from the gym sweating like a potbellied pig. In a gruff voice choked with emotion, his father announced that Wally had just been elected this year's king of the Krewe of Mirth. At first Wally thought the voice mail was a joke or some kind of mistake, so he played it again, never imagining that it would lead to the most humiliating night of his life.

He knew, of course, that everyone in the uptown Carnival organization owed his wheeler-dealer father a favor, and wondered how many arms he had to twist to engineer this unlikely coup. Last year, after Wally's krewe membership had lapsed for quite a while, his father restored it as a fortieth birthday present, muttering that time was a wasting and he was waiting for his only son to accomplish something that would do the family proud. In their social circles in New Orleans, that could only mean becoming an Episcopal priest, making several million dollars, marrying a debutante, or reigning as the king of a Mardi Gras parade.

"Or are you waiting to be elected queen?" his father once asked, eying his son's blousy shirt, tight denims, and maroon kid boots.

That had hurt Wally. It really did. He was a Wiggins, after all, not some queer on Bourbon Street.

His father, a ball-bearing baron and past king of Mirth himself, never stopped telling his son that "the position for my heir apparent is still open." Wally was used to his father's disappointment in him, but lately it had become his own. Maybe he really didn't try. He lived with his boyfriend, Nelson, in a drab apartment complex in Metairie, maintained the appearance of a lackluster decorating business on the Internet, and was still drinking far too much. No matter how regularly he worked out on the gym's cardio machines, he had an ample spare tire and slumped shoulders, and except when he studied himself in a full-length mirror, his father's thundering admonitions to stand up straight went unheeded.

After listening to the message for a third time, he vowed to stop boozing, but then—wait a minute—reminded himself that heavy drinking was part of the royal duties of a Carnival king. So he toweled his face, ran a pudgy hand through his spiky buzz cut, and poured himself a double Johnny Walker Black Label on the rocks before calling Daddy.

"Sorry I missed the krewe meeting," he lied, "but I was consulting with some rich clients about their new solarium." Wally only had three steady customers, all of them penny-pinching Presbyterian bridge partners of his mother's. Without his grandparents' trust fund that Daddy doled out to him each month, he couldn't pay the rent.

"Just as well you weren't there," his father said, clearing his throat. "The vote was easier that way. Now I'm really doing this for your mother, so she can finally see you sitting up there on the throne where she raised you. And I'm only asking one thing in return."

"What?" Wally's father was a shrewd negotiator. "That I lose weight?"

"Of course not. There you go again sounding like your mother. Real men don't worry about their figures, son."

"Well then, what?"

"That if the feds are pussy enough to pass this gay marriage business, you won't marry that bum you're living with. If you did that, swear to God, I'd cut you off without a cent. And take back the Honda Accord."

Wally cast a long look at Nelson, slumped on the sofa with wet hair in front of the TV. Wet hair in the middle of the day usually meant one thing. Often when Wally went to the gym, his boyfriend slunk off to a skanky bathhouse in the French Quarter, where he engaged in God knows what acts with hustlers, tourists, and other riffraff. Nelson's sculpted pecs had sagged into tits, his hairline of springy curls was receding into a widow's peak, and his default expression had become a sullen pout, like a baby denied its bottle. True, at one time he really knew how to make Wally grab the headboard and beg for more, but lately he seemed nothing but a bad habit, like smoking or video poker.

"Don't worry, Daddy," Wally said. "That's the last thing I'd ever do."

"I couldn't bear to introduce that loser as my son-in-law to neighbors here on the North Shore or friends at the Pickwick Club."

"Good riddance to bad rubbish, if you know what I mean." Wally rattled the ice cubes in his glass.

"Congratulations, son. Your mother and I can't wait to see you on that float. It'll make our lives complete."

Wally hung up the phone, and glancing at himself in the mirror, squared his shoulders. "Hey, Nelson," he shouted like a drill sergeant, "don't you think it's time you started dinner? Tonight's your turn. And not to get into it again, but where the hell were you this afternoon?"

THIS WAS IN EARLY January, just after Twelfth Night, when in great secrecy the Carnival organizations chose their royal courts. Then the city sprang into action. With basting pins between their lips and measuring tapes around their necks, seamstresses plugged in their idle sewing machines and, in a frenzy of tulle, satin, and sequins, took measurements for the queens' and maids' ball gowns, as well as for the tunics worn by pages, dukes, and kings. Parade routes were mapped out while the viewing stands went up in front of Gallier Hall and the exclusive social clubs along St. Charles Avenue. These preparations added a certain champagne fizz to the cold, damp air, and people drank an extra cocktail before dinner because—what the hell—it was Carnival. How could they ever get through a whole winter without it?

For Wally and Nelson in their cinderblock one-bedroom overlooking the cracked, empty swimming pool, things weren't going well. At the moment, Nelson was packing his belongings into empty liquor boxes, preparing to move back in with his former roommate in the French Quarter, a skinny guy named Kirby.

"At least Kirby has a job," Wally said, downing his third scotch. "But how long do you expect him to carry you on his phone company salary? Are you two still, you know . . . ?"

"Get out of here, you jealous bitch. At least I won't have to put up with somebody snooping around in my sock drawer, looking for other guys' phone numbers."

"You yourself said—"

"No I didn't."

Wally threw his highball glass against the living room wall, where it shattered over the TV. "Damn it, I want you to stay."

Nelson folded beefy biceps over his melting pecs. "Make me."

"I need your help to get through this . . . king thing."

"Okay. But as the king's consort, can I watch the parade from the balcony of the Pickwick Club with your parents?"

Wally stared at this former supermarket clerk and wondered how he had ever considered him the love of his life. That was where he'd met him, working in the nine-items-or-less checkout line at Winn-Dixie, and for a long time his life revolved around dating Nelson. Once Nelson lost his job and moved in with him, Wally distanced himself from the Uptown world where he grew up, a snooty milieu of private schools and charity organizations in which the new boyfriend, happy with his action movies, six-packs, and pizza, stuck out like a sore thumb. Now Wally tried to picture express-line Nelson standing in a circle of bankers next to his father on the balcony of the fancy men's club. "Out of the question," he sputtered.

"So I'm supposed to watch Miss High-and-Mighty parade by from a street corner while I scrabble with drunk tourists over throws?"

A brilliant inspiration popped into Wally's mind. In any case, it seemed like a good idea at the time. He picked up the phone to dial his mother, whom he hoped could cajole the old man into honoring her son's request.

Eventually it was decided, over Mr. Wiggins dead body, that Nelson would ride on the king's float as page captain, the adult in charge of keeping in line the ten-year-old pages surrounding the throne. Wally reasoned that if he planned to drink, he'd need Nelson's help in climbing on and off the monstrous float, and besides, he wanted somehow to share this moment of glory with him. Better things were on the way for Wally, of that he was sure, but for the moment he needed Nelson at his side.

Later that evening, after Nelson unpacked his boxes, Wally was looking forward to some great make-up sex. "Everything of yours can stay except for that pole lamp," he said, surveying the minimalist living room with a decorator's eye.

"But that was my mother's," Nelson said, "the only thing of hers I have."

Wally threw open the door. "Out with it."

"Bitch."

ON THE FRIDAY afternoon of the Mirth parade, while Wally was putting the finishing touches on his regal pancake makeup, Nelson came home with wet hair. That did it. Wally hadn't eaten anything all day and his nerves couldn't take it.

"I know where you've been," Wally shouted, draining a glass of Johnny Walker rimmed with smudges of lip liner. "Start putting on your costume."

"Man, what a hunk that guy was. You should've seen—"

Wally dove for this throat.

They stumbled out of the cramped bathroom and into the

bedroom, where Nelson picked up a bronze table lamp and threatened to brain Wally unless he settled down. Wally turned to face the mirror, where he smoothed out his makeup and fastened the pageboy wig in place on his throbbing head. He draped the burgundy velvet cape over his shoulders, took a nip from the pocket flask of scotch secreted in an inside pocket of his gold lamé tunic, and turned to face the miserable excuse for a man to whom he felt unbearably yoked.

"All hail His Majesty, King of Mirth," Nelson said, trying to fasten behind his back the tunic he was struggling to put on.

"Let me help you," Wally said, pulling at the stuck zipper. Then he ran his fingers through his partner's wet curls and, face frozen in a grease-paint grimace, yanked as hard as he could. "Whore," he hissed into Nelson's ear.

"Lemme go, you hysterical queen."

"King," Wally said.

"Get out of my life, you big fat . . . flop. Your old man is right about you."

"First get your sleazy ass out my house."

They were still going at each other like this at four when the black stretch limousine pulled up in front of the apartment complex to bring them to the beginning of the parade route. And they continued to pummel each other with insults and slaps like quarreling school boys, as Wally got drunker and drunker and Nelson grew more incensed. Finally the chauffeur turned up the car radio until Al Johnson's "It's Carnival Time" drowned out the two bickering royals in the back seat, their wigs askew and makeup smeared.

WHILE THE KEROSENE flambeaux were being lit with great ceremony at the corner of Napoleon and Tchoupitoulas, Nelson managed to shove the butt of the besotted King of Mirth up the shaky ladder, giving him a slap on the rump as Wally staggered onto the tinseled float. The pages, already in place, looked at each other, giggling. Then the tractor-drawn float jolted into motion, and following the strutting flambeaux carriers, swayed under a canopy of oak limbs as crowds gathered to cheer the parade on its way down the darkened Uptown avenue.

With a golden scepter in one hand and the pocket flask hidden in the folds of his cape in the other, Wally gestured and waved to the throngs, gestured and waved, already impatient to reach the Pickwick Club at St. Charles and Canal. That was where he would rise from his carved gilt throne to toast his parents on the balcony, which, after all, was the point of this whole ordeal. He should have eaten something this afternoon before he started drinking, and he really needed to pee, but ancestral duty called, even as he calculated the number of major intersections the parade had to cross before getting to Canal Street. Yet he knew that his life would be different from this moment on, when he'd assume his rightful place in the world as a Wiggins.

If only he didn't need to pee so badly. Wally glanced up at Nelson standing by his side, obviously having the time of his life, and blinked, certain that he saw him naked except for a skimpy white towel wrapped around his waist. Was this what he looked like at that Quarter bathhouse? Wally couldn't shake this soused vision of his boyfriend, and startling the pink-cheeked pages, began screaming "you whore" as he gestured and waved, gestured and waved, his shouts drowned out by the high-school band ahead marching to their brassy version of "Thriller."

By the time they reached Washington Avenue, the King of Mirth was sitting with legs crossed, concentrating on his bladder. When the parade stalled a few blocks down the avenue, Wally saw it was time to act. The marching band stopped playing, then its members broke formation and milled around, high-fiving each other. The flambeaux carriers extinguished their torches and lit up cigarettes. Word soon spread along the street that the tractor of the dukes' float ahead had broken down, and that it would take a few minutes for a replacement to arrive. Tourists checked their watches and looked concerned, but most of the crowd along the curb shrugged, as if used to how things worked—or didn't work—in New Orleans.

At that moment Wally spotted the Dunkin' Donuts on the corner.

"Get the ladder and help me down off this thing," he commanded Nelson, pointing. "I'm going to use the bathroom in the donut shop."

"But it's closed," Nelson said.

True, the overhead lights were off inside and a "closed" sign hung on the door, but the tilted trays of donuts were still back-lit inside their glass display cases. Wally could swear he glimpsed a lady in a white dress moving around among them.

"The ladder," Wally insisted. Once again he saw Nelson dressed only in the bathhouse towel, and spit out, "whore."

When the King of Mirth swung his legs over the edge of the papier-mâche float as if about to climb down without any help, Nelson lowered the ladder in place. Descending one unsteady step at a time, Wally made it to the street, and then staggered toward the Dunkin' Donuts, waving his scepter and straightening his crown.

He banged and banged on the locked plate-glass door, screaming, "Lemme in."

Inside, a frumpy lady in a smudged white apron was mopping the floor in the dark, her round, creased face a moon reflecting the spectral light from the lit donut cases. When she made it to the door, she mimed *closed* with crossed arms and a shaking head. Wally pointed to his golden crown and then steepled his fingers in prayer.

The door cracked open, and her frizzy red hair poked out. "What you want?"

"Need to use the rest room," Wally said. "Bad."

She looked him up and down, from the glittery leotards to the auburn page-boy wig. And then, as if for the first time, she seemed to notice the parade stalled along St. Charles Avenue.

"Make it snappy," she said. "I should've been home a half-hour ago."

The fluorescent overheads snapped on, flooding the donut shop with an icy glare. Wally scurried to the men's room, and the lady went back to mopping the floor, turning up the volume on her portable radio.

After a couple of thumping blues songs came on the air, banging resumed on the glass door. Mop in hand, she trudged to the front of the shop, and there stood Nelson, eyes frantic.

"Where's the guy dressed like a king?" he asked.

"Sitting on the throne, I guess," she said, pointing to the men's room.

"I've got to get him. The parade is about to take off."

Nelson raced inside, where he collided with Wally shuffling out of the bathroom. He was still wearing his crown, but the tunic was on backwards and the burgundy cape trailed along the wet tile floor behind him.

"Sit down," he said to Nelson, cross-eyed. "I need to talk to you."

"But the parade—"

"Screw the parade," Wally said, plopping down at a Formica table and resting the heavy crown on a sugar dispenser. "Hey," he called to the red-headed lady, "any of that coffee still hot?"

"You look like you could use a cup, baby." She walked behind the counter and placed a paper cup under the coffee-urn spigot.

"How about one of those glazed crullers to go with it?"

"Coming right up, your royal heinie."

"The parade is about to take off," Nelson said, banging on the table, "and here you are, having breakfast?"

"Time you and me had a talk." Wally could barely hold himself up in the chair.

Nelson blanched. "You idiot—"

"You know, I was really in love with you for a long time," Wally slurred, "but you don't respect me any more, wearing that bathhouse towel in my Carnival parade."

"What the fuck are you talking about?"

On the other side of the plate-glass window, the flambeaux were being relit and the marching band was falling back into formation.

"It's time for us to call it quits," Wally said, taking a long slurp of his coffee. "You've broken my heart."

The band blasted into a full-throttled marching version of "When You're Smiling" as the crowd roared back to life. Nelson tugged at the king's tunic, but Wally wouldn't budge. Then the royal consort made a dash for the door, swung it open, and Wally's mournful brown eyes followed his back as he scampered up the ladder, dragging it onto the float behind him.

Then float by dazzling float, the parade continued to pass along St. Charles Avenue. For a moment an enormous white swan hovered under the oak branches, ridden like a bronco by a busty papier-mâché Leda with yellow foil tresses. Then other illustrations of the krewe's "Greek Shenanigans" theme rolled by, reflected in the glass window of the donut shop where Wally sat saucer-eyed, gazing out. And in the distance, the empty throne on the king's float rounded Lee Circle and then disappeared down the avenue.

FOR A LONG WHILE Wally said nothing, slumped over his coffee and cruller at a table in the Dunkin' Donuts, as the parade that he had waited for his whole life rolled by outside. The muffled cheers from the crowd along the route faded into the insistent buzz inside his head. He figured that by now the king's float must have stopped in front of Gallier Hall, where he should have been toasting the mayor. And ten minutes later it should be passing under the eyes of his parents standing on the balcony of the Pickwick Club. He replaced the crown on top of his wig as muddy tears oozed down his cheeks, blotching the makeup and pooling on the tabletop in tan puddles.

"Trouble back home at the castle?" the donut lady asked, eyebrows raised.

"What's your name, sweetheart?"

"Evelyn," she said.

"I don't know what . . . ." Wally blew his nose with a honk.

"That's okay, baby," she said, coming around to join him at the table. "It's not much better at my house. My husband left me this week, after twelve years. Mind if I sit down?"

"Why'd he do that?"

"Split with a younger woman," she said, taking a seat, "some dame he met Cajun dancing at Rock n' Bowl while I was here working the night shift."

"That's not fair."

"Like they say about love and war. What's your story?"

"My daddy has always run roughshod over my momma," Wally said, "but in some ways they have the perfect marriage. And I always thought one day I'd have something rock solid like that, but you saw what I'm stuck with."

"He's not so bad, considering what's out there."

"Plays around on me. To my face."

"Maybe it's time to trade him in." Evelyn shot him a wicked grin.

"The stupid part is," Wally said, wiping his eyes with the velvet cape, "not being with him would be like cutting off my leg. I really love that damn man."

"I can tell you do. And I adore my husband," she said, shaking her head, "but I ain't taking him back when he gets tired of two-stepping."

"And what will Daddy and Momma say now that I've screwed up this?" He rapped his scepter on the table, knocking over the sugar dispenser. "I couldn't even sit on a throne with a crown on my head. That's all they asked of me."

"Well, Your Majesty, some jobs are tough, and this one better be here tomorrow," Evelyn said, rising from the table and reaching for the light switch, "or my two kids will starve." The overheads went out.

The opening organ chords of Toussaint McCall's "Nothing Takes the Place of You" were swelling from the radio as Evelyn returned her mop and sloshing bucket to the broom closet. Wally hoisted himself to his feet, wondering what he was going to do now. Nelson was the steady hand that anchored him, the only person who could calm him down and lead him home. Where was he?

"Want to dance?" he asked.

"With you?" Evelyn asked, eyes widening.

"Why not? It's Carnival."

He wrapped an arm around her waist, and she snuggled close to him.

"Don't be getting any ideas," he said.

"Oh honey, you're just like my sissy brother. I know you go to another church."

"Why, what you got against Episcopalians?"

While the red lights of a crash truck flashed outside, announcing the tail end of the Krewe of Mirth, Wally and Evelyn slow-danced to the smoldering torch song along the slippery floor in front of the illuminated donut cases, watery eyes closed tight as if dancing alone with lost dreams.

I moved your picture
from my walls
and I replaced them
both large and small.
And each new day
finds me so blue
because nothing, oh nothing
takes the place of you.

"You are my queen . . . ," he murmured.

"And you my king . . . ."

"For a day. . . ."

"Or tonight," said the donut lady, pulling him closer.

WALLY DIDN'T KNOW he could walk so fast. Maybe it was the coffee or a sugar rush from the cruller or the sweet kiss Evelyn planted on his cheek as he left the Dunkin' Donuts, but now he bounced along Tchoupitoulas Street, steadying the crown on his head while the velvet cape ballooned behind him with wintry gusts of fog blowing in from the river. He simply had to make it to Poydras Street, where the parade would be disbanding, to catch the limo waiting there to take him home. He'd left his cell and wallet in the car, and now with no money, ID, or credit cards, he could foresee an even more demeaning night ahead, with the King of Mirth wandering up and down Canal Street trying to cage cab fare from tourists.

The first thing he spotted was the enormous flying goose or swan or whatever in the hell it was, looming over a stalled float on the other side of the intersection. By now most of the riders must have already dispersed to the krewe's after-party at the Sheraton, where in his present circumstances Wally wouldn't have been caught dead. He couldn't imagine the hubbub that the empty throne probably caused when the king's float pulled up in front of the mayor's viewing stand or under the balcony of the Pickwick Club, where his parents would have been waiting.

His head hung so low that the crown tumbled off. He picked it up and kept on walking, wondering if Nelson would go with him to live in Atlanta or Houston, wherever Wally didn't have to live up to anything. His life was over in this town, where he'd never be his daddy's son.

Just as he was crossing Poydras, a limo cut him off and then screeched to a halt. The back window slid down as Nelson's widow's peak emerged. When their glances locked, they both froze, staring at each other for a long while. Nelson's slate eyes softened as his face turned tender, and whether the expression conveyed love, understanding, or only pity, Wally fell into it as though coming home. Nelson swung open the limo door and scooted over. While climbing inside, Wally's flask slipped from his tunic pocket and clanked into the gutter, which was right where he left it.

He inched closer to Nelson, fidgeting with the crown and cape and scepter, not daring to speak. Nelson reached for his fingers and they sat there, hand-in-hand, not saying a word as the limo plowed through the honking post-parade traffic on Poydras.

Wally's cell phone lit up, vibrating on the tray table next to him.

He recognized the number. Daddy.

"It's the queen mum," his mother's voice said, breathless, "and Wally, we're so sorry. Will you ever forgive us? The Causeway was fogged in tonight, so we had to take the long way into town from the North Shore, through Slidell. We've just left our car in the parking garage next to the club, but missed the whole parade. We're devastated that we didn't see you on that king's float. I told your father we should have left by four, what with the Carnival traffic, but listen to me making excuses. I'm sure other members took loads of pictures. How was your ride?"

"Fine," Wally muttered.

"We're so proud of you. Look, let me give you to your father. He's bursting, I tell you, just bursting."

Wally winced. "Okay."

His father's booming voice seemed to fill the entire limousine. "So, son, how did it feel to toast the mayor of New Orleans from the king's throne of Mirth?"

Wally calculated how long it would take, once his parents made it into the Pickwick Club, for word to reach them that the throne on the king's float was empty as it passed under the balcony tonight.

Maybe five, ten minutes at most.

"Daddy, thanks so much for everything," Wally said. "I've never been so happy and proud as I was waving up there on that throne."

They were still his, these five or ten minutes he had left as his father's son, all he'd ever have.

And he knew that now they would have to last him a lifetime.

ABIDE WITH ME

I FIRST HEARD about that bitch Consuelo, my mother's roommate, one moonless night in August while rocking on my slave-quarter balcony in the dark. At eight that evening, an electrical transformer had exploded inside a manhole in front of Rouses Supermarket on Royal Street, shooting flames ten feet into the air. My portable radio said the blackout in the French Quarter would last all night. Or longer.

An unsettling stillness descended upon the neighborhood as air conditioners choked off, fan blades spun to a standstill, and TVs fell silent. At first all I could hear were tree frogs croaking under the banana trees and water dripping from a rotten corner of the balcony. Then people poured outside, voices shouting across balconies as if trying to dispel the darkness. A police siren wailed on the other side of the brick courtyard wall. To see me through the night I only had a few candle stubs and a bottle of Bacardi Gold.

No wonder the transformer had exploded. For three weeks straight the temperature topped a hundred, so everyone's air conditioners had been running on high. Now here we were, fanning ourselves with magazines, mopping our faces with handkerchiefs, and swatting at blood-thirsty mosquitoes. I was drenched in sweat and covered with itching welts. I'd already scratched the stubble on my unshaven face into an ugly rash.

The scent of night-blooming jasmine was taking over, its sweetness almost visible in the impenetrable darkness. For the first time, stars gleamed in the night sky above the Quarter, stars that had been there all along, watching over us. And there was comfort in the rum, in rocking back and forth over creaky floorboards in my great-grandfather's oak chair. My mother told me I'd been breast-fed in this chair, where four generations of my family had been nursed. Yet like most people in the Quarter, I was always packing my suitcase with one hand while planting eternal live oaks with the other. I vowed to stay in New Orleans only as long as my mother lasted. But with her heart condition, that wouldn't be long.

A devilish stage laugh, eerily familiar, echoed from a neighboring patio. How young the dead still look, I marveled, conjuring up Aaron's cherubic face when I first met him. Aaron Hunter had been my neighbor in the downstairs slave quarter for almost ten years, until the coroner's office carried his corpse away three months ago. The last time Aaron sat up to look at the world, I'd just walked in carrying a tray of coffee with two rattling demitasses. He bolted upright in bed and stared straight at me with eyes as intense as the moons of Jupiter. Then he collapsed into the coma caused by the morphine drip with which we were slowly—to be blunt—killing him.

"Poor guy smells the coffee and thinks its time to rise and shine," said his roommate Darren.

I'd imagined morphine would come in an IV bottle we'd hang over the hospital bed that crowded his murky bedroom. But when we finally scored it from an AIDS hospice, it was more like a TV remote control, with buttons to measure the dosage spelled out in red digital numbers. His breathing was gasping, raspy, and waves of convulsions wracked his body. Little was left of him but translucent skin stretched over a skeleton of wire clothes hangers.

Darren passed me a joint and leaned over to whisper into Aaron's ear. "Look, we're having a goodbye party just like you'd want," he said. "Lucian just brought down some coffee and we're smoking a doobie and you're on pure morphine, you lucky dog."

I had no inkling Aaron was dying of AIDS, or was even HIV-positive. He was from one of those old Savannah families and I was from one of those old New Orleans families that just didn't discuss their blood work over cocktails. I thought if he'd tell anyone, it would have been me, but then again, he spent his whole life in the theater. He knew how to put on a good show.

In the past few years he had withdrawn into his packrat apartment chockablock with theater memorabilia. Most of the small houses he'd stage-managed in the Quarter and Faubourg Marigny were closed, and it humiliated him to work the box office for national touring companies at the Saenger. After their curtain calls at Le Petit Théâtre on Jackson Square, his theater friends would sometimes burst onto his patio like a traveling opera troupe, striking poses and belting out show tunes. And still, on occasion, I'd hear Aaron's Mephistophelian guffaws below.

But after Darren moved in, the friends stopped visiting.

Darren Mullen weighed almost three hundred pounds and had a complexion the color of pickled pigs' feet. He kept inflating, and in his red Eddie Bauer jacket, looked like a Macy's parade balloon of a Boy Scout. No, they weren't lovers, I assure you, although that was what everyone assumed. Yet why else would the flamboyant Aaron Hunter, unofficial mayor of the Vieux Carré, keep around a yahoo like that? Darren had never heard of Tennessee Williams or Oscar Wilde, and emptied six packs rooting in front of TV football games, which Aaron drowned out by blasting *Carmina Burana.*

Whatever bond they shared seemed so . . . unlikely.

Darren had been a nurse in the army. That much I knew. He was a member of some lost platoon of single vets floating around the country on Greyhound buses and in junker cars, unable to attach themselves to anything or anyone, scurrying from one borrowed shell to another like hermit crabs. Exactly how he and Aaron met is uncertain. What I heard is that Darren came over one afternoon for a drink. And never left.

Now the place felt so abandoned without Aaron Hunter. It

was as if some huge flowering magnolia tree at the center of our courtyard had been chopped down, and these days we neighbors kept to ourselves. As I rocked on the darkened balcony, Spike, the goateed new neighbor downstairs, crept out with a flashlight on his way to the late night shift at the Dungeon, a goth club where he worked as a bouncer. The night he moved in he rode his bicycle nude around the courtyard at 3 a.m. I normally avoided Spike, but couldn't resist calling down toward his bald head.

"Hey, Spike, I've got rum. Got any candles? Come on up awhile. This could go on all night." *We can talk about anything you like,* I almost added, *growing up in Old Metairie, your girlfriend from the tattoo parlor.* But he slipped off into the shadows on his bike, slamming the gate behind him. The candle sputtered in a breeze, and I leaned over to cup my hand around it. Then the heat, rum, and rocking finally got to me, and I gave in to the darkness.

THE BLEATING LANDLINE woke me up. I stumbled in through the screen door and tripped over the long phone cord, following it like Ariadne's thread from the living room through the hall into the kitchen and then into my suffocating bedroom. The answering machine was out with the lights, so the phone kept ringing. I slipped on a throw rug next to the bed and, down on my hands and knees, snatched the receiver.

"Lucian! Why'd you let it ring so long? Doesn't the machine usually switch—"

"Momma, hey. The electricity's been off all evening. Didn't you hear about the explosion?" Pulling on the cord, I retraced my path to the balcony. "Wait a sec. The candle's gone out. Now I can't find a light." I ran my fingertips along the scaly paint under the rocker, grabbing for the Bic lighter.

"The lights aren't off here. I'm worried about you living by yourself down there." My mother's house was in Kenner, a fifty-dollar roundtrip cab ride from here. After wrecking her car, she didn't drive anymore, and I couldn't keep a car in the Quarter. So we mostly talked on the phone.

"Yeah, streetlights are out, and so are stoplights." A pack of marauding kids passed in front of the gate, hooting and hollering. A beer can sailed over the wall, clattering into the courtyard.

"I've never told you about that nice nurse's aid, Consuelo, the Spanish one," Momma began. "She says I'm her favorite patient. Every time I walk into cardiology she runs up to hug me and says how much I remind her of her mother. Guess I'm in a situation like you'd get yourself into—"

"Your doctor is putting you in rehab?"

"No, silly. Consuelo will be moving in for a month."

"Much worse," I groaned. "How long have you known her?"

"She's only been at the hospital for two months, from Denver. Her husband works with computers and they move around a lot. They're being evicted, so he has to go back to Denver." I couldn't follow any of this so, as usual, just let her talk. "And somehow it was agreed on without her asking or me saying yes. She insists on paying me something, although I said it wasn't necessary. She doesn't have any other friends and, really, neither do I. We'll have so much fun together at the Esplanade Mall."

"Don't you know about the smooth-talking con artists who prey on the sick and elderly? Didn't I tell you what just happened to my neighbor Aaron? They move from city to city. You'd have to give her the key to your house. And when you're not there? Your jewelry and silver?"

"But she has a good job. And lovely jewelry herself."

"It's a terrible idea." A cat crashed through the garbage cans below, and then a neighbor's Spitz started howling.

"Since your daddy passed, I've been so lonely out here," she said.

"Everybody's lonely," I said, shielding the candle flame from a welcome breeze. Of course, what Momma was telling her only child made me feel terribly guilty, but she could no sooner move into a second-story French Quarter apartment than I could survive in her ranch house in the suburbs. "We all live alone."

"I'm reading in the papers how we have so much prosperity now, not like when I was growing up during the Depression and everyone had to live together. Why is everyone so alone now?"

"Because we can afford to be. The Mexicans and Indians don't have the luxury of feeling lonely. They live stacked six to a room in Mexico City and Bombay." I worked as a buyer for the Safari Bazaar at Canal Place, a job that took me to sweatshops all over the world, where the scrawny hordes knocked off cheap doodads to fill the lives of fat, lonely Americans.

"So what should I tell Consuelo?" she asked.

AFTER MOMMA AND I hung up, I sat studying the shadows of dangling ferns elongated by the flicker from a candle stub, not knowing how long this darkness was going to last.

What if it went on forever? I wondered, feeling my way along the wall to plink the last of the ice cubes into another drink. What if I had to sit here every night, worrying about kids on crack from the projects four blocks away jumping the wall, about Gulf shrimp rotting in the refrigerator, about the milk curdling, about how to scrub by hand the sweaty sheets I couldn't fall asleep on because the windows were bolted shut to keep intruders out? Then I found myself staggering around the kitchen, hot wax splotching the floor and scorching my bare feet. I was throwing open cupboards looking for birthday candles, votive candles, candles from a chafing dish my mother gave me.

One candle, I knew, would keep me safe. Any one would do.

"The candles must have burned down by now," Aaron had told me during one of his first visits upstairs. When he came up to tell me about our lost garbage can, I asked him in for a glass of wine. "Sorry, have to go," he said, checking his watch after half an hour. "I left a guest tied up downstairs."

"Tied up?"

"A twinkie I picked up. I stuck lit candles on his chest, and they should be burning down to the flesh by now." Aaron confessed that he was a sadist, as in S&M. That explained the handcuffs dangling from the black leather epaulets of one of the sweetest men I'd ever met. But I thought they were jewels, not tools.

"Look, this isn't about sex but power," he said. "And the complete possession of another human is based on trust. The bottom's got to trust the top not to go too far. And really hurt him."

"I'm all about pleasure, me." I reached under my T-shirt to rub my paunch.

"For some people," he said with a cackle, "pain is pleasure."

Often, well into the night, I could hear chains rattling below, slaps and groans. It sounded like a wrestling match inside a hardware store down there.

The last time I came back from a buying trip to Mexico City, I brought Aaron an onyx reproduction of an Aztec sacrificial victim. I thought he'd get a kick out of it. He had souvenir knickknacks like this displayed in lit curio cabinets around his apartment, and I could already hear him telling everyone it was pre-Columbian. His gentlemanly airs of a Savannah connoisseur amused me, considering we lived in a Sicilian tenement with exposed pipes and painted floors.

A skeletal Aaron swung open the door. He had *that look.*

"You've lost so much weight," I blurted out after a hug, handing him the present.

"I'm eating smaller portions," he explained with a tight half-smile. Inside Darren was roaring in front of a football game. Aaron didn't ask me in, and later declined my invitations to have dinner or a glass of wine upstairs—without Darren.

I'm sorry, but the minute Darren opened his mouth about sports or computers my mind went numb. Yet Darren seemed to own him, and Aaron did nothing without him. Whenever I'd ask Aaron if he wanted to go out for a bite, his eyes would cut to Darren, as if asking permission. Then I noticed the hospital bed inside his apartment. I grilled Darren on the patio one morning until he confided that Aaron, well, had been diagnosed with brain cancer. But I wasn't supposed to let on that anything was wrong.

"Brain cancer? Shouldn't he be in a nursing home?" I asked.

"Don't even mention it to him. He refuses. Why do you think I'm here?"

After the third convulsion, Aaron slipped into a coma. Then

the truth came out: he had AIDS. I lit the silver candelabrum in his bedroom and filled the incense burner with frankincense. I'd read that smell was the last sense to go. As a soundtrack, I added Gregorian chants.

Darren made himself a sausage po'boy and then looked for the key to the trunk.

While I read to Aaron from a copy of *The Tibetan Book of the Dead* he'd been studying, Darren knelt on the living room floor, sorting through Aaron's trunk of family heirlooms. Aaron had ritually unpacked and caressed the treasures in that trunk in front of Darren ever since his roommate moved in. Every once in a while Darren would come in to make sure Aaron was comfortable and punch up the dose of morphine. Then he'd go back to fingering the solid gold pocket watch and sterling antebellum comb-and-brush set that I'd been hearing about for years.

Aaron died at dawn in a cloud of incense, listening to a bad translation, while Darren snored on the sofa, the pocket watch ticking beside him. During the next few days, he maxed out Aaron's ATM card until he exhausted the account. He had the contents in the trunk of so-called heirlooms appraised at only $250, and found out that the pre-Columbian artifacts in the curio cabinets were just tourist reproductions. On the morning before Darren left, I stepped through the sidewalk sale he had set up in front of our carriageway on Orleans Avenue. The Quarter was lost in a fog sweeping in from the Mississippi, and as I glanced back, all I could make out was the arm of his red Eddie Bauer jacket waving at me. And the grin on his beefy face. There he stood, hoping to make a killing, heir to a mound of junk Aaron had purchased piece-by-piece at similar sidewalk sales over the years.

Within a month, I received a postcard from St. Petersburg, Florida, where Darren had moved in with an eighty-year-old widow. Obviously, Aaron had just been practice. I pictured Darren dining by candlelight with some old snow-bird, discussing her stock portfolio.

Now the chains of hanging ferns creaked while shadows lunged toward me. I lit the ragtag collection of foraged candles on the balcony table in a gorgeous, short-lived blaze of molten wax. The lyrics to a hymn I'd learned at Baptist Sunday school came back to me, and in a shaky, off-key voice, I sang:

Abide with me, fast falls the eventide.
The darkness deepens, Lord with me abide.
When other helpers fail and comforts flee,
Help of the helpless ones, abide with me.

The courtyard gate rattled, as if someone were trying to force his way in. The doorbells were out, so I stumbled downstairs with a chafing-dish candle melting on a pie pan, convinced that a friend had come to visit. Maybe somebody was worried and wanted to keep me company, someone else who knew this night would never end. Sometime after dawn I woke seated in the rocking chair on the balcony. The world had roared back to life: air conditioners were humming, TVs booming, and chandeliers spilling their wastrel wattage into the glare. An early-morning message was winking at me from the answering machine.

Momma couldn't wait to tell me the good news.

Consuelo was moving in.

A MONTH AFTER THE blackout, when my mother was down to eighty pounds, I invited her and the new roommate to dinner in the courtyard. In the speckled moonlight I studied Consuelo Lobo from behind a mask of polite detachment. A Dominican raised in Miami, she was about my age, plump, no children, dressed in a maroon outfit color-coordinated with her hair tint. I sensed burnt edges a millimeter beneath the warm, round contours that she radiated like the red globular candle holder glowing at the center of the patio table. But I passed bread pudding and demitasses of coffee, figuring maybe my mother did need a live-in companion. I was just sorry that it couldn't be me.

"Go for it," I told Momma. "If you trust her."

During the next few weeks, my mother's daily calls stopped.

When I phoned her, I usually got a message recorded in Consuelo's voice.

"We're really on the go," Momma explained one afternoon when I finally reached her. "Consuelo lost her job, so every evening we eat an early-bird special at Piccadilly in the Esplanade Mall, where Consuelo found me a new bank with higher interest rates. She's a whiz with taxes, those quarterly things your daddy always did. She even massages me when I'm worn out."

I called the new bank. My mother had turned over her banking to Consuelo. The accounts were now in both of their names.

The next day I took the afternoon off from the Safari Bazaar and caught a cab to Momma's squat brick house in Kenner. Odd, but my mother was an obsessive gardener, and now the lawn was uncut, her garden weedy and overgrown.

"Surprise, surprise," I said, letting myself in with a key. The TV set that my mother never watched was blasting. Consuelo swiveled around from the stove, where she was frying tortillas. Momma hated Mexican food, but pecked me on the cheek with a mouthful of taco.

"Just in time for lunch," Consuelo said, handing me a taco. For the first time ever, the furniture had been rearranged. Momma wouldn't let me decorate the house with the knickknacks I'd brought her from my buying trips, and every time I'd tried to shift even a chair or houseplant, she'd squawk, "Put that back where it belongs."

"You must have had to tie my mother up for her to let you redecorate," I told Consuelo. Consuelo shot my mother a look.

"It's so much better this way." Momma smoothed her napkin. "Even though I can't find a darn thing," she muttered to herself.

Consuelo wouldn't leave us alone for one second. She even followed my mother into the bathroom. We sat eating from TV trays in front of "Oprah" while Momma fidgeted, her gaze wandering. She usually chattered like a parakeet, but suddenly was mum. Finally, when Consuelo stepped into the bathroom, I turned to her.

"Who the hell is in charge here?" I bellowed.

"Shush," she whispered, waving a hand in front of her mouth.

I reached over to turn up "Oprah."

"I talked to your new bank yesterday, and they informed me—"

"Now don't say a *word*." Momma began to whimper. "Oh Lucian, I'm so afraid."

I took her bony hand. "Then we'll kick her out right now."

The toilet flushed.

"No, you don't understand. I'm scared she'll leave. Every time I tell her no—about anything—she says, 'Well, maybe it's time for me to go back to Denver,' and calls her husband on the cell phone."

"So let her."

My mother shook her head until I was afraid it would fall off. "Think I want to wind up like my sister," she hissed, "dying alone at Hope House? Because that's where my doctors say I need to go, some place like that."

I could understand why she didn't tell me that her doctors recommended a facility. When Aunt Earline had started to vomit blood during the final phase of liver cancer, her cold-blooded daughter dumped her in a septic snake pit on the Airline Highway called Hope House, a nursing home that my mother found too depressing to visit. She swore that she'd never end up anywhere like that.

As Consuelo bounced back into the room, Momma placed a finger across her lips and her face lit up like a child's.

"It's time for our drive," Consuelo announced, clapping her hands. Then she turned toward me with a chilly smile. "And where can we drop you?"

I never managed to talk with my mother about the joint bank accounts. She got much worse. "She's lying down now," Consuelo would whisper whenever I phoned. "I'll tell her to call you back."

But she never did.

IT WASN'T UNTIL months later, when I peeled the duct tape from Momma's mouth inside of her ransacked house, that I recognized Aaron's terror in her immense eyes. At the inquest, my mother's doctor said that she had suffered a massive heart attack, and he suspected that her medication had been tampered with. We went through the pill bottles and discovered that the bitch had gone to the trouble of emptying out half of every one of the beta-blocker capsules that were keeping Momma alive. Consuelo made off with a lot more than Darren did, including all the cash from the bank accounts and the contents of the safety-deposit box.

Evidently, what brought on the heart attack was when my mother refused to sign a new will Consuelo had drawn up. Then things probably turned ugly, Consuelo threatening to leave, Momma pleading. I called the hospital where Consuelo had worked. Turned out her Social Security number belonged to some Chicana in Los Angeles whose purse had been snatched two years ago, and the rest of Consuelo Lobo was a fiction, too, from top to bottom. Then I phoned the lawyer whose name appeared on the unsigned will I found tucked inside my mother's Bible. The lawyer said he smelled something fishy the afternoon they appeared to sign the revised will, which he refused to notarize, and then he notified the police just after they left, my mother in tears. The cops pulled up to my mother's house the next morning to find Consuelo gone, Momma's lifeless body bound and gagged. At least Consuelo didn't torch the place, they told me, to cover up the struggle. That was the way it was usually done.

I've been working with a detective from the Jefferson Parish Police Department but so far—nothing. Unlike Darren, Consuelo was a real pro, and left no trace.

At times I try to picture a moonless night in August years from now when I might well be rocking on this same balcony in my great-grandfather's chair. "Help me up," I'll say, and out of nowhere a hand will reach out to lift me to my feet. Whose hand will it be? I hope it won't be Spike's, the goth-club bouncer from downstairs.

But if it is his, I'll take it.

Make no mistake about it, end-of-life hustlers can spot *that look* from across a crowded room. The minute you need them, there they are, materialized from a stray puff of smoke. And, no, they're never quite the person you would have imagined. But no matter how proud and independent you may be, you'll be delighted to watch a football game with someone named Darren or eat an early-bird special with somebody called Consuelo. If only because they allow you to avoid that dismal ward at some place called Hope House, to die at home with your dignity intact. I'll blame myself forever for what I failed to acknowledge in those panicked eyes that still haunt me, staring up from emaciated faces. Maybe it was a look I won't understand until I catch it in a mirror brushing my teeth after a frightening diagnosis, or shaving after some grim lab report. And one day I also may fall under the comforting spell of some unlikely Charon as he rows me across the River Styx, helping me to shuffle from the balcony to the bathroom and then into bed.

And do you know something? In those darkest of hours, any candle will do. Like Aaron and Momma, I'll probably hand over everything I own, too, when only the stars abide, invisible by day.

Overpass

EVEN BEFORE Mr. Claude started planning the blast, he liked to set up his aluminum folding chair to face the statue of General Lee on its pedestal rather than the Claiborne Avenue expressway that loomed above the doorway where they sat. Miss Lottie didn't seem to mind watching the overpass since she couldn't see much any way, and appeared to enjoy listening to the cars whiz by up ahead.

"I wonder where all them people going," she told him one Friday, as if genuinely puzzled. "They sure in a hurry. Must be giving out money someplace we don't know about."

Mr. Claude stretched back in the chair and tilted the lid of a John Deere baseball cap over his forehead, blocking out the modern world that buzzed around him. He'd outlived his money, unlike his neighbors in the other project apartments, who never had any to begin with. Actually, the building where he and Miss Lottie lived wasn't the projects, although that was how he thought of it. It was an eight-story brick edifice of studio bed-sitters constructed in the fifties as swank apartments on St. Charles Avenue near Lee Circle. When the overpass went up half a block away during the sixties, the bachelor pads at Excelsior Place went straight to seed, and now they were federally subsidized housing for the elderly kicked out of the demolished projects. Mr. Claude figured that he probably paid more in rent than other residents—a third of his monthly Social Security check, for Christ's sake—but at his age he didn't have many other expenses, just groceries, beer money, cab fare to doctor appointments, and adding to the arsenal of explosives he stored under his bed.

Mr. Claude was mad about a lot of things—don't get him started—although these days the only person he confided in was Miss Lottie, his next-door neighbor in 42-B. Truth be known, he was sweet on cross-eyed Miss Lottie, an old-lady version of his mother's hot-to-trot housekeeper when he was a boy. She was a wheezing little pecan of a woman, doll-faced and wide-bottomed, with arthritic fingers that ended in persimmon nail polish. When she wanted to—and only when she wanted—she would flash a gap-toothed smile that could melt distant glaciers. She baked him sweet-potato pies and cooked him collard greens, and he changed her light bulbs and unstopped her sink. It was like that between them, flirty and jokey but with no hanky-panky. The closest they ever got was to snuggle together under a blanket in front of her TV, although sometimes Mr. Claude tried a smooch to her neck or a pinch on the butt. Then her caramel-colored forehead would wrinkle, her eyes would cross, and she'd push him away.

"Get out of here," she'd say. "In all my seventy-five years I never had me no white man and I ain't gonna start now. You keep that *couchez-cou* to your own self. I'm way past the time for that kind of monkey business." Then, as if secretly pleased, she'd zap him with her gap-toothed smile.

There weren't many men in the building to begin with, and Mr. Claude was the only white one. But after living in downtown New Orleans most of his life, he was used to being the only white face at the public hospital, on the bus, or at the grocery, like a single navy bean in a big pot of red ones. Some of the other ladies in the building seemed jealous of Miss Lottie because of the white man's attentions, so they snubbed her in the elevator or on the sidewalk in front of the building. That was where many of the residents sat on lawn chairs lined up against the granite and plate-glass façade, as if still on the porches of their shotgun houses in the Seventh Ward.

"Claiborne Avenue sure was different back then," Miss Lottie said, studying the rush-hour traffic on the overpass, "before they put up that thing."

"Don't get me going," he said with a groan. "We were living near North Claiborne when they showed up the summer of sixty-six with buzz saws to cut down those beautiful old live oaks along the Avenue."

Miss Lottie shook her head. "I remember. Every family had them they own tree they used to meet under. Ours was at Ursulines, right across from Mr. Alphonse Picou's barroom. Where was y'alls'?"

"At the corner of Governor Nicholls, two blocks from where we lived." Mr. Claude raised the cap, his face softening around twinkling eyes. "When me and my sister were teenagers, that was how we got to Canal Street to go to the picture shows, meeting up under that tree after school and then strolling along the shade of the neutral ground. After they mowed down the trees, that street was a war zone of cement trucks and pile drivers for two solid years while they put up that damn ugly thing. The city didn't ask any of us neighbors what we thought but just flushed the Tremé down the crapper while nobody said a peep. Even my mamma wanted to move, and her family went way back in that area. But my daddy said the house was finally paid for, so they stayed put. By then I was a married man living around the corner with two babies of my own, and the whole thing made me so mad that I started slitting the tires of the construction workers parked there."

Miss Lottie nodded as if she'd heard all this before. "But it was progress, wasn't it? What they call it, 'urban renewal?'"

"'Renewal' my ass. More like urban destruction. All those shops of well-to-do Negroes closed, and their big houses fell to ruins. Now the area is blighted for two blocks on either side of that overpass."

"Why they call that progress then?"

"Cause rich people can get out to the burbs faster. That's

progress."

"Well," she said, blinking into the sunlight, "look like it here to stay.

"I wouldn't be so sure about that."

ON A WHIM, Mr. Claude had started to hoard sacks of ammonium nitrate and cans of diesel fuel two years ago when the government moved him into this studio apartment after he maxed out on his pension fund. He'd worked as a road-crew manager at the Sewerage and Water Board his whole life, so he understood about potholes and pipes and explosives. At first he considered blowing up the dismal building where he was condemned to live out his final years, but soon realized that he liked the people there, as cantankerous as some of them could be. Most of them had suffered enough for one lifetime. Even with their insulin shots and rolling walker seats, he could tell that it felt like a second childhood to the residents, a geriatric boarding school. They sang songs he knew by heart, told stories he'd heard before, and cooked the dishes he loved. He didn't want to hurt these people, didn't want to hurt anyone, really.

But every time he walked outside and stood in the shadow of that towering cement monument to progress at the end of the block, his fists clenched. That was what he hated, not those folks whose lives it ruined. The way he saw it, an overpass was meant to literally *pass over* people like them, as if they didn't exist, like the "forgotten men" during the Depression when he was a boy. Years ago, after his wife died and their two kids went up North to college, it was as if he'd woken up after a long dream with empty pockets. He'd never managed to accomplish much of anything in life, and longed to do something important before he was gone, if only to bring his corner of the world back to the way it was meant to be. So he checked out books on fertilizer bombs from the library, which he read with a magnifying glass under a 150 watt bulb screwed into the table lamp balanced on the rattling air conditioner over his bed. Of course, he couldn't blow up the overpass with all those drivers racing along on top of it. That much he understood.

He had to wait for the right moment.

And what would happen to him after he blew up the Interstate-10 overpass? Maybe he'd get lucky and have a heart attack or another stroke. Either that or go to jail, which he thought of as free assisted living. He had no idea what the government would do with an almost blind eighty-two-year-old terrorist with blocked arteries and swollen knees. Waterboard him? Ship him off to Guantánamo Bay with those towel heads? At this point, what did he have to lose? He just hoped they'd let him make a statement and print it up in the paper. Maybe part of the manifesto he was busy scribbling in the spiral notebook he kept on the kitchen table. Of course, his son and daughter would be a major pain in the ass. They were always butting in and trying to bring him up to Michigan or Wyoming or wherever in the hell they lived now. He'd take jail here over that any day. The food might be better.

Miss Lottie was another problem. She had asthma so bad that she carried an inhaler wherever she went. The dust cloud from the explosion could do her in.

Last year the city had blown up an old rat-infested hotel right next to the overpass on Canal Street, at one time as snazzy as Excelsior Place used to be, that is, until the elevated freeway went up and the hotel also turned into crapola. On the day of the blast the respiratory threat from the explosion was so severe that residents within three blocks were relocated. Of course, Mr. Claude was on the front lines of those who gathered to watch, as close as the police barricades would allow. The city closed down the Interstate that morning, and Mr. Claude stood there frozen with regret that he hadn't used that opportunity to blow up the overpass, too. But he was trembling with excitement at the moment when the old hotel's façade splintered into a million jigsaw-puzzle pieces and in a snap, still maintaining its rectangular outline, vertically collapsed in on itself, leaving only a cloud of dust floating over a massive heap of rubble.

Now that was what he called progress.

But when he glanced to the left, the overpass was still rising to the heavens on elephantine legs of poured cement smeared with graffiti, its metal guardrails gleaming. That morning, when he'd invited Miss Lottie to catch the streetcar with him to go watch the explosion, she'd really given him the dickens.

"You stupid old man, all that dust would send me straight to the hospital, if it didn't kill me flat out," she said, taking a pull on her inhaler. "I done seen enough stuff fall apart in my time withouts having to go look for it. I'm gonna stay inside all day with the windows closed tight."

Inspired by the spectacle, that afternoon he bought another gallon of diesel from the gas station at Lee Circle. Dressed in his usual baggy bermudas flapping above bandy legs ending in thin white socks tucked into marshmallow sneakers, he lugged the sloshing gas can as best he could across the neutral ground. Then stumbling out of the elevator, he ran smack into Miss Lottie in the hallway.

He swept off his John Deere cap and beamed, aglow with the explosion he'd just witnessed.

"Where you going with that evil smelling stuff?" she said, batting at the air in front of her face. "You ain't even got no car."

"It's an experiment," he said, jostling the gasoline in the can.

"You keep your experiments away from me," she said, wheezing. Then she scurried across the spongy gray carpeting back into her apartment. "By the way, I got a sweet-potato pie in the oven."

IT WAS DURING a rare phone call that weekend from his nephew Bradley that Mr. Claude first heard about the temporary closing of the overpass. Years ago the young knucklehead had left town to live in a squat brick box stuck on a slab foundation in Magnolia Estates, a gated subdivision constructed on reclaimed swamp land off the Airline Highway. Since Mr. Claude's sister passed away, he and his nephew seldom spoke or visited, even though Bradley was his only relative in town.

"Just this Wednesday morning," Bradley explained, "while they reinforce the girding on a downtown section of the Interstate. As luck would have it, that's my day off and I was thinking I'd stop by and we could do lunch. But traffic on I-10 will be closed in both directions around where you live."

"*Do* lunch? Do *what* to it?" Mr. Claude barked. "Eat it?" He was all ears, even while wondering what his nephew was babbling about now.

"I'm not getting into the middle of that mess. So plan postponed."

"Yeah, you might have to actually drive along a city street instead of dropping down out of the concrete sky." Concrete. Mr. Claude could already picture the overpass blasted into a gazillion pieces, like the old hotel. He glanced under his bed at the sacks of ammonium nitrate. After he finished what he'd planned, maybe he and Bradley could do lunch over at Parish Prison.

Wednesday was the day he'd been waiting for.

He pulled out his dog-eared booklet from the Louisiana Conservation Department called *Pothole Blasting for Wildlife.* When he was managing road crews, they'd used a similar recipe for making explosives. The formula for ANFO called for 94 percent porous prilled ammonium nitrate to 6 percent number-two fuel oil, which in this case would be the cans of diesel he'd been collecting. He also had stacks of old *Times-Picayunes* he'd saved and a drawer stuffed with cotton batting that he could soak with fuel to detonate the mixture. The extension ladder was in the closet, the one he'd mount to wedge the newspaper cones of ANFO into the gaps between the electrical tubing and the overpass support beams. And the spool of wicking he'd use to ignite the whole thing from below, now where was that? He checked to see if it was still in his sock drawer.

He'd have to start at dawn on Wednesday, when St. Charles was deserted, just after the overpass traffic was blocked. If only his knees would hold out while he climbed the shaky ladder. If he heard workers above, of course, he wouldn't do it, but usually traffic was stopped at either end long before the crew arrived at first daylight, and the men were always late, as he well remembered from his own road-crew days. But this mixture of fuel to fertilizer had to be just right or the bombs wouldn't go off. And now he had only five days to perfect the recipe, make the paper cones topped with cotton, and attach the wicks. If he could just fire off a practice one on the roof or the neutral ground, but that was out of the question.

And then there was Miss Lottie.

Would the dust from the explosion send her gasping to the hospital? The overpass was right at the corner, separated from their building by a parking lot, and her window faced the Interstate. Even with her windows shut and the air conditioner running, the explosion could crack the panes and shoot a cloud of fine concrete particles right into her apartment. After Wednesday morning, he wouldn't be seeing her much anyway, but what if she took sick and it was his fault?

Mr. Claude put away *Pothole Blasting*, plopping down into his arm chair to take a blood-pressure pill and think over his plan. No matter how much preservationists squawked, he was sure that city leaders would never decide to tear down the overpass on their own. Yet he'd read somewhere that after the 1989 earthquake in San Francisco, when a chunk of the elevated Embarcadero Freeway had fallen down, the city razed the whole structure rather than repair it. Ever since, the once dingy waterfront there had blossomed with farmers' markets, apartment buildings, and a new streetcar line basking in the light. Like in Frisco, what New Orleans needed was a push in the right direction, an accident that sure as hell wouldn't be coming from Mother Nature.

Like an ANFO bomb. Or at least this was Mr. Claude's line of reasoning.

The health of a tart old lady seemed a small price to pay, even if it was Miss Lottie. If only Mr. Claude could convince her to go stay in Gentilly for a few days with her artist daughter, even though she didn't get along with her. To do that, he'd have to warn her—how could he put it?—that a big old dust cloud was on the horizon, one that could do her in.

Mr. Claude slid into his slippers, donned his John Deere cap, and scrubbed his fingers to wash away any lingering chemical scent. Swishing a swig of Listerine, he glanced in the bathroom mirror at his ruddy complexion and bushy white eyebrows.

How could she resist the old devil?

"YOU HAD DINNER YET?" Miss Lottie asked, beckoning him inside with her gap-toothed smile.

Mr. Claude didn't know it yet, but this would be the last time he'd ever see that smile. "Just a po'boy for lunch," he said.

"Lemme set you a place." She fidgeted around inside her Pullman kitchen, flicking on the stove and rattling pot covers. "I got some shrimp Creole simmering, and just put on the rice."

Mr. Claude perched on a dinette chair by the window, taking in a whiff of potpourri cut with joint liniment. He parted the ruffled curtains to take a peek at the planetary arc lights of the overpass, eerie as a landing strip for spaceships. Once visible, the rumbling hum of freeway traffic drowned out his thoughts, so he let the curtain drop back into place as a flimsy screen between the lemony glow inside and the alien glare out there.

"How's your daughter Marie Louise over in Gentilly?" he asked.

"Hincty as ever." She slapped a dish towel on the counter. "Why you ask?"

"You should go stay by her sometime, get to know her better." The crows-feet around his piercing blue eyes creased into a wide, denture-bright smile. "She's probably got a couple of good points you've overlooked during the past fifty years."

Miss Lottie swiveled around from the stove in her cayenne-stained apron, brandishing a long wooden spoon. "She ashamed of me, always correct how I talk. Like I the child and she the momma. Cause she ain't had none of her own, you know. And that boyfriend, what with his three kids and no job." She grunted. "Where she get off fussing with me?"

Mr. Claude could see that this attempt at family reconciliation was going nowhere, so he dove in. "Heard over by the gas station at Lee Circle that some terrorists are plotting to blow up the Claiborne Avenue overpass this Wednesday, and that could make you real sick."

"Get outta here!" She threw back her head and laughed. "Why don't you go tell J. Edgar Hoover, not me? Looks like our rice almost done," she said, peering into a pot.

"I can't tell the government," he said, hoisting his bulk up from the table with both hands and tottering to his feet, "because I'm the one gonna do it."

There. The cat was out of the bag.

"Oh Lord." Eyes narrowing, she let out a high-pitched chuckle. "You done joined up with that Been Loadin fellow or what they call him?"

"We've talked about this before." Hadn't she heard a single word he'd said over the past two years? "You know how that overpass ruined the neighborhood we grew up in."

She shot him a snake-eyed look. "You damn fool. So that why you been carrying all that smelly stuff into your apartment? To use it to blow up the overpass? Why white men got to go around blowing up everything they don't understand, like over in Europe and Vietnam and Iraq. You crazy, y'all."

Mr. Claude reached out to take her hand. "I want to see the street come back to what it was when we were young."

She flinched from his touch. "Well, we ain't young no more. Other people young now, and they made a life for they selves around that overpass. Done painted oak trees on the posts. That where the Mardi Gras Indians parade. Where folks go to get out the hot sun."

"And to shoot each other and deal drugs."

"Don't save nothing by blowing people up."

"But I won't hurt anyone." In a conspiratorial hush, Mr. Claude explained his plan.

"You serious," she said, eyes widening, "and I scared."

"Damn right." Mr. Claude was losing patience with this headstrong old lady. He pointed at the door. "Go pack your grip and get over to Marie Louise's by Tuesday night, hear?"

"Me, I'm calling the po-lice, that what I'm doing." She raced toward a white princess phone on top of her chiffarobe. In the rush, the back of her bedroom slipper snagged on a chair leg, her ankle twisted, and she stumbled backwards, crumpling into a heap on the tile floor.

"Now look what you made me do," she screamed, grabbing her thigh and wincing. Her face shriveled into an angry raisin as she called on the good Lord to help her. "Turn off the fire under that rice," she hissed between clenched teeth, "after you call 911. Then get the hell out my house, you."

Dazed with remorse, Mr. Claude did as he was told, but paced the corridor waiting for the emergency medical team to arrive. Soon pulsing red lights flashed up through the hallway window from the ambulance parked in the lot below. Stepping back inside her apartment, he watched bug-eyed as the paramedics slipped a board under Miss Lottie, her shoulders shuddering with sobs, and then transferred her to a wheeled gurney.

"See it every day," the young crew-cut nurse told Mr. Claude, glancing around the cramped room filled with framed family photos and ceramic knickknacks. "Lady her age break a hip, and she won't be living here anymore."

MR. CLAUDE'S NEPHEW wanted to help his uncle. He really did. Along with his cousins from up North, Bradley had been flabbergasted when Uncle Claude insisted on moving into a shabby, federally-subsidized apartment rather than accepting his nephew's generous offer to come live in the spic-and-span renovated laundry room behind his carport in Magnolia Estates. But Uncle Claude wouldn't listen to reason or accept assistance from anyone, even from his own two kids. After his wife died Uncle Claude even up and sold his car, refusing to drive anymore. Said that it made the world an uglier place. Now what could Bradley do with somebody like that? His uncle always wanted to live life on his own terms, according to Bradley's mom, so nobody expected the old fart to change, even toward the end.

So imagine Bradley's surprise when out of the blue his uncle called him from Ochsner Hospital, where for two days and nights he'd been hovering over the bedside of some old lady from his building who broke her hip. Uncle Claude said that he hadn't slept or eaten much the whole time and claimed how hard it was now to get his damn knees to work right. Because he wouldn't be able to make it into a cab by himself, he asked his nephew to give him a ride home. So like a squat tin soldier in Dockers and a Lacoste golf shirt, Bradley rolled him in a wheelchair from the hospital lobby into the parking lot, just as his mom would have wanted him to do.

Eventually they made it to his uncle's building on St. Charles, but the whole time on I-10 Uncle Claude wouldn't look at him or say a word. Bradley had never seen a more defeated expression on anyone in his life. Uncle Claude just sat there, squinting straight ahead into the morning glare, not glancing to the right or the left, treating the entire city below them as if it simply wasn't there. Bradley kept asking him about his friend who broke her hip, but his uncle would only say her name was Miss Lottie.

And then he'd clam up.

Two days later his uncle called to beg Bradley to take him to see Miss Lottie at the Good Shepherd nursing home on the Airline Highway, only two miles from his subdivision. Uncle Claude said that he had a terrible headache, and Bradley had never heard him complain about his health before. He told the old man that he could only do it on Tuesday afternoon, when he could ask to take the afternoon off from the Honda dealership where he worked. He reminded his uncle that on Wednesday morning, his regular day off, it'd be no dice: they were closing down the I-10 for repairs, still trying to bring the old overpass back up to code.

"Look, Uncle Claude," he said, trying to be as patient as possible, "what you're asking me for is two roundtrips from Magnolia Estates to downtown, one to come get you and one to bring you back home. Exactly who is this lady you need to see so much?"

Uncle Claude sounded choked up, fishing for the right word. "Miss Lottie is my neighbor . . . I mean my close friend. You know, my girlfriend."

Bradley didn't know men his uncle's age had girlfriends, but guessed with all the pills out there these days, anything was possible. He'd wanted to get to know his uncle better before he passed away—after all, he'd been trying for years—so he reluctantly told him okay. That Tuesday his uncle appeared even more frail and withdrawn than when he'd brought him back from the hospital. Uncle Claude kept rubbing his forehead and muttering about a headache, so he told the old man he should go have his head examined. What he meant, of course, was by a doctor at the Good Shepherd, but somehow it came out wrong. When they got to the nursing home his uncle slammed the car door and told Bradley he'd phone when he was ready to leave, as if his nephew were the chauffeur.

At six that evening Bradley did get a call from the Good Shepherd, but it wasn't from Uncle Claude. A nurse reported that at his friend's bedside his uncle had suffered a mild stroke, and that although resting well now he was still experiencing some mobility and speech problems.

Early on Wednesday morning the nurse called again to tell Bradley that at dawn his uncle had another stroke—a "massive cerebral hemorrhage," as she described it—and passed away.

And guess who had to deal with the alarming mess Uncle Claude left in his apartment at Lee Circle? Bradley couldn't believe the sacks of ammonium nitrate hoarded under his bed, the cans of diesel fuel, the stacks of old newspapers, and the cotton. At first it baffled him, and he thought that maybe the dotty old man was trying to relive his road-crew days by setting up a funky home workshop. But when he took a good look at the bomb-making books on his kitchen table, along with the diagrams Uncle Claude had drawn of the overpass, and then flipped through a few pages of the invective he'd written in a spiral notebook, Bradley had no choice.

His uncle was a terrorist.

So he called in the F.B.I.

The government agents finally ascertained that his uncle was, as they put it, "a lone wolf," and wasn't associated with the network of violent environmentalists prevalent on the West Coast. Poor Uncle Claude didn't even know how to turn on a computer, so the F.B.I. had no hard drive to seize and seemed at a genuine loss about what to do with a terrorist they couldn't Google. The story made the Channel 4 news, with a photo of a younger Uncle Claude together with a scary shot of the bomb-making materials from under his bed and a close up of the two newspaper cones of ANFO that he'd already assembled. The report even quoted a few sentences from the notebook Bradley found on the kitchen table, some gibberish about how the Claiborne Avenue overpass had destroyed a once beautiful neighborhood, how the city needed a shove in the right direction to get rid of it, let a million oak trees bloom, et cetera, et cetera.

He had to hand it to old Uncle Claude: sounded like a regular Mao Tse-tung.

Immediately after their father's funeral, Bradley's cousins flew back up North, obviously more embarrassed than bereaved. That was when he entered Uncle Claude's room armed with plastic bags, disinfectant, and air freshener. Throwing open the windows, he gagged on the stink of unwashed bedclothes, moldy bread, and gasoline fumes. While he was sorting through his uncle's junk, most of which he carted to trash bins on the first floor, someone rapped on the opened door of the apartment. There stood a trim, put-together lady, head wrapped in an African scarf and ears jangling with gold hoops, who asked if he was any kin to Mr. Claude.

"I'm Bradley, his nephew," he said.

She reached over to shake hands. "I'm Marie Louise, Miss Lottie's daughter, and I'm cleaning out my mother's place, too. I'm sorry for your loss. Mama speaks so highly of your uncle."

"He was a good man, although he had some kooky ideas."

"I saw the news report." She lowered her eyes. "Mama swears he wouldn't have gone through with it, that he never could have made it up that huge ladder."

"You didn't know my uncle. So, how's your mother?"

"She can't take care of herself anymore. No matter how loudly Mama complains, this weekend I'm moving her into my house in Gentilly."

"Boy, my uncle would never hear of coming to stay with us in Magnolia Estates."

"Well, it'll be a lot cheaper to hire a sitter during the day while I'm in the studio painting than keeping her in that nursing home. Besides, our people don't put their old folks in homes. After your uncle passed, Mama vowed she'd never come back here to live. She was really broken up that she couldn't make it to his funeral." A sly smile played across her face. "She says the Lord may have broken her hip, but Mr. Claude broke her heart. They were old fools, Mr. Bradley," she said, reaching over to squeeze his shoulder, "old fools in love."

And then she disappeared through the open door into the apartment next door.

Among the dust balls under the bed where his uncle stored the explosives, Bradley found a yellowed black-and-white family photograph, one he'd never seen before. He flipped the photo over and on the back was scrawled "on our way to the show!" There, posing under an oak tree on what looked like North Claiborne Avenue, were his mom and Uncle Claude as teenagers dressed in their Sunday best. It must have been taken in the late forties or early fifties, and Bradley could tell that the street was bustling with life back then. Everyone was wearing stylish hats of one kind or another, the men were in dapper suits and ties, and the women dolled up in fitted jackets with shoulder pads. In the dappled sunlight filtered down through the tree limbs, a group of black men stood in the background, also in suits and ties, flashing toothy smiles as one of them raised a trumpet to his lips. With grins plastered on their faces, everybody looked so proud and prosperous, as if they had everything in the world to look forward to.

They'd won the war, and now nothing could stop them.

That photo was one of the few of his uncle's possessions that

Bradley decided to keep. He wasn't sure what it meant to him, happier days, he supposed, from a more carefree era than he'd ever known. On his last trip to Lee Circle, while he was walking to the parking lot with the photo, the codgers sitting outside Uncle Claude's building in their lawn chairs gave him the stink eye. They probably weren't too thrilled about having a terrorist neighbor—and a white guy at that—and then having to evacuate the building for a whole day while the F.B.I. agents disassembled the explosives and carted them off. Bradley waved to the sour-faced old folks and thought that some of them could have been the smiling faces in Uncle Claude's photo. One moment they were young, strolling under oak trees, and then—in a flash—sixty years later they were old, sitting in lawn chairs in front of federal housing staring up at an overpass that covered the street where they grew up. Hard as it was to admit, that might have made Bradley want to blow up something, too.

He tossed the photo onto the dashboard before taking the on-ramp for the long drive home on the Interstate. Somewhere around Claiborne and Governor Nicholls, the photo got caught up in a gust of air and fluttered out the open window on the passenger side. He glanced up in the rearview mirror and spotted it dancing along the overpass guardrail behind him. And for a second he considered pulling the car over to go chasing after it.

But traffic was terrible, he was making good time, and he didn't stop.

II.

from *Perpetual Care*

Parce que le temps passe, je prie pour vous.

Why Isn't Everything Where It Used To Be?

AT AN AGE WHEN there was little to look forward to except getting into movies cheap, BouBou Glapion got married for the first time. After the modest wedding, she retired at fifty-nine from teaching in parochial schools and moved into her husband's house in River Ridge. For six years she sat in an aluminum lawn chair in the carport, drinking bourbon and crying to herself before the neighbors spoke a word to her. And by the time they did, she'd already begun to forget where she was and how she got there.

Unlike the Victorian shotguns in which she'd grown up in uptown New Orleans, these bungalows were squat brick boxes arranged around circles. This was where World War II veterans and their brides had raised children who then got married—two or three times each, at latest count—expired in boozy car crashes, or otherwise moved on to further glory. Now walkers replaced tricycles, and home oxygen delivery, the Pepsi-Cola man. Shade trees planted in the 1950s had grown tall enough to lend a leafy grace to the stark grid of streets. The dream of gracious suburban living finally had come true, but unfortunately, not until everyone there was widowed, bedridden, or in a permanent bad mood.

Never in her younger years had BouBou ever imagined that

she would wind up living way out here, even though she was the first person in her family to purchase an automobile and learn to drive. After Sunday dessert, the family would pile into her Studebaker to go visit the "new subdivisions" featured in the *Dixie Roto* magazine. From the parked car, they'd peer out at manicured lawns and split-level ranch houses, studying a future they both longed for and dreaded.

"It's real modren," her nearly blind mother would squeak, trying to get in the swing.

"Naw, MawMaw," a niece would correct. "It's ultra-modren."

BouBou's tipsy father would lumber out of the car and try to take a stroll through the new neighborhood. He'd set out jauntily only to trudge back five minutes later, muttering that not only weren't there any coffee shops, barrooms, or news vendors, but there weren't even any sidewalks. He didn't understand, never would, and died one afternoon with his checkered vest on, fedora in place, waiting for the Canal streetcar.

These days BouBou couldn't get to sleep at night until she found out who had been shot in New Orleans. She remained glued to the ten o'clock news so she could thank the Blesséd Mother in her prayers for not getting mugged or gang-raped in River Ridge. She secretly thrilled at scenes of the neighborhood she grew up in, people rocking on front galleries or chatting at streetcar stops. For years, as a young woman, she went everywhere on the bus for seven cents. That part of her life had been erased like an old videotape, only to resurface years later on the Channel 4 "Crime Watch." These days, of course, you'd get shot in the head the minute you set foot in the city.

Out here, she thought, were just hard-working white Christians like herself.

The trouble was, people in River Ridge were so bored they often got drunk and took potshots at each other. Three years ago was the Christmas Carol War. The Hendricks and the Bordelons, with houses on opposite sides of the circle, had each mounted garish Christmas displays with outdoor speakers broadcasting carols. And each kept turning up their volume to drown out the other's speaker, until the cacophony from competing versions of "Silent Night" and "Away in a Manger" was getting on everyone's nerves. But people didn't feel it would be Christmasy to complain.

On Christmas Eve Gus Bordelon got drunk on eggnog and shot out the red and green lights of the reindeers leaping in a flashing arch over Bernard Hendrick's carport. Then Hendrick rushed out in a Santa Claus hat with his shotgun and let loose at the life-size plastic nativity scene on the Bordelon lawn, blowing Mary, Jesus, and a couple of shepherds halfway down the block.

That was when BouBou had dialed 911. The sheriff cited the husbands for disturbing the peace, and they were sent to bed to sleep it off. Then she, Bessie Bordelon, and Raylene Hendrick wound up sobbing over a half-gallon of Seagram's in her kitchen until dawn.

After that, she was in like Flynn in the neighborhood.

"WHERE WOULD WE be without you?" the butterball Bessie Bordelon gushed as they unloaded Raylene's groceries from BouBou's Pinto. The recently widowed Raylene had come down with acute asthma, and on bad days couldn't move more than a few feet from her oxygen machine. She looked like an extraterrestial in her translucent oxygen mask and metal rollers, gesturing at them through the picture window.

"Hell, I gotta do something. I can't sit inside with that old man all day, the TV blaring and that schnauzer yapping underfoot. I wish I'd never retired, but after Mama . . . went, and I had to put Sissy in the Good Shepherd with Alzheimer's, well it near about killed me." BouBou adjusted her lustrous white pageboy and smoothed her piqué shirtwaist, proud of keeping up her appearance among the baggy shorts and extra-extra-large T-shirts around her. How could people be seen in public like that?

The life of the neighborhood had begun to emanate from BouBou's house. She crossed the circle twenty times a day as peacemaker, practical nurse, and chauffeur. At dusk, when crickets and tree frogs began to chorus from the swamps, she would sashay from house to house with a go-cup of bourbon in one hand and a filter-tip wand of Merits in the other, cheering up shut-ins with gossip and a raucous laugh.

"That Theresa Comeaux driving me nuts. All she wants me to bring her is a gallon of wine a night and a *TV Guide.* She hasn't cleaned that house in a year, and won't have anything to do with her children. Poor thing. We gonna have to turn the hose on her. That, or put her in a nursing home."

Nursing homes were a disturbing subject on Blue Bird Drive. Everyone in the neighborhood had to visit a relative in one, and privately believed they too would end up there.

"Why the last time I went to visit Sissy," BouBou recounted, "they were walking into walls and colliding with each other like bumper cars. It turns out they all were wearing each other's glasses. So-and-so couldn't find hers on her nightstand, so she put on someone else's, who did the same, and so on. It took days to sort them out."

"Oh, Gawd, one time I visited my poor mama," chimed in Bessie Bordelon, "she was tied into her wheelchair in the hall, and this woman on a walker with Alzerheimer's keeps coming over and saying, 'Daddy, can I come in? Daddy, can I come in?' And so finally I says, 'Sure, sugar, I ain't your daddy, but come on in.' So she starts raising Cain with me like I'm her daddy, wanting to know why I beat up on her mama, and my own mama sitting there with a Whitman Sampler on her lap, taking a bite out of each chocolate then throwing it down on the floor. By the time I got out that place I was bawling."

"Like I used to tell Bernard, may he rest in peace, long as you got your mind, you all right," Raylene said. "But the minute that go, somebody shoot me, quick." Bessie shot her a slit-eyed glance to shut up. For months now they'd been whispering about BouBou's memory. It had all started with little things. But after the weekend spent ransacking BouBou's house, searching for her lost wedding ring that they finally came across wrapped in Kleenex in the vegetable drawer of the refrigerator, they knew it wouldn't be long.

"Don't forget, BouBou, Raylene has her doctor's appointment tomorrow at ten and you promised to take her. So we'll see you around nine-thirty. Remember?"

BouBou went right home to write that down on one of the many lists she kept Scotch-taped around the kitchen. The next morning, she remembered she had to do something, but she forgot which list it was on. At quarter to ten Bessie was ringing her doorbell, shaking her head.

AFTER THE THIRD call from Jefferson Parish police about a disoriented lady found weeping, pulled over on the side of the highway, BouBou's husband Luke Leggio, a retired mechanic, hid her car at his cousin's across the river. BouBou reported it stolen, and Luke wouldn't let her use his, complaining she stripped the gears on his stick shift. He offered to drive her anywhere she wanted to go, but there was nowhere she wanted to go with him.

She spent a week moping on the aluminum lawn chair in the carport, then set out at a brisk pace one Tuesday morning for the Pak-'N-Save on Jefferson. Waves of heat were shimmering from the tarmac as she made her way along the edge of the highway, past Texaco stations, used car lots, McDonald's, and motels. Until she spotted the parking lot of the convenience store, she had no idea what she was doing stepping in tan Payless tennis shoes along the weedy ridges above highway drainage ditches.

It was as if she suddenly woke from a reverie of shady galleries, frilly skirts, and lemonade to find herself in a glarey Martian landscape of gas fumes and whizzing metallic blurs. *Whooosh*, the sound went straight through her, *whooosh*, drawing her in spirals of vertigo toward a distant vortex. Maybe she had already died and gone to hell.

Wherever she was, she needed to lie down.

Inside the Pak-'N-Save, she floated up and down aisles of shiny packages lurching out to grab her, trying to remember what she wanted. She concentrated on the Muzak version of "Mr. Bojangles" as her mind blinked off and on like a wincing fluorescent tube. In a bright moment she paid for a bottle of Windex and hurried outside, feeling as if she were late—terribly late—for a big test she had to take.

She rummaged inside her taupe handbag for car keys, but found only house keys. She had forgotten the car keys on the kitchen table, and now she would have to take the bus home. Well, Luke could come pick up her car later, so she went back into the Pak-'N-Save to explain this to a puzzled clerk, a stocky young man with a bad complexion who accompanied her across the highway to wait for the Kenner Local bus.

She rode in silence for forty minutes in the wrong direction, following the intestinal curves of the Mississippi, fidgeting with her house keys and peering out the window, unable to identify a single landmark. All of the gas stations, fast food joints, motels, and billboards swirled together into a whirl of red and yellow lights, like little Sambo's tigers turning into butter. The tigers raced around and around the tree until BouBou could taste butter on the dry toast of her tongue, and realized she was hungry.

At the end of the Kenner line, when she spotted the St. Charles streetcar waiting at the intersection of Carrollton and Claiborne, she smiled to herself and realized why she was hungry: she was supposed to meet her mother on Canal Street for lunch at D.H. Holmes. Why was she carrying a paper bag with Windex in it? Did Mama ask her to buy it? Never be late for Mama.

Why, that streetcar conductor robbed her, insisting she put a whole dollar and a quarter in the box! She couldn't afford such extravagances on her schoolteacher's salary. She took a window seat, catching her own reflection in the grimy glass. Oh, my, she would have to run by Godchaux's before she met Mama to buy a hat, gloves, and heels. She couldn't be seen like this on Canal Street with her mother. She looked like she'd just come from weeding the garden.

She settled into the swaying of the urban relic, humming under her breath and emitting puffs of air like the little engine that could. As pillared mansions fell into place along St. Charles Avenue, one after the other, an itinerary so familar it felt encoded in her DNA, she knew who she was and where she was going. The farther she rode along the oak-shaded avenue, the further back she was carried, as if the gnarled branches of live oaks were passing her, like tired old nurses, from one pair of rocking arms to another, back to her source.

Her sudden vitality woke up the middle-aged woman in white shoes and stockings dozing on the seat next to her. "Excuse me, miss, we passed by Napoleon yet?" the woman murmured, trying to rouse herself.

"Oh, no," BouBou answered with a burst of confidence. "This is only Joseph Street. It's about eight stops from here."

"I been on my feet all day by the cosmetics counter at Walgreens, and I can't wait to get home, know what I mean?"

"Oh, yes, indeed. Neither can I."

MISS GLAPION'S HEART leaped into her throat as the clanging streetcar swerved from Carondelet onto Canal Street, a wide elegant avenue bustling with businessmen and well-dressed people carrying shopping bags marked Godchaux's and Kreeger's. This is where she came shopping with her mother and sisters every Saturday, when they would search for Violet's sheet music at Werlein's and have Sissy's hair done at Maison Blanche and lunch at the coffee shop at the Roosevelt Hotel and then maybe go to a show at the Loew's State Theater.

BouBou stumbled in a daze toward the corner of St. Charles and Canal, still carrying the bottle of Windex. She was looking for Canal Street, the one she had just glimpsed as the streetcar looped back onto St. Charles. Obviously she'd gotten off at the wrong stop. This must be Magazine Street, a shabby thoroughfare of boarded-up storefronts and winos. Mama warned her to be careful on Magazine.

A gristled man with a red knit cap walked in front of her pushing a shopping cart filled with aluminum cans.

"Where's Canal Street?" she barked at him.

"Right here last time I looked, lady," he replied. "Spare any change?"

When BouBou reached to secure her purse, she realized she wasn't carrying it. The taupe handbag was propped next to the conductor's feet as the streetcar rattled around Lee Circle. At that moment, Luke Leggio had gotten up from his doughnut cushion in front of the TV to phone the Jefferson Parish police, and Bessie Bordelon was creeping along in the righthand lane of Jefferson Highway toward the airport, peering down sidestreets and into ditches.

This isn't Canal Street, BouBou thought, as she studied her reflection in the window of a running-shoe store called The Footlocker. And I'm not this old lady. There's been some mistake. I'm here to lunch with my mother and there's death all over the floor and no salt on the table and the rice in my gumbo is burned black. Take it back, I don't want it, take it back.

She trudged up and down Canal Street, past more running-shoe stores, chintzy gift centers selling French Quarter T-shirts, and cut-rate camera shops with "Going Out of Business" banners. Everywhere she walked smelled like piss. The D.H. Holmes clock was gone, the department store boarded up. So was McCrory's dime store. Where Godchaux's had been was a store selling football jerseys and baseball caps. The people were poor, dressed as if they were at the beach. The Loew's State Theater, where she saw *Gone with the Wind* twelve times, was a graffiti-covered place called The Palace. "Butthole Surfers—live tonite!" was advertised on its marquee.

That was a picture she didn't want to see.

She wavered in dark doorways of narrow pizza parlors covered with grease, where teenage boys in tank tops and Reeboks looked up from their slices with menacing glances. She wanted to blurt out *I'm here to meet my mother for lunch but Holmes is boarded up and I've lost my purse and I'm hungry and tired.* Finally she found herself in a McDonald's, where she grabbed a handful of ketchup packets from the self-service counter and stuffed them into the Windex bag. Outside, she tore them open with her teeth and sucked out the contents, ketchup dribbling from her mouth and running down the front of her yellow seersucker dress. She tried to rub out the stains with Windex, creating an enormous orange blotch that looked like a map of South America.

Since there was no D.H. Holmes clock to wait under, she decided to wait for her mother in front of The Dollar Store. She slumped to the sidewalk against the window, huddling with her skirt stretched over her knees. Standing in front of her, a man with a rainbow umbrella hat was screaming into a megaphone about Jesus. At the curb, a young woman in a violet sari stood watch over a card table draped in purple velvet, ecstatically waving sticks of frangipani incense with her eyes closed.

BouBou's eyes were also closed, studying the white crinoline petticoats of the other girls making their first communion march down the aisle of Mater Dolorosa. She was near the end of the procession, and saw the altar moving toward her in a flash of gold and crimson, grandfatherly apostles floating over the church on clouds of frankincense.

Then her eyes blinked open into the fulminant gaze of an enormous head, its smile exposing one gold tooth with a champagne glass etched into it, and another with a cross.

"Hey, lady," the head said, "gimme a swig of yours, give you a swig of mine."

The pecan-colored head was of indeterminate age, set without a neck onto a muscular torso perched in the seat of a wheelchair, where the fabric of empty pant legs bunched into a lap just below the navel. A thick arm was holding out a brown paper bag twisted around a bottle.

"Go on, take a swig, the wine'll wake you up. Now gimme your bottle." She handed over her own paper bag, surprised to be carrying it. The head erupted into an uproarious laughter that made the wheels of his chair swivel from side to side.

"Woowee, Windex, now I seen it all! You getting high on this shit, or using it to wipe car windshields? First time I ever see an old white lady hustling that game."

"It's for my mother. To clean the mirror of her vanity."

"Yeah, where your vain mama at?"

"She's coming to meet me at D.H. Holmes."

"She better hurry, honey, cause the place been closed for twenty-five years. Where you stay by?"

"We live at 1232 Upperline Street."

"How you gonna get home? Got any carfare?" he asked with pointed interest.

"I left my purse at Mass."

"Tossed your whole purse in the offering plate? Hey, loony-tune, gimme back my wine," he demanded, tucking the bottle of Windex into the side pouch of the wheelchair. "First, go head, unscrew the top and take a swig."

In one deft maneuver, he spun the wheelchair alongside of BouBou, and they began to pass the Thunderbird back and forth.

His name was Breeze, he told her, and he'd been on the streets for twelve years. He knew the ropes, the best places to sleep and how to dodge the cops. She stared at him blankly, mesmerized by the champagne glass and the cross flashing between his fleshy lips. That smile. A much darker color, different clothes, and no fedora, but it was her daddy, that dapper gentleman smelling of bourbon who knew every doorman and sales clerk on Canal Street.

Out of the bulging wheelchair pouch Breeze produced a Hostess cupcake and offered it to her, just as her father would have from the pocket of a rumpled linen jacket. The wine fumes reminded her that it wasn't her mother she was supposed to meet, but him.

"Don't worry, grammaw," Breeze told her. "You sweet. I take care of you." Then ornate street lamps flicked on under the palm trees, and the light inside The Dollar Store dimmed and went out.

ON BLUE BIRD DRIVE the policeman leaned his potbelly against the squad car's hood, filling out a green form with painstaking slowness under a streetlight. "I forget—how you spell Alzheimer's?" he asked Luke, who threw his hands up in the air.

"Just write demented," Bessie broke in shrilly. "It means the same damn thing. D-E-M-M-E-N—"

"Yeah, yeah, I know. Look, we can send this missing person description to Orleans Parish if you think she got that far. But if we haven't picked her up in a week—"

"She wouldn't set foot in no New Orleans," Bessie protested. "She don't want a bullet in her head. She probably just got lost wandering around River Ridge. These circles are confusing. I hope she isn't stupid enough to walk into the swamp."

"Of course she ain't. She was a schoolteacher, a very educated individual," wheezed Raylene. The neighbors were milling around the circle, even Theresa Comeaux staggering in her plaid bathrobe. Most of them had already taken turns driving in and out of River Ridge's labyrinthine dead ends.

"When they find her," Bessie whispered, nudging Raylene, "it's either bars on the windows or the Good Shepherd for her. I don't think Luke can handle watching her twenty-four hours a day. Ain't it a crying shame?"

The police got several snapshots of BouBou smiling over a birthday cake, and issued Luke a report number. The only lead they found the whole evening was when they stopped by the Pak-'N-Save to buy some Hubig pies and showed the photos to a pimply clerk bleary-eyed from a double shift.

"I could swear that the lady I helped put on the Kenner Local about noon . . . No, sir, the bus was going thataway, toward New Orleans. She goes, like, 'I gotta get home,' and points across the street. Weird how someone from New Orleans would come all this way to buy a bottle of glass cleaner but, hey. . . ," he said with a chuckle, downing a swallow of Gatorade.

BOUBOU PUSHED BREEZE down Tchoupitoulas Street toward the Vision of Zion soup kitchen, both drunk on wine and singing hymns at the top of their lungs. His rich baritone and her off-key contralto bounced off the brick walls of abandoned warehouses and echoed under overpasses.

. . . to save a wretch like me.
I once was lost but now I'm found,
was blind but now I see.

She knew what she was doing. Why was she pushing this legless man in a creaking wheelchair down a deserted street at eight o'clock at night? Because her daddy needed her to.

At the Vision of Zion they feasted on macaroni and cheese, cole slaw, and slices of white bread, then listened to a preacher say we are all children of God, and held hands in a circle. They sang "The Old Rugged Cross" and other hymns, then straggled out of the old storefront. Most of the communicants headed toward the nearby homeless shelter.

"Some rough shit go down at that homeless shelter, grammaw," Breeze told her. "We better off bedding down by that church what got St. Jude over by North Rampart, where I stash my blankets. There a chapel outside filled with candles where the Virgin Mary look after you. They lock the gates up at ten, so we better get a move on."

The lights along the wharf were greenish-violet and cast iridescent patterns on the damp concrete. It was a balmy May night with a breeze blowing in from the river. BouBou was used to seeing the world through a TV screen, a picture window, or a windshield, and walking through the city made her feel like a young woman again. For a change, she felt inside the picture, at home in her own body. She was pushing her little sister Violet in a stroller down St. Charles Avenue, pretending to be the mama. The freedom of being here, a loose-limbed, grown-up girl made her so giddy she almost skipped when she walked. Where had she been all these years? For a second she closed her eyes, trying hard to concentrate on that glary, horizonless parking lot where she'd sat watching the world like a TV program but couldn't remember, from minute to minute, a single thing she'd seen.

With each step she took, pieces of herself sprang back to life, and they were halfway down Canal to North Rampart before she realized she'd turned the corner, and was almost home.

The iron gates of Our Lady of Guadalupe were still open, and Breeze wheeled himself into an outside grotto filled with candles lit under a statue of the Virgin of Guadalupe. The stone walls were plastered with small plaques that read "Merci, Maurice," or "Gracias, Juana," or "In Loving Memory." He unearthed a bed roll from a cavity between the rocks under the altar, and BouBou hoisted him out of the chair and helped to situate his torso between two blankets on the cement floor.

"In here, you sleep like a babe. Every night there's someone to tuck me in, and every morning the sexton help me back in my chair. She look out for me," Breeze said, pointing at the Virgin. "Tonight she sent me you." The gold champagne glass and cross were glimmering in his wide drunken smile, reflecting the pulsing flames of votive candles. Breeze handed her a third blanket and patted the floor beside him.

"Bedtime, baby." He looked up at her once, then turned away.

Entering the church, BouBou clutched the tattered pink blanket to her breasts as she shuffled down the aisle toward the altar with tears welling in her eyes. St. Jude was decked with wilted red carnations, beckoning her with an incandescent flame shooting from the top of his head. A bronze plaque under the statue read: "Saint of Impossible Cases." She hesitated, then reached down to touch the saint's plaster foot, worn smooth by so many hands.

AT SIX THAT MORNING two New Orleans police officers located Mrs. Leggio from River Ridge wrapped in a blanket under the floor-to-ceiling shelves of red and blue novena candles blazing around St. Jude. She had fallen asleep in the alcove behind the statue, directly under a huge Byzantine mosaic in which St. Jude was bearing a golden chalice and Jesus a golden cross. Between them a dove was descending in a shower of gilded tiles.

Her fingers were curled into tight fists, blood oozing from her palms. The intoxicating waxy odor of this oven of faith was translated into a serene paraffin expression on her wrinkled face.

They found her lying on her side, bare feet tucked under the hem of a stained seersucker dress, in what the doctor at the Good Shepherd Nursing Home later that day described as a fetal position. Conscious but shaky, she was escorted from the church while the sleepy sexton, who had notified the police, stood wringing his hands at the gate.

Propped up in the back seat of the squad car, her head lay to one side and her mouth hung open. Her final vision of the city of New Orleans was through the limpid police car window. The city disappeared into shadows below her as a golden champagne glass and a cross glinted through the bruise of dawn streaking above the Claiborne Avenue overpass.

It was a miracle, Bessie Bordelon declared that morning, that they found BouBou alive in the French Quarter without a bullet in her head.

PERPETUAL CARE

THE EASTER SUNDAY that Miss Estelle Arceneaux heard someone singing inside the tomb was the first time she'd been back to the cemetery since All Saints Day, and everything was a real mess. With a grimace, she emptied dried cockroaches from a glass vase and turned on the spigot full force, careful not to splash the white crochet handbag hanging from her elbow. Algae caked around the rim was the hardest to clean, and the paper towel turned to mush between her fingers. This part of the ritual was for the men of the family, but they were all either in the crypt waiting for their gladiolas or way out in California playing in some kind of band.

As the last of the Arceneaux women who could both walk and see, she took her family duties seriously. Opalescent plastic earrings marked the formality of the occasion. It was a shame, she thought as she spun the spigot shut, how fast things went to ruin if you let them.

She squinted in the overexposed New Orleans sunlight reflected off the whitewashed tombs, noticing for the first time the profusion of day-old wreaths piled around the corner crypt. Shielding her eyes from the glare, she could barely make out the name: Famille Lemoine. The Lemoines. She knew them. One had married a Dordain and lived on North Miro near Esplanade back before the war. The last Lemoine was buried there years ago, and the family hadn't engraved the marble slab yet with the recently deceased's name. Wedging the vase under one arm and securing her pocketbook under the other, she turned to walk on when she heard an echo from somewhere inside the tomb, a tinny, rasping wail.

At first she thought it might be the previous coffin moved from the shelf inside settling to the bottom of that pit—or whatever they have down there—the endless darkness she had tried not to peer down into during a lifetime of burials. Once she had dreamed it was filled with giant crawfish clattering their claws against coffins, trying to open us up for a change. When she was a little girl she had asked her Pepère if it led to China, and he told her no, chère, back to France, an answer that satisfied her until she had made her second communion. There was nothing about underground funerary passages to France in her catechism, and one of the LeBlanc boys had told her that down there was where the devil went to the rest room.

Stepping through spongy grass in her oxfords, she mounted the first marble step of the Lemoine tomb, sticking her silver perm into the alcove of the plastered brick bread-oven styled like a little Greek Revival house. Immediately she was blasted by a crescendo of horns and a roll of drums. She jumped back, almost knocking over an enormous basket of Easter lilies with a ribbon marked "From the Senior Class, McMain High School."

She could swear a Negro was inside singing, "I been loooving you toooo looong to stop nooow. . . ."

"You are tiiired and you wanna be freeee," he was moaning in falsetto. "My looove's growing strooonger as you become a habit to meee." She had eaten a banana this morning, and bananas made her dizzy. That was it. She had forgotten to take the potassium Dr. Schumaker prescribed. She would put the white gladiolas in the clean vase, pray for the souls of her family kneeling on the steps of their tomb, sweep around it, get back in the car, drive carefully home, and lie down on the daybed in the back room with the blinds closed.

A brass cascade of pleading followed her as she scurried away. "Don't make me stop nooow oh puhlease don't make me stop, don't make me stop nooow. . . ."

"Papa," she murmured to herself, "I can't do this all alone any more."

GOD KNOWS HE HAD done everything he could for the boy. So Easter morning found Dr. Lemoine speeding in a pearl-blue Cadillac DeVille toward Bay St. Louis, where he hoped to console himself over the blackjack tables of the Casino Magic Inn at the $29-a-night suckers' rate. And the getaway would do a world of good for Sybil, who hadn't spoken a word all morning. His wife sat sphinx-like with her flipped shoulder-length hair, staring straight ahead into the morning traffic, tapping an enameled fingernail against the cream vinyl seat-bucket to a medley on the Easy Listening station. Her debutante-ball mask had gotten her through the autopsy, funeral, and burial. And now Dr. Lemoine could picture her floating in a turquoise pool, hair fanned out in a nimbus around her face, that taut mask dissolving into tears like a lump of sugar.

No one could reach them at the Casino, not the hospital, insurance company, police, or well-meaning friends and family. None of the psychiatrists blamed either of them, of course. The hospital, well, just hadn't worked out, but it was the only choice left after all of those . . . shenanigans the boy pulled. Running away from home to go live in the Tremé. Brass bands. Drugs. He could have gotten shot. Yes, he had musical talent, but that shouldn't lead him into the middle of a black neighborhood and—whatever in the world was that place called?—the Little People's Club!

"You took the wrong exit," his wife announced.

"I'm going to take the scenic route, along the coast." He turned his bearded, marmot-like bulk toward her, stunned at the first words she had uttered all day. She looked back at him as if that was the saddest thing anyone had ever told her. The scenic route—the day after they buried their only son who jumped out of the window of the Rosary Three ward at St. Vincent DePaul Hospital on Holy Thursday.

Why couldn't Jay have become a normal gutter-punk, Dr. Lemoine had often wondered, with green hair and a shirt-stud in his tongue to click against his front teeth for attention? Those kids at least had a reasonable cure rate. A little therapy. Extra spending money. And an upscale party college. But what could you do with a boy from a good French Catholic family who thought he was black?

As the Cadillac swerved onto the coastal highway, his wife gasped at the first raucous screech, bracing her vermilion fingernail extensions against the padded dashboard as if the seagulls were about to nosedive through the windshield.

THE DEVIL WAS busy beating his wife over the clapboard office of St. Louis Number Three Cemetery on Esplanade Avenue. Despite tentative morning sunlight, a persistant drizzle had driven the director inside, where Mr. Broussard felt comfortably alone with his sinuses and hemorrhoid. He was just biting into his second McKenzie doughnut when Miss Arceneaux stomped up the steps in a no-nonsense stride. He wasn't in the mood to talk about Perpetual Care.

"Mr. Broussard," she informed him, "there are colored people singing inside the Lemoine tomb."

"Where they at?"

"I said I hear the voices of Negroes coming out of the Lemoine family tomb. You must do something."

"Miss Arceneaux, always a pleasure to see you. Set yourself down right here next to one of these glazed doughnuts I got over by McKenzie. They nice and fresh."

"I had breakfast early, thank you. I couldn't sleep a wink last night. I kept thinking about what I heard here yesterday, inside the Lemoine tomb, when I brought a bunch of glads to my poor papa, who had a hard time of it, let me tell you."

Mr. Broussard nodded sympathetically and nibbled on his

doughnut, pushing the box toward her. "They good."

"I don't care for doughnuts, Mr. Broussard. They raise my blood sugar. So I came back this morning and heard puh-lenty more. What I'm trying to say is there's some . . . dis-TUR-bance," she said, enunciating the word like the retired public school teacher she was, "at the Lemoine tomb."

Remembering her mention of colored people, at "disturbance" Mr. Broussard jumped up as if for a fire drill, closing the box of doughnuts and grabbing his massive ring of keys.

"There's clapping, singing . . . and a trumpet," she continued, like a student trying to remember her lesson, "and then a man's voice saying something over and over about . . . ."

Holding the office door open, Mr. Broussard fidgeted while she finished her report.

". . . the fun butt bar, or funky butter. You better go see."

"We'll get to the bottom of this," he assured her, as they walked out into the middle of a busload of wet German tourists pointing cameras at each other in front of marble angels, the day after Easter, in the rain.

"HELLO, WWOZ, NEW ORLEANS' jazz and heritage station. Travis Refuge on the air. Do you have a request?" Travis cradled the receiver between ear and shoulder as he began to line up CDs for his Afro-Caribbean program.

"You hear WWOZ coming out where? Out what tomb?. . . No, we don't have no transmitters down in there. What you talking about, man? . . . In his teeth? No, I never heard nothing about that, Mr. Broussard . . . Yeah, I'd like to hear that for my own self. Maybe Marie Laveau down there at St. Louis doing her some hoodoo. I'm on the air. Catch you later."

Travis hung up, swiveling his chair back to the mike to bleed his voice over the final percussion of a souk song. "And those are Les Poivres Rouges from Martinque, with 'Moucher Ma Bouche,' here on Afro-Caribbean rhythms this rainy Monday morning, at WWOZ, your jazz and heritage station, in La Nouvelle Orléans." Travis went on to give another plug to the Tremé Brass Band playing this evening at the Funky Butt Bar and Vietnamese Vegetarian Restaurant on North Rampart Street. Then he spun around and shut off the mike.

"Man from the cemetery call up," he blurted out to Shantrell Cousin, a Creole administrator tiptoeing through the sound studio with a file under her arm, "to say WWOZ being broadcast from a *tomb.* Say he sit there on the stoop of that tomb and hear me talking and the music I playing. Say he think the silver filling in this boy teeth they bury Saturday picking up the radio signals or something. I been working here for seven years and *that,*" he said, shaking his beaded dreadlocks until they rattled, "is the *weirdest motherfucker* ever called up this station, and they been some. It give me the willie to think my voice coming out some white kid tomb."

Shantrell lowered her tinted John Lennon frames to peer out at Travis with a "what you been smoking?" inquisitive bugeye. As she rummaged through a drawer, her back to him, she winced at what he intoned into the mike with a dungeon tremelo.

"This is Travis Refuge, the voice from *beyooond,* on WWOZ, live from the (*crrreaak*) *crypt. . . .*"

NINE HUNDRED SEVENTY-two pairs of wet Nikes squeaked down the freshly waxed corridors of Eleanor McMain High School on the day after Easter vacation. As the first homeroom bell sliced through the banging of lockers, the stampede up the granite staircases left a group in the corner of the girls' gym, in front of the windows on Nashville Avenue. With looseleaf binders joined at their hips, the students were speaking in whispers and shrieks that echoed up to the exposed pipes on the ceiling.

"It was so gross. On Saturday I walk up to his mother at Schoen to go like how sorry I was, and she goes, 'Who are *you*? You didn't love him.' And I go like, '*Wait a minute,* Mrs. Lemoine, Jay was my boyfriend since eleventh grade and like what do you know about who he was? You the one made him leave NOCCA and stop playing the trumpet and then put him in that insane asylum.' And she like completely loses it right there. Goes ballistic and orders me out of Schoen, but there were so many people from McMain with us I just ducked into another viewing room where these Cajuns from Breaux Bridge are having a wake with an accordion. And suddenly I'm dancing a two-step with this fat man who's crying to beat the band about his mama."

"Cool," the listeners murmured in unison.

"When they called me up on Good Friday to tell me about Jay," chimed in Andrea, blowing wisps of frosted mane from her face with puffs of air, "I was like no way. I felt so bummed for you, Lynnette. And the next thing I know, I'm in Mass at Holy Redeemer with the statues all covered in purple and staring up at the crucifix obsessing on Lynnette and Jay, Jay and Lynnette. I was sniffling and my mawmaw goes, 'Finally you got religion, girl.'"

"I swear to God I don't know what come over me," Lynnette Terramina burst out, her Sicilian features taking on tragic ancestral proportions uncommon to a seventeen-year-old with a nose ring and fuchsia highlights. "After Mrs. Lemoine ran me out into the wake with those coonasses, I grabbed this tiny clock radio I keep in my purse so I can take naps in my car when I cut, maxed out the volume, set it to WWOZ for midnight on the dot, when Jay and I were usually doing it on Saturday night, ran back into the Lemoine wake like—*excuussse* me, I have to say good-bye to my boyfriend, if you don't mind—and threw myself over the open casket, carrying on like a banshee from hell. It took Dr. Lemoine and two security guards to carry me out that fucking place, but not before I jammed that radio as far as I could down into the closed half of the casket."

Giggles all around, followed by the hyena laugh of Chaz, a tall thin black kid who squatted down to beat his palms in a staccato rhythm on the gym floor, chanting "yeah (*boom*), yeah (*boom*) yeah (*boom*)!" Thumbs shot up around a smiling circle.

"So when was, you know, the burial?"

"The bitch goes don't you dare show up for the burial at three o'clock, but I followed the procession to the cemetery, my car radio blaring Clarence 'Gatemouth' Brown all the way."

"And did your radio like go off at midnight?"

"I don't know." Lynnette was sobbing as the second homeroom bell sounded and the girls' gym teacher bounded toward them, a volleyball under her arm, pointing at the staircase with the mock severity of someone who had just spent a week in a bikini across the lake, far from the crumbling gray building on Nashville Avenue.

MR. BROUSSARD REARRANGED the pillow on his office chair, took a bracing whiff from his inhaler, and hunched forward like a chief of staff manning a battle station. Word had come down that morning from the Archdiocese lawyer on Carrollton Avenue that under no circumstances was St. Louis Cemetery authorized to enter a tomb without the consent of its owners, even though X-rays confirmed an electrical device inside the coffin, presumably a portable radio. The petition to disinter the burial in the Lemoine tomb "due to unusual circumstances affecting the security of cemetery property" was denied. And he had already left three messages on Dr. Lemoine's home answering machine that had not been returned.

No one at Touro Infirmary knew where he was. The obstetrics nurse he spoke with explained that the doctor had taken a two-week bereavement leave. Where were those assholes? he wondered. If they wanted their boy to have some company in there, why didn't they toss in a teddy bear or a half-dead hooker from the Airline Highway?

The Archdiocese lawyer had been adamant, breaking off his legalese to thunder into the phone with a Chalmette accent that "we can't dig up some guy's dead kid even if they got the whole filly-monia orchestra in there. They can turn around and sue the pants off the Church. You get them people to sign on the dotted line, or we wait till them batries go dead, hear? Jeez, we got enough going on here with that priest in Houma diddling them altar boys."

But by Wednesday, the batteries hadn't gone dead. It seemed the radio was getting louder, broadcasting from an infernal echo chamber, the marble slab vibrating with jazz. Whole carloads of high school students dressed in black had started turning up in the afternoons, sitting in a semicircle around the tomb hung with yellowing wreaths of white roses, chain-smoking cigarettes and passing skinny joints. They said they were from McMain and the performing arts high school, where the dead boy had gone. Only his mama, they said, made him quit the artsy place on account of some monkey business in Tremé. The girlfriend had pink hair, and if you asked Mr. Broussard, looked like a little dago slut.

The telephone was ringing off the hook ever since that "Blues from the Tomb" article had come out in the "Living" section of the *Times-Picayune.* The place was a nuthouse. Gator Holiday had called to add three busloads of tourists a day to their contract, CNN was threatening to send someone to New Orleans, and WWOZ was in an executive meeting with the Board of Directors of the Jazz and Heritage Foundation. Mr. Broussard was secretly tuning in to the station from a radio he kept in the bottom drawer of a file cabinet, and he knew the DJs were addressing comments to the kids around the tomb, clapping and hooting. Jay Lemoine was mentioned frequently, along with some guys named Jim Morrison and James Booker, who he assumed were dead, although he was sure they weren't buried in St. Louis Number Three.

His only ray of hope was the article had mentioned that this Jay Lemoine character committed suicide. Catholic cemetery bylaws prohibited the burial of a suicide on consecrated ground. The Archdiocese lawyer advised that to exhume a suicide required permission from the Vatican, no less, so Mr. Broussard was writing a letter to His Holiness over in Rome, Italy. He was stuck on the salutation. He had already scratched out "Your Holiness (and Mine)" and "My Dear Pope."

Pushing the letter aside, Mr. Broussard glanced out the Venetian blinds. A Lucky Dog hot dog vendor had set up his cart outside of the cemetery gate, in front of two parked Gator Holiday buses disgorging stout ladies with sun visors and fanny packs. Gangly goth teenagers, wiggling to spectral rhythms from i-Pods, were slouched against the fence, handing pieces of paper to tourists. And two black kids had put out a cardboard box top and were squatting on the sidewalk, adjusting the taps on their running shoes.

He dialed the Archdiocese for the fifth time that day, to ask if they had the Pope's email.

IT TOOK ALL afternoon to decide, but the project was a go.

The Executive Board of the Jazz and Heritage Foundation, meeting at their offices on North Rampart Street, felt it would be a unique way to kick off the Jazz Fest. The bone of contention was whether it would be "appropriate," a soothing word from California where people had transcended right and wrong. But they had just taken Marvin, a city councilman's cousin and the Fest's marketing consultant from Los Angeles, to a three-hour lunch at Dooky Chase, and he had convinced them to "go for it."

"What we got here is a tomb with a view," Marvin enthused over crab claws with greens. "The damn thing sits but five yards from the fence that's right next to the Fair Grounds, where it all gonna happen. It's got all the classic New Orleans themes. Death. Cemeteries. Music. Sex."

"Where the sex come in?" Travis asked, sucking on a claw without looking up.

"Here's the pitch. It's Romeo and Juliet, man. He's a trumpet player, imprisoned in a tower, then driven to suicide by his high-tone folks who don't understand him. She's a seventeen-year-old gutter-punk from the wrong side of the tracks, devoted to her man and his music. She waits in front of his tomb all day, listening to all these beautiful sounds coming right from the spot where her love lies rotting. That swing, or what?"

"I don't know," said Shantrell, clearing her throat. "It doesn't seem appropriate to broadcast our program from a cemetery. This is a really Catholic city. It'll offend people."

"Where we at? Some French fishing village?" Marvin sneered. "Or the City That Care Forgot?"

When the vote was taken later at Jazz Fest headquarters, it was decided to broadcast, on the second Thursday after Easter, the day before the first Friday of the Festival, a special "Live from the Crypt" program of WWOZ. The master of ceremonies would stand before the tomb, where he would introduce the Rebirth Brass Band. Lynnette Terramina would talk about her boyfriend, and specially orchestrated acoustic effects would transmit the echo from the tomb to a hundred and fifty thousand listeners. The public was invited.

The mayor expressed his doubts. But when he learned that the local Romanian radio commentator with a Transylvanian accent would step in as the celebrity emcee, and the famous Gothic romance writer would lend her presence as a tie-in with the Save Our Cemeteries campaign and her new novel, he was sold. Reluctantly, he placed a call to his old friend the Archbishop. When he got him on the line, and met some resistance, the mayor of New Orleans rubbed his bald head, grabbed his crotch, and reminded the Archbishop of New Orleans of promises a then-simple parish priest had made during the 1970s to an altar boy in Broadmoor.

In the meantime, Mr. Broussard had already sent his email addressed TO: His Most Holy See, Leader of the Christian World; FROM: Elwood P. Broussard, Jr., Director, St. Louis Cemetery No. 3, 3421 Esplanade Avenue, New Orleans, Louisiana 70119, U.S.A.

TUESDAY BEFORE THE live broadcast, the ten o'clock news on WDSU featured a spot with Thadeus Ribbit, the celebrated reincarnation of Louis Armstrong. "Jazz Fest kicks off on a solemn note this year" was the crisp lead-in voiced over a snazzy neon Jazz Fest logo, cutting to Ribbit, dressed in fedora and double-breasted suit, caressing his trumpet in front of a peeling shotgun in the Upper Ninth Ward.

"I don't know what to tell you all about him," he said sweetly, looking down at his trumpet. "He come in all the places we play. I see him by Little People, Vaughn, Funky Butt, tall white kid with a trumpet case standing in back the crowd every night, big old white T-shirt, smart-boy glasses, just looking, really digging it, but I mean in a quiet way, you know. He always there, sometime with a chick what got pink hair. One night late at Vaughn he let loose with his horn, when we was packing up our axe and barbecue, and he *goooood*, you know what I mean, just a kid, but he all right. Then he hanging with a crowd from NOCCA, and I think one day I gonna hear from this cat. Sorry to learn he passed, and I be there tomorrow at the cemetery to say good-bye before I play my ten o'clock gig at the House of Blues."

This was followed by a fade-out to the tomb, covered with bleached wreaths and surrounded by bleary-eyed teenagers, bleeding into a closeup of a petulant girl with pink hair, blowing fierce jets of smoke at the camera, backed by Aaron Neville singing "Mona Lisa" from a staticky transistor radio inside someplace that sounded like St. Louis Cathedral.

Minutes later, the Casino Magic house doctor was called from an evening consultation with a transvestite with silicone implants to administer 10 mg. of Ativan to a woman who had collapsed in hysterics off a high bar stool in front of the TV in the Wild Card Lounge. The cause of her attack was unknown, but her almost inaudible words before going under were something like "fuck the priest" and "even if I have to walk to New Orleans."

MISS ARCENEAUX STOOD at the edge of the crowd in a daisy-patterned sun hat, staring over the bony shoulders of a group of high school students in black tank tops who were circulating what looked like photocopies of a poem through the crowd. When they turned to look back at her, they did a collective double-take and began to chant "Oooh nooo, Miss Arceneaux, oooh nooo, Miss Arceneaux." Their retired English teacher stepped back to size up her former students, who seemed to have turned out even worse than she had imagined possible. Of course, they let them run wild as alley cats these days.

She was still in a state of shock from trying to maneuver her politely beeping Toyota through the Lucky Dog vendors and hot tamale wagons blocking the gate of St. Louis Cemetery. Scrambling between them were children with Styrofoam gumbo bowls Scotch-taped over their heads hawking beers and Cokes from ice-filled garbage pails resting in the shade of illegally parked vans. The wrought-iron fence was lined with scraggly Quarter-types selling handmade earrings stuck to red velveteen display cards. A mime playing an imaginary trumpet was walking through the crowd with a half-sad, half-happy face painted on, and a bald young man with elaborately tattooed biceps was distributing pamphlets about teen suicide from a card table.

Mr. Broussard, still waiting for an email from the Pope and livid that the Archdiocese had authorized this display of bad taste, had hired an off-duty New Orleans policewoman as a security guard, confident that she could prevent any mayhem. Early that morning, he and his crew had stripped the Lemoine tomb of dead flowers, as stipulated in the Perpetual Care contract the family had purchased, and he had done as little as possible to cooperate with the radio people. Thick orange cables ran like writhing anacondas from their truck through the alleyways behind adjacent tombs to the front of the Lemoine tomb.

The news commentator with the Transylvanian accent was seated in the grass leafing through a copy of *Playboy* while technicians in African-print drawstring pants were taping special sound-sensitive mikes to the marble slab of the tomb. The arts high school Jazz Ensemble had assembled on the lawn, where the efficient blond principal was going over details with Travis Refuge. The Gothic romance novelist from uptown, a slight woman in a black cowl, was curled up on the stoop of a tomb with her arm draped over a plaster urn, gossiping with the grotesque writer from downtown, a tall woman dressed in billowy white, lounging on the steps of the next tomb. The visiting poet at Tulane was already drunk, and Babs Godoy, the beaming society columnist, was mingling like there was no tomorrow.

Then the Rebirth Brass Band blared in at full throttle down a broad grassy avenue of the cemetery, playing "The Shiek of Araby." Those following along began to second-line, sashaying in and out of the narrow alleys behind and between tombs, waving white handkerchiefs high in the air and boisterously colliding with each other as they joined together in a throng approaching the Lemoine tomb like a Southern Baptist vision of the Day of Resurrection.

Travis raised his palm to silence the band and to still the bobbing white handkerchiefs, then tapped his mike, sending an ear-splitting electronic screech bouncing back from inside the tomb. Wild applause. He gave a final signal for "on the air" and welcomed WWOZ listeners to the "Live from the Crypt" kickoff of the Jazz and Heritage Festival, broadcast from inside a tomb in the historic St. Louis Cemetery overlooking the Festival site at the lovely Fair Grounds. He was introducing the celebrity emcee from Transylvania when his voice suddenly turned thin and sailed off, light as a paper plate, lost in the meringue clouds of a cerulean April afternoon.

The echo had disappeared.

He tapped his mike.

Nothing.

A sepuchral silence was etched in the glare between row after row of taciturn tombs, festivities poised in midair. "Shit," said Travis in a stage whisper, staring at the pyramid of blinking equipment. "I guess those batteries in there finally wore out."

At that moment Thadeus Ribbit lifted his horn, stepped in front of the tomb, and in the lithest tones ever seduced from a trumpet, began to play a taps rendition of "May the Circle Be Unbroken." Lynnette Terramina collapsed. "Gone," she kept mumbling, "he's really gone," as Andrea and Chaz wrapped their arms around her waist and lumbered with her behind Thadeus, who was heading toward the gate with his horn held high in the air, playing as slowly as a late afternoon stroll through a New Orleans cemetery might inspire.

Everyone followed him out of the cemetery, walking arm-in-arm. Even plastic plates and go-cups trailed after him as if bewitched, swept along in a melancholic trance, and orange radio cables and studio trucks and disappointed high-school musicians who didn't get to play, holding their instruments over their shoulders like tired children. No one spoke a word until they were out of the gates, milling down Esplanade Avenue in the speckled sunlight under the shady arches of live oaks. And for weeks to come, many still didn't speak, afraid they would somehow find their own voices abruptly, irrevocably, gone.

Miss Arceneaux was the last to leave. She stooped to pick up the only piece of paper that hadn't sailed out of the cemetery in the wake of Thadeus Ribbit, one of the photocopied poems the students had been handing out. She fished her reading glasses out of her purse and when she recognized what was scrawled there, her lizardy skin bunched into a broad smile. There it was, an unpunctuated, wildly misspelled rendering of the poem by Miss Emily Dickinson that she had required her tenth-grade English students to recite. "I died for Beauty—but was scarce / Adjusted in the Tomb," she declaimed, with chin up and chest out, as she had taught her students, "When One who died for Truth, was lain / In an adjoining Room—." Softly to herself, she spoke the last stanza from memory as she folded her glasses and this final homework from her teaching career into her crochet purse:

And so, as Kinsmen, met at Night—
We talked between the Rooms—
Until the Moss had reached our lips—
And covered up—our names—

BY THE TIME Dr. Lemoine made it through the bumper-to-bumper traffic on Esplanade, after having his wife admitted to St. Vincent DePaul Hospital on Henry Clay Avenue, it was almost four, and the massive iron cemetery gates were about to swing shut.

He braced himself as he approached his family tomb, but when he dashed out, leaving the car door ajar, he saw nothing and no one. He stood sweaty and disheveled, ready to be judged by ranks of seraphim and cherubim, by CNN and a waiting nation, by generations of pregnant mothers astride rows of tombs, by the only baby he had ever lost, his own. The mute marble slab remained as it had always been.

The stone had not been rolled away.

It bore the name of his father, Numa Eugéne Lemoine, and stuck to the death date was a sliver of silver duct tape. That was all. Next week, he promised, he would have his son's name sandblasted into the marble. He imagined it there already, followed by his own.

Weaving his way back to the car through the trellis of lengthening shadows, he passed behind an old lady in a sun bonnet kneeling in front of a tomb. She looked like she had been there a long time, and he shook his head at how absorbed she seemed in saying out loud prayers he remembered from childhood. "Holy Mary, Mother of God, pray for us sinners," he repeated with her under his breath, "now and at the hour of our death."

The Jew Who Founded Memphis

IN BELLIGERENT silence, Jake pushed his mother's wheelchair up the steep ramp to the cemetery office, her right leg sticking straight out like the prow of a frigate. They were visiting Memphis to clean the angel on her family plot, and as Mrs. Hokum had told her son on many occasions, she intended to make sure the people who ran Oak Grove Cemetery knew exactly who she was.

Three days before they left their fallow farm in Bossier, Louisiana, an arthritic knee joint had frozen on her. Then she read in the Saturday religion section of the *Shreveport Times* that fifty thousand black Pentecostals would also be in Memphis for a Church of God in Christ convocation. This, Jake had hoped, would do it, but she stuck to her guns. He rolled his eyes as he wheeled her through the screen door into the cramped office, dominated by a grandfather clock on one side and a red Coca-Cola machine on the other.

Like an ostrich, Mrs. Hokum strained her wrinkled, pointy face to the height of a long, curved neck, trying to see over the top of a paneled counter. Finally she cleared her throat several times and chimed in a cheerful singsong, "Guess who's here?"

A chinless head shaped like a white china doorknob rose over the counter, ice-blue eyes staring down at the plaid pant leg jutting out of the wheelchair. Holding up half of an egg-salad sandwich, the young woman had a full mouth and was trying hard to swallow.

"Hello. I'm Rebecca Berkow Hokum and my great-grandfather, Colonel Abraham Berkow, founded this cemetery in 1852."

The chinless woman managed to swallow. "Care for a Co'Cola?"

Jake's mother was undaunted. She removed a white glove and held out a claw-like hand. "This is one of Colonel Abraham Berkow's very own solid-gold cufflinks made into a signet ring. And here's the other cufflink," she said, tugging at the charm bracelet on her bony wrist that she couldn't get turned around.

Behind the wheelchair, Jake shifted his stooped shoulders, chuckling to himself. His mother had been rehearsing this speech for three years, ever since she'd begun receiving the Polaroids that her third-cousin Gloria in Memphis enclosed in Christmas cards of the "sadly deteriorating angel" at Oak Grove. He'd seen the life-sized statue only once, when he was a child. He remembered the fragile face looking down at him shyly, bathed in a fairy-tale light. A mane of curls cascaded down her back, disappearing into a pair of crushed wings folded around the lower half of her body. Originally the statue had been covered by a glass dome, but an ice storm had shattered that decades ago. Now a fungus was eating it and had turned the angel pockmarked and black.

"And this is my son, Jacob Berkow Hokum," Mrs. Hokum said, pointing with her ungloved hand. "He's the artist in the family and is going to clean our angel just as good as new. That statue was a memorial to my aunt Rachel, Colonel Berkow's granddaughter, who expired on her wedding day. It's marble. Genuine Italian marble."

"Too bad the director's at lunch," the woman said, feeding quarters into the Coke machine. "He's real historic."

The screen door creaked, and the shining dark face of a teenager in an ill-fitting black suit and stiff white shirt was framed in the doorway. His hair stood up in a three-inch wedge on top, the sides shaved close. Suddenly the office smelled of drugstore cologne. "Excuse me, but where Mrs. Wardell Ticker bury at?

Her funeral this afternoon."

Mrs. Hokum flashed a stricken look at her son that he refused to acknowledge.

"Been no burial so far today," the chinless woman said, "but will be one in about ten minutes. It's the Ticker party, I reckon. So hold your horses till I ring the plantation bell when the hearse passes over the drawbridge."

"I'm Rebecca Berkow Hokum," Mrs. Hokum said, swerving the wheelchair around to aim her extended blue oxford at the young man's crotch. "My great-grandfather founded this cemetery."

"Yes, ma'am."

"Are you attending a burial?"

"Yes, ma'am." The young man was backing out of the door.

"I'm so sorry. Who is it, may I ask?"

"My mama. Ma'am."

"You mean to tell me your mother—"

Jake grabbed the handles of the chair and wheeled his mother out of harm's way, next to the Coca-Cola machine. This would have been the perfect moment to finally inform her about his brother Ed's brood of caramel-colored children that he and his wife Judy, a former Black Muslim, were raising on their pot farm in Northern California. That would have shut her up.

The chinless woman accompanied the young man to the porch, where she stood staring at her watch. At a certain moment, she bounded down the steps in spongy running shoes, and a bell tolled as a hearse, followed by a procession of cars, nosed its way over a frail wooden drawbridge. The young man stood by the side of the road, waving his arms at the second car.

Mrs. Hokum sat erect, half-closed eyelids fluttering. The building vibrated with each slow, penetrating peal of the bell.

"What would Colonel Berkow say," she asked in a hoarse whisper, "if he knew colored people were using his cemetery now?"

Jake allowed the bell to answer with its solemn, relentless tolling.

"Don't you remember what Gloria found out last Christmas,"

he asked, trying to change the subject, "from the Mormons on the Internet? The name's really Berkowitz. Supposedly they were Polish Jews who immigrated to Tennessee in the early 1800s, then finally settled in the Pinchback district. Berko*witz*, Mama."

"'Partly Hebrew,'" Mrs. Hokum quoted, twisting the signet ring on her finger. "Who in creation would send you a Christmas card saying you're really Jewish?"

"EVERYONE'S JEWISH," Ed had commented that Christmas. "Aren't we all descended from Adam's rib?"

"So should we still put up the tree?" Mrs. Hokum looked exasperated, glancing from one son's face to the other as she tried to untangle a string of electric lights. She had just opened Gloria's Christmas card.

"Those of us who aren't descended from monkeys," Jake spit out of the side of his mouth.

"Jacob, stop it." Mrs. Hokum said. "I want peace in this house for the first Christmas without your father. And your brother Edom wouldn't look like an orangutan if he'd just cut all that mess off top his head."

The two brothers had been trading insults of "nerd" and "orangutan" ever since Ed arrived for his visit. Ed was burly, ruddy-faced, and bearded, with a matted shock of graying dreadlocks twisted up into a rainbow-striped Rastafarian cap. Jake had solved his prematurely receding hairline by shaving his head bald. Ed lived in a commune that produced the largest marijuana crop in Mendocino County, although he'd always told his parents he made a living from telemarketing. Jake, who designed graphic software for Adobe, was pale, gaunt, and always dressed in black. Together on the sofa, they looked like a Neanderthal seated next to a Star Trek character.

The only stage missing in their evolutionary diorama was the human.

This was the last time Ed would be invited home for Christmas, Jake had decided. His brother moped about like their father's vengeful ghost, tossing bridles and saddles around the empty stalls then trudging off into the woods to hunt, startling everyone in the new subdivision with rifle blasts. Ed had been livid about his younger brother selling off his father's pine woods to Partridge Estates, and about Jake's plans to convert the now empty barn into his design studio. Jake's cyber startup in Austin had gone bust, and four years ago he'd moved back in with his parents, "temporarily."

"I was planning to come home one day and run the old horse farm like Daddy would have wanted, and now you've taken everything away," Ed said when they were alone in the kitchen, mixing up eggnog.

Jake banged down the bottle of bourbon. "Then why didn't you stay?" There were no more family farms in northern Louisiana. Everyone who hadn't sold to developers had to make it in some other way. "I mean, you could be raising emus and daylilies like the Trotters next door," Jake taunted, "or maybe Christmas trees and Easter bunnies like the Finneys down the way."

The final showdown had occurred ten years earlier. Home again after being kicked out of the third college, Ed had taken LSD, then walked naked into the woods with a gun, a Bible, and a frying pan, screaming that was all he needed from his goddam family to survive.

"Daddy was blind when you had him sign those papers."

"He could see pretty good when his son went back-to-nature, buck-naked in the woods waving Mama's electric skillet. What were you planning to do, run an extension cord to the house?" Jake hissed, trying to calm the hysteria in his voice. "And he could see good enough to find that pot field you planted in the back pasture. And he could see that picture of your 'Sufi bride' you mailed us, which he tore into tiny pieces before Mama could find it. You really thought he'd turn over the farm to you? You broke his hard-shell Baptist heart."

While Ed stood tucking stray dreads into the knit bagful of hair sagging to his shoulders, Jake bolted from the kitchen with a tray of filled glasses.

"Now boys, not everybody in every generation gets along," Mrs. Hokum said, lifting a glass of eggnog. "But having kids helps to iron out everyone's differences. The future belongs to people who have children. Thought by this time I'd have me some darling grandchildren."

Ed looked away, and Jake glared down at him from the aluminum ladder, placing a frilly lace angel on top of the Christmas tree.

THE WINGED STATUE was a smudge on the horizon, standing out in the coppery fall landscape like a huge rotten tooth. Mrs. Hokum winced when it fell into view, but Jake kept propelling his mother along the curved cemetery path, her stiff leg pointing them toward a meeting with origins.

"Think somebody threw black paint on it?" Mrs. Hokum asked, as they drew nearer. "I mean, because we're 'partly Hebrew?'"

"No, this is the mold of the ages," Jake said as he moved closer, chipping away at the darkened crust with his fingernail. The wistful features of the young woman with the flowing locks faced downward, as if contemplating the sere ground in which she lay buried. She carried a profusion of lilies on her lap, tangled with the finely textured down of feathery wings drooping like an opera cloak from her shoulders. Perched on a block of stone, she was an angel at rest, weighed down by the earth's bounty and her own beauty, unable to soar. Now the dank loam surrounding her was taking her back. "Vengeance is Mine." Jake barely remembered the verses he'd had to memorize. "Sayeth the Lord."

"Think you can save her, sugar?"

"Don't worry. I have those special brushes and marble cleansing powders from the preservation group in New Orleans. See what I can do tomorrow," he said, scrutinizing the statue with a squint. No way was this going to work, he decided.

The white eye sockets stared out from behind scabs of decay so dark that the angel appeared to be wearing minstrel blackface. She was a nurse, a perpetual sitter, keeping watch over the oval bathtubs sunken into the ground in front of her—the grassy graves of all the Berkows—as though they were filled with bathing babies.

"So awful," Mrs. Hokum said. "She was bitten by a brown recluse spider on the morning of her wedding in 1911. Say she was allergic and swole up like a hog. That was long before my time. So she never had children, and I'm an only child. None of my father's brothers had any children, so except for third-cousin Gloria, an old maid schoolteacher, it looks like you and me are the last Berkows left." Mrs. Hokum looked at her son as if they were stranded alone in a lifeboat in the middle of the Atlantic. "Not that Edom doesn't count, but he takes after your daddy. Countrified."

Jake knew what was coming: the apocalyptic importance his mother placed on the end of her family line. "Go forth and multiply," she kept misquoting the Bible, "and ye shall be like the dirt of the earth." Dirt. That's what she'd consider Ed and Judy's four clay-toned kids frolicking naked in the backwoods of Northern California, their nappy heads dusted with marijuana pollen. Edom claimed to have transcended money, Jake thought with a snort, imagining all the dough he must have socked away from wholesale dealing. After all, marijuana was to California what cotton used to be to the South.

"Is there anybody special in your life?" His mother tilted her head, glancing up at him with a flirtatious smile. "You just made thirty-two. Time's a wasting."

Jake grabbed the wheelchair handles and carted his mother between the other graves, avoiding the already canned "somebody special" conversation. The truth was, he didn't believe any more in romance than he did in religion. He had tried various women and even experimented with men. But being part of a two-headed beast just didn't suit him. He counted himself lucky to be free of the delusional convulsions he watched his friends suffer through. Several heartbreaks later, they all wound up alone and childless anyway. Men were extraneous to reproduction, he'd decided. Women gave birth to women who gave birth to women. Where did he fit in? Whenever a woman happened to be ready, the perfect mate was around the next corner. But fewer and fewer women seemed ready these days, at least among those his age in the computer world.

They meandered along chill walkways among the garish funerary monuments of the Gilded Age, bronze statues corroded green, chipped obelisks, the crumbling columns of miniature plantation houses, and iron-lace settees rusting into the ground. Jake couldn't believe what grandiose dreams of permanence these people had once entertained. By contrast, he felt like a wisp of dandelion, a mutant seed bouncing along the ground, the mysteries of where, when, and what he was to become shifting with the seasons. A brilliant abundance of vermilion, ochre, and golden foliage whispered above him as the tires of his mother's wheelchair crunched through dried leaves swept into mounds by the wind.

In the distance Jake spotted what at first seemed like a carnival float moving toward them. He then realized they were hats—wide-brimmed lime, fuchsia, and magenta feathered chapeaux, of the most fanciful confection—perched on the heads of a group of women accompanied by somber-suited men, and followed by a dozen squealing children playing tag around the tombs. This must be the Ticker family returning from their burial. By the time he made out the wedged head of the son leaning on the shoulder of an eggplant-shaped woman, the loud procession was upon them. The woman's face was covered by a black veil studded with teardrop rhinestones.

Suddenly Rebecca Hokum's wheelchair was surrounded by pastel pinafores with matching head bows, and little boys with clip-on ties making monkey faces. They seemed delighted to see the half-stiff corpse of a living white lady being paraded through the cemetery, one who hadn't been buried yet.

"Mister," said a girl with pigtail plaits looking up at Jake, "you sure do look like a hard-boil egg."

"Hey, Humpty-Dumpty," a boy blurted out, covering his mouth. This set off another round of stifled giggles.

"You all having a good old time here in the cemetery?" Mrs. Hokum asked, her birdlike features softening. Her craggy hand reached out to grab the fingers of the pigtailed girl, and didn't let go. The young man with the wedge-shaped haircut drew up beside them.

"I met your brother here at the office," Mrs. Hokum said.

"He our uncle," several children chimed in unison, pulling at his coat tails.

"Sure are a lot of you." Mrs. Hokum's head swiveled around to take them all in with a wide flash of dentures.

"Yes, ma'am. We a family."

"I'm real sorry, son," Mrs. Hokum said, her clouded gray eyes watering. "My mother's buried here. It's a terrible thing to lose a mother. Makes you feel like you got nowhere to go."

"You said it, lady."

"Come on, Mama. We'd better get back to the bed and breakfast. I have to clean that angel tomorrow."

"There's our family tomb." Mrs. Hokum pointed out the statue to the rhinestone-veiled woman. "We've come to clean the angel."

"That's my most favorite statue in the cemetery," the woman said in a deep contralto. "Just looking at her give me the unburdening."

Then the Wardell Ticker party was behind them, the ladies adjusting their hats, the children turning around to peek at the old white woman in the wheelchair with her foot pointing through the trees toward the setting sun.

THE NEXT MORNING, when Jake turned from Jackson Street onto Front, he saw plenty more hats outside of the Cook Convention Center. Women were prancing arm-in-arm up and down the street, crowned with elaborately beaded hats, felt ones wrapped with chiffon or gold metallic lace, zebra-striped, leopard-spotted, some frothy, others ferocious, no two alike, all peaked with feathers waving in the breeze. Jake smiled and shook his head, reminded of an aviary of exotic birds preening in tropical sunlight. A big banner announced in red: WELCOME CHURCH OF GOD IN CHRIST. PRAISE THE LORD. WE GOT SOME CREATION GOING ON HERE!

He and his mother were lodged in a Victorian bed and breakfast in the Pinch Historic District, where Mrs. Hokum's father grew up. Sitting around in the flouncy parlor of the old mansion, Jake's mother had reminisced about her grandmother presiding over her silver coffee service. The old lady had been such a devout Episcopalian she could afford to tell people, Mrs. Hokum finally recollected, that—way back—her family had been Jewish.

"Now the truth comes out," Jake said.

"She used to joke about Jews and Episcopalians, claiming in her heart she was still one of God's frozen people." This grandmother had grown up in a plantation house, a Daughter of the Confederacy. And her father, Colonel Berkow, had made a fortune in cotton trading, then established the most fashionable dry goods store on Beale Street. "They say the Colonel helped start that country over in Africa for freed slaves. Liberia? But his own son was a slaveholder. Why I bet those two had words. I suspect families didn't get along any better then than they do now."

Mrs. Hokum eventually had talked herself to sleep, reliving a glorious past she'd never known. Her purse was stuffed with Ziploc bags filled with half-eaten sandwiches and packets of cookies so she wouldn't have to waste money on restaurants. She had grown up during the Depression, and her gentleman father, who never held a full-time job after 1932, had been happy enough to marry her off to a Louisiana horse breeder with a tenth-grade education.

Jake had dropped his mother off for a tour of the Hunt-Phelan plantation home with Gloria, and now was on his way to clean the angel. As he drove under the colonnade of oaks arching over the cemetery, sunlight dappling the car hood made him long to pick up a paintbrush again. After art school, he'd done little else for eight years but fiddle with cursors on a computer screen, submerged in a cartoonish blur of primary colors and beeping boxes that accordioned out. He felt like the boy living in the plastic bubble who could only touch the world through Gore-Tex gloves. The textures of the real world terrified him with their mystical concreteness that couldn't be clicked away.

Yet he was anxious to lay his hands on something—anything—real. And he figured rot was real enough.

The dark angel was waiting for him, gazing at the ground with her wings gathered around her in a gesture of distilled grief. He mixed the powders into a paste, then tried out a patch on the cheek, dabbing on the solution as if he were making up a bride. He covered the face, then the smooth neck above the pleated folds of cloth draping the body. The wings would have to wait until he had mastered the technique.

Jake worked all afternoon, mixing, dabbing, flaking off the dried mixture, and then reapplying a second coat. The last time he'd done anything so physical was during his only visit to Ed's, when he'd helped his brother install a sunburst stained-glass window in the group dining room. The commune had been buzzing with activity: Judy baked her own bread and made their clothes, and Ed was always at work composting the vegetable garden. Jake had been so stoned the entire time he didn't remember much from his visit, except carving and sanding fragrant redwood while a tangle of kids and mutts played underfoot to the cacophonous drone of an eternal drum circle. And every event had been an occasion for them to join hands for a Sufi song or some made-up Muslim ritual. He slept in a tree house lit by a kerosene lamp. Not a bad life, he'd decided, if you didn't mind being a grown man still playing Indian fort, watching your life disappear in curlicues of marijuana smoke.

The lazy warmth of the sunny afternoon made Jake drowsy, so waiting for the cleansing solution to dry on the intricate carving of the lily garland, he stretched out in the grass, his head against the statue's stone base. He drifted into a deep sleep, as if the angel had reached over to cover his face with her wings.

In his dream he saw twin escalators side-by-side, one going down, one going up and reaching far into the sky.

The escalator steps were crowded with stout women in church hats, clapping and swaying. Ed and Judy in knitted Rasta caps were playing conga drums, and motley-hued children raced between everybody's legs, singing a cappella. Those going down were waving at those going up, as if seeing them off at the airport on some marvelous trip. At the top of the up-escalator, Jake recognized the sepia features of Colonel Abraham Berkow looking quite pleased with himself, standing in a yarmulke like a department store manager greeting his customers. Rachel was in a wedding gown with a pearl-studded veil, wings fanned out behind her, and people were tossing rice at her.

"Jacob, Jacob, help me get to the next floor. I want to go where they're going."

His mother was calling to him, stuck at the bottom of the up-escalator in her wheelchair. She was wearing a ribboned plantation bonnet, her frozen leg sticking out. He was just about to lift her out of the wheelchair and sling her onto his back to mount the escalator when he was seized by a childhood fear of bare toes getting caught between the meshing teeth of the mechanical staircase. He looked down, and was naked. A series of high-pitched notes—*ding, ding, ding*—rang like a department store intercom as he yawned, neck against the stone, waking to the tolling of the cemetery bell that announced the final burial of the day.

One hand shot to the top of his head, rubbing his baldness. His head was smooth as a baby's bottom. He felt uncovered in the presence of the All Knowing, and shook himself to dispel the awe and shame.

Caw, caw, caw.

All around him in the violet twilight an enormous flock of shiny crows had descended on the cemetery with angry shrieks. They were perched in branches and on the tops of mausoleums, swooping to the ground to peck among shadows at the withered grass for whatever specks of stray life they could unearth. He planted himself in front of the statue, kicking at a few scavengers scuttling toward him, their reptilian heads all bulging eyes and greedy beaks. Their fluttering darkness covered the cemetery as far as he could see, deep into nightfall, far into the future.

Batting at the crows, he took out a hefty flashlight from his canvas tool bag and studied Colonel Berkow's statue. While he slept, as if by magic, the powders had done their work. Everywhere he had touched was now sparkling, as if the lustrous marble were freshly minted flesh. Rachel Berkow seemed to come alive, translucent, shielding virginal eyes from the beams of his light. He pulled on a sweater, tied a red bandana over his head, then buffed the lilies with fine steel wool before beginning on the wings. He was supposed to meet his mother and Gloria at the Peabody Hotel at five o'clock to watch the ducks parade through the lobby and into the elevator. Let them wait.

Losing track of time, he continued scrubbing like a man possessed, arching over the statue as purposefully as prayer, covering her with hands warm as a lover's. All of the gazes that had ever fallen here searching for something lost, all of those eyes hungry as empty plates, bore down upon him. He thought of his mother with her Ziploc bags, of Edom in his stoned exile, of the eggplant-shaped lady with the rhinestone-teared veil and her unburdening. Ever so softly, he hummed an off-key version of "Rock of Ages." Then lifting up a voice long choked inside, he began to sing.

Knock Knock

BEFORE MICHAEL got mixed up with the old sailor, Mr. Malone, he'd wanted to be a streetcar. When he turned ten, he tried to explain this to Miss Francis on the Ding-Dong School TV show for birthday kids. He'd been chosen for the Butch-waxed blond crew cut, blue eyes, and dimpled smile that made him look like the boy eating cereal on the Rice Crispies box. "Such a pretty boy," ladies at church always told him, making his rosy cheeks blush even redder. "What a shame to waste such coloring on a boy," the ladies clucked to his mother, Maxine. Michael had appeared in Schwinn, Ford, and RCA Victor commercials since he was five. That was after his father had left for good, and Maxine began to enter him in modeling contests to make ends meet.

"And what do you want to be when you grow up?" Miss Francis had asked, tilting a lollipop microphone toward Michael.

"A streetcar."

"You mean a streetcar conductor?"

"No." He glared into the camera. "A streetcar."

That summer Michael claimed the streetcars as his own. His post was at the side-window next to the conductor, where he imagined himself clanging the bell and twisting the handles. He would board at Willow Street, and then brace himself for the abrupt turn as the streetcar swung from Carrollton onto St.

Charles, changing its course to follow a bend in the Mississippi. St. Charles Avenue seemed like another universe, a broad oak-lined thoroughfare of shadowy mansions far from the weedy shotgun-doubles on Michael's street. He would ride almost until the end of the avenue and get off at the YMCA on Lee Circle, where his mother had enrolled him in the day camp for boys aged nine to sixteen.

Mr. Malone always had a Snickers in his pocket and a knock-knock joke up his sleeve, and was the only one at the Y who could distract Michael from the window that opened onto St. Charles. Michael would stand there for hours tugging at the Venetian blind cord, pretending to ring the bell as he drove his streetcar. Mr. Malone would wait for him in the lobby, reading the newspaper in a leather armchair. For years he'd rented a room upstairs, since he first came to visit his old Navy friend, Coach Harley, who directed the summer program. Mr. Malone had a gray crew cut, a slightly bent, bulbous nose, and a jagged-tooth smile, and was at least fifty or a hundred years old, Michael figured. A retired merchant marine, he had been to every country in the world and had taken a special interest in the boy. Mr. Malone swore that Michael was the spitting image of Biff, his nephew in California.

"Biff favors my mother's side of the family," Mr. Malone told him. "You and me could be related. Cute little fellow, a real boy."

Michael loved looking like a real boy named Biff in California. Especially since he felt like such a fake boy in New Orleans, Louisiana. California was where TV shows came from, and he hoped one day to make it there to become as real as the people on the black-and-white screen who mesmerized him.

Streetcar conductors began to notice Michael, too. They nicknamed him "Shotgun" because that was where he always rode, a skinny kid with a paper bag containing a clean towel, red YMCA gym shorts, and a sandwich, usually baloney with chow-chow.

"What's your dad do, Shotgun?" the conductors would ask.

"He's away at sea." Once he'd heard his mother tell that to Mrs. Friedman at church.

"So he's a sailor?"

"On a big ship," Michael lied. His father lived in Chicago and called home whenever he was drunk.

The name Shotgun made Michael feel full of "Snap, Crackle, and Pop," even though his world was as gauzy and faraway as a pastel diorama tucked inside a sugar Easter egg. He had stared out of the window so much in fifth grade that one afternoon Miss Umholtz made him count all the cars that passed by. Once he overheard Aunt Jewell, a grammar-school teacher herself, describe him as a "quiet boy." He tried to ape the screaming and jostling of other boys, jumping up and down on cue. Just as in high school, years later, before he stopped pretending, he would cheer and boo with the crowd at the stadium when he didn't know where the ball was, or even which game they were playing.

He was happiest working on his stamp collection, daydreaming of a triangular purple country called Malaysia, or a regal emerald country called Ceylon. For almost a year, he'd spent most of his time in the company of an imaginary Dutch friend named Derrick—Holland had such beautiful stamps. He and Derrick would listen for hours to his *Bozo the Clown Goes Around the World* record on the portable Victrola that looked like a little white valise. In April, Derrick sailed away with Bozo to plant tulips under windmills, just like in the record's picture book. And never came back. Maxine put Bozo in the box with Michael's loopy kindergarten drawings and said, "Time for the real world, kiddo."

So every day she sent Michael to the Y with fourteen cents in his Daniel Boone wallet for carfare. This was when a ten-year-old could ride public transportation by himself throughout the city of New Orleans. And when children did exactly what grown-ups told them to do.

They had no idea things could be any other way.

THIRTY NAKED TROOPERS stormed through the showers and scummy footbath, screams ricocheting off the swimming pool walls in a piercing echo. Coach Harley stuck fingers in his ears and grimaced as if the noise were cracking the enamel on his teeth, then blew his whistle. The boys crouched in orderly rows along the bleachers.

"Look at this, Michael," Stanley Friedman said. He was a fat, freckled kid, the only boy Michael ever talked to—their mothers were friends at church. Somehow, on its own, Stanley's peepee was wagging back and forth like a metronome. Michael studied the swollen knob under Stanley's belly as if it were a gizzard in the poultry shop.

"Hey, you big fruit, knock it off." Jet Musso was looming over them, a Commando, one of the thirteen-to-sixteen-year-olds who worked as lifeguards. They strutted around as if they owned the place, their pimply butts sticking out of jockstraps the coach made older boys wear in the pool area. Michael was speechless in the presence of Jet Musso and his Brillcreamed black hair. Jet's fleshy lips, curled into a perpetual sneer, obliterated any trace of Michael's existence.

Days before he met Mr. Malone, Michael had noticed Jet leering at him with eyes green as the panther's at the Audubon Park Zoo. Then one afternoon Jet grabbed Michael by the back of his T-shirt and dragged him across the gym floor. Michael flinched, sure he'd done something wrong, but Jet's touch made his skin tingle, and he went limp in the sweaty Commando's grip.

"This the boy I been telling you about," Jet said, depositing Michael like an offering at Mr. Malone's feet. Now Michael knew he was in trouble. Raised by indulgent women, he suspected men were there to punish you. He could sense Mr. Malone's furrowed brow appraising him, as though the old man could see through to his inner-most secrets, like God. Michael flashed a crooked smile, trying to look harmless and cute.

Mr. Malone's eyes lit up, his ruddy face crinkling. "Knock knock," he said.

"Who's there?" Michael stared down at his Converse high-tops.

"You."

"You who?" Michael asked, barely audible.

"Yoohoo!" Mr. Malone boomed. "Hey, no need to shout. I'm

right here," he cackled, slapping the boy on the back, then handing him a Snickers. When Jet disappeared, Michael relaxed.

Michael had spotted Mr. Malone and Jet together before, joking and whispering next to the candy machines. Now whenever he and Mr. Malone were alone talking and Jet approached, the words pouring out of Michael's mouth froze in midair like comic-book bubbles. Jet made him feel puny and ridiculous. Why would Mr. Malone want to be friends with him when he had someone like Jet?

"Tuck that midget weenie inside your fat thighs," Jet barked at Stanley, snapping the elastic strap of his badge of authority.

Then the Troopers jumped in the pool, splashing and ducking each other with vindictive savagery. Michael waded alone toward the shallow section, and Jet squatted in front of him. Michael didn't dare look up. All he could see were the curly black hairs sprouting on Jet's wet red toes.

"Hey, little buddy," Jet said hoarsely. "Mr. Malone says he'll meet you by the Ping-Pong table after lunch, okie-dokie?"

Michael bobbed from one foot to the other, flapping his hands with nervous energy, and then felt it starting to happen. Ian Vickers was swimming around him underwater, shimmering like a minnow. He torpedoed to the surface, shrieking at the top of his lungs, "Michael Higgins got a bone-on." Then the fluorescent-lit ceiling seemed to fall on top of Michael amid squeals of laughter.

MICHAEL DREADED THE end-of-the-summer award ceremony, and couldn't believe his mother planned to attend. Maxine worked downtown all day as a dentist's receptionist and was too tired at night to do anything except cook dinner, wash her mane of red hair, press clothes, and go to bed after Milton Berle.

"Just kids doing jumping jacks, then the coach hands out some stupid trophies."

"I'll be so proud," Maxine said, testing the iron with her fingertip. Her nails were chewed, with chipped vermilion polish.

"But I'm the biggest spastic in Troopers."

"Have faith in yourself," she said, starting on a shirt collar. "You can do anything you set your mind to. When I was a girl, I wanted a pair of roller skates so bad I borrowed my friend Emily's and entered a skating contest in City Park. The first prize was—guess what?"

"A pair of skates?"

"You bet, kiddo. And I'd never been on skates in my life. You should have seen how wobbly my ankles were, like a puppy taking its first steps. I fell down three times, skinned my knees, but golly, I wanted those skates. So I picked myself up—*zoom*—off I rolled. And I won, Michael. Your mother won."

Maxine had also taken apart a refrigerator motor and placed second in a talent show singing "High Hopes" with laryngitis. She had hundreds of stories that illustrated her pep and pluck, and all of them distressed her son, like being too close to a fan rattling at high-speed that any minute might spin out of control.

When the Troopers paraded double-file into the gym, a Sousa march blaring out of scratchy speakers, Maxine was perched high in the bleachers, wearing the shabby, shoulder-padded jacket of the business suit she'd been married in. With her gaunt face framed by a flowered scarf done into a turban, she stood out among the Mamie perms and Ike golf-shirts around her, a figure leftover from a black-and-white movie, a reminder of hard times. Her broad, expectant grin matched the red clutch purse balanced on her knees.

Michael wilted with embarrassment. If only he didn't look at her, he thought, he could get through this.

Trophies gleamed in rows along a table covered with a crisp white tablecloth. The gym swelled with order and optimism, smelling like floor wax and pencil erasers. With other Troopers, Michael drifted through choreographed calisthenics while Coach Harley counted "one, *two*, three, *four*." Michael flailed his arms doing jumping jacks and stiffened pale, froggy legs to complete twenty sit-ups. The eyes of all the parents in the world were burning a hole at the center of his crew cut, studying his shaky limbs and flushed face.

"In third place for Troopers," Coach Harley announced when the awards began, "Billy Blondeau." If I didn't get third, nothing, Michael thought.

"In second place, Ian Vickers," the coach boomed. Ian leaped from the floor and sprinted toward the glittering table.

"And in first place . . . Michael Higgins." Michael wasn't sure he'd heard correctly, and didn't rise until Stanley and Billy started kicking him. Michael floated across the floor to receive the golden statue, a muscular angel with outstretched wings arched over its head, as if it were doing jumping jacks to heaven. His mother sprang to her feet, applauding. Michael blinked, and for a second saw his father beside her, dressed in a streetcar conductor's uniform.

Mr. Malone was approaching the table, where he held up his hand to silence the applause.

"This summer Michael has made the most progress of any Trooper and has shown the strength of Christian character that makes this the greatest country in the world," Mr. Malone declaimed in his broad Boston accent. "To further recognize his achievements, I'd like to present him with this Timex watch."

Then Mr. Malone winked at him, and Sousa started up again.

Michael's first impulse was to see if his father really was there in a streetcar conductor's uniform. Soon his mother was standing over him with enormous shoulders, red lips puckered to devour him with kisses. She was alone.

He brushed her off, and she leaned over to embrace Mr. Malone, her eyes moist and glistening.

"Mrs. Higgins, I want to tell you again what a fine young man you're raising," Mr. Malone began. Michael tried on the watch. The chunky stretch band was ten times too large for his pencil-thin wrist. The face was yellowed, the crystal cracked, and it wasn't ticking. Michael tried to wind the stem, but Mr. Malone's Timex was frozen at another moment.

Jet Musso slouched against the gym wall, smoking one of the cigarettes Mr. Malone always bought him. Panther-eyes narrowed, he watched Michael, smoke drifting lazily from his nostrils. He was snickering, as if this were some sick joke only he understood.

"DON'T LOOK AT ME. I feel like a gerbil," Michael sputtered, averting his right cheek so Mr. Malone couldn't see the swollen jaw. Michael had been riding shotgun on the way home from the dentist's office on Barrone Street where his mother worked, and Dr. Roche had just pulled an impacted baby tooth. When Michael spotted Mr. Malone seated by a window in the streetcar, he'd abandoned the conductor and almost leapt into the old sailor's arms.

"Must hurt like the dickens," Mr. Malone said with a slow whistle.

"Where are you heading?" Michael couldn't imagine Mr. Malone's grown-up life.

"Over to see an apartment for rent. You could come visit, and we'd raise a little hell together."

"Neat." Michael's mother and Aunt Jewell never cursed. "Hell" thrilled him. His jaw throbbed and he winced, biting down on the gauze pad. Something was missing.

"Try not to talk." Mr. Malone put his arm around Michael's shoulder, drawing the boy toward him. Michael smiled and closed his eyes, auditioning for the part: everybody thinks I'm sick, and this is my daddy taking me home.

Yes, you can be my daddy.

"Chin up, champ. I'll ring you tomorrow," Mr. Malone said, getting off at Erato Street.

Through the open window, Michael watched the back of the gray crew cut crossing the intersection under a street lamp. He started waving, waving, and suddenly Mr. Malone turned and, with a huge gap-toothed smile, waved back.

Yes, you can. . . .

"Later, gator," Mr. Malone shouted to Michael from across the street. A lopsided grin spread across the boy's distorted face.

Heads turned, nodding, giving him the odd sensation that he was part of the boisterous world around him.

Yes.

"JEEZ, THIS *PUTA* in Lima had the loosest twat I ever seen." When Mr. Malone chuckled, his turkey-wattle jiggled.

Michael squirmed, cutting his steak into tiny pieces at the dinette set in Mr. Malone's new apartment in the Dorian Arms, a brick building with fake columns at Erato and St. Charles. He didn't understand most of Mr. Malone's dirty talk, but they never had steak at home, only red beans or brisket soup. So every Wednesday after school he came to spend the afternoon at the Dorian Arms with Mr. Malone, who told him tales about Malaysia, Ceylon, and Holland, every country he ever imagined.

Mr. Malone would prance around the kitchenette, sipping whiskey and grilling steaks. In spite of his bellowing, Michael noticed something old-ladyish about how he fussed with tin foil and dish towels. Everything had to be just-so, like at his aunt's house: which chair he sat in, the rooster salt-and-pepper shakers so far apart, the plastic place mats to the edge of the table.

First they would play Ping-Pong in the spare bedroom with the door closed, and afterward Mr. Malone would fix dinner and they would eat. Then Mr. Malone would start with the stories and jokes: big-tittied ladies in various ports, priests and altar boys and what fruits on the wharves had wanted to do to him. A queer in San Francisco had told him, "If you got a pickle, I got a nickel." Michael laughed and laughed with a whinnying gasp, the laughter choked down inside him, trying to get out. It all sounded so funny, although he wasn't sure why.

Michael was most fascinated by the Buddha on the end table near the sofa. Mr. Malone said it was from a country called Formosa. He was a Buddhist.

"Think that sad sack nailed to the planks over the altar is going to bring you peace? Look at him!" Mr. Malone said, stretching the YMCA sweatshirt over his protruding belly. "He wants us to suffer like him, get all bent out of shape by right and wrong. He needs to be goosed. Lighten up, for Christ's sake."

"But Jesus is the Son of God, who so loved the world . . . ," Michael protested, reciting from the catechism he was learning.

"Save it for the priests. One thing I learned as a kid, when their mouths are full you can say any damn thing you want. Hey, how about some cherry pie with vanilla ice cream?"

Michael brightened. The old sailor was his best friend, even though he was devastated about Mr. Malone and Jesus.

That evening he didn't ride shotgun, but huddled on the side-seat of the swaying streetcar. The conductor had pulled a ribbed black curtain around himself like bat wings so that he wouldn't be blinded by the glare inside reflecting off his window. Michael contemplated the conductor's oxfords beneath the curtain and thought about the Buddha on Mr. Malone's end table, so ageless and sexless. And with that knowing smile.

"YOUR T-SHIRT IS in the way," Mr. Malone had said at first.

The next week Michael's blue jeans had to go. After playing Ping-Pong, Mr. Malone had been massaging him on top of the Ping-Pong table. Gives muscle tone, he promised.

"This is what real athletes do after a game," Mr. Malone said, rubbing his hands together. Unlike most boys, who collected baseball cards and memorized batting averages, Michael couldn't name a single athlete. And he wasn't used to being touched. The pounding and pulling hurt. Other parts tickled. Mr. Malone's calloused hands were rough, but Michael didn't want to complain like a big sissy. He balled his hands into fists and thought of Shotgun, the boy on the Rice Krispies box.

The Ping-Pong table was in the middle of an empty bedroom. As usual, Mr. Malone had closed the door. Michael was lying on a rose towel at the center of the table in white underpants, staring at a stain in the ceiling.

Touch me where?

One of Mr. Malone's hands swept down and grabbed Michael's crotch. Michael shot a glance straight up. Mr. Malone's lower lip was wet and quivering, and his breath smelled like whiskey and peppermints.

Put your mouth where?

A clock was ticking behind the closed door, and a faint roar of traffic filtered in from St. Charles. The ceiling lowered, and the windowless white box dimmed, airless as an engine room. Mr. Malone's hand glided down Michael's smooth stomach.

Make it feel good where?

Michael tensed, eyes watering and toes twitching as in the dentist's chair. Was the old sailor going to punish him? Our Father, make this go away.

No, I won't. . . .

Michael sat up and reached for his T-shirt, unsure where the words were coming from. "It would be—against God."

"Now I want you to know I've never asked any other boy to do that. You remind me of myself as a kid. You're specially chosen, you know?" Michael saw Jet Musso's lip curl, aiming a cynical stream of smoke at the ceiling.

"Not even Jet?" It just slipped out. Was this what those two did together?

Mr. Malone folded the towel into a perfect square. "I've known Jet since he was your age. We used to be a lot closer, like you and me are now. He said you were the kind of boy who. . . . Why, what did he tell you?"

"He said you were an old fart who bought him lots of stuff," Michael lied, striking back. He kicked on his jeans, then threw open the door.

"I could eat a goddamn horse," Mr. Malone announced to the empty daylight outside.

Touch me where?

The bronze Buddha gleamed on the end table, silent as the Three Monkeys Aunt Jewell had given him: Think No Evil, Hear No Evil, Speak No Evil. Michael was no longer sure that what he thought had happened actually had. He'd made it up in his own twisted mind. While Mr. Malone banged pots in the kitchenette, Michael stared through Venetian blinds slats at the street, thinking about Mr. Malone's red Keds, his nylon gym shorts, his "Go, Tigers!" sweatshirt. Now it seemed like some Halloween costume. He wasn't really a father but some comic-book monster of an overgrown kid.

No, you can't be. . . .

Michael fidgeted on the turquoise section-sofa wrapped around a corner of the room. Outside a streetcar clacked past. He wished he were on it, but felt hungry and knew his mother wasn't expecting him for dinner. Putting on his socks, he could taste disgust on his dry tongue. This was what it felt like to be his father: angry, jumpy, ready to eat and run. He laced up his high tops, and then flipped on the transistor radio lying on the kidney-shaped coffee table. Frankie Avalon filled the room singing "Only the Lonely."

Then steaks hit the pan and started to sizzle.

BEES WERE BUZZING in and out of wisteria blossoms drooping from the vine that grew across the rusty screen of Michael's bedroom window. His desk faced the window, where he squinted with a stubby pencil in hand, filling in the blanks of his sixth-grade science workbook. "(B) Phototropism" matched "(7) Growing toward the light."

Maxine was squealing with girlish laughter next to the squat black phone in the hall, so different from the strict-Mom voice, the tired-Mom voice she used with Michael. The only time she sounded serious on the phone was when his father called. Then she spit out syllables. Afterward her bedroom door slammed and bedsprings sank.

Her radiant face appeared in the doorway, frizzy red hair gathered by a rubber band into a ponytail. "High hopes, I've got high hopes," she was singing in off-key soprano, "high, apple-pie-in-the-sky hopes."

"That guy is a stitch," she said, sitting cross-legged on Michael's bed in a baggy man's dress shirt.

"Dr. Roche?"

"Mr. Malone. And guess what?"

"I've got homework to do." Michael hadn't seen Mr. Malone in months, but knew he still kept in touch with his mother.

"He's going to take you to *Disneyland* after school is out next month," she said, clapping. "He has a sister in Long Beach he's dying to visit, then *you two* can spend a few days in Disneyland. He'll pay for the plane and motel and *everything*, honest Indian. It's like winning a prize on TV. This could be your big chance for the movies."

No, I won't. . . .

The lavender scent of wisteria wafted through the window along with the *Father Knows Best* theme from the neighbor's TV. "Starring Robert Young," the announcer said.

No, you can't be. . . .

"California!" Maxine reached over to shake Michael's shoulders. "Hollywood. And a room in some swank motel with a swimming pool full of movie stars. Wish I could go."

Touch me where?

Michael's cheeks flushed crimson.

"What do you say?"

Michael stiffened and turned around to face his mother.

Put your mouth where?

"You'd get to fly in an air-o-plane." She stretched out her arms, waving them up and down.

"So why don't *you* go?" he asked.

"He didn't invite *me* along." Maxine's arms fell, and her eyes teared. "Look, honey, I'm sorry you don't have a real daddy. Believe me, nobody's sorrier. But sometimes in this life we don't get what we need from the same people we want it from. So now this perfectly swell man, who's been like a father to you, wants to take you on a trip—"

"Words are all blurry. I think I need glasses." Michael looked up at his mother, and then yanked the silence around himself like a streetcar conductor's curtain.

Mr. Malone and the trip to Disneyland came up every day for

a week, then Maxine let it drop. Michael spent that summer lying next to the window abuzz with bees, polishing his new black-framed glasses and reading every book he could lay his hands on. He haunted the neighborhood branch of the library, checking out books from the grown-up section then sprawling in the tan La-Z Boy his father had left behind, not even closing his book when Maxine came home, plunked down grocery bags, and rattled dishes.

"Such a quiet boy," his mother and Aunt Jewell would comment.

Michael put the golden trophy of the angel reaching toward heaven, the Timex, a plastic sports ring with a genuine ruby Mr. Malone had given him, his YMCA T-shirt and shorts, and the stamp album into a Campbell's soup box.

Then he shoved the box under his bed as far as it would go.

ONE EVENING SOON after his sixteenth birthday, Michael Higgins sat by a window in the St. Charles streetcar, on his way to a bar called La Casa de los Marinos in the French Quarter to meet Hermine, the girl from English he was in love with. In a faded black turtleneck, he was reading a fat paperback titled *Atlas Shrugged*, scratching the bristly head of hair he had singed the night before with a cigarette lighter and candle.

At Erato Street, the streetcar stopped in front of the Dorian Arms. As far as he knew, Mr. Malone still lived there. After the summer of his eleventh year, he'd lost touch with the old sailor, except for one drunken evening last October with Hermine. Driving past Erato Street, he'd made Hermine stop her Mercury, insisting he wanted her to meet another Buddhist. At the beginning, what had attracted him to Hermine was the bronze Buddha she wore on a leather thong around her neck, and her honey-colored hair and olive corduroys that always smelled of incense. A mutual interest in Nietzsche and Cutty Sark developed later.

"Knock knock," Michael had said as a milky eye appeared through a cracked door.

Mr. Malone blinked. He didn't seem to recognize the scrawny student dressed like Woody Guthrie, but invited them both in.

"This is Hermine, a fellow Buddhist," Michael blurted out, bouncing from one foot to another along the shag carpet. It was important for him to be there with Hermine, although he didn't know why. She'd already met his mother at Dr. Roche's office.

The Buddha was still on the end table, and the door to the Ping-Pong room closed. Two young men lounged on the turquoise sofa watching *77 Sunset Strip* on a color TV. The one in the tight black jeans turned out to be Jet Musso.

While Hermine crouched in front of Mr. Malone's Buddha, Jet cornered Michael in the kitchenette, draping an arm around his shoulder. His shirt was maroon velour, unbuttoned to the waist, exposing a hairy chest. "Turned out different than I figured," he slurred with boozy bravado in Michael's ear.

Michael gave a full-throated laugh at what he saw: Jet the mighty Commando through the wrong end of a telescope. His English Leather cologne and stale whiskey breath smelled of youth gone sour, stuck at a certain hour like the Timex. Jet was still one of Mr. Malone's boys—and always would be—until someday he turned into Mr. Malone.

"After all the grief you put the old man through, I thought you'd be little Miss Priss. You're more like a hobo," Jet said, stroking the wispy hairs on Michael's chin, "but still chicken."

Jet's eyes were hooded and bloodshot, and his raw mouth looked as if he'd been making out with sandpaper.

"Tell you one thing," Jet said, raising his voice, "your girlfriend's got one fine pair of tits on her."

Michael blushed and turned around to survey the living room.

"Everything is just the way it used to be," Michael said. "I remember how—"

"Don't let memory play tricks on you," Mr. Malone cut in, busying himself with ice cubes and cocktail napkins. When he asked Michael for the third time about his mother, Jet's friend disappeared without a word into the Ping-Pong room, clicking the door closed behind him.

That had been Michael's signal to leave.

The streetcar's accordion doors folded shut in front of the Dorian Arms, and then it lurched forward. Michael had spotted Jet Musso only once since, sliding into a silver-haired gentleman's Cadillac in front of a bar on Bourbon Street.

Dog-earing his page, Michael stared past his own sullen reflection in the window pane, into invisible crevices of the darkness outside. The box with the golden trophy and gym clothes and stamp album was still under his bed, bearded with dust balls, and his mother was after him to clean it out. She complained that her child-model and award-winning athlete had become an unkempt stranger who gulped his food, read at the table like a boarder, then slammed closed the door to his room. "Like a complete unknown, like a rolling stone" were the words of a whiny harmonica music seeping at all hours from under his door with the scent of sandalwood incense. Michael had no idea who the things belonged to in that box his mother kept harping on.

They were somebody else's.

Michael sank back into *Atlas Shrugged*, lulled into a trance. Approaching the lights at Lee Circle, the streetcar conductor wrapped himself behind his night drape. Michael glanced up from his book as the streetcar swung past the YMCA then veered right onto Carondolet Street, the second place it changed course to follow a sudden bend in the Mississippi. Again, it was as if the river had said *no* to the land but continued flowing, in a different direction. The conductor, a silhouette as mysterious as fate behind his curtain, clanged the bell as the streetcar rattled through a corridor of office buildings, bringing Michael toward the Greek and Latino sailor bars that lined the dark, narrow streets of the port.

La Vie en Rose Construction Co.

"NEW ORLEANS A CITY built on top a swamp," the airport shuttle driver recited as the Garden of Memories loomed to the right. "Bodies are sealed above ground in them little white houses. You can't put 'em in the ground account of the water table."

The haggard man winced behind dark glasses as the driver's spiel worked its magic with the rowdy conventioneers in the van, who began to sing off-key choruses of "When the Saints Go Marching In." Every time he flew in or out of New Orleans, this information was there to greet him like a gargoyle at the gate. He had just bid goodbye to a friend dying of breast cancer, and now he was coming home to his ailing mother. This gargoyle and he were old friends, but he hoped this once to be spared acknowledging it.

The pirate Dominican taxi had been by at five that morning to pick him up for LaGuardia, and still flush with Cuba Libres and goodbyes, he had maintained an animated discussion with the driver about—what else?—how the hell could anyone live in New York. He had been gone the whole month of August, hadn't slept in two nights, and now all he wanted was to sip a glass of wine in his courtyard and crawl asleep between the sheets.

Over the past three years he gradually had been moving back to New Orleans, and in his suitcases was the last load of rugs, papers, and photographs. This time he had even taken the silverware. He was hanging up his freelance photography business in New York, capitulating to origins. He had won every battle, but had lost the war for independence from this place. And as the shuttle turned onto a narrow street of wrought-iron balconies spilling over with begonias, he was relieved to admit it.

With his last burst of strength, he trundled the bulging suitcases from the van and threw them against a green gate, behind which was a serene rose-colored courtyard. He identified with this aspect of Mediterranean architecture, nondescript on the outside, like this shabby fence, but with a luxuriant interior landscape hidden behind walls. He couldn't wait to slam the gate shut onto the world, with its incurable diseases, honking horns, and aggrieved parties.

Unlocking the wooden gate, he was met by the glare of eight men in purple T-shirts, black pants, and gold baseball caps. Slouching on patio chairs in the shade of the live oak that dominated the courtyard, they were sitting around a battered blue water cooler set on his grandmother's oak table, leisurely chipping mortar from bricks heaped in piles at their feet. In the shock of intrusion, he and the men just stared at each other, as once, while washing dishes at his sink on West 14th Street, he had locked eyes with a cat burglar passing along the fire escape. His own resentment wilted in the waves of misgiving he felt coming at him. Lowering his eyes, he wheeled his suitcases one by one across wobbly bridges scattered over dank trenches of corroded pipes. The purple T-shirts read, in flowery script, La Vie en Rose Construction Co.

"How's it going?" a portly man growled. "You Mr. Weems in apartment B, right?"

"Yes I am, and I'm real tired. You all doing a little work out here?" Mr. Weems ventured, defying the obvious.

"All these pipes in the courtyard gotta come up. They a gas leak here, big time. We been at it for a month, be at it for another one to come. Just got the toe-mice out your kitchen. Had to tear down a coupla walls."

Hoisting the largest suitcase over the apartment threshold, the wheels popped off. He bent down to scoop them up with pale, shaking hands while the eight men studied him. Then he walked inside, choking on the fine white dust that covered everything. All the family antiques he had so carefully restored were stacked in one corner under a shroud of cement chips. His table lamp squatted on the floor with the shade ripped off, an outdoor spotlight beaming into his eyes.

He kicked the door closed and sat down on a suitcase to survey the damage as, on the other side of the green storm shutter, an electric saw blade cut into a length of pipe.

DERWOOD WEEMS DIDN'T even begin to unpack his suitcases for three days. Most of that time he spent in bed in chili pepper boxer shorts eating fudge-ripple ice cream with ear plugs in.

Halfheartedly he studied the "for rent" classifieds in the *Times-Picayune*, but in the end, didn't make a single call. He hauled the construction debris out of his bedroom, swabbed the floor three times, then closed off the rest of the apartment. He kept the jalousie shutters shut and the bedroom air conditioner running, sealing himself inside like an eggplant forgotten at the bottom of the refrigerator. He cancelled his photographic shoots and didn't return calls.

Beep. "Hello, Woody honey, Mama. Guess you decided to stay longer in New York, because I been ringing you forever. Your number up there's been disconnected, so I don't know where in the world you are. Everything's fine here. That new medicine is working real good, and I don't have so much fluid. Now you ring me soon as you get in, hear?" *Beep*.

He let the message erase.

Like people enduring a siege, his neighbors only emerged at dusk to scamper to the corner store or dry cleaners, then bolted themselves inside, away from clanging pipes, jackhammers, and crashing loads of bricks. On the second evening home, when Derwood at last stumbled outside after the workers had packed up, he ran into his neighbor, Irene Guidry. Fingering the leaves of her shriveled bougainvillea, she reminded him of a photo he printed last spring of a Bosnian woman who had endured the shelling in Sarajevo by hiding for two years in a crawl space.

"Guess the dust smothered these," she was murmuring to herself. "I see you're back, Derwood. Bet you wish you weren't."

"Irene, when are they going to turn the water and gas back on? How long is this going to last? I'm definitely moving."

"That's all I thought of . . . for the first month," she snorted. "That's when I asked the workers about their progress and tried to reason with Eustice."

Eustice LaRose, their landlady's light-skinned handyman, had been in and out of the courtyard flashing his gold tooth and dusting off his chinos ever since Derwood moved in. He was the kind of fast-talking man his father had taught him to avoid at the racetrack.

"The day after you left," Irene began with a deep breath, already exhausted by the litany of disasters she was about to recount, "Eustice found what he calls 'toe-mice' in your kitchen wall and proceeded to call the termite man. The termite man drilled into the courtyard to bury bug poison and proceeded to hit a gas pipe. The gas man came and proceeded to impound the meter, and Eustice sweet-talked Conchita into replacing all the service pipes in the courtyard and the woodwork in our kitchens, though most of this doesn't need to be done. He started his own company and will be a millionaire by Christmas."

"By Christmas?"

"You know Eustice. Every night he probably runs home to study the *Time-Life* books on plumbing and carpentry so he can tell his crew what to do the next day. Now I just accept it as Allah's will and hide upstairs all day while they tear out my kitchen floor, looking for Formosan termites. I haven't had a bath in ten days. Yesterday at Mass they offered me literature on the parish homeless shelter."

"Isn't this an awful mess? Hi, Woody, welcome home, sugar."

They were joined by their landlady Conchita, tiptoeing in stiletto heels along the plywood over the trenches with her blind Lhasa apso waddling behind. "Over here, hon. Come on, Choo-Choo."

Conchita Claret Charbonnet, from Hammond, was accustomed to tour the courtyard at dusk every evening with a highball in hand, surveying her kingdom. She was a sixtyish former Strawberry Queen whose hair got bigger and bigger as it turned blacker and blacker. Conchita had been a secretary who retired to marry her boss and lover, Monsieur Charbonnet. The elderly Parisian dressed up every day in a loop bow tie and double-breasted brown suit, as if he were about to promenade along the Champs Elysées, although he never moved from his glass of Johnny Walker Red in front of the blaring TV. Nobody knew how old he was, but if it was any indication, he claimed Edith Piaf as an early conquest. "After she make sex with me," he told Derwood last Mardi Gras, "her voice it really improve."

An engineer, Monsieur Charbonnet had been invited by Governor Huey P. Long to teach Louisiana how to drill for oil. During that era he bought this Creole cottage, built in the 1820's, and fixed up the slave quarters behind it into apartments. His first wife, an artist, had made the complex beautiful, and it appeared in several Vieux Carré patio books. Conchita had made it interesting for herself, filling it with the handsomest young men she could lay her hands on, including Eustice LaRose.

"That fat plumber, the minister, thought I was flirting with him," she confided hoarsely to Derwood and Irene. "He said 'I do believe you flirting with me, Miss Conchita. You and me should step out some time. I like white women.' The nerve. I told him, 'Look, Reverend, I'm a married lady, and besides, I don't date nigras.'" She furrowed her clown-white brow to whisper in mock horror, "You think I want to get Ebola?"

Sniffing among the rubble, the Lhasa apso almost slid into a ditch. Conchita screamed, "Choo-Choo, remember you've had your bath!" Derwood yanked the yelping animal by its collar back onto the bricks as Monsieur Charbonnet appeared through the shutters, grasping a cane in each hand.

"Stop this sheeet!"

"Sweetheart, Choo-Choo almost fell in a ditch. His cataracts won't let him see where he's going to make peepee."

"I bet he can still smell pussy," Monsieur Charbonnet remarked. "I am so tired of this sheeet. All day long, *boom boom boom.* If they are not finish by Friday, I fire them all." And swiveling his toothpick body around on two canes, he faced Conchita. "And you, too!"

Derwood led the dog by its collar across the courtyard to the Charbonnets' door. Irene scurried into her kitchen, and Derwood let the gate slam behind him as he burst onto Burgundy Street, where the gay bars were hosting a weekend celebration called Southern Decadence.

THE DEVIL SURE WAS flexing the biceps in his left arm tonight, Derwood thought, stepping out of the gate into a group of balding men in black leather chaps and bare butts with hardware dangling from every crevice and joint of their bodies. They were carrying go-cups of beer toward a corner bar called The Rough House, where a crowd of identical creatures milled under a canopy of white and baby-blue helium balloons. Derwood decided he might as well stroll in that direction toward Rouses.

Once, while fixing the kitchen sink drain, Eustice LaRose had told Derwood his vision about homosexuals. Eustice was not only an ordained Pentecostal minister, but also considered himself a prophet. "When homosexuals die," he explained, loosening a socket with a wrench and looking straight at Derwood, "they go straight into the left arm of the devil down in hell." Then he tightened the socket with a grimace.

"Now a while back, I had me a woman who was mighty fine in bed," Eustice continued, cleaning the drain trap, "best I ever did have. But I gave her up to please the Lord, and to marry a woman who'd be a good mother to my children."

Derwood thought about what unhappy people plumbers always were, mucking around in other people's waste all day. And he suspected, trying to make sense of this conversation, that the woman who was so mighty fine in bed probably wasn't a woman at all.

Derwood's trip to the grocery on Royal Street was waylaid into an all-night drunk on dollar-fifty well drinks at a bar called Your Little Red Wagon on North Rampart. That night the club featured an ancient drag queen who looked like a tax auditor and sang "We're in the Money" in pig Latin in front of a gold lamé backdrop tacked across the storefront window. You can lead a whore to water but you can't make her drown, Derwood chuckled to himself as he fell into the hairy arms of a bald man with no eyebrows named Earl. Earl's keys jangled when he walked, and his slow smile exposed rotten front teeth. "Duke, Duke, Duke," he kept singing, "Duke of Earl," a song that Derwood hadn't heard since high school.

"I'd love to invite you home for a drink, Earl," Derwood protested, coming to his senses, "but they're tearing the damn courtyard apart to put in new plumbing and didn't even have the decency to turn my water back on before they split this evening. I won't have water all weekend."

"For true? Who's doing the job?" the Duke of Earl asked, with a sudden professional interest.

"Some outfit Eustice LaRose put together called La Vie en Rose."

"That Vie en Rose don't know shit. I'm a plumber, hear, and it ain't nothing to turn someone's water back on if the pipes is laid right while you working on them. Lemme go by my daddy's on Dauphine," he said, shooting Derwood a sweetly rotten smile as he massaged his thigh, "and get my wrench, know what I mean, Woody? Gimme your address on this napkin."

Oh God, what had he gone and done? Of all things, a plumber! Derwood's head was spinning as he lay stretched out on his crummy sheets, hoping the doorbell wouldn't ring. But it did. He stumbled barefoot in his shorts across the plywood bridges toward the courtyard gate, ready to make any excuse. When he opened it, there stood an enormous woman with a cascade of curly red locks in a kelly-green dress, hand on hip.

"Woody, where y'at? It's me. So whatcha think, cher? Pretty foxy?" the figure gushed, doing a runway twirl and voguing in through the gate.

"Man, look at this mess. Them guys don't know they ass from a hole in the ground," Earl mumbled in disgust, swaggering bow-legged in beige half-heel pumps that went *tap-tap-tapping* across the plywood bridges. Yanking a wrench out of a beaded handbag, he hiked the slip up to his crotch and squatted like a bull frog to inspect the water main.

"Piece of cake," Earl said.

Leaning over too far, his thin soles slipped on the mucky plywood, and he skidded feetfirst into a sinkhole under the pipes, up to his knees in fetid water. With a sucking sound, he step-kicked one meaty calf over the pipes to strike a vampish pose with one bare foot resting demurely on his knee.

"I'll get you out. Here, grab my hand."

"Whoa, not so fast. Where my shoe at? Don't rip them twenty-dollar panty hose, hear?"

As Derwood and Earl grappled over the ditch, Conchita's pale yellow kimono appeared framed in the French door of the Charbonnets' apartment. "Woody, is that you, honey? Who's that lady in the ditch? She with you?"

Conchita padded out in velour slippers to get a better look.

"It's the plumber, Conchita. Everything's all right," Derwood boomed in a businesslike baritone. "We're just trying to turn my water on."

"Turn *who* on? At this hour of the morning? Hey, she's a redhead. She's a redheaded plumber! I never seen such a redheaded plumber before." Conchita thought this a hilarious observation and insisted on helping hoist Earl out of the ditch, her mascara-smudged eyes widening as she grabbed hold of his thick, tattooed forearm. "How would you and the plumber like to come in for a teensy-weensy nightcap?" she slurred. "My husband's gone beddy-bye."

Heavy-lidded, she gave the mud-splattered Duchess of Earl a

slow up-and-down. "You sure you a plumber?"

Earl seemed furious. He'd lost a new Dillard's pump in the sinkhole and wanted to go straight home to change his dress. The offer of a shower tempted Derwood, but when he considered the Duchess's other charms, he declined. They exchanged phone numbers, and for the next few days—during which Derwood was on the phone to New York every minute of the day and night telling everybody he was moving back—Earl didn't call.

"MAMA, I'VE TRIED everything to come home, but it isn't working out . . . No, I don't want to own a house here anymore . . . Because my expectations have changed. I expect things to work, and for things to work people have got to. It takes more than a pound of crawfish, a couple of beers, and a Carnival parade to make me happy these days. I guess New York has changed me . . . Thanks, but you don't need to remind me this is where I'm from—it's a great place to be *from*. And a great place to come *back to*, once in a while. In the meantime . . . Permanently? Inside that tomb with you. That's where I'll end up permanently. Then I'll settle down for a century or two. But right now, to find another apartment and move again, I might as well move to Paris for all the trouble. I don't know. Something tells me I may never get out of here. How you feeling? . . . Well, why did he change the medication if the other one was working so well? Try it for awhile, I guess . . . Yeah, I'll be out to see you this weekend. First thing I'll do is check out your hot water . . . I love you, too."

Derwood always knew New Orleans would be his undoing, he thought as he hung up. It had taken him twenty years to get out, and another twenty to get back, transformed from a blond catalog model into a mature photographer. Unlike most New Yorkers, who thought they could take the slow, sensual Crescent City by storm, Derwood understood the value of lifelong contacts. No, here he wouldn't edit and print for the World News Service, but at least he could shoot the right weddings and Mardi Gras courts. And this would leave him time for his own projects, like the photo essay on New Orleans cemeteries. The creative possibilities here seemed endless.

And so did the destructive.

At night he could feel the city sinking back into the swamp it rose from, a miasma of hereditary alcoholism, violence, and dementia. He could sense hideous tumors blooming like bayou orchids inside the lethargic bodies that sleepwalked the streets. Swatting at mosquitoes on his balcony, he stared down into the Venice of trenches in the moonlit courtyard below, examining for signs and portents the brackish entrails that lay two feet beneath the surface of a city that so charmed visitors. Just below the pipes floated a soggy bed of cypress logs placed by French settlers and their slaves on top of a snake-infested swamp.

I know where I'm from, he thought.

Mosquitoes already had begun to breed in the stagnant ditches, and Formosan termites were devouring the city alive. The termites could only be stopped here and there, a bathroom or kitchen at a time, by endless restorations like this one. Sixty percent of the primordial live oaks shading the city were already being hollowed out from below by these insects brought over from Taiwan aboard World War II freighters. This species only swarmed during three or four evenings in May, ferocious to fuck each other and then nest before their double wings fell off at 10 p.m. like a Darwinian Last Call.

The wrought-iron courtyard furniture had been abandoned to the August rains, and in a matter of weeks was as barnacled with rust as the heaps of corroded pipes that lay next to it. The spongy night drove Derwood back into the air conditioning, where he slipped into a deep sleep. He dreamed of a dark reservoir filled with naked swimmers. They were clamoring for him to *jump in, jump in* but he knew the tank was bottomless, stretching into the bowels of the earth. He hesitated at the edge of the water that wound deeper and deeper down into nowhere, and woke with a start at the first low rumblings of thunder.

It was about to storm.

FOR TWO NIGHTS Derwood Weems was held prisoner in his slave quarter. All lines to the outside world were cut—electricity, gas, water, and telephone. He survived on sardine sandwiches and brushed his teeth with Dr. Pepper. The hurricane had passed yesterday, but still the shutters were locked tightly from the outside. Through the louvers, he could see the courtyard was nothing but flooded moats with pipes sticking out at jagged angles.

All of his neigbors had escaped days ago, when the workers from La Vie En Rose Construction Co. got into a violent argument with Eustice. After they had done the most backbreaking part of the job, digging ditches and pulling up old pipes, Eustice wanted to lower their wages, or he threatened to fire them and bring in even cheaper workers. That was their side. Eustice, on the other hand, admitted these guys were just preachers and homeless men he'd recruited at the Vision of Zion soup kitchen on Perdido Street. Now that he had to connect new pipes, he needed trained plumbers and electricians, and these other men could continue working as assistants. Derwood didn't know whom to believe.

For several mornings leading up to the blow out, Derwood was woken up by the stentorian voice of a minister gesturing in the shade under the live oak, preaching about Joshua. "Now Jericho was an old city, and Jericho was an evil city, eaten up by weevils and sin. And Joshua had him a trumpet and stood outside them gates, blowing to let a little *light* in, blowing to let a little *justice* in, blowing to let a little bro-ther-ly *love* in . . . ."

"And the wall come tumbling down," was the uproarious response of the men, listening with shovels and pipes in hand.

This was not a good sign.

Work came to a standstill, and within a few days, Eustice fired the crew. But without a week's severance, they refused to allow new workers in. They camped out in the courtyard overnight, so Derwood heard more about corrupt Jericho, Joshua, and his golden horn. He let them keep beer in his refrigerator and call home from his phone, and only stopped short of offering them space on the floor.

That evening Conchita waltzed in from Arnaud's in a lilac mother-of-the-bride's dress and marched around and around the courtyard with a tumbler of scotch in her hand. "Go home and go to bed, you naughty boys," she screeched, "before I call the cops."

At three in the morning Eustice brought over the sheriff to evict them for trespassing. Conchita told him that the takeover had driven off all her tenants, which was almost true, although Derwood didn't know how much longer he could have taken it. So early the next morning, when a hurricane unexpectedly veered west from Pensacola and headed toward southeastern Louisiana, Eustice came by to test the storm shutters. He double-latched all door and window shutters from the outside while Derwood was upstairs sleeping off the battle of Jericho.

By the time Derwood got up and stumbled to a balcony door, the hurricane was already starting to hit. He noticed a broken wire flapping in the wind outside. When he tried to call Conchita, his line was dead. The last time he saw her, from between the louvers, she was trying to fold Monsieur Charbonnet's palsied limbs into the Buick in the driveway. A suitcase had blown open, and undergarments were twirling furiously around the courtyard. Conchita was screaming "Choo-Choo, Choo-choo," trying to find the Lhasa apso. Later Derwood heard the car start up, and after ramming every shutter in the apartment with a solid brass coat stand, he curled up in bed to listen to stinging sheets of rain whip across the house, bombarding the roof with tiny green acorns.

THE BLOATED LHASA apso with a rhinestone barette was floating belly-up in a trench, next to a beige pump. A mandarin silk pajama top, an alarming red, dangled from a top branch of the live oak.

The waters had receded, coating everything with a primal gray slime.

Derwood kicked through the acorns and branches that matted the slick courtyard, his blue eyes blinded by morning glare. He'd leapt up to embrace the flashing grin of his jailer and liberator when Eustice arrived to unfasten the storm shutters the second morning after the storm hit. Like a trapped animal, Derwood had almost destroyed the apartment trying to gnaw his way out. In one particular hole, over the stove, he had burrowed with a butcher knife as far as the original brick wall of the slave quarter.

Eustice apologized for his terrible mistake, but otherwise was all business.

"Yes sirree, it's a new day for me," he kept repeating, as he tossed tools into canvas sacks. "Lucky the Charbonnets asked me to come by to look for they pooch," he said, glancing at the dead dog floating in a trench, "or you could've been locked in there till kingdom come. They staying out by her sister's house across the lake till Thanksgiving. Mr. Charbonnet ailing and Miss Conchita ain't about to drag him back to this holeful of toe-mice."

"When will the work start up again?" Derwood wanted to know, calculating how long it would take to haul his things out.

"Not for a long time now. I'm bailing out of this town and following the storm down the coast. La Vie en Rose got a brand new bag, and we gonna be cleaning up after the hurricane. We're talking exclusive home reconstruction and insurance megabucks, get me? You should see Biloxi. It a mess. By the way, babe, got a plumber gonna work with us name of Earl who says if I see Woody over by Miss Conchita, be sure to tell him 'way to go!'"

A flock of sparrows, driven off by the construction project, had returned to the live oak, now split to one side. Morning birdsong joined the high whine of an air conditioner in allegro accompaniment to the Creole Queen's calliope on the levee, belting out "Do You Know What It Means to Miss New Orleans?" The worst part of his incarceration was Derwood had run out of cigarettes, so he and Eustice sat smoking on the rusted patio chairs under the tree, Derwood plotting how to revive his career in New York, Eustice flush with plans to make a killing on the devastated Gulf Coast.

Suddenly the sparrows surged all at once from the tree top into a black funnel of wings shrieking to a nearby roof. The sound almost tore the top of Derwood's head off. The two men jerked backward, gazing up into the quivering branches, but before Derwood knew what was happening, the quivering became a massive sway.

And then a splintering.

The tree trunk split open like papier-mâché, tumbling down on top of the two natives smoking together after the storm. Derwood could feel the warmth of Eustice's limbs entwined with his own, but couldn't lift either his arms or legs as a salty syrup that tasted like blood seeped into his mouth. He thrashed his head in the struggle to free himself, finally surrendering his panic to a familiar comfort that closed over his head like dark water.

A group of early-morning revelers with sausage balloons tied around their heads stopped to marvel. The top of a huge live oak had just come crashing to Burgundy Street through a green wooden fence, exposing the radiant pink flesh of a French Quarter courtyard. "Whoa, did you see that?" they asked each other, as a parked car smacked by a gnarled limb let out its supersonic wail. Then, checking their map, they ambled toward the Mississippi, looking for the blackjack tables and another cold one.

Open Mike

THERE MUST BE hundreds of kids who have wound up dead in the French Quarter. Eva Pierce was just one of them. Everywhere you walk in the neighborhood you see fliers about them Scotch-taped to lamp posts: *Information Wanted* or *$5,000 Reward.* And below is a blurry snapshot of some scruffy young person. After Eva's body was discovered, bundled inside a blue Tommy Hilfiger comforter floating in Bayou St. John, the girl's mother moved down here from Idaho or Iowa or Ohio—however you pronounce it—and blanketed the Quarter with those signs. She even printed her daughter's final poem on the flier, but no dice. The fifteen hours between when Eva was last seen and when her body was found in the bayou remained a blank.

That was when the mother rang me. I'm listed in the Yellow Pages as *Need to Know, Inc.: Off-Duty Homicide Detective—Missing Persons—Surveillance.*

Mrs. Pierce met me under the bingo board at Fiorella's restaurant at the French Market. It wasn't my suggestion. I hadn't been to the market since I was a kid, when my daddy used to take me on Saturday mornings to squabble with his wop relatives while we loaded up at a discount on their fruits and vegetables. On my daddy's side I'm related to everyone who ever sold a pastry, an eggplant, or a bottle of dago red in the Quarter, and on my mother's side, to everyone who ever ran the numbers, pimped girls, or took a kickback. I peeked inside the rotting old market but sure didn't see any Italians or tomatoes. Now it was just Chinese selling knockoff sunglasses to tourists.

Mrs. Pierce was short and round as a cannoli, with a stiff gray bouffant and a complexion like powdered sugar. With those cat's-eye bifocals, she looked like someone who might be playing bingo at Fiorella's. But when she opened her mouth . . . *Twilight Zone.* Mrs. Pierce said it wasn't drugs or sex that did her daughter in but—get this—poetry.

"And the police aren't doing anything," she said with a flat Midwestern whine that made me want to go suck a lemon.

"Look, lady, I'm a cop—Lieutenant Vincent Panarello, Sixth District—and the police have more trouble than they can handle in New Orleans. They don't pay us much, I got a wife and three kids in Terrytown, so that's why I moonlight as a detective."

"My daughter loved moonlight."

"I bet."

"She read her own original poetry every Tuesday night at that rodent-infested bar on Esplanade Avenue called the Dragon's Den." She was twisting the wrapper from her straw into a noose.

"Yeah, that used to be Ruby Red's in my day. A college joint, the floor all covered with sawdust and peanut shells." I didn't tell her how drunk I used to get there in high school with a fake I.D. While I was going to night school at Tulane, Ruby Red's was where I met my first wife Janice, may she rest in peace.

"Well, the place has gone beatniky." Mrs. Pierce leaned forward, her eyes watering. "And do you know what I think, Lieutenant Panarello?'

"Shoot."

"I think one of those poets murdered my daughter. One of those characters who read at the open mike. And that's where I want you to start. To listen for clues when the poets read. Eventually one of them will give himself away."

"Listening to the perms will cost you extra." And so will the

French Quarter, but I'd already averaged that in when I quoted her my fee.

"I'll meet you there Tuesday at 9 p.m. It's above that Thai restaurant. Just go through the alley—"

"I know how to get up there." I could have climbed those worn wooden steps next to the crumbling brick wall in my sleep. That was where I first kissed Janice. Funny, but she also wrote poems she read to me on the sagging wrought-iron balcony. The life I really wanted was the one I planned with her. The life I settled for is the one I got.

Mrs. Pierce handed me a picture of her daughter, a list of her friends, and a check. I eyed the amount. Local bank.

"What your daughter do for a living?" I pushed back my chair, antsy to blow Fiorella's. I could already smell the fried-chicken grease on my clothes.

"Why, she was a poet and interpretive dancer."

"Interpretive dancer. Gotcha."

I studied the photo. Eva was about twenty-four, pretty, with skin as pale and powdery as a moth's wing. But she was dressed in a ratty red sweater over a pink print dress over black sweat pants. Her dyed black hair was hanging in two stringy hanks of pigtail like a cocker spaniel's ears. Who would want to kill her, I wondered, except the fashion police?

When I got down to the station I pulled the report. Eva was last seen at Molly's bar on Decatur Street at 4 a.m on a Tuesday, where she told her roommate, Pogo Lamont, that she was going home to feed their one-eyed dog named Welfare. They lived on Ursulines at Bourbon, upper slave quarter, uptown side. She never made it home. After an anonymous 911 tip, her body was hoisted out of the bayou at 7 p.m. the next evening. One clean shot through the temple, real professional. No forced sexual entry. Her purse was lying open on the grassy bank, surrounded by a gaggle of ducks trying to get at the bag of stale popcorn inside. A cell phone and twenty-five dollars were tucked in the bag, so the motive wasn't robbery. Also inside the purse were a red lipstick, a flea collar, a black notebook filled with poems, two Vicodins, an

Ohio picture I.D., a plastic straw that tested positive for cocaine residue, and a worn-out restraining order against Brack Self, a bartender and "performance artist" who turned out to have been locked up the whole time in Tampa for beating on his present girlfriend. That, and an Egyptian scarab, a petrified dung beetle supposed to be a symbol of immortality.

Which didn't seem to have worked for Eva Pierce, poet and stripper.

I MADE IT TO THE Dragon's Den on a sticky Tuesday evening, with a woolly sky trapping humidity inside the city like a soggy blanket. It had been trying to rain for two weeks. The air was always just about to clear but never did, as if old Mother Nature were working on her orgasm. I carried an umbrella, expecting a downpour. The place was right next to the river and hadn't seen a drop of paint since I last walked in the door thirty years ago, with all my hair and a young man's cocky swagger. A whistle was moaning as a freight train clacked along the nearby tracks, and the huge live oak out front shrouded the crumbling façade in a tangle of shadows. An old rickshaw was parked outside, where an elfin creature with orange hair sat scribbling in a notebook. He shot me a look through thick black plastic glasses, and then went back to writing.

Guess I'd found the poets.

I slapped a black beret on my head as I headed through the clammy alley, the bricks so decrepit that ferns were sprouting from the walls. I needed to blend in with the artsy crowd here, so I wore a blousy purple shirt and tight black pants, and carried a paperback by some poet called Oscar Wilde that I'd had to read at night school. A wizened old Chinese guy was squatting over a tub of vegetables in the patio, and the air smelled like spices. Something was sizzling in the kitchen. I felt like I was in Hong Kong looking for my Shanghai Lil.

Except for the Far East decor, the bar upstairs hadn't changed that much. A small stage and dance floor had been added at the center, and the tables were low, surrounded by pillows on the floor. Was that where poets ate, I wondered, on the floor?

"I'll have something light and refreshing, with a twist of lime," I lisped to the two-ton oriental gal behind the bar, waving my pinky. A biker type in a leather cowboy hat was observing me from across the bar.

"You a cop?" he yelled.

"Why no," I said, batting my eyelashes, holding up the lavender book so he could read the cover. "I've come for the poultry."

"Hey, Miss Ping," he shouted to the bartender. "Give Lieutenant Girlfriend here a wine spritzer on my tab."

Just as I lurched forward to knock this asshole's block off, in walked Mrs. Pierce with that orange-haired garden gnome from out front.

"Here you go, Lieutenant Girlfriend," Miss Ping said, setting down the drink.

"Lieutenant," Mrs. Pierce said, "this was Eva's roommate, Pogo Lamont."

"Lieutenant Girlfriend," Pogo cackled, extending his hand.

"Come on, son, I want to talk to you on the balcony," I said, grabbing him by the shoulder.

"Unhand me this instant!" the little creep cried out.

"Watch out," grunted the joker in the leather cowboy hat, "Lieutenant Girlfriend's already hitting on the chicken." Miss Ping barked a throaty laugh.

The kid followed me onto the balcony, which was pitching precariously away from the building. I steadied myself as if stepping into a boat, not trusting the rusted iron-lace railing to keep all 250 pounds of me from rolling off.

"OK, you know why I'm here," I said, plunking down my drink on a wobbly table. "Who's this Brack Self character that Eva took out a peace bond against?"

"Oh, that snarling beast," Pogo said, curling up like a cat into a chair. "A former beau who used his fists to make a point. Black and blue weren't Eva's most becoming colors."

"She liked it rough, huh?"

"Oooh, Lieutenant Girlfriend," Pogo squealed.

"Say, you little—" Play it cool, I thought. This was just a job.

"She met him here at the open mike when the poetry series first started. That first night he got so wasted he just unzipped, whipped it out, and pissed sitting right at a table. While I was performing, I might add. Now that, honey, is what I call literary criticism. Eva mopped it up, and never stopped. And ended up mothering him."

"How long they together?"

"Until the third occasion she summoned the police."

He couldn't have killed her from a jail cell in Tampa. Maybe he had friends.

"How long you been coming here?"

"Since I was a boy. When Mother couldn't find a babysitter, she'd haul me here when it was Ruby Red's—"

"I used to come here then, too. Who was your mom?"

"Lily."

"Lily Lamont?" She was the fancy-pants, Uptown debutante who used to cause scenes whenever I was here with Janice. In those days the port was right across the train tracks from the Quarter, and Lily Lamont was usually being held upright between a couple of Greek or Latino sailors. Once I swung open the door to the can to find her on her knees giving one of them a blow job while a rat looked on from the urinal. That was when I stopped bringing Janice to this dump.

"Did you know Mother?" Pogo squirmed in his seat.

"Only by sight." So this was the stunted offspring of one of those Ruby Red nights. If Janice were still here, we'd have children his age.

"Your mother still alive?" I asked.

"If you care to call it that. She's secluded inside her Xanadu on Pirate's Alley."

I softened to the little creep. He told me that as a kid, his mother would often show up at their apartment on Dumaine with a strange man, and they'd lock themselves inside her room for three days with a case of bourbon. Now Pogo lived on a trust fund from the Lamonts, which paid the rent on the apartment. He was finishing a book of poems dedicated to his mother titled *The Monster Cave.*

"Where did Eva strip?"

"At Les Girls on Iberville. She gave it up soon after she moved in with me. You see, I paid for everything. Because Eva was my teacher and muse."

"She ever bring any guys home from there?"

"Not guys. Other strippers sometimes."

"So she swung both ways?"

"Oooh, Lieutenant Girlfriend." Pogo nudged my leg with his foot. "Do you?"

I heard some ranting and raving from inside the bar, and edged my way in to listen. The place was packed, with a permanent cloud of cigarette smoke hovering in the spot light. First up was Millicent Tripplet, an obese woman with ruby lipstick, who recited a poem about how oppressed she felt when she was being fucked by a certain guy, and how depressed she felt when she wasn't. That got a howl of appreciation. Then a rapper named Pawnshop took the stage, coked out of his gourd, to blow the trumpet and rap about how all the bitches and ho's weren't down with his skinny black ass in the baggy jumpsuit. His rhymes were catchy but the rhythm was a snooze. Then came a comic from the racetrack who sounded like my Uncle Dominic; next up was some nerd in a plaid sports coat who read a sonnet about peat moss and death; and then some anorexic lady dressed in lilac who choked up in the middle and had to sit down. I couldn't figure out what her poem was about. I think her pooch died.

One thing I clocked: the better the poet, the shorter the spiel. The worst ones droned on forever. I gave Mrs. Pierce an empty shrug, as if to say, *No clues here, lady.* Then she took the stage, hands folded, looking like a Methodist Sunday school teacher. She held up the flier and announced that she would read the last poem her daughter ever wrote:

Open Mike

I've always known you
though we haven't met.
I know how your name tastes
though I've never said it.
You linger on the last step
of stairs I never descend,
I stand with my address book
on a landing to which you never
climb, and every day we stop
just short of each other.

I invoke you to appear,
to kiss childhood back
into my skeptical mouth,
rain into this parched air.
I invoke you at the sudden angle
of smoke, secrets, and zippers,
at the hour when ear lobes,
skin along inner thighs,
a smooth chest is tenderest,
love unfolding like a hammock
to fit whatever is nearest.
I invoke your breath's fur
on my neck, your curve of lips,
the blue seaweed of your hair where
we'll weave a nest of lost mornings.

The words sent a chill down my spine. It was as if Eva had been waiting for her murderer. Had a date with death. All I could see was Janice, her face bent over a glowing red candle holder, her straight blond hair swaying as she read poems to me. I had to rush out onto the balcony where I could sit alone and be twenty again, if only for a moment, and remember what a love so fragile felt like.

Finally it was raining, coming down in torrents, the oak branches and curlicues of iron lace dripping fat, dirty tears. "Drip drop, drip drop." That was how the Irma Thomas song began, the one we were always listening to in those days. "It's raining so hard, brings back memories." An ambulance raced past, its flashing red lights hellish on the slick street. And I had to endure it all over again, her body dragged from the driver's seat of our crumpled red Chevy. She had been coming home with a birthday surprise for me, and the McKenzie cake box was soaked with her blood. I never thought I'd be sitting again with Janice on the balcony at Ruby Red's, listening to the rain.

I BEGAN TO HAUNT the Quarter for the first time in years, trying to get a handle on Eva's world. Mostly she hung out in what they used to call Little Sicily, around the French Market and lower Decatur Street, where my daddy grew up. Like all the Sicilians in this town, his family had lived over their corner grocery store, Angelo's Superette at Decatur and Governor Nicholls. My only relative left in the neighborhood was Aunt Olivia, a butch little old maid who used to run a laundromat with her mama on Dauphine Street. She owned half the Quarter, and my Uncle Dominic, who hadn't worn anything but pajamas for the past twenty years, owned the other half. When I was young, everyone was always going *Oh, jeez, you got family in the Quarter, you should visit them.* But like my mama always said, "Me, I don't go by them dagos none. They just as soon stick a knife in your back."

The neighborhood was a different place now, and I couldn't understand what anyone down here did to make a living. You hardly saw any grocery stores or dry cleaners or fruit vendors or florists or printing offices or notions stores. Mostly the shops were Pakistani joints selling Mardi Gras masks made in China. Even the criminals were candy-assed, just a bunch of two-bit drug dealers and purse snatchers, nothing like the outfit my mama's family used to run. In those days, if a girl didn't cough up to her pimp, she got a Saturday-night makeover with acid splashed in her face. The girls used to roll the sailors right and left, slipping mickeys in their drinks or switch blades between their ribs.

Now I walked around at night unarmed with a couple hundred bucks in my pocket. The streets were filled with gutter punks, their mangy mutts, and older kids playing dress up. These kids thought they were being *bad bad bad.* They'd snort their little powders and do their little humpety-hump on somebody's futon. Then they'd ride their bikes and eat their vegetables, just like their mamas told them. They even recycled.

I figured with all these Pollyannas floating around, older predators were bound to be lurking in the shadows, dying to take a bite out of this innocent flesh. So the first place I hit was where Eva used to strip, Les Girls de Paree on Iberville between Royal and Chartres. This block of seedy dives was the real thing, the way the whole Quarter used to look when I was coming up. The Vieux Carré Commission must have preserved it as a historical diorama. A hulking bozo with a mullet haircut held the doors open onto the pulsing red lights of a dark pit belting out bump-and-grind. Inside, Les Girls smelled like dirty drawers in a hamper. Or to put it less delicately, like ass.

Some skanky brunette with zits on her behind was rubbing her crotch on an aluminum pole and jiggling her store-bought titties. You'd have to be pretty desperate to throw a boner for a rancid slice of luncheon meat like that. Only two old guys were sitting in the shadows, and I couldn't figure out how this joint sucked in any bucks. Finally Mullet Head waltzed over to ask what I wanted.

"I want to talk about Eva Pierce."

"Miss Ivonne," he called out, eyeballing me up and down. "Copper here."

This over-the-hill fluffball with champagne hair clopped over to my table. I couldn't take my eyes off her lips. "What can I do for you, officer?"

"Eva Pierce" is all I said. Her lips were pink and puffed out like Vienna Sausages. They must have kept a vat of collagen under the bar.

"I've been waiting for this little bereavement call," she said, sliding into a chair. "I'm still broke up about Eva. She didn't belong here, and I was glad to see her leave. All she ever did was write poetry and sip 7-Up. But she sure attracted the chicken hawks."

"Anyone in particular?"

"I don't rat out my customers."

"Eva liked it rough, and swung both ways, right?"

"Where you hear that, babe?" She yanked a Vantage from inside her bra and lipped it.

"Her roommate Pogo."

"Me and his momma used to have the best damn time," she shrieked, pounding the table. "But don't ever cross that woman. No, siree."

"You know Lily Lamont?"

She slit her eyes at me. "You sure get around for a cop."

"Some people pay me to."

"Look, officer," she said, shooting a stream of smoke toward the ceiling through those lips, "Eva went home with a couple of the girls here, but they just wanted somebody's shoulder to cry on. Eva was a mommy, not a dyke. She took care of stray animals and people. Like that Brack creature and poor Pogo. She was like Dorothy in the goddamn *Wizard of Oz*. All she ever talked about was that farm in Ohio."

"So who'd want to kill her?"

"You got me," she said. "Maybe the wicked witch with her flying monkeys. Or the blue guy."

"The blue guy?"

Miss Yvonne stifled a laugh. "Buffed up psycho used to come in here, hair and beard dyed cobalt blue. He wore a cat of nine tails around his neck. Sure took a liking to Eva, but I run him off."

I WAS WALKING BACK down Chartres Street, thinking about Janice, when I heard a dog leash rattling behind me.

"Oh, Lieutenant Girlfriend." It was Pogo walking this dust mop named Welfare, now squatting at the curb. I hadn't seen Pogo since last Tuesday at the Dragon's Den. I was becoming a regular at the open mike and starting to get a kick out of it. It was like a cross between a gong show and the observation room on Acutely Disturbed at DePaul's.

"Been meaning to ask you," I said. "Eva go to the movies a lot?"

"Never," he said, picking up a dog turd between two fingers with a plastic baggie. "She preferred to star in her own epic drama."

"So why was she carrying popcorn the night she died?"

He stopped. "Popcorn? I never thought about that. Maybe she swung by the Cloister after she said goodnight at Molly's. Sometimes the bartender there hands out bags of popcorn. Just before dawn."

I smiled. The Cloister. A few doors down Decatur from Molly's.

Pogo put the plastic baggie in his pocket. Who would've ever thought that one day the Quarter would be filled with rich people walking around with dog turds in their pockets? The dagos moved to Kenner just in time.

"Ever see Eva around a man with a blue beard. Blue hair and beard. And a whip?"

"Oh, him."

"She date him?"

"He followed her to the open mike from Les Girls. She wouldn't have anything to do with him. Now we have to listen to his poetry."

"His perms any good?"

Pogo pulled out the baggie of dog mess and waved it in my face. "See you at the open mike, Lieutenant Girlfriend."

IF THE GARAGE ROCK band at the Cloister banged out one more song, I thought my skull would pop. I nursed several Seven and Sevens while I jotted down random thoughts in my notebook, hoping Swamp Gas would finally run out of steam. The crowd was twenty-somethings dressed in black with all the hardware in Home Depot dangling off their mugs. I wondered if they got snared in each other's rings and things when they got down to business and had to use a wire cutter to separate themselves. Nobody seemed to be having a particularly good time. Janice and I'd had more fun eating thirty-five-cent plates of red beans and rice at Buster Holmes. A steady stream of couples was going in and out of the bathrooms in back, but not for any lovey-dovey. They were wiping their noses and clenching their jaws when they walked out. That explained the coke residue on the straw in Eva's purse.

Finally I was getting somewhere.

Swamp Gas petered out at about five in the morning. I was getting ready to leave when I spotted this geezer with a snowy white pompadour hobbling around in his bathrobe and slippers. When he turned around, I had to laugh.

"Hey, Uncle Dominic, it's me, Vinnie. Chetta's boy." I hadn't seen the old guy since my daddy's funeral.

"Vinnie, let me get a look at you." He cuffed my head and patted my cheeks. "Not a day goes by I don't think of my sweet little sister. How she making?"

"Same old same old." Mama was still fuming about how Uncle Dominic had gypped her on the inheritance. *He stuck a knife in my back*, she growled whenever his name came up.

"Remind her she still owes me three hundred bucks for property taxes the year she sold out."

"What you doing here at this hour," I asked, swiveling my hips, "getting down with the girlies?" His robe was covered with lint balls.

"Just checking on my investment. Got six, seven other buildings to see this morning. You?" he asked, swiveling his own hips. "Thought you was married. You just like your papa."

"Here on a murder case. Know this young lady?" I flipped out the picture of Eva, and he fished glasses out of his robe pocket. "Killed the night of March 28th."

"Let me think," he said, staring at the snapshot. "Yeah, yeah, I seen her here that morning. Last time I come in to check on my investment. Around this time. I axed her what she was writing down in her little book, and she says 'a perm.' Looked like a bunny with them funny pigtails."

"She leave alone?"

"Yeah, yeah. No, wait—" He slapped his forehead. "Madonna, how could I forget? She left with that *pazzo* what got the blue beard."

Blue Beard.

Bingo.

Then somebody handed me popcorn still warm in the bag.

THE NEXT MORNING I radioed Blue Beard's description in to the Eighth District station in the Quarter, and rang Pogo, Miss Ivonne, Miss Ping, and Uncle Dominic to ask them to contact me the minute they spotted him. Uncle Dominic told me he wanted a cut of the reward, and lost interest fast when I told him there wasn't any. But both he and Miss Ivonne promised to make a few phone calls to help locate Blue Beard. Mrs. Pierce sputtered "God bless you" when I reported that I was zeroing in on the killer.

Where the hell could he be? It wasn't like a man with blue hair could hide just anywhere, even in the French Quarter.

That afternoon I got a staticky message on my cell phone.

Lily Lamont.

A husky, spaced-out voice said she needed to talk with me in person. That evening. She left an address that at first she couldn't remember right.

My heels echoed on the flagstones in deserted Pirate's Alley like the approaching footsteps in those radio plays my daddy used to listen to. A mist had rolled in from the river, wrapping St. Louis Cathedral in fog, and I squinted to make out the address under the halo of a streetlamp. I pictured Lily Lamont blowzy and toothless now, passed out on a filthy mattress cradling an empty bourbon bottle.

Nothing could have prepared me for what I found.

After I was buzzed in, I mounted a curved mahogany staircase that swept me up into a cavernous Creole ballroom under a spidery bronze chandelier. In a zebra upholstered throne, there sat a mummified lady with white hair pulled back tight from her porcelain face, buttering a slice of raisin-bread toast.

"I'm famished," Lily Lamont said, taking a bite. "Would you care for some toast and tea? That's all I ever, *ever* eat."

I shook my head. Perched in the zebra chair next to hers was a bulky goon with a body like a boxer's gone to seed. He was caressing the top of his shiny bald head, several shades paler than his face.

"I don't believe we've ever formally met, Lieutenant Panarello," she said. Her bones, thin as chopsticks, were swallowed by a red silk kimono fastened by a dragon brooch.

"Not face-to-face." What was I supposed to say, tell this lady I saw her on her knees in a men's room thirty years ago?

"And this is my associate, Lucas," she said, gesturing to Baldie.

I nodded, taking a seat in an elaborately carved bishop's chair under an alabaster lamp of entwined snakes.

"Nice place," I said. The floor-to-ceiling windows were draped with damask swags. Outside, shadows from the extended arms of a spot-lit Jesus loomed over the cathedral garden.

"I bought this house last year from your uncle, Dominic Zuppardo." Her sharp little teeth gnawed on the toast like a rat's. "At a pretty penny. Actually, I paid him twice as much as the sale price we registered. That helped with my property assessment and his capital gains taxes. Smart man."

Bet Uncle Dominic is kissing her butt now, I thought. So that was who tipped her off to my investigation.

"Met your friend Miss Ivonne," I said, since we were having a family reunion. "Place where Eva Pierce used to strip."

"How is Ivonne?" Lily asked with a tight smile. "I set her up with that club. I've never been in it, of course." Her frail shoulders shuddered.

Ditto, I thought. Miss Ivonne probably called her, too.

"Look, I won't beat around the bush," Lily Lamont said, brushing toast crumbs from her finger tips. "I want you to call off your investigation into Eva Pierce's death. The killer is probably in Timbuktu by now. Questioning all of these people is silly."

"But I know who did it. A guy with blue hair and beard."

"Have you ever seen him?" Her enormous hazel eyes studied me slyly over the gold rim of an ornate tea cup.

"No, but he used to come to the open mike at the Dragon's Den all the time to read his lousy perms."

Baldie winced. Then a shit-eating grin spread across his face. Why the hell would he care about Blue Beard's poems?

Unless he wrote them.

"Do you have children, lieutenant?" Lily's voice was filling with church choirs.

"Three. A boy at De la Salle, a girl at Mount Carmel, and another girl starting out at Loyola University next year." That was why I moonlighted, to pay all those tuitions. The older girl worked at a pizza parlor after school to save up for Loyola. Her dad, you see, was a New Orleans cop.

"And wouldn't you do anything to help your children?"

"Anything short of—"

"Eva Pierce was a horrible influence on my son." Lily swayed like a cobra as she mouthed the words in a slow, woozy monotone. "She turned him against me. You should read the venomous words about me she inspired him to pen. She was just using him."

"Maybe he liked being used," I said, locking eyes with Pogo's mother. "Maybe it's all he's ever known."

"Here, this is for you." Her long indigo fingernail flicked an ivory envelope across the coffee table toward me. "It's a check for $25,000. Eva's mother hired you to investigate. I'm hiring you to stop the investigation." She arched a penciled eyebrow. "Simple."

I stood up. "Can I use the john?"

"Lucas will show you the way."

I studied the rolls of skin on the back of Baldie's head as I followed him down a long corridor, trying to picture him with blue hair and beard. The smartest thugs know the best disguise is something attention-getting but dispensable. And who would testify against Lily and this hit man? My uncle? Miss Ivonne?

Trust-fund Pogo? The whole Quarter owed Lily Lamont a favor.

In the bathroom I tore open the envelope with an Egyptian scarab embossed on the flap: 25,000 smackers, made out to cash. I folded the check into my wallet. It was five times what Mrs. Pierce was paying me. I splashed water on my face and took a long look in the mirror. The jowly, unshaven mug of my daddy stared back at me, the face of three generations of Italian shopkeepers who worked like hell and never managed to get ahead. *What, you crazy or something,* they screamed at me. *You want your daughter to graduate from college? Take the damn dough and run, Vinnie.*

I picked up the plush blue bath towel folded next to the mirror. Underneath was a syringe, a packet of white powder, and a silver iced-tea spoon.

I rang Mrs. Pierce as soon as I'd escaped the junkie fog in Pirate's Alley.

"Look, lady," I told her, "the investigation is off. Your daughter just got mixed up with the wrong crowd, that's all. Blue Beard is probably unidentifiable by now. He could be anywhere. I can't, in good conscience, waste any more of your money." All true.

Mrs. Pierce started sobbing and then hung up. She'd been right. It wasn't sex or drugs that got her daughter killed, but poetry. Me, I was never so glad to drive home to Terrytown, to the wife and life that I've got.

I DIDN'T MAKE IT back to the Dragon's Den until one sweltering August night later that year. The air smelled like river sludge, and the façade was shimmering in the heat like a mirage made of shadows and memories. The old Chinese guy was still hanging over his tub of vegetables in the patio. He shot me a thumbs up as I mounted the stairs, mopping my face with a handkerchief.

Every step was an effort.

"Look what the cat drug in," Miss Ping said, setting me up with my Seven and Seven.

"Where's that sign-up sheet for the open mike?" I asked her. She pushed a clipboard toward me. With a shaky hand I scrawled

Vinnie P., third name on the list. I couldn't believe what I was about to do. It seemed like jerking off in public. So I sat on the balcony to calm myself down and go over what I'd written.

"Hey honey, what you doing in the den with the TV off?" my wife had asked me. "You sick?"

"Writing a report." I swatted her away.

What I'd been writing for two weeks wasn't exactly a report but some buried feelings—poems, I guess you'd call them. I couldn't sleep or concentrate, and had even thought of going to Saturday confession, but then nixed that dumb-cluck idea. I couldn't tell the Father who would marry my kids and christen my grand babies that I, a cop, was the accessory to a murder. Those poets that I'd listen to during the open mike, something like this was eating them up, too. Their girlfriends left them or their parents never loved them or they felt lonely and empty—I don't know—they just needed to spill their guts and be heard. By anyone. Just *heard.* They didn't tell it straight but in a symbolic way, you know, twisting it up enough so that it wouldn't be only their story but everybody's. So that was what I'd been writing: what happened to me investigating Eva Pierce's murder. And with Janice. Where it all went wrong and how I wound up feeling the way I did, as old, corrupt, and dirty as this French Quarter.

I had to get it off my chest.

Pogo stuck his face onto the balcony, eyes popping out at the sight of me.

"She's a vile bitch," he hissed, biting his lip. Then he waved me inside.

Only about ten of the usual suspects were sprawled around the room. The first two poets went on forever. I was so wound up I couldn't concentrate on a word they said.

Finally the clown with the leather cowboy hat held up the clipboard.

"And here, ladies and gentlemen," he announced, "is a rising star in the Quarter poetry scene. A man of the law who will grace us with his debut reading. He came to bust us, and now he's one of us. Put your hands together to welcome Lieutenant Girlfriend."

Everyone clapped like crazy as I stepped onto the stage feeling like a horse's ass. Pogo was jumping up and down, waving his arms like a cheerleader. I shuffled through the pages to get them in order. My voice caught as I started to speak.

Miss Ping plinked an ice cube into a glass. The air conditioner coughed.

Then a huge gray rat scurried across the room, stopped in the middle of the floor to take in the audience, and disappeared under the stage I was standing on.

Everyone jumped to their feet.

"OK, you assholes, sit down," I said, adjusting the mike. "That rat has to wait its turn just like all us other poets. This is called 'Janice and Eva Swap Lipsticks in the Changing Room to Hell.' I bet you lunkheads aren't going to get it, but here goes."

All Spiders, No Flies

TOMORROW I'VE GOT to bail my boyfriend out of jail. As if I'm made of money, which is what everybody thinks. But he's better than some of the people who have crashed here. Like that one-armed carpenter who begged me to go on jobs with him to hold the damn nails. Finally, I said look, honey, and gave him four hundred dollars to lease a fruit stand in a truck parked in front of St. Louis Cemetery. First week someone ripped off all four tires. Now it just sits there propped up on cinder blocks with ratty cardboard signs advertising strawberries from the country.

And everytime he gets a hard-on he takes the day off.

They call me a "remittance man." Means my family pays me to stay away. That's how come I'm back in New Orleans, where years ago I finally finished at Tulane with a thesis called "Madonna: A Woman of Gender," which I won't go into now. If I hadn't gone to Tulane, I wouldn't know who I am. I mean, socially. Even if I do live with a penniless old alcoholic and am in love with a dreamy hustler named Ernest Royal Breaux, who's in for assault.

Like everyone I meet these days, I had a miserable childhood. My mama was a drunk, my daddy chased women, and my grandfather was the governor of the state of Louisiana.

I'm not telling you which one he was—I'm too ashamed—but I will say PawPaw escaped over the state line with a paper bag over his head after my grandmother Mimi tried to have him committed. Then he gave a press conference from a motel in his drawers, eating grits without his teeth in. They broadcast that over the whole world, and I just about died. Especially about the teeth, which PawPaw forgot on the back of a commode in the capitol washroom, he was in such a hurry to get the hell out of Louisiana.

When they brought him back, Mimi was like, "You go play bourrée with him, boy, and keep him quiet." This was around when Mama and Daddy were getting their divorce, so I was staying in the mansion a lot. PawPaw and I had played bourrée together while he decided on some important legislation, emptying a bottle of bourbon in the process. One thing I can say, he cheated at bourrée.

That's only part of my miserable childhood. Fact is I'm a flaming faggot.

"We don't care if you a hoMOsexual, Bib," my big sister always goes, "but why you have to turn out a flaming faggot."

Then I go, "We don't care if you a WOman, but why you have to turn out a fat sow with a kid hanging off each of your six tits. Or those supposed to be your knees and elbows?" That gets her every time. She really does need to reduce.

Daddy caught me the first time. I'd managed to hogtie myself in the stable, bare-assed except for Mama's bra, and was rolling around in horse shit. He beat the tar out of me because he said I was aroused. What really got him: so was his favorite thoroughbred. That was the beginning of shrinks and military schools.

They said they wanted to make a man out of me but really just wanted me out of sight, like PawPaw when he wound up with the paper bag over his head.

"Puh-lease," I pleaded, flipping bug-eyed through a military school yearbook, "don't send me away to be locked up with all these muscle-bound boys in uniforms." But they wouldn't listen to reason. So by the time I was kicked out of the last one, Culver Military Academy in Indiana, for starting the midnight action in the wheelchair-access bathroom, everyone was calling me Long-john. Cadets are a bunch of size queens, if you want to know the truth. My first name is John, though everyone calls me Bib.

And I'm not telling you what my last name is.

I'VE BEEN BACK IN the French Quarter ever since I broke up with my second husband, a dentist named Bernard I lived with in Daytona Beach. Why a dentist? I ask myself in moments of introspection. But after the plastic surgery, I feel comfortable with doctors. They can see me for who I really am, beyond all the glamour.

Only with the Percodan and coke we were doing, Bernie and I started working each other's nerves. After smashing every piece of glass in his condo one night, I took off with a guard who had just been fired for running a security golf cart into the lagoon looking for a bottle of vodka he'd stashed behind a philodendrum.

Too Too is a sixty-two-year-old alkie I used to pal around with while Bernie was off doing root canals. Too Too listens to opera and is into butt plugs, one of the sweetest men I've ever known. I drink a lot, too, if you want to know the truth, so I took him hostage and caught the Amtrak to Baton Rouge. We got there just in time for my thirty-fifth birthday. After two nights at Mama's, she made a few brisk calls that set me up with an apartment in the Quarter and a check every month. She had discovered one of Too Too's playthings wedged into her La-Z-Boy.

"I'm getting too old for so much commotion," Mama says. She dried out a long time ago.

"Rehab is for quitters," I tell her. She just shakes her head, says stay in touch.

One thing, as the daughter-in-law of a former governor, Mama has flawless taste. The apartment she got me on Dauphine is a restored shotgun with crown moldings, bronze fixtures, hardwood floors, and glass chandeliers. I really didn't mean to trash the place. Things have just gotten out of hand.

The day I moved in I met Crystal, a forty-year-old crack whore who strips at Les Girls de Paree. She had just been evicted and was circling the Quarter with a U-Haul filled with all her stuff. Her fourth husband, a teenager who works as a clown on Jackson Square, bought me a half-gallon of vodka and convinced me to let them keep everything here for just one night. I didn't have much to move in except for a boom box, my Madonna poster, and Too Too, who had managed to lose his suitcase on the Greyhound.

Our welcome to the neighborhood wasn't exactly cordial. The director of the Vieux Carré Commission, who lives across the street, said he didn't particularly object to Crystal's five-foot cage on the gallery with the squirrel inside who thought it was a human being. Or to her mangy white cockatoo in another cage. What got him was her leatherette couch we couldn't fit through the door. Said it was tacky and had to go, and suggested cane rockers or a swing or a loveseat in white rattan. All my new friends were on the floor next to the dishwasher getting high. I didn't want to ruin my first evening fussing with that old queen.

Now you know how the Quarter is on a July night.

At dusk everybody comes scampering out like roaches hiding from the scorching light. Then the neighborhood is one big cocktail party. Music blares out of open bar doors. Hunky guys in tank tops and cutoffs lean against car hoods sucking on ice cubes, rattling go-cups at you as you pass. People scream to each other from balcony to balcony, hang out on their stoops, draining beers and mopping their brows and shooting the shit with everyone who walks by.

It's too hot to touch. And too hot not to.

So I slipped on bathing trunks and some Mardi Gras beads Crystal gave me, found a garden hose, and wet my curly self down every half hour. Dauphine Street was the only place I ever wanted to be, stoned on the steps with a Screwdriver and my boom box, carrying on with everyone in the street. I kept turning up the Stones, singing "Wild, wild horses couldn't drag me away."

That first night I was drunk as a monkey, rolled up in one of Crystal's old sheets in front of the floor-to-ceiling window that opens onto the gallery, when somebody crawled inside on all fours. I said to myself, "Bib, honey, prepare to expire." But then the intruder curled up beside me like a lost lamb—or should I say ram? He was sporting a monster down there, and it wasn't until the first rays crept in through the jalousies that I realized he didn't have any top front teeth and smelled like a free box. But by then I didn't care. It was a new morning, and he was mine.

Said he grew up in Crowley and his name is Ernest Royal Breaux—I do believe that's the only true thing he's ever told me—and he's a veterinarian at the Audubon Park Zoo. He's twentyish with wavy chestnut hair and soft green eyes, tanned and built like he's been doing hard labor, not another gym bunny hanging out in the free-weight room like those Muscle Marys in Daytona.

"So what's a veterinarian from the zoo doing crawling into my cage in the middle of the night?" I wanted to know.

"Last week three assholes mugged me at the ATM," he explained with a coonass accent. "Niggers punch my teeth down my throat, take all the money out my account, then leave me broke and bleeding in Pirate's Alley."

"So you crawl in anybody's window you please like a dog in heat?" I don't fall in love before breakfast. That's my policy.

While I was in the shower, I heard Royal in the kitchen informing Crystal and her clown, who was putting on his makeup, that he's a golf pro who will be judging an open competition at Elmwood Country Club. I was some mad. Then, tossing everything out my suitcase trying to find something to wear, I hear the golf pro tell Too Too—get this—he's the director of the Vieux Carré Commission.

I maxed Madonna on the boom box, sashayed onto the gallery, and threw myself onto the leatherette couch. Everybody was already high and talking to that stupid squirrel like it was a human being.

"Let's get something straight, Royal," I hissed, lighting a Kool and tossing the burnt match in his direction. "The director of the Vieux Carré Commision lives right across the street, and yesterday him and me had a little tête-à-tête. And I know you're not him or a golf pro or a fucking veterinarian at the goddam zoo.

You can't con a con man. Who are you really?"

Now whenever you ask anyone in the Quarter who they really are, pull up a chair, loosen your girdle, and get ready for a real pack of lies. Ernest Royal Breaux said before he won the "New Meat Night" contest at The Rough House and became a hustler, he was a member of a white militia on his sister's survivalist ranch in Alabama.

"If PawPaw could see me now, he'd be so proud," I said, casting my eyes heavenward.

Like all hustlers, he said he has a girlfriend he adores who serves him champagne barefoot, but he just can't stay off the pipe. And in his sick mind, he becomes his tricks. Takes on their identities. Ever since that time he ripped off a trick's wallet and impersonated him across the country on a drug-crazed credit-card spree.

"Last night I tricked across the street," he said, pointing at the door of the director of the Vieux Carré Commission. "That guy has a security camera that's not a prop, like most around here. Lays in bed jerking off, watching his front steps on video, and when he sees someone setting there he likes, he comes out and yanks him in. He's into spanking, so we have to tell him how bad we been while he spanks our butts. So he throws me out at five in the morning and tells me I can probably crash on that tacky sofa cross the way. Then I see you sleeping in there like an angel and come in to keep you company. Tricking's lonely."

That afternoon we hung out on the gallery and organized Crystal's stuff into a sidewalk sale. And met more neighbors, like Earl the bald drag queen who lives in the slave quarter out back with his eighty-two-year-old father. Royal stayed around until evening, when he took his shirt off, stuffed it in his back pocket, and went to stand on the corner. And around dawn, he crawled back in through the window to curl up with me, and in the morning handed me a twenty and a bunch of change.

That was how I got started with Ernest Royal Breaux. Believe me, walking on the street with him is like being with Mae West. Everybody's like in awe until they check out the teeth. At least he pays his own way.

Too Too, on the other hand, doesn't have a dime to his name and plans to retire on Social Security in Mexico next year. He only has one shirt and a pair of pleated gray slacks, so he started spending the day dressed in nothing but a beach towel. He's the one who cooks, so he sleeps on the floor by the stove. Until Earl showed up one day with a cot after the ambulance left. That girl was a mess.

"Dad just died," Earl said, all puffy-eyed. "Can y'all use his bed? I can't stand to look at it no more."

"You mean that's where he died?" Too Too wanted to know. He opened it up to inspect the mattress for stains. "Hey, you want a drink?"

So they had a good bawl, and now Too Too lolls around on the Bed of Death all day like a beached whale, listening to opera, wrapped in a towel that says *Surf's Up!* When the black football players drop by to see him, he closes the kitchen door. But it still drives Royal crazy. Last week he threw a hissy-fit.

"Take your tricks out to the alley," he screamed. "Decent people have to eat in here."

But then Royal started scoring rocks off Too Too's tricks, and on New Year's, some defensive end from LSU even brought over a bottle of Dom Perignon. And that's made an uneasy peace between the watermelon queen and the white survivalist.

In the meantime, I've kicked everybody else out, the one-armed carpenter, Crystal and her clown, and the eighteen-year-olds who would hang out all day rolling joints and grabbing my remote. I can't take it anymore. I started feeling like the Mother Teresa of hustlers and con artists, running a soup kitchen in the quarter of lost men.

Wherever I go, they find me, and like PawPaw, I never learned to say no until it's too late. They fall in love with me because I listen to their stories about who they were, or who they think they are. No one else bothers. Just fuck 'em, pay 'em, and throw 'em out. Their raps are all lies, I guess. Although sometimes they're telling the truth, sprawled on my scuzzy mattress and staring up at the chandelier. They go on about their grandmas and their dogs, stuff like that. And know I don't want anything from them except maybe a hit off their joints. I can't help it. I like damaged people because I'm one of them.

Like that blues song goes, don't roll those bloodshot eyes at me.

EARL, THE ONLY neighbor I get along with, has moved out.

After his dad died, he went on a bender and emptied all the drag out the armoires and chiffarobes into the middle of his bedroom floor. He threw the scarves, skirts, wigs, and padded bras into Seagram boxes, along with makeup, tweezers, and everything else he called his "woman's stuff." Then he took the day off from his plumbing job, stacked the boxes in the back of his pickup, drove them to the Goodwill, shoved them across the counter and announced, "I quit."

I see Earl in the bars, and his eyebrows have grown back in. He took his dad's death real hard.

So except for Royal and Too Too, no one's left to hang out with this January. It's damp and cold, and I feel like a lizard at the bottom of a well. Tonight I stopped by Your Little Red Wagon to say hello to Miss Mamou behind the bar and find Royal. Just a bunch of hustlers playing video-poker or nursing beers in the corner—waiting for a ride to their mama's wake, it looked like.

It was all spiders, no flies.

Except for an old black gentleman who comes in every night—a choir director or voice teacher, something like that—who was trying to have a birthday party. Half-eaten paper plates of gooey cake were all over the bar, and he was wrapping the leftovers up in the McKenzie box, tying it again and again and looking at each of the guys like, *now what?* He kept twisting the red string around the box like he couldn't believe nobody loved him on his birthday because he was old.

I mean he couldn't keep his hands off his cake.

So I went over and hugged him and told him happy birthday

and how handsome he was. One day I'll be wrapping up my cake in a bar like this, after the party has been over for twenty-five years but nobody's told me. So while this guy is revving up the story of his life, Miss Mamou comes over to tell me Royal has been popped.

"Dude's a beeper queen," Royal cackled. I'm his one call, and the phone was ringing when I walked in.

"A new one on me." I never believe a word he says, but I listen. "What happened this time?"

"I tie him up in his bed, just like he says, set his beeper to *vibrate*, slip it in a condom and shove it up his ass. Then I shut the door, go into the kitchen, crack open a cold one, dial his number, and hit redial every few minutes."

"Ever do a three-way with Call Waiting?" I asked.

"Hey, no shit. He works for the phone company, so he's got all kind of gadgets and beaucoup bucks. But tries to pass me a twenty when we settled on fifty. So I punch out his lights and he gets the cops to pick me up. Says the jab to his kisser wasn't 'consensual.'"

"Look, this is the last time I bail Ernest Royal Breaux out of jail. Try to stay out of trouble till I see the bail bondsman in the morning."

So I just got off the phone to Baton Rouge. And tomorrow I have to hightail it over to Merrill Lynch on Poydras, then take the bus to Parish Prison on Tulane and North Broad. I told Mama I need some dental work. God forbid I tell her the truth. Not that she'd recognize it if I did. Or anyone in this town, for that matter. Everytime I start what Too Too calls that "governor's grandson bullshit," he walks out of the room. I don't care if he or anyone else believes me. It only costs a drink or a joint for someone to believe you. Or at least listen to you.

And I haven't run out of people yet.

The Night After Christmas

MOTHER LEANED OVER inside the vinyl booth, all the diamonds on her arthritic fingers glinting at once. "Think your sister's on dope?"

"Mary Ellen?" I snickered. "Come on, she's an ex-therapist on Prozac. She doesn't need anything else to make her crazy."

It was the night after Christmas and freezing-ass cold outside. Mother had picked me up at Louis Armstrong International Airport, so shrunken she could barely see over the dashboard. Through alternating gusts of sleet and rain, we inched our way down deserted suburban streets lined with the tinselly skeletons of Christmas trees tossed on their sides and plastic bags disgorging tangled red ribbons and crushed toy boxes. Now, over my dead body, we were sitting under a golden Buddha strung with blinking red and green lights at the Hao Tai-Tai restaurant in the Metairie Plaza Shopping Center. The last time I'd eaten in a Chinese restaurant, during a late-afternoon lunch with my lover Don, he hit me with his diagnosis. At that exact moment, the manager decided to drain and clean the tropical fish tank next to our table. While one waiter served our meal, another was suctioning up stinky strands of green goop as my mind reeled with Don's treatment plans.

"After that," I told Mother, "I swore I'd never set foot inside a

Chinese restaurant again."

"Just because your roommate died?" Mother's eyebrows shot up. "That's no excuse."

"But for months I've been dreaming of oyster dressing and candied yams."

"Don't they know how to bake a turkey up North?"

"Not like yours."

"Well you're too late," Mother said, unwrapping her chopsticks. "I don't cook anymore. I gave all my pots and pans to Mary Ellen, who never uses them. That daughter of hers is being raised on fast food, and now only eats shrimp fried rice. So Chinese it has to be."

We were waiting on my sister and her eight-year-old daughter Brittany, an hour late and due in any minute from Lake Charles. My mother was sipping a Mai Tai with a red umbrella in it and had a copy of my historical novel about New Orleans on the table in front of her.

"My son here wrote this book," Mother informed the Cantonese waitress in the brocade jacket as she handed us menus. "It's a story about his grandparents—my mama and daddy—and their parents, too. He's even got the Civil War in it."

"Wah, the Silver War." The young woman giggled. "Make a lot of money, I bet."

Leafing through the menu, Mother started back in on Mary Ellen. "Promise me one thing. That you'll never put anything in those story books about your sister."

"You think she's a fascinating nut case because she's your daughter," I blurted out, tired of the subject before we even started. We'd already picked over censored details of my life.

"One thing I want to know," Mother had asked the minute we sat down, "does your principal allow you to wear those gold earrings?"

"My principal? These," I said, tugging at my ear lobes, "are acceptable male dress in university teaching."

"A male dress? That's not acceptable. I don't even wear a dress anymore."

Now it was my sister's turn for Mother's scrutiny. "I wouldn't want it to get out what she said about your father after he died. That's something they could trace back to me." My mother straightened her frail frame with dignity. She had shriveled to the size of a fifth-grader sticking out of a baggy pink pants suit. The air around us was bubbling with hilarity. Booths were filling with elderly ladies wearing too much lipstick and plastic candy-cane corsages, escorted by jocular old gentlemen in plaid sport coats. A bovine woman with a bouffant hairdo and a name tag was wandering among tables with a clipboard.

"Mary Ellen isn't the only one," I assured Mother, "who paid some hypnotist to make up a recovered memory."

"Your father worshipped the ground she walked on," she enunciated, rapping her knuckles on the table.

According to the therapists, Daddy's whole generation liberated concentration camps, saved Europe from fascism, studied on the GI bill, bought ranch houses, and then raped their daughters. Every so often my sister would present Mother with yet another theory about why she turned out like she did, smug as a cat dragging home a dead mouse. "My life is your fault" was the jist of her line of therapy. The latest dead mouse she'd dumped in my mother's lap was that Mary Ellen broke up with her boyfriend because she was the "adult child of alcoholics."

"I'll drink to that," Mother told me she'd said, lifting a tumbler of Sprite. Once every six months my parents managed to finish a fifth of discount bourbon, if that, which they kept on a kitchen top shelf along with a dusty bottle of pink champange they'd saved for over twelve years, waiting for some special occasion that never arrived. Yet Mother was bawling when she phoned to tell me that my sister had called her a drunk.

"Like they say, the statute of limitations on blaming your parents," I said, "runs out at thirty." That made Mother cackle. Then shrieks of laughter arose from the booths around us, followed by a spatter of applause.

"MOTHER, FRANKLIN, Merry Christmas! Look, let me get off the phone, and I'll be with you in a sec." Mary Ellen finally made her entrance, dragging two bulging Saks shopping bags with one hand and cradling a cell phone to her ear with the other. Scowling, her daughter Brittany lagged behind, a sweater stuffed between the shoulders under her jacket.

"Nick, listen, where I'm at now is the Hao Tai-Tai in Metairie Plaza. Why don't you come by and have a drink with us so I can reimburse you. You saved my life . . . Sure, I'd love to see you again, too . . . In a while, then. Bye."

Mary Ellen slid into the booth with an exasperated sigh and then slipped the cell phone into her purse. I barely recognized my sister from last summer. Her new hair color illuminated the booth like a klieg light.

"You'll never guess what happened to us. We ran out of gas five miles from here in a sleet storm. The car just—*ploop*—died. And all I had was seventy-eight cents. This nice man, Nick, comes along. . . ."

"He's hooor-rible!" Brittany shrieked. "Got a big thing like this on his back."

Bent over like a crone, she was scurrying between the tables with the sweater bunched up under her jacket.

"OK, when Nick was a substance abuser in the French Quarter, he was run over by a beer truck so now he's just five feet tall. Before he was six something. Anyway, his spine collapsed so he's sort of like a hunchback."

Brittany was down on all fours now, screeching, with her butt up in the air. "He drives to get us ten dollars of gas at Texaco," Mary Ellen said, "puts it in the tank, and I invited him to come have a drink with us so I can pay him back. Mother, can you lend me ten dollars? Take it out of my Christmas money, all right?" Mary Ellen lowered her eyes to arrange the shopping bags under the table with a defeated look I'd never seen before on my little sister.

"You mean to tell me," Mother shouted, gathering strength from her stomach like a Sumo wrestler, "you set out on an automobile trip from Lake Charles on these icy roads with seventy-eight cents to your name and not enough gas in your car to get to Metairie? Traveling alone with that baby? And now you've invited a dwarf to have dinner with us?"

"Care for cocktail?"

The waitress was back, placing a menu in my sister's hands and staring down with a forced smile at her little hunchback daughter. "She need special facility?"

I grabbed Brittany by the collar and placed her howling on the seat next to me. She was squirming monkey-faced as I yanked the sweater out from under her denim jacket. Mary Ellen cooed, "Go kiss Mémère hello, sweetheart," as she excused herself to the restroom with a Louis Vuitton bag slung over her shoulder. I passed the sobbing child to my mother, who assumed a familiar expression as she gathered the crumpled girl into her matchstick arms.

After she had quieted her granddaughter and was taking a comb to her matted mane, Mother looked at me with a grimace halfway between mock gravity and irrepressible laughter, and then called back the waitress.

"Might as well have a second one of these Mai Tais, hon, since my daughter thinks I'm such a big lush."

Brittany asked for some quarters and went to play the claw machine in the lobby. The piano struck up "Happy Days Are Here Again" and several couples slid out of their booths. The ladies took the gentlemen's arms as they high-stepped it into the bar, wiggling their polyester behinds.

I hadn't eaten a bite since I stuffed a croissant into my face at the Newark airport at nine that morning. Then in Atlanta I had to scamper from Concourse A to D to make the connection. Mother had promised we'd drive straight to a restaurant, but nobody seemed interested in eating. I flicked open the heavy menu, and then caught the waitress's eye. She held up her hand, as if to say *just a moment.* The place was packed. I couldn't order a platter of scallops in black bean sauce just for myself in a family-style Chinese restaurant. That wouldn't be right.

"What's this, a convention?" I asked, looking around.

"Must be a holiday package," Mother said, "like the tour I took with your Uncle Goozy's third wife last spring. I noticed they have a piano and dance floor in the bar when we came in."

I waved the menu at another waitress as she marched straight past us. Maybe we could start with the fried calamari.

"Mary Ellen's probably in there right now, " I said, "fox-trotting with the dwarf."

"I'd rather see her fox-trotting with dwarves than sitting around the house all the livelong day steaming about how everyone else has ruined her life. I mean, she's the one who decided to take her student loan to study poor people and spend it on that nose job. Don't look at me. Now that would make a good story, don't you think?"

"We're not even Jewish. Catholic girl gets nose job to better serve the needy? Get a load of that nozzle on Mother Teresa. It wouldn't sell."

A waitress finally scurried over, pen poised.

"We'll start with an order of egg rolls." I slapped the menu down.

"Anything else?" she asked, glancing at Mother. "Want entree now?"

"Not now, honey. We'll wait until my daughter and granddaughter get back. They're off somewhere in there." She waved her hand toward the bar, then turned to face me. "Come on. That's an interesting story. Put in that part about how she had to advertise those abused twins on the TV show in Lafourche Parish."

"My sister, the incest worker. Until she realizes she forgot to have a baby, hooks an oil-platform engineer, who she divorces a few months after the child is born because . . . . What was it little Brittney asked me a few years ago? 'What's a mature jaculator? Mommy says Daddy's a mature jaculator.' Mary Ellen said that in front of her five-year-old."

I fished around inside the pockets of my blazer for the packet of pretzels the stewardess had handed me with the Coke, then ripped open the cellophane with my teeth.

Mother bristled, staring straight ahead. "Talk about child abuse. Imagine having to spend half the week with one parent, half with the other. What do you call that? Shared . . . ?"

"Custody." I crammed a pretzel into my mouth, running my tongue over the salty crust. "And do you know what your darling granddaughter did in my custody last summer when I took her to the petting zoo at Audubon Park?"

"What?"

"She kicked the llama," I sputtered with a mouthful of pretzel.

"She didn't."

"She did. She said the animals on TV were much better." I balled up the cellophane, searching my pockets again.

"I know better than to expect any more grandkids," Mother said, shaking her head as she studied my receding hairline and salt-and-pepper goatee for any signs of potential lingering in her hopeless bachelor.

"Would the lovely lady care to dance?" This florid geezer in an emerald blazer was shifting from one foot to the other in front of us with a Bud Light in his hand. His tag read: "Hello! My Name's Napoleon Tatum."

"That's so sweet of you," Mother gushed, "but we're all set to have a family reunion. This is my son Franklin who flew in this evening from New Jersey, where he teaches history at the community college. And my daughter Mary Ellen just drove in from Lake Charles."

"People call me Uncle Na' Tatum, and we're senior citizens getting together after having to put up with our children all day yesterday. Just kidding. We call ourselves the Turkey Trotters and decided to come to a Chinese place 'cause we couldn't stand to look at no leftover turkey today."

I peered over the old man's shoulder, scanning the room for my eggrolls. I could almost taste a sandwich of leftover turkey, slathered with mayonnaise and scarfed in front of an opened refrigerator the night after Christmas.

"I'm Vergie Dordain." Mother's taut face lit up as she twirled the umbrella in her Mai Tai. "Looks like y'all having a lot of fun. My son won't believe me, but we cut up more than the young folks when we go out. They're so serious these days. Everything has to be such a big deal, a 'relationship' or whatever they call it."

"We didn't have all of them communicative diseases like they got now," Mr. Tatum said.

Here was the waitress, at last. The egg rolls were charred, but I picked one up. On its way to the mustard dip, the greasy egg roll slipped out of my chopsticks and skidded onto the floor.

From the bar swelled a chorus of "Bye, Bye Black Bird." There was hooting and applause, as if some old dame had claimed the dance floor with a shimmy. I reached down to the carpeting, grabbed the egg roll between two fingers, and bit into it. Mother's eyebrows shot up to her hairline.

"Come on, Mr. Tatum." She hoisted herself up with both hands. "Let's go show them how to do it. Looks like those Mai Tais just reached my arch supports."

TWO BURNED EGG rolls did not hit the spot. As I started to peel the label off my Heineken, I was carried back to the smells of fresh pine and simmering gravy in my grandparents' shotgun house on Christmas day, a gas heater flaring under the chimney hung with chunky red stockings embroidered in green with our names. The roasting turkey would draw everyone toward the linoleum-floored kitchen, until Mémère shooed us out. After Don's funeral in November, I'd hoped Christmas at home would be . . . Christmas, but Brittany had to spend the big day with her father and his new girlfriend's family.

My luggage was still in the trunk of Mother's car. Our lives didn't fit together anymore.

I drifted through the bar, where Mother and Mr. Tatum had joined a group at the piano. "I'm dreaming of a white Christmas," they were singing, "just like the ones I used to know." Mary Ellen waved me over to where she was flirting with Quasimodo in a Santa Claus cap. I pretended to misunderstand, waved vigorously back, and rushed into the lobby, where a fat, freckled kid was playing the claw machine.

"The little girl went thataway," he said, pointing.

I found Brittany back near the kitchen door, hiding in the shadow of a plastic dieffenbachia. She was staring at the round table in the corner where the elderly owners were having dinner with their children, who did the cooking, and with their grandchildren, who were the waiters. A moon-faced baby was being bounced on laps and chopsticks were flying over round white bowls as steaming platters of shrimp, chicken, and clams revolved on a lazy-Susan at the center. They glanced around at each other as they were eating, but no one interrupted the nurturing silence of clacking chopsticks. Our waitress caught my eye and stood up, embarrassed. She said something in Cantonese to her family then rushed toward me.

"Ready to order yet?"

"As soon as everybody gets together. I'm starving. You hungry yet, Brittany?" I took her hand, smiled and winked. "Why don't you go round up Mémère and your mother so we can eat?"

"Nooooo," she whined, pulling away from me into the dieffenbachia. I gave up, leaving her to gawk at a real family sitting down to eat a meal together as if they were some rare species of crustacean masticating on the Discovery Channel.

I slipped out to the parking lot, my breath hanging in a cloud before me, leaving my family parked in the restaurant like Christmas trash on the curb. At the moment, I was toying with the idea of catching a cab to the French Quarter, where I could bite down into a shrimp po'boy or something else that tasted like home. Stepping behind the Scenicruiser that must have bused in the Turkey Trotters, I unwrapped a thin joint from my United boarding pass. Time to run away from home again, I told myself, firing it up.

When we were kids, Mary Ellen and I had run away from home. One afternoon we just packed a little red valise and skedaddled to the bus stop, just like that, then hid under an oleander bush in front of a raised double. We checked out people's shoes getting on and off the bus, but didn't have fourteen cents between us to get on. Mary Ellen was clutching the red valise, and I was doodling with a stick in the mud. The damp ground was littered with cigarette butts and gum wrappers, and we crouched there way past suppertime, streetlight filtering down through white blossoms that smelled like birthday-cake icing. We wanted every day to be our birthday, and we'd just figured out it wasn't. Somewhere down the line, we learned the luscious oleander flowers were poisonous.

Where else but home, I wondered, did we think there was to go?

Just as I yanked out the cell phone to call a taxi, a snowflake settled on the sleeve of my navy-blue blazer. I looked up, blinking, as the sky filled with fuzzy white chips fluttering down through the glaring security lights. Turning in a circle, I stood in the middle of the parking lot as the snow drifted down around me. The last time it snowed in New Orleans on Christmas had been when I was seven. Awestruck, I'd scooped up the cold white powder from the sidewalk to make a snowball that I kept in the freezer until my mother asked what that dirty hunk of ice was doing there. She thought it would make the hamburger meat go bad.

"Oh my gawd," shrieked a woman in a black rabbit coat walking out of the restaurant. "It's snowing." Then she raced back inside.

The snow was beginning to nestle inside the gigantic cupped leaves of the elephant-ear plants next to the door. Soon everyone inside the restaurant was out in the parking lot with their cocktails, looking up at the sky and reaching out to touch snowflakes with their fingertips.

"It's snowing, Uncle Franklin." Brittany raced up to grab my legs. "I've never seen it snow in real life." Then she ran around trying to catch snowflakes on the tip of her tongue.

Of course, I was used to slugging through the yucky stuff in Newark, but to see it snow in the parking lot of a Chinese restaurant in New Orleans the night after Christmas was like witnessing it for the first time, too. Even the rowdy Turkey Trotters had fallen silent, arms tentatively outstretched, as if trying to caress a lacy wraith that had suddenly appeared among us.

Soon I was joined by Mother and a flushed Mr. Tatum, by Mary Ellen with her dwarf in a ratty Santa Claus cap. We were beaming like fools, embracing each other and jigging around on top of the crunchy tarmac.

"Wait a minute," Mother said. "Nobody is ever going to believe this." Out of her handbag came the old Brownie, then she and I and Mary Ellen and Brittany were entwining arms in a pose in front of glistening elephant ears as Mr. Tatum snapped a picture.

And let me tell you something about that photograph. Although it was the last photo ever taken of us together, believe it or not, we look like the happiest family in the world. That was why I had it enlarged and framed, and then hung it in my living room. The picture elicits a smile from everyone who sees it. "You must come from a great family," people say, or "You guys look so close-knit." The snow is flurrying around us, dusting our shoulders and heads with sparkling cut crystal as we hug in a snug mass of pink cheeks, flashing eyes, and gaping grins. If I close my eyes, I can still see the flurries of snow spiraling around in the parking lot of that Chinese restaurant. It's like the glass snow dome I used to take down off the chimney mantel at my grandparents' house on Christmas Eve, turning it upside down over and over again, mesmerized by those old-timey carolers under the street lantern, the flakes whirling and whirling as if they would never stop.

Lucille LeBlanc's Last Stand

ONE DECEMBER, Celestine lay down in the middle of the parlor and stayed there for three weeks. "I don't know whether to call a priest or a crash truck," Lucille complained to my grandmother on the phone. "How I'm gonna move her without a hook and ladder? I can't have y'all over for Christmas with that woman moaning between the Motorola and the piano."

"Jack, go over there and see what you can do," my grandmother urged me. But trying to do anything about the LeBlancs was like trying to do something about the Civil War. It was over, and I was just getting started.

Celestine was a massive, gold-toothed woman who shook the floorboards when she walked. Lucille was wiry and smart-mouthed, with mottled skin two shades of white and one of brown. She was better off than her sister Mignonne, who used a walker and was so deaf she couldn't hear the telephone ring. But standing up made Lucille so dizzy she couldn't wait to sit back down. All three were over seventy-five years old and, as Lucille liked to say, had one good pair of legs, ears, and eyes between them.

For twenty-five years Celestine had worked for the LeBlanc family in their dilapidated West Indian plantation house on Bayou Road. She'd kept order and cooked grillades among the squawking eccentricities of six Creole brothers and sisters, none of whom had ever married or held a job. Celestine's voice thundered from the kitchen to the front gallery, commanding everyone in its path. On Sundays while we ate in the dining room, she'd perch on a high stool in front of her stove, engaged in an ongoing conversation through the door with everyone at the table, telling us what to eat and how much, and serving up side dishes of advice and gossip. Any difference of opinion at the table awaited her final word, which came booming in with the next course. Lucille would change the subject rather than give in to Celestine.

Yet Celestine was as terrified as the LeBlancs of the deteriorating neighborhood beyond the picket fence on Bayou Road, and ventured out even less than they did. She was afraid, she said, some young fellow with a loud radio and a big stick would knock her down at the bus stop. Except for the walk to morning Mass at St. Rose de Lima, during those final years only Lucille ever left the house, putting on her hat and pearls to "go to town" (as she still called Canal Street) to visit with the lawyer and banker or to fight another battle with the "big monkey-monks" at City Hall.

First the Department of Public Health condemned the chicken and duck coops the LeBlancs had always kept in the yard, forcing them to eat store-bought meat. Then the city sealed the well and cistern, obliging them to wash down store-bought meat with tap water from the Mississippi River. "Them health people trying to make us sick for sure," Lucille ranted to anyone who would listen. The last straw was when the city condemned the fireplaces. Then they had to huddle all winter in the cavernous rooms around electric space heaters connected by dangling extension cords to the crystal chandeliers.

None of the old downtown families still kept chickens or drank rainwater from a cistern, my grandmother told me, although she remembered doing so as a girl when they lived next-door to the LeBlancs. My grandmother had gone to convent school with the LeBlanc sisters, but compared to Lucille and Mignonne, she was a Thoroughly Modern Mémère. She smoked Salems, drove a car, and probably owned the first MixMaster and electric rotisserie oven in the state of Louisiana. "Times have changed" was her motto. Long before he became president, she liked that handsome actor on the General Electric TV show who said every week, "Progress is our most important product."

Around the time the city condemned the fireplaces, the remaining LeBlancs went into mourning and never emerged. They continued eating a long, leisurely dinner at one o'clock in the afternoon and then napping, as though the buzzing nine-to-five world of rush hours and freeways didn't exist. Meanwhile, the house fell apart around them, jerry-rigged in that style of managed decay endemic to the tropics. Burst pipes were wrapped with rags and duct tape, swatches of mismatched linoleum covered termite holes in the floors, and broken shutters were wired closed. The garden grew wild, and when I got older, after Sunday dinner I'd change into an old pair of jeans and do what I could to weed and trim. They often threatened to sell the house and move to the country, where their cousins had a sugar plantation, but the plantation eventually was bought by an oil company, one thing led to another, and they never did.

First Euphèmie, the youngest LeBlanc, became convinced that her sisters were trying to poison her. During our Sunday visits, she would suddenly appear at the creaky pocket doors between the dining room and parlor, her oval eyes lowered to the floor like a novitiate, hands wrapped around her elbows at the small of her back. Her downy gray hair was cropped short as a boy's, and she must have weighed no more than seventy-five pounds. She spoke in a loud whining voice, making sounds like a deaf girl mouthing her first words.

Once, when I was about fourteen, she came in, curtsied, and kissed me shyly on the cheek. "Why did Miss Euphie do that?" I asked Lucille, blushing.

"She thinks you that good-looking boy Auguste used to call on her from Bayou St. John. But Papa ran him off, and then he went over there and got himself killed by the Kaiser. Euphie Marie, she never got over that boy, I hope to tell you."

The next time Euphèmie made one of her appearances between the pocket doors, I gallantly kissed her hand, playing my part as the ghost of a Creole suitor. Euphèmie ran shrieking from the room, and we could hear Celestine tussling with her in the kitchen. When she finally got her quieted and tied down into bed, I asked Celestine what happened.

"She thinks you the trash man. Come back here screaming something about how the trash man done licked her hand, and make me wash it five or four time to get the smell off."

Lucille refused to have her sister put away, as her cousins thought she should, and always said she couldn't sell the house as long as Euphèmie was alive. Where else could she find a place big enough so that neighbors couldn't hear her scream?

After Euphèmie starved herself to death, Sylver, the older brother, started up. He took to his bed, refusing to move until he died. He would sit propped up, wild-eyed and unshaven, and demand Dixie beer and Lucky Strikes. To catch the ashes, Celestine held a silver tray under the cigarette drooping from his mouth, terrified he would set the bed on fire. He called and called on the merciful Lord Jesus to take him, until one Sunday I heard Celestine march in to tell him—in no uncertain terms—he should be ashamed for calling on the Lord to do something He had no mind to do at the moment.

That was the night Sylver died.

THOSE VISITS TO the nineteenth century lasted all afternoon, especially the formal gatherings after Christmas dinner, when my grandmother, mother, sister, and I would come to exchange presents with the dwindling circle of LeBlancs. Tart-tongued Estelle Arceneaux, a retired English teacher, would always be there because she'd grown up with the LeBlancs and her tomb was right next to theirs in St. Louis Number Three Cemetery. The parlor smelled like the inside of an old leather suitcase, and I sat up straight for hours with red foil wrapping from a new pair of cuff links balanced on my lap. My grandfather had knotted my tie so tight I could barely swallow the cherry bounce in a cordial glass.

Everyone spoke at once, to no one in particular, in French,

in English, and in both. To American ears, they always sounded as if they were arguing, even when they were agreeing. This was a conversational style known as *cancan*, as boisterous as the dance but not as naughty. Nodding in the direction of the cancan, I would run my hands against the nap of the prickly horsehair chair I was sitting on.

"Margot, dites-moi encore l'âge de ce garçon, oh la, il est grand." Then Lucille would turn to me. "I say, Ti-Jacques, you want a Barq's or Big Shot? Maybe you not big enough for cherry bounce. *Ma cousine le fait en la campagne pour la famille toutes les fêtes de Noël mais* maybe it too strong for you."

I was in a cage filled with giant lady parakeets dressed in flowered rayon dresses with clunky black shoes and long wisps of white hair held in ornate barrettes. They were chirping and shrieking and filling the cage with feathers, beating their wings and hopping from perch to perch. Balanced on the edges of their chairs, they'd dip their beaks rapidly into tiny glasses in their hands. Outside, I could hear pine cones dropping onto the rockers on the front gallery and sense the sun motionless at the center of the pewter sky.

Inside the crystal ball from the whatnot cabinet, it was always snowing when I wanted it to be.

The whatnot cabinet was also lined with cut glass bowls reflected in beveled mirrors. The high ceiling was the color of pages from an old book, the paint peeling back in long strips. The parlor reminded me of an antique shop on Royal Street, overflowing with china urns, candelabra lamps, still lifes of blowzy dahlias in gold frames, chairs with caning the color of tobacco-stained teeth, and an obstacle course of back tables and end tables. Overhead hung a huge ceiling fan like an ornamental propeller that didn't move. The piano seat did move, and my sister spun around and around on it in her yellow pinafore with starched petticoats underneath, her new Mary Janes almost touching the floor. A small Christmas tree glimmered on top of the piano, and the plaster Magi and camel crossed the piano lid—nailed shut—in search of their blinking silver star.

The Christmas after the city condemned the LeBlancs' fireplaces, their cousin Goozy Dordain ordered for them from the Montgomery Ward catalogue a cardboard fireplace with a revolving spotlight behind a sheet of red cellophane. Not to hurt his feelings, Lucille set it up every year, and we sat in chilly parlor shadows with red light wavering across our faces as we sipped cherry bounce, rearranged space heaters, and silently watched snow falling in New York on the new Motorola TV.

"It's real pretty," everyone said. And we left early.

LUCILLE HAD THE MONTGOMERY Ward fireplace box in the front hall, ready to set it up, when Celestine lay down in the middle of the parlor. For years each brother or sister had lined up to be the next to die, until only Lucille, Mignonne, and Celestine were left. Out of the blue, Celestine decided it was her turn.

Like the white ladies she worked for, Celestine had never married. "Who would have her?" was the way Lucille always answered the question, out of earshot. Celestine was from the country in Assumption Parish, and was given to odd beliefs. She kept an assortment of small animals in and around the house, which she claimed were her spirits. Looking for sugar inside the screened cupboard in the pantry one day, I was bitten by a box turtle hiding among the canisters. Rubbing my hand with alcohol, Celestine said the turtle was curing her.

I was in my first year of college by this time, had long hair, and went to civil rights demonstrations. And so, smarting from my turtle bite and guilt about segregation, I sat face to face with Celestine at the kitchen table—I'd never done that before—and we talked about reincarnation. We both believed in it.

"Nothing die," Celestine told me. "It all go on from one thing to the next. These animals I brung here are my people from the country. They can suck the misery out me and put it back in the ground. One day I be them, or they be me or Miss Lucille or your Mémère. They our people, too."

My sit-in in the kitchen with Celestine discussing hippie ideas didn't go over too big with the LeBlancs or my family. They made Celestine put the turtle in a hole under the house and get rid of the lizards, field mice, and garden snakes she kept tucked away in every nook and cranny of the kitchen. And the next time I visited, Lucille exploded. "I hope you don't mind if I tell you to your face that you'd look a lot better without all that hair hanging off your head." As she lurched to the sideboard for her barber shears, I excused myself to jump on the bus.

Whatever Celestine was trying to cure with the box turtle was awfully real, because the house smelled so foul that all but their most faithful friends and family stopped visiting. I first noticed the stench when my grandmother explained in a stage whisper, "Celestine has soiled herself." We exited the kitchen onto the back gallery. But an odor of stale urine began to seep into the woodwork, linen, and marquisette curtains. The smell was aggravated by a Creole fear of drafts, so the shutters were kept tightly shut. Lucille and Mignonne didn't notice it; they lived with it. But the first blast on entering the house on a summer afternoon was . . . well, I asked myself how could people live like this?

After the smell came the trash. I was amazed at the number of shopping bags my grandmother kept carrying out of the house and stuffing into her car after visiting the LeBlancs. One afternoon I lugged three, she, two, and they weighed a ton. At first I didn't ask, thinking they were old clothes for the Sisters' Home for the Incurables or a lifetime supply of fig preserves and cherry bounce. Finally I couldn't resist.

"Don't tell anyone, Jack, but Celestine won't let Lucille or Mignonne throw out anything. She's got it into her head that the garbage is invaluable. Newspapers, milk cartons, tin cans, it's all piling up in the house to the point where Lucille has to sleep on the couch in the parlor because her room's filled with stacks and stacks of trash."

I reached around to the back seat to peer into a shopping bag. It was filled with Holsom bread wrappers and French Market Coffee & Chicory cans.

"And so we decided each visit I would, you know, make like

I was just coming from Maison Blanche with shopping, and get rid of the trash that way. Sad thing is, we didn't know Celestine banks her money between the old newspapers until six one-dollar bills slipped out. Now we have to thumb through the papers first and put her money under the Bible she keeps on the mantle in her room. That's where she saves the money for her funeral."

The garbage smuggling went on for several months, until the day Celestine made her pallet in the parlor and lay down to die.

Lucille called us every day with the latest report. "She likes to sleep on the floor . . . like you"—Lucille paused for emphasis, exposing once more our hippie conspiracy—"but usually sleeps in the back hall next to the kitchen. Lord knows it'd take me till next Easter to clean out that room of hers. For ten years I been begging her to see a doctor but she say she don't have no use for doctors. And every time I mention an ambulance, she commences to holler. You hear, there she goes again. I got to go. I'm waiting on that woman like she was the Queen of Sheba. Tell your Mémère I'll ring her later. Pray for me."

Seated on the gossip-bench next to the square black telephone, Lucille went down the list, asking each of her relatives what to do. Her cousin Vergie Dordain suggested that Lucille "launder Celestine's step-ins." Lucille performed this chore every night in the bathtub, diapering her with a fresh pair of drawers every morning. Celestine moaned and cussed and called on her Maker as Lucille struggled to change her, but a least the smell wasn't as suffocating during our last visit with Celestine.

She lay sprawled under a pile of patched blankets, even though it was an unusually warm December day. The acrid piss smell lingered, in spite of laundered step-ins. Rays of strong sunlight, strained through closed shutters, cast a zebra-pattern across the room, catching motes of dust falling in slow currents from the overhead fan. The air had an exhausted gray tinge. We stood over Celestine as though over an impromtu grave.

At first the deathbed seemed like a mound of rags with a big green rock balanced on top, heaving up and down. When I looked closer, only Celestine's ashen-blue face was exposed, pocked with beads of sweat, eyes rolled back in her head. The turtle rested on her formidable stomach, tail and legs withdrawn inside its parched shell, its head protruding with yellow carmine eyes staring defiantly at us. It seemed to be guarding her, and I remembered it bit.

I thought I heard it hiss. I didn't get too close.

Lucille ushered us out onto the gallery, and Mignonne clanked after us on her walker. "She says it draws the misery from her, that turtle. Says her soul going to go in it when she pass, and then I should put it back under the house," Lucille said. "I got enough on my hands without fooling with no dirty *caouanne.* I tell her I'm gonna make a soup out of that *caouanne,* and she holler some more."

Mignonne, rocking herself into a trance in her worn rattan rocker, stared down the long shaded walkway that led to the gate, as if imagining her own last exit from Bayou Road. Shaking her wilted head, she cut in at regular intervals with "Lucille's right!" and "We done all we could."

"Have you tried to make other arrangements, called a nursing home or something?" my grandmother asked, trying to bring the conversation back to earth. "I hear the Good Shepherd has wonderful care, for white and colored both."

Lucille swept the suggestion aside as if it came from another planet. "Every day I get down on my knees and ask the Blesséd Mother what to do. And yesterday I got an answer loud and clear: *call her family.* So finally I talk to some woman in Assumption Parish who claims Celestine as her great-aunt. She says, 'You got Tante Celestine?' and I say, 'If she your kin, come get her. That woman suffering bad. Us, we got one foot each in the grave, my sister and me.'"

Three days before Christmas, I'd just finished my final exams when Lucille called to tell us Celestine had died, and that her niece had taken the body to Assumption Parish. On the morning of Christmas Eve, my grandmother drove Lucille and Mignonne in her turquoise Plymouth to the country for the funeral. I heard that at one point Lucille hung her head out of the window, carsick in her new rose hat. Before she left, she asked me to do something with that turtle. I coaxed it into a shoe box and carried it back to its hole under the house, where I had my own funeral rite for Celestine with votive candles and a mayonnaise jar of holy water I took from Mignonne's prie-dieu.

While I was scurrying under the brick pillars that raised the house above the flood line, a crack of thunder announced one of those flash Louisiana storms that unexpectedly sets the moment in parentheses from the rest of the day. So I spent a while under the cypress floorboards, lighting votive candles and singing a Choctaw poem I'd ripped out of my literature textbook, hypnotized by the torrential downpour. The damp, loamy smell reminded me that Bayou Road had first been a muddy Indian portage between the Mississippi and Bayou St. John, bricked over into a street at the end of the nineteenth century. I imagined a procession of Houmas with bark pirogues hoisted over their heads treading toward the bayou, shook a few more drops of holy water from Mignonne's jar into the turtle's hole, and buried them there, too.

Lucille had often told me her mother's story of how a rich voodoo named Jean Bayou had buried gold under the house. And to my boyish fascination, she'd promised that before she ever sold the place, she and I would rent one of those metal detectors and crawl under the house to search for it. Studying the recession in the ground where the intractable turtle lay, I figured that must be where the gold was. So I sprinkled the rest of the holy water there and buried Jean Bayou along with his gold for the turtle to guard, and Celestine with her misery and—although I didn't know it at the moment—the past, both my own and one from long before I was born.

LUCILLE AND I NEVER did rent a metal detector to dig for Jean Bayou's gold. The day of the thunderstorm was my last visit to Bayou Road. We didn't celebrate Christmas there the next day, and within a month Lucille and Mignonne, abandoned in what suddenly felt like a drafty ruin, put the house up for sale. They moved into a cinderblock room their cousin Goozy constructed behind his tract bungalow in Destrehan, connected to the main house by a corrugated tin breezeway. With a suppressed shudder my grandmother discouraged me from visiting, reporting that Mignonne wasn't responding and Lucille was becoming disoriented, packing her suitcase to walk back to Bayou Road to pass the dust mop, or something like that. I was in college; I couldn't relate.

Both Lucille and Mignonne died in the cinderblock room within a year after leaving Bayou Road, and my grandmother said it was for the best. I now live in another city of another state, where free-range chickens, bilingualism, drinking rainwater, recycling trash, and dying at home are the cutting edge. I have to shake my head and laugh out loud, imagining what Lucille would think. She always had something memorable to say as she stubbornly dragged the nineteenth century by a mule harness halfway into this one.

Just before my grandmother died she mailed me a clipping from the *Times-Picayune* about how some dot-com baron from San Francisco had turned the house into a bed and breakfast where TV stars stayed when they visited New Orleans. "Times have changed!" she scrawled under a color picture of Mary Tyler Moore sitting on the front gallery. There were photos of beige wall-to-wall carpeting around a sunken whirlpool bath in Mignonne's room, and of a swimming pool where the chicken coop used to be. I could drive into any suburb and see the same thing, so I threw the article away.

After Mémère passed away, we had the piano the LeBlancs gave her shipped up here. The fragile upright was delivered during a snow flurry, a week before Christmas, and my wife wanted to pry up the rusty spikes right away, have it tuned, and play carols on it. But I shook my head, insisting we keep it nailed shut. If only to humor me, she gave in after I told her what that Yankee soldier did the night Lincoln was shot.

The story went that the LeBlancs' grandmother had been playing it that evening, when New Orleans was an occupied city.

When a Union soldier came by to warn her to stop playing because the city was in mourning, she kept right on because she didn't understand a word of English. He came around a second time, and she showed him to the door, smiling, and resumed playing. The third time he returned with a hammer and nailed the lid shut. Not a note has been played on the piano since the night Lincoln was shot, and the dank silence and defeat should stay buried in there like a ghost sonata.

For whatever it's worth, that's all I have left of home.

Every Christmas we have a small to-do here. Friends come over for something to drink, and I usually wind up seated on the revolving stool at the mute piano, telling this story about the last December on Bayou Road. And for my little boy I line up the Magi and camel along the piano lid, still searching for their star.

WHAT FLOATS

"SHE'S LYING DOWN."

That was what I told Miss Viola from down the block when she stopped by to see my mother. Miss Viola straightened the strap on her flowered sundress, peering through the half-opened screen door into our messy kitchen. She held a pack of Kools in one hand and looked like she expected coffee.

"Jonathan," asked Miss Viola, squinting her mascaraed eyes, "is your mother sick?"

"No. I mean, yes. A little."

"One of those headaches?" Miss Viola wrinkled her brow, waiting for a response. I said nothing. "Well, tell her to ring me when she feels better."

I closed and locked the door, and went back to washing dishes. This was the first Wednesday after it happened, and I'd never cooked for myself before. I didn't even know you had to defrost hamburgers from the freezer before you fried them. The charred lump of meat that I gobbled took an hour to cook. I put a lot of mustard on it. There was no bread.

I still had homework to do. I tiptoed into Mother's room and turned up the air conditioner. I didn't know why I tiptoed, but it was awfully quiet in there. I flicked on the lamp next to the bed and tried to tug the covers out from under her, but they were tucked tight and wouldn't budge. So I ripped the pages out of my fifth-grade arithmetic workbook and spread them on top of her in case she was chilly. She looked so peaceful in the blue rayon dress she'd been wearing when she rushed home from work on Monday evening.

"Just need to lie down for a few minutes," she'd said, sweeping past me into her bedroom. Lately she'd had a lot of headaches, so I knew how to take care of myself while she rested. I peeked into her room every half hour. Usually she asked for a glass of water, but now she wasn't asking for any water. I brought her a glass anyway.

She was still lying down.

I shook her. She moaned.

Then I shook her again. She didn't moan.

Her eyes were wide open, staring straight at the ceiling.

I let the phone ring and ring, and latched the doors. She was afraid of burglars and murderers in Gentilly, our neighborhood of raised wooden bungalows behind the racetrack in New Orleans. Mostly there were just kids like me with moms like her, except the other houses had daddies. We lived in my grandparents' house, where my mother had grown up. After my father left us, MawMaw and PawPaw moved to Jackson, Mississippi, and let us live there. But my grandparents thought I was a big mistake.

"Look how that boy is growing up." MawMaw would shake her head. "A nine-year-old needs a father and brothers and sisters. He can't live alone with a woman who works in a drugstore all day. And kids shouldn't be raised around a man with a temper like that. Should have known that before you started."

Whenever I sassed or wouldn't go to bed on time, my mother would say she couldn't do a thing with me.

"I'll have to send you to live with your father. He could make you listen."

That was my worst fear, that I'd have to go live with my father in California. When he left, he busted up everything. It took us a week to pick the broken glass out of the carpet. He didn't remember my birthday, and when he called he was gruff and grouchy and didn't ask to talk with me. "Put your mother on," he'd say when I answered. I was just a nuisance in the way.

I climbed into bed and tried to read the chapter in *Faraway Lands and Peoples* about the Egyptian pyramids, but I couldn't keep my eyes on the page. So I slid under the bed where no bad thoughts or murderers could get me. Late at night I'd often hidden there listening to clicks and thumps and footsteps echoing through the four-room house. Closet doors creaked open and closed, drawers slammed shut. Shoe shadows shuffled past the slit of light under the bedroom door. Sometimes I heard a suitcase being packed. I was convinced my parents were stealing away to leave me alone under the bed. But in the morning they were both at the breakfast table.

Except for the morning after my father left. It looked like a hurricane had hit. There wasn't a single unbroken dish in the house.

I lay there under the dusty box springs for the longest time, wondering what was going to happen to me. When I spotted daylight creeping across the carpet, I crawled out, ate some Coco Puffs, and got ready for school. I still had clean clothes in the chifforobe, only I wasn't used to picking out what to wear. I climbed on a chair and stuck my hand into the big pickle jar on top of the refrigerator, taking whatever money I would need for busfare and lunch at school.

I checked on mother. Her hand was stiff as a baseball mitt, but I needed to hold it while I talked with her. I told her I'd see her at 3:30. Then I kissed her on the forehead. Before I left, I switched the overhead light on and off about a hundred times. Darkness, light, darkness, light. The light was never gone for good. I could always get it back when I wanted it.

Then I amped up the air conditioner to high.

The room was already starting to smell.

"WHAT'S THAT YOU'RE fooling with, Jonathan?"

"A mosquito hawk." I was petting its crackly head while fussy

Miss Avery was telling us how Egyptians buried Pharaohs in the pyramids.

"But it's dead," she said, staring into my hands.

"How do you know?" When I picked it up off the playground, it was twitching.

"Go put that thing in the trash."

I walked to the garbage can, but tucked the brittle wings inside my shirt's breast pocket.

"Now, class. After the Pharaoh was mummified, he was placed into a sarcophagus." Miss Avery wrote "sarcophagus" on the blackboard. I wrote "mommyfi" in my notebook. This was starting to make some sense. "Then food and water were placed in bowls to give him something to eat and drink during the long journey to the underworld."

"What's the underworld?" Eileen Gusman asked.

"Hell," shouted the redheaded kid from the back of the room.

"He cussed," Eileen said. Everybody exploded. Only I wasn't laughing. I was almost crying. I had to excuse myself to the bathroom to think this over. Where is hell, I wondered, and how do you know if you're there?

After school I walked the six blocks to City Park. Mother wouldn't miss me. I perched on a big gnarled root under a live oak and studied the mosquito hawk. How could a mother or a mosquito hawk or a Pharaoh be alive one minute, and not alive the next? What was the spark inside something that made it alive? Was it like the on/off switch for a light bulb or air conditioner? If you turned it off, couldn't you turn it back on again? Forever was the part I couldn't get. How long did forever last? Did it go on and on and on and then stop somewhere in the middle of the sky?

Was a star the end of forever?

I'd never really known anybody who just stopped. I'd seen sparrows rotting in the backyard, but mother said don't touch them, they had diseases. I wondered if the mosquito hawk had a disease now that it was dead. Was disease what you got when you stopped moving, like Mother?

When I arrived home, Miss Viola was standing in front of the kitchen door with her arms crossed.

"Your mother doesn't answer the phone or my knocking. Where is she?"

"She's at work."

"But you said she was sick."

"She felt better today, and went to work."

Miss Viola looked me straight in the eye. "Tell her to call me as soon as she gets home."

"Sure."

"Promise?"

As soon as I got inside, I put the mosquito hawk next to my school books on the kitchen table. I didn't promise Miss Viola anything. Mother never really liked her anyway.

The key to keeping our secret was not answering the telephone, and some nights it rang and rang. I knew the minute I spoke with MawMaw or PawPaw they would insist on talking to Mother. I couldn't just say she was lying down. I couldn't just say she was still at work. I couldn't even say she was in the bathroom. I needed to wait until Mother got to the end of forever and came back. I hoped it didn't last past the weekend.

I was running out of everything.

I took whatever money was left and bought milk, cereal, Cokes, and cookies at the corner store. I put a Coke and cookies on Mother's night table, like the Egyptians did for the Pharaoh's mommies to eat and drink on their trips to forever. Mother didn't eat or drink much, but once a bite of Oreo was nibbled away. Maybe she was hungry and ready to come back.

At night I would stare at the stars and wonder if she'd gotten there yet. The mosquito hawk was flaking to pieces, and I really had to take a deep breath every time I stepped into Mother's room. I pictured it as her pyramid, and her bed as a boat that the dog god Anubis rowed to the other side.

I wanted her back so bad. But when I looked up in the sky, forever was far away.

Miss Avery said I smelled, so I had to remember to take a bath. And comb my hair. I tried to avoid my friends at school, afraid I would burst out crying. I told them I had a disease, and they shouldn't get near me. During recess I walked along the outside walls of the building with a pencil in one hand, marking a continuous line in the gray cement of Jean Gordon Grammar School that got darker and darker every time I circled around.

That was my map to forever.

MY GRANDPARENTS RAISED me in Jackson, and never took me back to New Orleans except once, to visit my mother's tomb. They said the city was too dangerous. The story of the boy who stayed with his mother's corpse for ten days after she died of a stroke made the newspapers, but my grandparents never showed me the clippings. I found them stuffed in a yellowed envelope with my mother's death certificate after my grandparents passed on, when I was already in college in Massachusetts. Not once did MawMaw and PawPaw ever mention my mother or father in front of me. My childhood split into two separate hemispheres, like a peeled orange.

The first half, the nine years I spent in New Orleans with my mother, eventually shriveled and dried up. I seldom thought of it. Soon after I arrived in Mississippi, my grandparents treated me as if I'd been born yesterday. Their only therapy was complete erasure, and it worked. The second half of my childhood I ate up greedily, sucking out every last drop of juice. I was an honors student and star athlete. To this day I speak with the hint of a Mississippi drawl. I haven't talked with my father in twenty years, since the first time he was sent to jail. I've never felt the slightest curiosity to look him up. I'm an agnostic, a Democrat, and an architect, divorced and with two kids of my own. Up here in the North, I'm considered a colorful character, a self-styled Mississippi redneck, a personality I exaggerate whenever possible. Except for my ex-wife, I've never told anyone about my origins in New Orleans, or about my mother. In my white-wine circles, I'm already considered enough of a lunatic because I eat boiled peanuts and listen to country western.

What Floats

Why go overboard by telling people the truth?

Like everyone up here, I was riveted to the TV coverage of the hurricane that just devastated the Gulf Coast. I watched it day and night for two weeks, and became a source of firsthand commentary among friends. I was even interviewed on the radio as a Mississippian. I paid special attention to the details about New Orleans. I studied the city floodmaps posted neighborhood by neighborhood on the Internet and finally located the block where I used to live on Gardena Drive. My grandparents had sold the house years ago, after my mother died. I tried to picture it flooded up to the roof.

I recognized familiar landmarks in TV footage of the rescue boats patrolling the neighborhood. People died on nearby rooftops or suffocated in attics. I stopped eating and began to lose sleep. When I did manage to sleep, I'd often sleepwalk, and once woke up at three in the morning behind the wheel of my truck in the garage. I dreamed of my mother's house, of Miss Viola and Miss Avery. My mother was floating down the street on her bed holding a pyramid. She kept calling and calling for me, warning me not to let anyone in. I waded through water up to my waist looking for her but could never find her bedroom.

Her death took New Orleans away from me for the first time. But all these years a nine-year-old boy had been waiting there inside a sealed room for his mother to return. Then the hurricane washed that room away. Strange, but when a tragedy strikes once, you think what tough luck. But when the same tragedy is repeated, you crumble, reliving both at once. I couldn't concentrate on blueprints and spoke out of turn at meetings. I'd wake up dazed and confused. Nobody could understand why I took what was happening in New Orleans so hard.

My ex-wife suggested therapy.

I said *naw.*

AS SOON AS I stepped out of the doors of Louis Armstrong International Airport, the blanket of heat and humidity wrapped me from head to foot. At first I couldn't breathe, and then I sank into air as familiar as old bedclothes. My long-sleeved Oxford shirt was soaked with sweat. Immediately I began to sneeze and cough, and the cough followed me during the next three days I spent in New Orleans.

I had booked my seat at the last minute, on impulse. It was Easter week in April, eight months after the storm. I justified the trip at the office with some architectural gobbledegook about studying "paradigms of restoration in flood-impacted urban centers." There was nothing I could do for the city. I knew that. But I hadn't even gone to my mother's funeral, if she had one, and I was being eaten alive by a sense of loss. I planned to visit my mother's tomb, walk around, scarf up some jambalaya, and then hightail it home.

And maybe drive down the street where I once lived.

"Where you from?" The man from the airport car rental agency was the first to greet me with that unnerving question.

"Originally from here," I shot back without thinking.

"How did y'all do?" That was the other question I heard everywhere. It didn't mean how was I feeling but how much of my life the storm had destroyed. I blinked my eyes.

"Where abouts in the city your people from?" he asked.

"Gentilly."

He shook his graying afro as he filled out the form. "Eight foot of water. Nothing left, baby. My mama stayed by there. Nothing left. Sign here. And welcome home."

It was late afternoon when I pulled up in front of 1327 Gardena Drive. I'd been circling the ashen streets of the ghost-town city all day. Even with the windows rolled up, I kept coughing. For mile after mile I'd been tracing the brown flood lines on houses: up to my knees in this block, up to my waist a few blocks down, over my head closer to Lake Pontchartrain. Most houses stood empty or boarded up. Others showed signs of gutting, with crusty belongings heaped in piles at the curb. Here and there I spotted a white FEMA trailer parked in a driveway, with masked people dragging Sheetrock across dead gray lawns. But in most neighborhoods, the houses sat abandoned, doors opened, windows askew, with ominous red *X*s painted on the outside. In the crux of the *X* was the number of dead bodies discovered inside.

I felt as if I were encased in a submarine bell, floating through the amber shadows of a submerged world. A giant horned toad looming on the horizon, or a python twined around a rusted swing set, wouldn't have surprised me more.

"If you get out the car," the gas station attendant had warned, "be careful of gators. They taking over."

I hadn't been to my mother's tomb yet, but I carried her photograph in my shirt's breast pocket. Now I was seeing the city through her eyes. When I drove past the cemetery, a Good Friday procession had been winding its way between the rows of little white houses. The entire city was my mother's tomb. I thought I'd spotted her once from the back, until the woman turned around, skull teeth bared, laughing.

A corroded tricycle sat in the walkway to my mother's front door.

The splintered door stood ajar. The *X* spray-painted on the side of the house indicated one body had been found inside.

I kicked open the door and stood on the threshold. Great splotches of mold blackened the walls, and the furniture was upside down, strewn across the floor. The curtains were shreds of rotting fabric hanging translucent in late afternoon sunlight. I swabbed my face with a handkerchief and stepped into the oven-like heat, kicking my way through a fetid nest of buckled books and broken crockery. This was how the room had felt the morning after my father left. I could see my mother and me on our knees, picking through the debris.

I walked into the kitchen. In a cleared area smelling of Clorox, Miss Viola was seated at the table. She was still young, younger than I appeared, wearing a flowered sundress. A white rose in a bud vase stood at the center of the table, next to two coffee cups. She smiled and beckoned me to sit down.

"You probably don't recognize me. I'm Jonathan."

"Your mother told me you were coming."

The blood drained from my face.

"She said you'd be tired and to fix up your room."

"Where is she?"

"She's lying down."

"Do you live here?"

"I look after all these places now."

"Miss Viola, I—"

"Hush. You've been gone a long time. You'll get used to it. We're all still here, just the way you left us. You take cream in your coffee?"

While I drank the coffee, she smoked a cigarette and then touched up her lipstick. The refrigerator was on its side, and the stove on top of it, the oven door hanging open like a panting tongue.

"Is Mother in her room?

"You remember where it is?"

I reached for the light switch when I stepped into the room. Off, on. Off, on. Nothing. Both windows were open, and a huge chunk of the wall was missing. The outside had moved inside. Leafy mirliton vines were climbing up the mildewed walls, and green garden lizards scampered through overturned furniture.

The irridescent wings of a blue mosquito hawk were vibrating on the bed post.

But the bed was empty. Fern fronds were sprouting out of the sodden mattress, the spiny kind that grew between the bricks of tombs.

"Good night," I told the bed. "Good night."

In my room I pictured where each piece of furniture had been. This still must have been a boy's room, I thought, stepping around a moldy catcher's mitt and plastic action figures strewn across the floor. The bed was in the same place mine had been, made up with fresh white sheets.

I slid under the bed. The carpet stank, but I felt safe. Next to me I found a red rubber ball and a vinyl children's book, an inflated bathtub book called *What Floats.* I paged through it.

It was amazing what floats and what sinks.

I wondered if I'd be arrested for trespassing. Did New Orleans even have a police force anymore? Sometime during the second week I had remained inside the house with my mother's body, a police car pulled up out front, and two officers banged on the door. I opened it just a sliver.

"You Jonathan?" they asked.

I nodded through the crack.

"Your grandma called a few days ago from Jackson to place a missing person's report. She can't reach y'all. Why's that?"

"The phone is broken."

"They had AT&T send a lineman out here yesterday. Said the line is clear. We need to speak with your mother, young man."

"She's at work."

"She hasn't been to work in ten days." The officer adjusted his belt with the holster on it. "Your grandma checked."

"She's lying down."

"Look, son—" The policemen pushed through the screen door, and I ran into my room, sliding in here, under the bed.

One policeman let out a slow whistle as he entered my mother's bedroom. "Hey, come look at this," he said, coughing.

The next thing I knew, a long flashlight was aimed at me under the bed. I kicked at it, and the policemen dragged me out by the feet, screaming. One of them held a fistful of crumpled workbook pages.

"You don't understand," I was shouting red-faced as they carried me squirming between them. "She's coming back. She said to wait here for her. She told me to *stay*."

But I didn't stay.

And here I was, a thirty-five-year-old man with a family of my own, hiding under the bed and sniveling like a nine-year-old.

I eased myself out from under the bed, stood up, and dusted myself off. In the kitchen the three-legged table was upside down, with no hint of Miss Viola or her ghostly coffee klatsch. I staggered from the house, eyes stinging, and stumbled onto the eerily silent street. Even the crickets were quiet.

Everything was poised, as if waiting for someone to return.

At dusk on my street in Massachusetts, boys would be playing softball in the street, toddlers careening up driveways on tricycles, and gravy smells wafting from kitchen windows. Men would be hosing lawns, listening to the TV news blaring through opened front doors. Here on Gardena Drive, above the darkened rooftops, a purple bruise marked the dying light in the sky. Then the first star of the evening appeared, faint and luminous, as far away as forever. All these years I had carried around this star inside while everyone else was hosing and cooking dinner and throwing softballs. As I walked past the sepulchral houses, I felt relieved. Now the star's planetary landscape was visible on the streets of the city where I was born. The outside view at last matched the one inside.

With no direction in mind, I set off into a darkness so remote that it had no shape or name. There at the corner, illuminated by a hurricane lamp, a group of people were seated in a carport around a card table. That was Miss Viola's house, the green one under the still standing live oak. Cigarette dangling in her mouth, a wrinkled old woman was slouched in a wheelchair, surrounded by three children and a middle-aged couple. They were listening to the radio and playing cards.

I waved across the street. They waved back. Nobody was going to recognize me now. I doubted that I even existed. I was a wraith floating along the cracked sidewalk, an inhabitant of another world. The lamp in their carport was the only light I could discern far into the distance.

I shook my head in disbelief. These folks weren't going anywhere. What in the world must it feel like to stay on in the pure abandon of this place? For one last time I cracked open the door to my mother's room.

And I remembered.

Acknowledgments

These new stories have appeared in the following publications: "Reconcile" in *Arkansas Review*; "Latins on the Loose" in *Saints and Sinners: New Fiction from the Festival* (Rebel Satori Press, 2010); "The Empty Throne" in *The Devils We Know: A Collection of Short Stories from New Orleans* (Grand Circus Publishing, 2013).

The ten stories in section II were first collected in *Perpetual Care: Stories* (Jefferson Press, 2008), and (in order of the table of contents) previously have been published in: *Hog Town Creek Review*; *Crab Orchard Review*; *Boulevard*; *Shenandoah*; *French Quarter Fiction* (Light of New Orleans Publishing, 2003); *New Orleans Noir* (Akashic Books, 2007); *Exquisite Corpse*; *Arkansas Review*; *Something in the Water: Twenty Louisiana Stories* (Portals Press, 2011); and *Callaloo: A Journal of African Diaspora Arts and Letters.*

My most appreciative gratitude goes to Louisiana artist Adrian Deckbar for the use of her painting "In the Foyer" as a cover image; to lawyer Lisa Brener for her efforts in reassigning the copyright to *Perpetual Care: Stories*; to photographer Doug Parker of the *Times-Picayune* and to the Landov Agency for the use of the author photo; to Carolyn Perry for her careful proofreading of the galley; and to Amy Conner for her suggestions regarding the selection of new stories for this volume. For their diligence and care with the publication of this book, I offer special thanks to editors James D. Wilson, Michael S. Martin, and Melissa G. Teutsch at the University of Louisiana at Lafayette Press, whose trustworthy support at every stage of the production process has proven invaluable.

PRAISE FOR JAMES NOLAN'S NOVEL *HIGHER GROUND*

WILLIAM FAULKNER-WISDOM GOLD MEDAL
2012 INDEPENDENT PUBLISHERS GOLD MEDAL IN SOUTHERN FICTION

"*Higher Ground* is the funniest book I've read in years. James Nolan gets New Orleans like no one but a born-and-bred native really can. No doubt there will be comparisons to John Kennedy Toole, and they'll be deserved."

-Julie Smith, author of the *Skip Langdon* mysteries

"Like the indomitable city it celebrates, *Higher Ground* is lively, sensuous, and hot."

-Valerie Martin, author of *Mary Reilly*

"If Flannery O'Connor were alive today, she would no doubt find James Nolan's *Higher Ground* well worth reading . . . James Nolan has proven himself a master storyteller."

-Terry Dalrymple, *Arkansas Review*

"This dazzling debut novel set in post-Katrina New Orleans pays both serious and satiric homage to the survivors. *Higher Ground* abounds in dark humor and comic hi-jinks."

-Philip K. Jason, *Southern Literary Review*

"If John Kennedy Toole had lived through Katrina and could turn a phrase as well as James Nolan, he might have followed *Confederacy of Dunces* with a novel like *Higher Ground.* Read this and weep with laughter."

-Jed Horne, author of *Breach of Faith*

"In the frame of a page-turning noir, James Nolan has painted the most chillingly loving portrait of New Orleans. He is the Baudelaire of the post-Katrina city, and both its poetry and horror emanate from this story like a bouquet of carrion and jasmine."

-Andrei Codescscu, NPR commentator
and author of *The Blood Countess*

"*Higher Ground* is a deluge of delights—spectacular characters, fine mystery, astounding transformations . . . An instant classic of post-Katrina lit."

-Moira Crone, author of *What Gets into Us*